Freak Show

Alexa O'Brien Huntress Book 7

By Trina M. Lee

Freak Show
Copyright © 2013 by Trina M. Lee

Editor
B. Leigh Hogan

Cover Artist
Michael Hart

Published by
Dark Mountain Books

Chapter One

The loud clink of glasses was one of many sounds in the busy, fast-paced atmosphere. It was pushing three in the morning, yet the patrons of the Galleria Bar in Caesars Palace were nowhere near finished. I sat at a small round table with Shaz and Jez, trying to decide where I wanted to start. There was so much going on.

Jez held her cocktail up and with a bright smile, crashed it against my martini glass. "Cheers, wolf girl. Here's to making Sin City our bitch."

"I think you might have that backwards, Jezzy," I laughed as the high-strung, erratic energy of the hotel's occupants crawled over me. It was intense, intriguing and a little chaotic. "This city is going to chew us up and spit us out."

I sat back in the comfy chair, running a hand over the soft material. The scent of cigarettes and perfume quickly became irritating, and I wrinkled my nose in distaste. Coming to Las Vegas had been Jez's idea of a getaway, but it was more than that for Arys and me. This trip could prove to be downright deadly.

"I just hope I can keep up with the two of you." Shaz sipped a beer, his jade-green eyes scanning the vicinity with the wolf's calm curiosity.

I was happy he had come along on this trip. The time he'd recently spent in the mountains had been hard on both of us. Gone for about five weeks, his absence had been a gaping void in my life. I'd missed him desperately. Our relationship was complicated. Straightening it out was going to take time.

We arrived at the hotel well past a normal check in time, not that there was a whole lot of normal going on in Las Vegas. Arys had gone to the front desk to see about our rooms, while Jez had promptly led the way to the bar, bubbling over with excitement. She was an endless well of exuberance.

I watched her bounce in her chair as she tossed back the fruity drink. Though her enthusiasm was genuine, I couldn't help but wonder if she was trying extra hard to leave her emotions back at home. Suffering the loss of a lover can really screw up a person. Of course, she needed to cut loose and leave the real world behind for a while.

"We should go hit the slot machines," Jez said, abandoning her empty glass. She peered over the partition to the casino beyond. "It's still early."

I glanced down at the bags near our feet, glad I had packed relatively light. "Slow down there, wildcat. Lots of time for that. Let's get settled into our rooms first. I could use a few hours of sleep before Harley's crew knows we're here."

"Do you think they'll be a problem?" Shaz picked at the label on his beer bottle, but his eyes were on me. "It's not like you came here to make trouble for them. Did you?"

I squirmed a little under the weight of his gaze. There was so much going unsaid between us these days. Since he got back, neither of us had wanted to ruin the glow of his return by touching on past events.

"You're asking the wrong person." I shook my head and looked at a young couple falling all over each other in the corner. Anything to break eye contact. "Arys wasn't willing to let me come here without him. That should speak for itself."

"It does." Shaz followed my gaze, spying the smitten lovers. He looked back to me and raised a brow, flashing me a flirty grin.

A blush warmed my cheeks. In so many ways, it felt like we were starting over. The anticipation of every look and touch was strong. Things had changed, but we'd been so close once. The love we had for one another still existed, beneath the remnants of the mess we'd made. Perhaps we'd find our way back to each other. Eventually.

"If I have to watch you two slip shy glances back and forth all week, I may have to poke my eyes out." Jez groaned and pretended to vomit. "Just go bang your brains out already and get it out of your system."

"Jez," I admonished with a glare, flushing with the heat of embarrassment. A peek at Shaz revealed he was trying to suppress a laugh.

"Sorry," she said but clearly didn't mean it. "I'm just jealous and bitter. Seriously, though, somebody should be fucking like bunnies. Might as well be you guys."

It was a touchy subject for sure. Shaz and I hadn't been intimate in months. It wasn't something I wanted to rush. It had to happen in its own time.

"This is Vegas." Shaz spoke up. "I doubt it will take you long to find a sexy lady to rock your world, Jez. And if you're not ready, that's ok too. We'll happily drink ourselves stupid with you. Right, Lex?"

I opened my mouth to reply, but nothing came out. The vampire that had just walked into the bar transfixed me. Shit. Where was Arys?

Bracing for the moment the vampire would look our way, I held my breath. His dark gaze fell upon me immediately, and I froze. He was tall and burly. Bearded with long, shaggy hair, his dark eyes were piercing. Our gazes met, and he stared into me with a fierceness that made me defensive. In a show of blatant disrespect, he felt me out, reaching out metaphysically to get a taste of my power. It was invasive and beyond rude. Instead of resisting his appraisal, I took the brief opportunity to do the same.

I barely tasted his power when a blur of images hit me, flashes of the memories that lived deep within my subconscious. Arys's memories.

The vampire's strong pull of energy oozed eroticism and violent pleasure. It promised to draw me in, to make me lust's slave, to keep me begging no matter how bad it hurt. I knew that power very well; I possessed it. Whoever he was, he belonged to Harley's bloodline, just as Arys and I did.

I hadn't always been able to identify the vampires that shared Arys's sire. Now I could feel the strange metaphysical flavor that we all shared. It was both pleasing and startling to see how my power had grown.

Outwardly disaffected and nonchalant, I sat back in my seat and exuded a relaxed appearance. Inside I was coiling my power tight in my core, knowing I couldn't use it in a human place like this but ready just the same.

"Lex?" Jez spoke softly, her words for my ears only. "Is this gonna get ugly?"

"No." I didn't dare take my eyes off the vampire taking calculated steps toward our table. "It doesn't have to. We're not doing a damn thing. Just having a drink."

Shaz didn't move a muscle, yet his wolf was ready. I could feel it.

This city buzzed with supernatural energy from the monsters who called it home. I shouldn't have been surprised that we'd already encountered a vamp. I suppose it had been wishful thinking that we'd make it until tomorrow night without our arrival being discovered.

"May I?" The vampire pulled out the empty chair at our table, inclining his head in inquiry. The light flashed off something metallic in his mouth, and I realized one of his fangs was gold. I couldn't tell if his entire fang was gold, a replacement for the original tooth, or if it was merely gold plated. Either way, it gave his already rugged face an additional element of menace.

"Go right ahead." I gestured to the chair, studying our guest. It would be nice if Arys would reappear. I had hoped he would be the one to handle the locals.

The vampire glanced around the table, taking us all in one at a time. He ended with me. Propping his elbows on the table, he clasped his hands and grinned. "So it's true; Arys and his wolf are in town. I had to see for myself. Is this a personal visit?"

"News travels fast here, huh?" I refused to be intimidated. Obviously, the Vegas vamps had eyes and ears all over the place. "Just here to lose some money and drink a lot of booze. Like everyone else."

"Arys doesn't set foot in this city without a reason. Not anymore. We can't help but think he's here to make a play for Harley's old turf. Where is Arys anyway?" The vampire let his gaze travel over me, lingering on my cleavage and then on the pulse in my throat.

As much as I dreaded the day I would join the vampire ranks, I looked forward to having them look at me without seeing a super-charged snack. Ignoring his hungry stare, I reached out to Arys, opening the mental link between us.

'We have a visitor. Friend of yours I think.' I let him see through my eyes, showing him the undead man seated at the table next to me.

'Do not leave that bar. I'm coming.' His alarm sang through me, hitting notes of worry and apprehension.

"Arys is right around the corner, checking in," I said, my smile so tight it hurt. "He'll be here any moment."

"He left your side in this city? You must be stronger than you look. Or else he's grown careless."

"Come on now, Roscoe." The vampire's name fell from my lips, surfacing from my subconscious. "You know Arys better than that."

Roscoe was visibly surprised, but he hid it quickly. "So Harley was right after all. You're the one Arys was dreaming about all those years ago."

It was my turn to be surprised. I didn't know Harley's many vampire progeny knew that much about me. Since I couldn't willingly access each of Arys's memories—a blessing in disguise, I was sure, as having them all free flowing in my mind would likely be too much to handle—Arys clearly needed to tell me a few things.

"Whatever Harley said, I'm sure it was fabricated from his delusions." I scowled and sipped from my drink. Harley was a bitter subject for both Arys and I, each for different reasons. I doubted that would ever change.

Roscoe chuckled, a low throaty sound that struck another hidden chord in my memory. He shifted in his chair, his scent wafting to me. He smelled like expensive cologne, cigarettes and blood, all rolled into one nose-assaulting odor.

"Sounds like you really knew him." Roscoe leaned across the table, dangerously close. He ignored Shaz, who leaned in as well. "Before you killed him."

"We're not playing this game. I came here to escape masculine, pseudo-macho bullshit and head games. Spare me the crap." I held his gaze, letting the wolf show in my eyes. I kept my power tightly contained so it wouldn't change my brown eyes to Arys's vampire blue. This guy didn't need to see it.

Jez glanced nervously at the door as the cold wind of Arys's arrival swept over me. He strode into the bar with a cool, composed demeanor, but I could feel the storm building within him.

Arys was a dark dream in black leather. Blue jeans and a white t-shirt along with a leather jacket and his sexy mess of ebony hair gave him a slightly 50s greaser look. No matter how many times I saw him walk into a room, I couldn't help but swoon.

With the grace of the undead, he moved through the bar. His dark-blue gaze locked on Roscoe, who stood in time for Arys to grab him around the throat. He jerked the other vampire close and shook him.

"What the hell do you want, Roscoe?" Arys snarled. "You know what happens if any of you touch her."

Roscoe raised both hands and shook his head. "Hey, brother, take it easy. There's been no touching. Just scoping out the tip that you were in town."

"I have as much a right to be here as you do. We won't be around long, so just stay out of our way." Arys released his hold on Roscoe so they stood nose to nose.

"You know Jenner will want more than that. Why are you here?" Roscoe took a step back, an action that spoke volumes. The same vampire may have sired them, but Arys had dominance here.

Jenner…that name rang a bell though I couldn't put a face to it. When I killed Harley, I hadn't entertained the idea that I might have to face the vampires tied to him. It had been hard enough to face Arys. Nervous, I wished for a moment that we'd vacationed somewhere else, where nobody knew who I was.

"Tell Jenner he should be on his knees praying every night that I don't show my face in his club while I'm here. If he wants trouble, I'll bring him trouble." The atmosphere hummed with the intensity of Arys's growing ire.

Nobody in the bar paid him any attention. They were all too caught up in their own evasion of reality to notice or care that two men glared at one another like dogs about to fight.

Roscoe slid a glance my way. "You shouldn't have brought her here."

"Why? Are you afraid of her? You probably should be."

"Look, Arys, I have no issue with you, but I'm Jenner's right hand. I'm just here to deliver a message: Get out of town or be driven out." Roscoe shrugged, and his long brown hair fell over one eye. "Sorry. Gotta keep tabs on the city. Security, you know."

Arys caught my eye, and a mischievous grin lit up his face. "Be sure to remind Jenner that Alexa is the one who killed Harley. He should have considered that very carefully before he sent the welcome wagon with a threat."

Oh geez. My stomach flip-flopped, and I almost choked on my next sip of booze. Shaz regarded both vampires with curious interest. He didn't need to have Arys's memories to tell there was some serious history between them. Jez ran a finger around the edge of her glass, watching with trepidation as her hopes for a carefree party week shattered with the inevitable vampire pissing contest.

Roscoe took one last perusal of our table. He lingered on Shaz as the two of them had a predatory stare down. When he finally dragged his gaze back to Arys, he said, "If I were you, I'd hop the first flight out of here after sunset."

"That's not going to happen." Crossing his arms, Arys gave a halfhearted shrug.

"If you're here to move on Harley's turf—"

Arys cut in. "I'm not going anywhere."

Roscoe clamped his mouth shut. A glare made his tough features downright scary. He nodded curtly and shoved past Arys, exiting the bar.

I sighed and downed the rest of my drink in one swallow. Might as well keep 'em coming. If this was an indication of how the rest of the trip would go, I might need to stay drunk to get through it without having a nervous breakdown.

I flew fourteen hundred miles to have a few days to myself. So much for that.

Chapter Two

I shoved the door to our suite open, happy to be away from the hotel buzz below. I needed a quiet, safe place to gather my thoughts and interrogate Arys.

Jez had booked us two attached rooms in the Augustus Tower. The first door opened into a small foyer where Jez's room lay to the left and ours was straight ahead. We walked through both suites, checking out everything from the tubs to the minibar.

Immediately, I noticed a problem. I stood in the center of the living and dining room combo, taking in the warm colors and flat screen TV. Arys took our things to the bedroom while I tried to find a way to give voice to the issue.

"So, um, Jez?" I began awkwardly. "When you booked these rooms, did you realize there is only one bed in our suite?"

She popped back into our room after dropping her bags in her suite. "Uh, shit. I'm sorry, guys. I didn't think. I just assumed. Wow, I feel like an ass."

Shaz and I exchanged a look. He shrugged it off, but I knew he was as uncomfortable as I was. "It's no big deal," he said. "I can crash on the couch."

"You don't have to do that. There are two beds in my room but no separate living room, which is why I gave you guys this room." Jez helped herself to a beer from the minibar.

"Hey," I scolded. "You only get twenty seconds to put that back before we get charged for it."

"Um, what's your point?" She shot me an incredulous look and popped the top on the beer. "Wanna trade rooms? Or someone can crash in my room with me."

Arys reappeared wearing a devilish smile that revealed sharp fangs. His gaze slid from me to Shaz. "Or the two of you could get naked and get over this weird shit you've got going on."

"Arys," I scolded at the same time Jez quipped, "That's what I said."

I was mortified. The blood drained from my face. I wanted to drop through the floor to the suite below.

Shaz grabbed his bags and headed for the door. "It's cool. I'll take the extra bed in Jez's room."

I turned on Arys, shaking a finger at him. "Why the hell did you say that? Shaz and I can do this on our own in our own time. Without your help."

Arys snickered and grabbed my finger, pretending to bite it. "I guarantee you the wolf pup will be back in our bed by the end of this week."

I glanced toward the door, knowing damn well Shaz's wolf ears could hear our every word. Jez busied herself with the view, staring out the picture window at The Strip.

"Are you crazy?" I snapped, jerking my finger from his grasp. "We can't just all jump into bed together, Arys. It doesn't work that way. Besides, there can't be any blood sharing with him around. None."

Arys feigned a yawn, completely ignoring my irritation. "I'm not going to bleed your wolf, Alexa, but give him some credit. He's stronger than you think. He wouldn't be here if he wasn't."

I joined Jez at the window, watching the traffic down below. The city was a maze of lights as far as the eye could see. The Eiffel Tower at Paris Las Vegas stood bright against the skyline.

"I'm so sorry," Jez whispered, reaching to touch my hand. "I shouldn't have assumed anything."

"No worries. It's not your fault. It's my mess."

"Wanna go back downstairs to drink and gamble? It's not even dawn yet."

"No way," Arys cut in. "You can't go running around the hotel without me. It's not safe."

My temper flared, and I pinned him with a deadly glare. The angry energy spilled from me. I had to make a conscious effort not to slap him with it. "Don't start with that shit," I warned, a growl lacing my words. "I didn't come here to argue with you. I came for a good time with people I love. Don't ruin it."

"I won't let you put yourself in danger." Arys was noncommittal, refusing to argue. He held up his hands as if to say he was done and that was the final word.

"Then come with us," I said. "There's not a big sunlight risk inside the casino."

"And on that note," Jez announced, "I'm going to go to my room and unpack a few things."

Storming from the living room, I rounded the corner to the bathroom where I splashed some cold water on my face and checked my cell phone for messages. There was a text from Kylarai making sure we'd made it safely. While I typed a quick reply, I sat on the edge of the tub, fuming.

I wasn't really pissed at Arys but myself. I'd created the situation with Shaz that made me insecure, and I'd secured so much power that I couldn't even step into a city far from home without trouble from a damn vampire.

Being angry was easier than being afraid, and I realized I was scared, dammit. The last time I'd encountered Harley's vampires, a dear friend had died, and I'd had to fight to prove I was a force to be reckoned with. I wasn't sure I could do that here in their home territory.

Returning to the sink, I ran my fingers through my hair and took a few deep breaths. This trip was about having fun. I would not allow either Arys or his Vegas vampire family to ruin it for me. I was going to have a good time, goddammit, even if it killed me. Which it just might.

When I opened the door, Arys was standing in the hall waiting for me. He held out a glass of whiskey, which I gratefully accepted. What could I say? He knew me well.

"Sorry for being an asshole," he said, pulling me close for a soft kiss. "You can take care of yourself. I know that. It's just...Jenner doesn't make empty threats. And he isn't going to let us out of this city without rubbing my nose in the fact that he's taken over Harley's business. I'm sure he's going to want a look at you."

"Of course." I sipped the whiskey and made a face. "I'm really sick of Harley's vampires looking at me like I'm some kind of fucking carnival prize."

"They won't. Not for long anyway. Jenner won't take it too far. He doesn't have a personal stake in my connection to you the way Harley did. His biggest concern will be keeping us from taking what is rightfully ours." Arys held me tight, his embrace possessive.

I pulled back to look into his eyes. "Please tell me that's not why you came here."

"It's not. Not really." Arys smirked, and I knew he was up to something. "I might let him think so though."

I groaned and pushed a lock of long, ash-blonde hair back from my face. "I don't like the sound of that. We need to keep the peace while we're here. There's enough trouble waiting for us at home."

My gaze fell to the black dragon on my forearm. The demon mark ensured I could always be found by the demon that left it there. If I wanted to stay sane, having a few days away from Shya and his ridiculous demands was essential. I wasn't keen on filling the void with vampire politics and power struggles.

"Don't worry about anything. You want to go gamble with Jez? Go for it. I'll take the pup and do a little recon." Wrapping his hand gently around my forearm to cover the demon mark, Arys guided me back to the living room.

Jez was shoving my shoulder bag at me before I could change my mind. "We won't be gone long," I called to the guys as she dragged me toward the door. "Stay out of trouble. I mean it, Arys."

His laughter followed me out, and I frowned. Maybe I was paranoid, but I never felt good about leaving the two of them alone together. His sudden willingness to let me wander off without him smacked of some suspicious, clandestine activity, but I wasn't about to question it. Not yet.

"They'll be fine," Jez admonished, catching me staring back at the closed hotel door. "They're grown men. And then some. I'm willing to bet we find more trouble than they do."

"Good Lord, I hope not. We've only been here a few hours."

"Then I'd say we're already behind." Jez linked her arm in mine and all but skipped her way to the elevator. I couldn't help but smile. Her enthusiasm was infectious.

We made our way to the casino where my senses were immediately overwhelmed. The noise hurt my sensitive wolf ears. Raised voices mingled with the clink of bottles and glasses, all topped off with the clang and ding of so many slot machines. I wasn't sure what was worse, the sound or the smell. So many people crammed into one large windowless room gave off the pungent aroma of sweat, perfume and booze. Among other things.

It took several minutes for me to adjust to the assault on my senses. Vegas may be a vampire's city, but it was not wolf friendly. The beast inside rebelled at the thought of staying in this place. It was harsh and raw, too much for my forest-loving, earth-bound wolf.

A glance at Jez revealed a wound up woman ready to gamble. For a werecat, she was completely unfazed in this environment. Perhaps it was the demon blood in her veins.

"How exciting," she gushed. "This city never sleeps. I missed it. I could totally live here."

"Not me. I couldn't survive in a city like this." I gazed about in wonder, finding each person more intriguing than the last. Vegas was many things, but you couldn't say it wasn't entertaining.

My gaze closed in on a lady seated at a nearby slot machine. Dark circles lined her eyes. Her hair was in disarray, and her outfit was far from laundry fresh. A few machines over, an older couple, dressed to the nines in fancy evening wear, laughed and joked as they pumped coin after coin into a machine. Contrasting them with the other lady, I realized this place was an enigma.

"What do you think, Lex? Are we high rollers tonight or what?" Jez eyed a small group of women giggling with drinks in hand, as she led me along.

Raoul, my former lover and the wolf who turned me, had left me more than enough money in his will. It had taken me a long time to bring myself to touch any of it. However, I did not have enough to call myself a high roller, nor was I the type to take that kind of risk. I regularly faced vampires and demons that wanted to kill me; gambling with all the money in the world couldn't replicate that level of danger.

"Hell no." I decided. "I'm a slot machine girl, myself."

"Seriously? Your man is a poker master, and you only play slots?" Jez shook her head and tsked at me. "Sad."

I followed her through the place, content to let her lead the way. A people-watcher could stay in this place round the clock and never run out of interesting things to see. The deeper we went into the casino, the more I felt like I was plunging into a human abyss. I scanned the crowd, feeling for anything present that wasn't human. The energy in the casino was incredibly scattered, creating a loud noise inside my head. I struggled to shut it out to save my sanity.

The demon seated at a nearby table was unexpected. He looked up as we passed, our eyes connected. For a split second, I saw through his human façade to the black-winged, black-eyed creature beneath. He looked us over, lingering on Jez. Then his gaze fell to the demon mark on my wrist, and he turned away.

"I guess I shouldn't be surprised that demons enjoy this city," I muttered.

"Goes without saying, I'd think," Jez quipped, pulling me along.

Once we got caught up in the buzz of playing and even won a few small jackpots, my tension eased, and I began to enjoy myself. Giggling like teenagers as we tossed back shooters; we became part of the room, just two more gamblers out to lose a crap load of dough. Despite our welcome wagon earlier, it felt damn good to unwind and leave my worries behind for a while.

"If you'd like some time alone with Shaz this week, I'm sure I can lure your vampire down here to play some poker." Jez pumped quarters into the machine, waiting while I pushed the button. Nothing. Another quarter.

"Actually, that would be great. We haven't had much time alone since he got home. It's been awkward. Makes me wonder if it will ever feel right again."

"He's had your back from the start, long before you and Arys made your connection. You just need some time together, a chance to remember what made you fall in love." Jez handed me another shooter and smiled. "You're damn lucky, you know, to have them both."

"Yeah," I nodded, taking the shot and grimacing as it burned its way down to my stomach. "I know. But how realistic is it?"

"What do you mean?" Pausing to gather our meager winnings, Jez gave me a critical once over.

I shouldn't say it, shouldn't even think it. But she was one of my best friends, a girlfriend, the one person I could say it to. "Is it selfish of me to want them both? Because it feels like it is. It feels like—" I stopped short, struggling to get the words out. "It feels like it's wrong. For Shaz. He deserves better. He deserves to be set free. Like Kale."

Jez turned to me, taking my hand in hers. "Take a look around you. Do it. Now." She waited expectantly for me to look around the noisy casino. "This is not the place to make those decisions. This is a place to put that shit to bed and go wild. No serious crap. Save it for when you get home. And don't bring Kale into this. That is a whole other fucked-up situation."

"Thanks." I rolled my eyes and stuck some of our winnings back into the machine. I watched the little pictures flip by, waiting for them to stop and proclaim us losers. That didn't happen. Instead, we hit a small jackpot and won five hundred bucks.

"Now that's what I'm talking about, baby!" Jez crowed with glee. "Now let's take this five hundred and play some blackjack."

It didn't take her long to settle at a table with two others. I hung back, content to watch. In no time, Jez was losing a little but winning more. Surrounded by noise and chaos, people getting off on the rush of the risk, she was clearly in her element.

Sunrise was approaching. The casino may be void of windows and clocks, but I could feel it in my bones. I was beginning to tire, in need of a bath and some uninterrupted sleep. Jez didn't appear to feel the same way.

Right about that time, two idiots at the next table over started shouting about cheating. The dealer was trying unsuccessfully to calm the commotion. A fist was thrown, and blood spilled. That's all it took to shatter my control and bring my bloodlust bubbling to the surface.

I was suddenly aware of every heartbeat in the place. They pounded in my skull, reverberating through me in a discombobulated rhythm. So much blood, pumping through the veins of every human present. More than enough to bathe in. How many could I consume before security took me down?

I shook my head, refusing to allow those thoughts to take hold. Not here. Not like this. Taking deep breaths was impossible due to the lack of fresh air. Breathing in the scent of smoke, liquor and lively humans was not going to help. *Stay calm. You got this.* But I didn't. A little personal pep talk wasn't going to give me the strength I needed. Security quickly dealt with the troublemakers. The bleeder was gone. Too late though. The damage was done.

I grabbed Jez's arm and leaned in close, whispering under my breath, "I'm leaving before I turn this place into a bloodbath."

Her head snapped up, and her eyes were huge. "You've got to be kidding me."

"I wish." I backed away, unable to be so close to the pureblooded Were. Only the knowledge that the blood was demon tainted kept me moving. After my stint on angel blood, no way in hell was I going to taste anything even remotely demon.

"Lex, wait. You can't go alone." She dropped her cards and held up her hands to show the dealer she was out before rushing after me.

"I feel so stupid for thinking I could come to a place like this and not totally lose my shit," I growled, balling my hands into fists so tight my nails dug into my palm. I moved fast for the exit, finding with each step it felt farther away. No idiots designed these places.

"What about Arys? Can he help?" Jez fell into step beside me, looking worried. She watched me closely, ready to tackle me if I gave her reason to.

I laughed bitterly. "Yeah he can help me hunt and kill someone."

Jez grimaced and surveyed our busy surroundings. "What about my blood?"

I stopped short, causing the waitress behind us to swerve to avoid a collision. I searched her emerald eyes. "You would do that for me? I don't even know what to say to that. Thank you. Unfortunately, I don't think I could if I wanted to. After what Falon's blood did to me, I don't think I should risk demon blood, even if it's just half."

She nodded, and obvious relief swept over her. Couldn't say I blamed her, though I would never forget that she offered. Her blood hadn't harmed Kale, but why take the chance? Besides, she was a friend. Not food.

"You can stay here if you want to keep playing," I said, feeling guilty. I shouldn't need my friends to babysit me.

"I can't let you wander the hotel alone like this. Come on; let's get back to Arys so he can bring you down. Or whatever."

It was growing harder to form words. My focus scattered. "I'm not sure it's a good idea for us to be locked in an elevator together right now." I watched the green of her iris bleed across the whites of her eyes. She was ready, defensive.

"It's cool. You don't have that insane undead strength yet. I think I can take you." She forced a smile, but it didn't reach her eyes.

Every person we passed was walking, talking food. I held myself on a tightly wound leash, knowing it would soon snap. I considered breaking into a run for the elevator. By the time we got there, I was perspiring from the effort it took to restrain myself. I wanted the sensation of my fangs sinking into flesh, the moment when the blood burst forth and the acrid scent of fear. The need for it made my stomach hurt.

The elevator door opened, and a man stepped out. I lunged at him, instinct overriding sense. Jez caught me around the waist, dragging me away. Her grip was firm. She held tight until he had hurried away, muttering after him, "Sorry. Sometimes the party just never stops for this one."

She shoved me into the elevator, forcing me into a back corner. She hit the button for our floor but never took her eyes off me. "I sure hope you can deal with this shit, Alexa. It's going to ruin the entire trip. We'll have to lock you in the hotel room so you can't run amok and terrorize the city."

I frowned, unable to find any humor in the visual she brought to mind. This trip was off to a shitty start so far. It was discouraging. I just wanted to have a little fun. Was that so wrong?

I stared at the floor, trying to memorize the strange flower pattern on the carpet. The back wall was mirrored, and I avoided looking at myself. I didn't want to see Arys's blue eyes on me. So when I tired of the carpet, I stared at the screen near the ceiling instead, trying to focus on the running ads for various live shows.

When the door opened, Jez went first, checking for anyone in the hall before allowing me out. We made it back to our room without incident. Ok, so that could have been far worse than it was.

My relief was short lived. My senses blazed as I became keenly aware of the heavy vampire energy burning inside the suite. It wasn't just Arys. Someone else was inside. My bloodlust was strong, but my fear was stronger.

"Somebody is in there with the guys," I said, my hand on the doorknob.

We exchanged a look, ready to confront the stranger inside. Jez slid the key card into the slot, and I shoved the door open. I strode into the suite, a mess of hunger and wariness. I took one step into the living room and stopped dead in my tracks.

Arys sat in the middle of the couch, straddled by a buxom blonde.

Chapter Three

"What the fuck?" I was stunned, but anger quickly followed the shock.

The blonde got to her feet, managing to look elegant and coy at the same time. Arys sprang off the couch as if he were on fire. Shaz sat as far away as he could get from both vampires without leaving the room. His expression was pensive but sour.

"Alexa, this is Sloane. She's one of Harley's, like me. She just came by to say hello." Arys stood between the tall, leggy vampiress and me as if he feared I might lunge for her. It was tempting. "She was just about to leave."

I stood with hands on my hips, glaring with a vengeance. "Save the crap. It sure didn't look that way."

I knew who she was. I recognized her from Arys's memories. She had played a significant role in his life. Having lured him in for Harley, one might say she was directly responsible for Arys's conversion to vampire.

Sloane shoved past Arys, extending a hand to me. A friendly smile lit up her face. "I'm Sloane. It's so nice to finally meet Arys's wolf. You are more beautiful than I was led to believe."

I stared at her hand, confused by her sugary sweet greeting. Was she for real? I was hesitant to take her hand, knowing she'd use the opportunity to taste my power. However, I was curious myself. I accepted her hand, boldly meeting her ocean blue gaze. Her energy hummed with that same tone I was coming to associate with Harley's bloodline. It crawled into my palm, a strong, warm but neutral pulse of power. She wasn't aggressive in any way, which made it especially hard not to send a little jolt into her.

"May I ask why the hell you were practically dry humping my lover?" I asked, my smile brittle and forced.

She turned to Arys with a laugh that had clearly been perfected over the centuries and a very subtle, hard to place accent that came through only on certain words. It sounded European. "She's feisty. I like her. Finally, Arys, a woman that can keep you in line." To me she said, "I apologize. It's been a long time since I've seen him. I let my excitement get the best of me. It won't happen again."

"You're damn right it won't." This time my smile was genuine, and it was vicious. My wolf looked out at her, promising very bad things for the woman that dared to climb all over my man.

"I told you, Sloane," Arys said, having a hard time meeting my eyes. "Alexa doesn't like to share. And I no longer enjoy being shared. Things have changed."

I bristled at that. It was impossible not to look Shaz's way. He remained motionless, void of any true emotion. I wondered how much I had missed.

Sloane saw the brief exchange and nodded in sudden understanding. "Oh, I see. Well, I can respect that. She is your other half after all. Not much room left for another in that tightly bound equation now is there?"

Shaz winced, though I wasn't sure she intended her words as a direct hit. Sloane was oblivious, rambling on again about how thrilled she was to meet the one woman who could tame Arys Knight. Tame him? She had no idea what she was talking about. There was no taming a vamp like Arys.

"You should go, Sloane. I'm sure Jenner would have a tantrum if he knew you came here to throw yourself at me." Arys gestured to the door, clearly not interested in having me in the same room as yet another of his old lovers. This was how many now?

Sloane retrieved a little black clutch from the couch. It matched the little black dress that hugged her curves like a second skin. I felt incredibly underdressed compared to the women of Vegas.

"Don't flatter yourself, sweetheart. You may be a bad ass in bed, but that's not why I came here." With a wink, she reached for Arys, grasping his hand tight. "I came to warn you, Arys. Get out of town. Jenner feels threatened by your arrival."

"Good," Arys said with a satisfied sneer. "He should be threatened. I could have this city if I wanted it."

"But you don't, do you? You left Vegas and everyone in it. You abandoned us. You don't belong here anymore." Sloane's lower lip trembled, a subtle but dramatic action that had me snorting in derision.

"Spare me the dramatics, Sloane." Arys pulled away from her and stalked over to the door. "I didn't abandon a damn thing. The way I remember it, you weren't exactly begging me to stay."

I was growing increasingly uneasy as I watched their exchange. A dull throb racked my brain as memories that didn't belong to me struggled to surface.

Sloane stood her ground, refusing to allow Arys to usher her out the door. "Harley and Jenner never understood your reasons for leaving. I did." Her cool blue gaze flicked to me. "But coming back was a really dumb move. It's dangerous. Go home, Arys. Please."

"Goodbye, Sloane." Jerking the door open, Arys ignored her pleas. He swung his arm in a gesture for her to get out. The two vampires had a stare down the way vampires often do. Arys won.

With a huff and a shrug, Sloane sashayed from the room. Lingering at the door, she cast a glance at each of us in turn, ending with Arys. "I was hoping you'd prove to be the more reasonable one. God knows it isn't Jenner. Your presence opens up old wounds. You should know better." Without another word, she disappeared into the hallway.

The door slammed behind her, and I faced Arys with a deadly glare. "Are you kidding me? What the hell was that?"

"I didn't know she was coming," Arys began to explain, continuing even as my glare darkened. "Sloane was just being Sloane. She's a bit over the top sometimes. She doesn't mean any harm though. I'm sure she's overreacting." Realizing he was rambling, he paused to study me. "Are you ok? You feel a little scattered."

"I wasn't ok before I walked in here. Now I'm not ok, and I'm pissed." Instead of allowing my temper to start a fight, I walked away. I went to the bedroom to dig through my suitcase. My hands shook from hunger and fury. Damn vampires and their touchy feely, cryptic crap.

From the living room came Joe's low murmur, telling Arys about my near attack on the man downstairs. Shaz's voice joined the mix, and I tuned them all out by crossing the hall to the bathroom.

The tub was nice and big, with jets. A quick perusal of the small bottles lined up on the bathroom counter revealed bubble bath. If I could relax and refocus my energy, perhaps it would help. The urgency and demand of the bloodlust had faded, though it remained as an ill twinge in the pit of my stomach.

I was expecting Arys when he knocked, then opened the door. I stood at the counter, tying my long locks up into a bun to keep them from getting wet. The mirror allowed me to watch him enter, closing the door behind him. Our eyes met through the reflection.

"How are you feeling?" He asked tentatively as if expecting me to tear his head off.

"I feel like a failure for losing control like that. I feel like bitch slapping you for flaunting another former lover in my face." I leaned over the tub to check the water temperature and turned the hot up a bit. "I won't though. I'm mostly just mad at myself. And that cheap blonde floozy."

Arys's lips twitched as he tried to hide his amusement at my jealousy. "There's only one blonde for me. You know that."

"I do. I know." I nodded, peeling my top off and tossing it on the floor. I saw the way his gaze traveled over me, lingering on my bra-covered breasts. It was a nice stroke of my ego, especially after seeing the knockout that just walked out of here. "Are you planning to stay and watch while I relax in a bath? Maybe tell me some lies about how this Vegas visit won't be a total mind fuck?"

"Oh, it will be that and more, I'm sure." Arys leaned against the counter, watching me strip down as if he hadn't seen my body countless times before. "I came to give you blood. It'll kill the urge for a while. Don't slap me for saying this, but you might have to, um, partake a little. Obviously, the ideal place would be Jenner's club. I believe I owe it a visit anyway."

Harley Kayson had owned a small franchise of nightclubs for those who wanted to give and take blood, among other things. The Edmonton club caused tons of trouble in my city, until Shaz and I killed Harley. Naturally, I took over control of that club, but that's where my control ended. Harley's other properties were scattered around North America, and Lord knows where else, each of them under someone else's control. Las Vegas was Jenner's.

I didn't need blood to survive. Not yet. But I did need it to keep the bloodlust at bay. Vampire blood was potent and powerful but a short term fix at best. It wasn't mortal, yet it would take the edge off. However, Arys was ludicrous to think we could walk into the club of the vampire who had told us to get the hell out of town.

"We didn't think this part through before leaving home." I turned off the water and stuck a toe in the tub. It was hot and welcoming. "I can't take blood from some Vegas blood whore. And most definitely not at a club owned by someone who hates you. We're not going in there."

"What about Shaz? You could take his blood. No power games."

I shot Arys a dirty look, surprised he would suggest such a thing. "Absolutely not. Totally out of the question. I can't use him as a blood source. It's far too dangerous."

"For who?" Arys challenged. "Him or you? It's just blood, Alexa. He can handle bleeding a little."

"It's never just blood!" My voice echoed, amplified by the bathroom acoustics. I lowered the volume, aware of the keen ears beyond the door. "You've said the same thing yourself."

Arys held his hands up in surrender. "Fine. I'll leave that between you and the pup. Eventually, it will come up again. But I'm out of it. Ok?" He held his wrist out to me in invitation.

I didn't want his wrist, but I accepted it anyway. I preferred a more intimate bite. There was nothing like feeling someone's jugular beneath my lips. My fangs sprang forth, yet I hesitated. Wolf fangs didn't pierce as neatly as vampire fangs. When Arys gestured for me to go ahead, I bit carefully into his wrist. The tangy vampire blood spilled from the wound, deliciously coating my tongue. I sucked hard on the bite, coaxing a groan from Arys.

With his free hand, he stroked my hair. His arousal was palpable, a heady desire that rolled off him like waves on the ocean. Arys was always ready and willing. However, he would never make a good victim. There was one thing missing. He didn't fear me.

Blood was just one part of the feed for a succubus like me. It was because of Arys's incubus nature, courtesy of his bloodline. We needed more than just blood. We needed to feast upon the lusty energy of our victim, and in turn, their fear aroused us. It all went hand in hand. Arys's blood tasted like power and eased my hunger, but it wasn't enough.

I gazed up at him, running my tongue over my lips. Shoving a hand into my hair, he kissed me with a primal passion. Arys slipped his tongue into my mouth, firm and commanding. My head spun, and I fell into him, my earlier irritation obliterated.

"Take your bath. Relax. We're here to enjoy ourselves." Arys pulled me into a hug, running his hands down my naked body.

"The tub is big enough for two," I taunted. I pulled away and climbed into the bathtub. Sinking below the bubbles into the soothing heat, I sighed with pleasure and crooked a finger to beckon to Arys.

He raised a dark brow, his expression playful. "Tempting. Very tempting. Might I suggest you extend that offer Shaz's way tonight instead?"

That I had certainly not expected to hear. I pursed my lips, trying hard not to frown. "That's definitely not an Arys comment. What's your deal? And anyway, I don't think Shaz and I are there yet. Too awkward."

"Which is exactly why I should send him in," Arys said, his gaze on the bubbles hiding my nudity. "I don't have a deal. I just want to see your relationship restored."

"Why? What's it to you?"

Arys maintained eye contact, but I saw the lie in his eyes. "I just want you to be happy. The pup too."

I squinted at him with my best scrutinizing stare. "You have an ulterior motive. I know you do. Why do you really want Shaz and me to reconnect? You were never so keen on sharing before, unless you got something out of it."

"He's the only one I trust to protect you." There it was. Arys's confession was no surprise. "That wolf would die for you if he had to. Loyalty like that only comes from love."

"So you're willing to exploit his feelings for me," I said with a nod. "Sounds about right."

Arys shrugged and headed for the door. "Be mad if you like. You're the most important thing to me. I'll do whatever it takes to protect you."

"I noticed." My tone dripped with acid. I was still bitter about Arys's recent stint dealing with a demon for my so-called protection.

"I've got to talk to the others about our visit to The Wicked Kiss. Enjoy your bath." He ignored my snarky remark but paused to add, "You may want to do some shopping. I want you dressed to kill."

He left swiftly, closing the bathroom door behind him before I could protest his latest bout of insanity. I squashed the urge to grab a towel and go after him. Screw it. If Arys was going to raise hell, then I might as well enjoy a hot bath first.

* * * *

"You don't have to come with us. Really. Don't feel obligated." I stood in front of the bathroom mirror the following evening, digging through my makeup bag. Jez was beside me, doing the same. There was more than enough counter space for the both of us.

"Are you kidding? I'm not missing out on a chance to see how Sin City does a club like The Wicked Kiss." Jez swept mascara onto her long lashes. Her hair was bound up high on her head in a towel. "Aren't you the least bit curious?"

I lined my eyes with black liner, creating a dramatic cat-eye effect. I paused to paw through my bag, looking for my favorite pale silver shadow. "No, I'm pretty much just scared. I think Arys is letting his history with these vampires cloud his judgment. I'm not sure what I dread more, meeting Jenner or seeing what goes on in his club. Harley was using that place in a blood ring operation. Some twisted shit."

Jez carefully applied her trademark red lipstick, pursing her lips to inspect her handy work. "Isn't Harley's stuff technically yours now? I mean, you killed him."

"Some might say that." I was hesitant to claim anything of Harley's as mine. I'd gotten my share. "I don't want it though. My hands are full as it is."

"Better make sure the new owner knows that."

"I intend to, when I'm not doing damage control for Arys. He's stubborn, but this time he's taken it to a whole new level." I finished my makeup, refusing when Jez tried to force me to wear red lipstick as well. She thought it went with everything at any time of day. It wouldn't surprise me if she wore it with PJs as well.

To appease her, I agreed to a light pink lip-gloss that smelled like candy. She huffed at me like the snooty cat she sometimes was but relented. After layering my lashes in volumizing mascara, I stared at my hair and shrugged.

"Leave it down," Jez suggested, eyeing me through the mirror. "It's so long and beautiful. It looks really bad ass down."

"Thanks." I pulled a brush through the tangled ash blonde mess until it lay smooth against my back. "Sometimes I think about hacking it all off and dying it black." Since trimming off the black tips I used to have, I hadn't added any color to it.

"Oh God, don't do that." Jez was aghast. "That's too drastic. And I don't have to be a shrink to tell you what that kind of sudden change often means."

"That I'm in need of control and can find it only in insignificant things like my hair style because I'm too neurotic to keep my shit together." I smiled, but I wasn't joking.

"Yeah, exactly that." She turned to face me, a serious light in her green eyes. "Please don't go off the rails on me, Alexa. I can't lose another friend like that."

I reached to touch her hand, a brief but poignant connection. "I won't. I promise."

She was thinking about Kale Sinclair, our friend and my one time lover. The three of us had been a tight knit group for several years. Recently, that had unraveled, primarily because of Kale's inability to maintain his sanity. Five hundred years of vampire hell could do that to a person.

"You know I'm always here for you, right? No matter what." Pulling me into a hug, Jez held tight. She hummed with pent up emotion that sought to escape her restraint.

"I know." I breathed in her earthy Were scent. It was comforting. "I love you, Jezzy."

Things had been tough for us both lately. She had lost the woman she loved. We had both lost Kale to his delusions. Worst of all, we'd lost our illusions: safety, peace, self-contentment. Gone. All of it.

"Ok, enough sappy shit." Jez pulled away and tugged the towel off, letting her damp golden locks tumble over her shoulders. "Should I flat iron or let it curl naturally?"

"Curls, definitely. I can never understand why women with curls straighten their hair." I studied my poker straight tresses. I was more than a little envious of Jez's gorgeous curls.

"Go get dressed," she commanded, grabbing the blow dryer. "Your boys will hit the floor when they see what you bought."

I still couldn't believe I'd let her talk me into buying the body-hugging dress. The bodice was a black corset that made my breasts look photoshopped. The skirt was fairy style, cut into black and white jagged edges that fell halfway down my thigh. It had looked pretty damn good in the dressing room before I bought it.

Now I wasn't so sure. I brought it from the bedroom into the bathroom so Jez could help me lace up the back. "I don't know about this. Maybe I should have bought pants."

"Don't start. Insecurity is not allowed for Arys Knight's queen," she snickered, tying the lacing securely but allowing me room to breathe properly. "I still think the red lipstick would top it all off. Think about it."

I ran a hand down the tight bodice to the skirt, reveling in the soft material. It was a knockout dress for sure. I felt good in it, sexy. As I gazed at my reflection, the insecurities began to fall away. I hoped this was what Arys had in mind when he said dressed to kill.

"No red lips," I said, grabbing my choker from the counter top.

I knew better than to walk into a place like The Wicked Kiss with a bare throat, especially one I didn't run. The choker was black velvet with an oval moonstone hanging from the center. I had found it in my friend Brogan's magic shop.

"Stilettos?" Jez tried, returning to the hair dryer.

"Not a chance." I spritzed on some French vanilla perfume and left the bathroom to fetch my boots from the bedroom. They were black leather and almost knee high. The three-inch heels were perfect, not as dangerously high as Jez would prefer but enough to add height to my petite five foot one frame.

I took a deep breath and left the bedroom, glad that the minibar was outside the door. I poured a few shots of vodka into a glass and stood in the small hallway listening to Arys and Shaz talk in the living room.

"And you're sure we're going to walk out of there in one piece?" Shaz asked, his tone heavy with concern. "The guy told us to get our asses on a plane out of here, and you really think going to his club is the best response to that?"

"Of course," came Arys's self-assured reply. "Jenner's bark has always been worse than his bite. Threats are his way of throwing his power around, making sure I know my place in his city."

"And do you?"

"What do you think, pup?"

Shaz chuckled. "You don't want to know what I think."

"Jenner was Harley's favorite after I left. He wants to make sure I remember that. There's nothing more to it." Arys sounded confident. Too confident.

I rounded the corner, drink in hand. "Harley had a favorite other than you? Great. So this is a case of spoiled sibling rivalry."

Both men looked up at my appearance, and their jaws dropped almost simultaneously. I hid a smile, enjoying their shared reaction.

Arys's blue gaze traveled over me, lingering on my thighs and then my covered throat. "I'm not sure I've ever wanted to bleed you as bad as I do right now." His lip curled in a sexy smirk, sending a tingle through me.

"That's a compliment, right?" I teased though I was keenly aware of the hunger lurking in his stare.

"You're smokin' hot, Lex." Shaz wore a predatory expression of desire that made my stomach flip. "But you could be wearing sweats with no makeup, and you'd still be the most beautiful woman I've ever seen."

An irrational urge to cry overcame me. I didn't. I just wanted to. I also wanted to run across the room and fling myself into Shaz's arms. It wasn't that we didn't touch. We did. It was that there was something missing. I wanted so desperately to rekindle our spark.

"Thank you, Shaz," I said with a slight blush. "You both look pretty damn fine yourselves."

They were each wearing a black suit, both of them slightly casual with no tie and an open collar. Shaz's platinum hair lay neatly, falling over his forehead. Arys's hair was tousled as always. I couldn't help but eat up the eye candy. It was rare that I saw either of them break from their usual casual attire. My mind wandered down a naughty path as I remembered what it felt like to be naked and writhing between them.

"So this is a big deal, huh?" I asked, swirling the vodka in my glass.

Arys shrugged, unwilling to let on how serious he was taking Jenner's threat. "Not so big. Just old friends reacquainting."

"What about this?" I held up the arm bearing the black dragon. "Should I cover it somehow?"

"No, leave it. As shitty as that mark is, it does have its advantages."

Unfortunately, that was true. Those who knew what it was were often reluctant to harm the one who bore it. They feared the wrath of the demon. Anyone who killed me would likely end up taking my debt as their own. Soon, however, this mark would become more of a hindrance than a help.

The worst part was that Arys had one too. Shya had put it on his back where Arys easily hid it from everyone but me. I had to see it in private moments, the one time we should be free of all that shit. But no, Shya had made sure he was never far from our thoughts.

Less than ten minutes later, Jez appeared, a golden vision in white leather. The halter-style dress clung to her like a second skin. It covered her behind but not much else, making her legs look longer than usual. Sky-high stilettos completed the look. Her curls bounced as she sashayed in.

"Can I be you?" I joked. "Just for a day. I want to know what it feels like to be that tall."

"It's the heels, baby," she replied with a wink.

"You look runway fabulous." I downed the rest of my drink and set the glass on the table.

Arys snickered, a low, evil sound. "Good enough to eat."

"Watch it, vampire." Jez wagged a finger at him in warning. "I'm flattered, really, but you're just not pretty enough for me."

Arys laughed but didn't reply. Nobody could out-snark Jez. Not even him. He rose from his seat on the couch and motioned toward the door in a grand sweeping gesture. "Everybody ready?"

I met Shaz's eyes across the room, and we shared a look. The two of us together had killed Harley. Two vampires had come after us, believing we were their ticket to claiming Harley's power. They had failed. If there were to be backlash for any of that, it would be tonight.

"Sure." I nodded. For the first time all evening a hint of apprehension crept in. "Walk into a place where we're not welcome, and I may be wanted for the murder of the former owner...what are we waiting for?"

Chapter Four

No amount of pleading, arguing or threatening would sway Arys. I did everything short of throttling him. Jenner's demand that we leave had only encouraged Arys. Wild horses couldn't drag him away now.

We started at Caesars, deciding it was a good place to get warmed up. Blackjack barely held Arys's interest. Neither the buffet of human treats nor the inviting poker tables caught his attention. Whatever had gone on between him and Jenner, it ran deep. I kept hoping for some clue or answer to pop up from the recesses of my subconscious, but my curiosity remained unsatisfied. I had a sneaking suspicion that would soon change.

The Wicked Kiss was closer than I expected. It was just off The Strip, down a side street. It was big, much bigger than my club back home. However, it was smaller than the other buildings in the area, which allowed it to blend in among them. The exterior of the building had a glassy appearance, reflecting back the street before it, ensuring nobody could see inside.

"Wow," Jez gazed at the vampire club and casino with a mix of awe and intrigue. "This place has got to be at least six times the size of your club, Lex."

"There's more. Underground." Arys led the way to the door. He reached to take my hand, pulling me into step beside him. A united front.

The door opened as we approached. A big, bald vampire who looked like he had never smiled a day in his life greeted us. He stopped us in the lobby, demanding our names. I was itching with curiosity, straining to see past him into the club beyond. The Vegas sounds of slot machines, music and voices spilled out toward us.

Sloane was visible, smiling like she was in a cosmetics commercial for youth serum. She was working the room, chatting up patrons and ensuring the blood and money kept flowing. What a good little hostess she was.

"You're not on the list," the doorman grunted. "Can't let you in without verification from the boss." He pulled a phone from his pocket and began dialing.

Maybe it was just me but having to phone in our arrival really stole the drama from this whole thing. It was hardly worth the risk. Sloane's gaze landed on us, and her eyes widened in alarm. She cleared the distance with inhuman speed.

"Arys, Alexa, hello! I'm so glad you decided to grace us with your presence," Sloane gushed with false enthusiasm that was so good an outsider would never have guessed she was faking it. Taking the phone from the doorman's hand, she ended the call and shook her head. "No need to bother Jenner. These are my guests."

She shoved the phone back into his hand and motioned for us to follow her. The skirt of her thigh length white dress hugged her behind as she walked. I couldn't figure out how it stayed in place without flashing a glimpse of her ass.

Jez's small gasp echoed my own. It was bigger inside than it had appeared. The luxurious quality of it smacked of cheap illusion yet remained stunning. A massive chandelier hung from the ceiling in the center of the room. The carpet was a deep, luscious red, and so firm that, as we walked, our heels did not sink in. A bar lined the full length of the wall to the right. Waitresses in skimpy outfits hurried back and forth with trays laden with drinks.

A stage at the back immediately drew my attention. Half a dozen showgirls danced in lingerie, feathered fans and headpieces popping with bright colors. Vampires, every single one of them. Several male vampires worked the room, dressed to the nines, seducing human women while the ladies on stage brought the men to their knees.

The red carpet wound its way through the casino and past small round tables and a series of private booths in the corners that were not tables at all but small sofa-like beds instead. The essence of sex hung on the air like the place had been built upon it. It rolled over me, a dizzying fog of erotic energy that stole my breath.

"What the hell are you doing here, Arys?" Sloane demanded, her eyes flashing angrily. "You just can't leave things alone, can you?"

"No, he can't," Shaz quipped, though his attention had been captured by our surroundings. "Heaven forbid his manhood be somehow threatened."

Arys scowled but ignored Shaz's comment, addressing Sloane instead. "Well, you know me. Naturally, I was curious. I had to see for myself why Jenner is so desperate to get rid of me."

"No, you can't be here. Just go." Placing her hands on Arys's chest, Sloane gave him a shove. "Hurry up, before he finds out."

He caught her wrists and pushed her back. "Where is Jenner, Sloane?"

"He's busy getting ready for a performance. Which is why you should leave now while you still can." She made as if to grab him again, and he warded her off with a raised hand that crackled with blue sparks.

"Take us to him, or I'll find him myself." Arys exuded a deadly calm. He was taking this all the way.

"Alright, alright!" she shouted, then glanced around frantically to make sure nobody was listening. "I'll take you to him. Just please settle the hell down. He really is busy at the moment. That's not a lie."

"That's fine." Arys surveyed the club, a mischievous grin adorning his handsome face. "I have plenty of time. Why don't you give us the grand tour? I'm sure Alexa would love to see it."

Sloane pouted as if we were crashing her party. Her extreme unease mirrored my own. Accepting defeat, she turned to lead us through the maze of tables. "As you can see," she said between gritted teeth. "This is the main floor where our guests enjoy entertainment, gamble and meet with their prospective dates for the evening. I'll show you the second floor."

We followed her through the crowded room, to the grand spiral staircase in the back left corner. Pale pink lights adorned each stair, lighting the way up. We passed a couple coming down, a female vampire and her male human toy. Bites covered his neck, and he wore an expression of confused joy.

I couldn't help but sneak a peek at Shaz. Not so long ago, he had been one of those lost in the pleasure of the vampire's bite. I hoped he was strong enough to resist this place. I hoped that I was too.

"As I'm sure you can see, the second floor is where our private rooms are. The club operates twenty-four hours so this floor is always busy." Sloane sauntered down the hall like the proud madam she was.

There was vampire security at each end of the hall. My skin prickled as the atmospheric energy marched over and through me. The scent of blood and sex tainted the air. It caused something low in me to tighten with arousal. I sent a panicked glance Arys's way, finding him watching me intently.

The doors had little gold name plaques stating such things as "Lady Angelina" or "Sir Antonio." And there were so many of them. I was willing to bet the inside of each room was far more lavish than at my own club. My club was beginning to look like a real dump compared to this place.

Returning to the main floor, Sloane led us to a well-concealed elevator hidden beneath the staircase. To access it, she produced a swipe card from within the bosom of her dress. The door opened, and we all stepped into the small metal container.

"Last chance to change your mind," Sloane offered, holding a finger over the elevator buttons. When Arys stubbornly shook his head, she gave an exasperated sigh and punched the down button. "Oh Arys, you will never change. You're still a conceited ass."

His laughter filled the small space. "Guilty."

For the first time since we arrived, I began to feel the telltale signs of trepidation. Arys was unmoved, showing no concern for whatever we were descending into. Jez and I exchanged a look and a shrug. I grasped my power, my fingers humming with readiness. I didn't give a damn who felt it.

The elevator stopped, and we entered an entirely different kind of party. The heavy vampire and werewolf energy overwhelmed me. The place reeked of it. The supernatural made up a lot of the crowd, though there was a heavy human presence as well.

The red carpet continued, but the entertainment had changed. The room was smaller than the main floor upstairs, leading me to believe we weren't seeing all of it. I would have looked around for a door or hallway, but the MMA-style ring in the center of the room captured my attention.

The crowd gathered around, shouting and cheering. The noise faded into the background as I realized what was taking place. Two wolves circled one another inside the cage. Lips peeled back in a deadly snarl, they lunged, meeting one another in the middle. The snap of jaws was audible over the crowd. The wolves went hard at one another, and the blood sprayed.

I was disgusted. Shaz and Jez wore matching expressions of shock and distaste. Arys watched with disinterest. I half expected him to feign a yawn and check his imaginary watch. This wasn't a surprise to him.

"What the fuck is this?" I turned my angry glare on Sloane, letting her see the wolf behind my eyes. My beast was not happy to be here.

"It's exactly what people come to this city for," she replied coolly. "Not every high roller is content to sit in the casino and play cards. Some of them come here for a taste of something a bit wilder."

"It's vile," Jez said, flashing cat eyes at Sloane.

"It's business." Sloane's flippant retort incited my wolf's rage.

Shaz was quiet, but the wolf eyes he was sporting indicated how he really felt. It was impossible not to react while two werewolves were tearing each other apart for the entertainment of humans and vampires. It took all of the self-control I possessed to keep from lashing out. Acting rashly would land my ass inside that ring; I was sure of it. So I fought back the surge of power that threated to burst forth.

"Is this supposed to impress us?" Arys asked, looking bored. "So you've replaced the screaming blood ring victims with wolves. Why so smug?"

Sloane grew defensive. Her hands clenched into fists at her sides. "You know how I felt about the blood ring Harley was running here. It was sick. You thought so too. When Harley died, Jenner put a stop to that. This is a business, and we need to turn a profit."

"I see. So you're proud of yourself for having a hand in that," Arys observed, his tone bitter. "But we both know Jenner will do anything for the right piece of pussy."

The tension between them was thick. Sloane held her head high and marched across the room, expecting us to follow. Arys chuckled, happy with himself for getting under her skin.

"What the hell was that about?" I grabbed his arm, forcing him to meet my eyes. "I want to walk out of here alive, Arys."

"No worries, my love. Nobody here is stupid enough to lay a hand on you." With an arm around my shoulders, he guided me along, down the hall where Sloane had disappeared.

"Seriously?" Jez piped up. "Do we really want to keep following this crazy bitch?"

I sure as hell didn't. I was ready to leave without ever seeing another inch of this place. Instead, we followed the vampire.

She was waiting for us at a door that opened into a small theatre. "Jenner will be performing in just a few minutes. Please, Arys, don't make an ass of yourself."

"Can't make any promises," he said.

Row upon row of ascending seats filled the theatre. She led us to the front row, issued a final warning to Arys and left. Many of the seats were already full. People sat talking quietly among themselves, waiting for the show to start.

Front and center was a well-lit stage. It was currently empty. The sounds of the angry wolf fight next door were gone. It had to be soundproofed down here. That did nothing to ease my growing apprehension.

Arys took the aisle seat. I sat next to him with Jez on my other side and Shaz next to her. Two waitresses made their way through the aisles, passing out drinks. To the mortals they handed out glasses of white wine. Arys, a few others and I received a glass of scarlet liquid that could only be one thing.

I tried to pass my glass back, but Arys stopped me with a hand on my arm. "Keep it. You might wish later that you had."

"What is going on here?" I demanded, unable to resist the urge to smell the contents of the wine glass. Human blood, fresh from the vein.

"I don't know. I guess we're about to see a show." Arys sat back, relaxed and waiting. Intrigue shone in his dark-blue eyes.

Shaz sat stiffly, surveying our surroundings. His energy was scattered. I could feel the frustration of his wolf. "If this little show involves werewolves, I'm taking Alexa and getting the fuck out of here." He gripped his wine so tight I expected the glass to shatter. "After what happened with Claire and Maxwell, I don't feel so great about this. The wolf fight next door doesn't help."

Claire and Maxwell were the Vegas vamps who had come to Edmonton for Shaz and me after we had killed Harley together. The way they saw it, we were their ticket to taking over Harley's position of power in Vegas. They figured that, by handing over Harley's killers, the rest of his vampires would reward them for their efforts. Now they were dead.

"Stay calm, pup. I can assure you, the vampires here are not missing Harley." Arys tipped his glass up and sipped the crimson contents. His tongue darted out to capture a drop from his bottom lip, and I found myself longing to lick the scarlet smear.

"Maybe not, but if they know his killers are here, that may change. If all hell breaks loose, it's all on you." Shaz shot Arys a look that was all wolf, pure predator. Then he offered his wine to Jez, refusing to take even a sip. She shrugged, downed the rest of hers and accepted.

"Oh, Shaz..." Arys forced an exasperated sigh. "It is *so* good to have you back."

Despite my nerves, I had to smile. The two of them had been so over the top polite to one another since Shaz's return, I'd begun to get suspicious. This was more like it. Oddly enough, I found their banter comforting.

Jez added, "I don't think we have anything to worry about. If anything happens to either of you, Shya will be here in a flash kicking some ass." Clinking her glass against mine, she gulped down the wine and deposited her empty glasses on the floor.

I peered into my glass. It was warm but cooling quickly. Did they have some human cattle they bled for this? Ugh.

The lights went out, and the chatter of voices immediately hushed. The audience of two hundred or so fell silent. Their excitement created a buzz that made my skin crawl.

"Here we go," Jez whispered at the same time Shaz muttered, "This should be painfully interesting."

A spotlight lit up center stage. A vampire stood there, staring out at the audience. It was Jenner. I felt it, an echo of a memory that wasn't mine.

In dark pants and a black V-neck t-shirt that revealed his tattooed arms, Jenner's pale blue eyes stood out with an eerie glow. They fell upon me, and I froze, afraid even to breathe while he watched me. His gaze lingered for only a second before passing over Arys and, finally, the rest of the audience.

His dark hair was short and trendy, slightly longer in front and gelled as if he'd merely pushed it around on his head and left it. Average height and build, he had a bit of facial scruff that gave him a rugged attractiveness.

"Good evening," he addressed the crowd. "It's a pleasure to have you all here tonight. What a fine looking group of people."

A few women at the other end of our row giggled when he flashed them a brilliant, fang-revealing smile. He was smooth, making eye contact with several audience members.

"Tonight is ladies night." He paused when a small cheer went up from the women gathered. "For those of you who have been here before, you know what that means. For the newcomers, let me welcome you to The Wicked Kiss. This is the place to make your darkest fantasies come true."

"I thought that's what upstairs was for," I whispered to Arys, knowing Jenner's sensitive ears would hear me.

"Let me make it clear. This is not an experience for the timid. What you see here may shock you. It may also excite you. It's up to you to decide if it's real or not." Jenner's smile grew impossibly wide. "Now, which of you ladies would like to make your vampire fantasy come true tonight?"

Ah, it was starting to make sense. I could see where this was going, and I didn't like it. This wasn't like the blood and sex fest going on upstairs because this was a performance. I sat stiffly, nervous about what was to come.

Jenner descended the steps at the front of the stage. Several women raised their hands and shouted their willingness to be his victim. He ambled up and down the aisles, pausing here and there to take a closer look at the volunteers. He passed before our seats and paused. Arys stared daggers at him, a challenge on his face.

Jenner leaned in, breathing deeply of my scent. "How about you, darlin'? Interested?"

I smirked, feeling unbearably uncomfortable. The sensual touch of his power sent a tickle down my spine, but I sat stiffly, refusing to show it. "Thanks anyway, but my vampire fantasy has already come true."

"Fair enough." With a nod, he moved on, but his unreadable gaze stayed locked on mine until he disappeared high in the crowd.

A high-pitched squeal rang out as Jenner made his selection. He led the excited brunette back to the stage. She pressed a hand to her mouth, glancing around nervously. The tense energy oozing from the audience thickened as they waited in restless anticipation.

In various colors and strengths, several spotlights blinked on at the same time, bathing the stage in a warm glow. The light chased the dark back, revealing a chaise lounge. Black velvet with silver trim, it was a pricey piece of furniture. Also on the stage stood a table with a bottle of champagne.

Jenner pressed a glass into her hand, encouraging her to drink. I could see her hand shaking from where I sat. Her energy was frantic and jumpy. It drew me the way wounded prey draws a predator. Everything about her screamed "easy target."

"Are you afraid, my dear?" Jenner asked, capturing her hand as it fluttered. He raised it to his lips, kissing her upturned wrist.

She nodded, her eyes darting around the room. She was like a deer in the headlights up there. "A little bit. I'm not changing my mind though."

"It's too late for that." Jenner's wicked chuckle rubbed me the wrong way. It grated on my nerves. I gritted my teeth and tried not to squirm in my seat. He sniffed her wrist, inhaling the aroma of her blood. "You're mine now. That's why you came here, isn't it?"

"Oh, yes." She giggled when he kissed her wrist.

"What's your name, beautiful?" Jenner cast a smirk our way, ensuring we were watching every move he made.

"Layna." The one word was a sigh. It didn't take much for a vampire of Harley's bloodline to seduce a woman. I knew firsthand.

Again, she peered out anxiously at the crowd. Jenner took her face in his hands and kissed her, a deep exploration of her mouth that was a hot display of passion and hunger. "They aren't here," he murmured against her lips. "They see you, but you no longer see them. All you see is me."

My stomach clenched, and I crossed one leg over the other, finding it hard to sit still. I was uneasy with my growing curiosity. I despised the fact that I wanted to see this.

Layna forgot all about the watching audience. She fell heavily under Jenner's thrall, seeing him as the undead master he painted himself as. Her eyes took on a strange glazed appearance. She moved robotically as he guided her to the chaise lounge. I don't think she even blinked.

Jenner's movements were smooth and calculated. He brushed the hair back from her face, smiling when she quivered at his touch. "Tell me how I make you feel."

A blush colored her cheeks. She sipped the champagne and giggled again. "You make me feel nervous but excited. I have butterflies."

"More like bats," I snickered. A woman in the next row shushed me. Jenner slowly swung his gaze my way; unspoken promises glittered in his strange eyes. I clamped my mouth shut and focused on shielding against the onslaught of feverish energy.

"There's no need to be nervous. You want this. Tell me you want this." Jenner plucked the empty glass from Layna's hand and set it aside.

"I do," she gushed, reaching for him. "I want it."

I rolled my eyes but kept my snide comments to myself. This was ridiculous. The people seated all around me were eating it up. When Jenner began to undress his victim, I realized why. A few gasps filled the silence, most likely from other newbies like me. Everyone else watched expectantly.

Layna welcomed his touch. With each caress, he freed her of another piece of clothing until she stood bared to us all. Jenner eased her back against the large, rounded arm of the chaise lounge. He sat between her legs and pulled her arm across. We all watched in silent wonder as he dragged his tongue over her wrist.

When he bit into her flesh, I flinched. The sudden intake of breath sounded all around me. Layna swooned, throwing her head back with a moan. She tried to pull him to her, spreading her legs wider in invitation.

"Patience, my sweet." Jenner laughed softly, licking the blood from his lips. He got up on his knees, leaning over to kiss her while sliding a hand up to cup her breast.

I tore my gaze away to stare into my glass. Maybe I would need it after all. Just to take the edge off. The scent of Layna's blood and arousal was tearing through my shields, stirring my bloodlust to life.

She paid no mind to the blood running from her wrist. All she saw was Jenner. I could relate to both of them, the predator and the prey. I had been both. He was a dark god to her in that moment, and she would allow him to do anything he wanted.

Jenner rose up to peel his shirt off, revealing a heavily tattooed but firm body. He was decorated in ink. A tiger snarled from its place on his back. Music notes adorned his side. There was more than one chunk of lettering that drew my curiosity.

The cloud of desire thickened as the women in the crowd reacted to him. It was his intent. The way he pushed his hypnotic power out in a wave made it difficult to resist. What made it worse was that I didn't want to. There was pleasure in that power, and I was as much a sucker for it as any hot-blooded woman.

A peek at Jez revealed she too was feeling it. Her brow furrowed in confusion, but there was awe in her eyes. I couldn't help but wonder how it felt for her to have a man manipulate her like that without even a touch.

Arys caught my eye and gave a slight shake of his head. He wasn't impressed with Jenner's blatant abuse of power though he himself was guilty of doing the same damn thing. Thankfully, without an audience, as far as I knew.

"I want to feel you, Layna. I want your legs wrapped around me while I make you cum. How does that sound?" There was absolute quiet as he took her nipple into his mouth. Her back arched, and her lips parted in a silent cry.

"Yes, yes please," she gasped.

My discomfort level rocketed off the charts. I searched the edges of the theatre, seeking an exit. I didn't want to watch this vampire porn despite the growing heat between my legs, which said otherwise.

The fire burning between the two on stage grew from a spark to a blaze. Jenner continued to draw her deeper under his spell. After decorating her body with small bites and kisses, he finally descended between her thighs.

"Oh my," Jez whispered, shaking her head in disbelief. Similar hushed words echoed from several others.

I snuck a glance at Shaz, finding his shoulders stiff and his expression blank. Only his eyes betrayed him. They glowed with the jade fire I recognized. That same lusty flame had burned for me once. How I missed it.

Jenner's oral attention had his victim writhing and shrieking. Her cries echoed inside the theatre, sending a shiver down my spine. I was ready to head back to the wolf fight, ready for anything to escape the overwhelming sensations.

Jenner was brewing a storm of energy. As he stirred the lust of the audience, he also fed upon it, creating a cycle of power that would carry us all higher. The mortals stared in hypnotic wonder. I could feel every nuance of the push and pull he created, despite my shields, which were weakening. With an inward groan, I dropped them completely, allowing the full effect of the rush to hit me.

I fell hard into the tornado of power twisting through the place. There was no controlling my response. The essence of vampire in my core rose up like lava to overflow in a wash of scorching energy. My four fangs filled my mouth, and my fingertips glowed blue and gold. The lust for body and blood was undeniable.

I watched Jenner make a show of removing the last of his clothing, and I panicked. He wasn't going to stop until it was all over. If I had to sit through that, I would end up killing someone. The scent of so many humans was tantalizing.

Without another thought, I lifted the glass in my hand to my lips and took a long swallow. The blood was cooling but a poor substitute for taking it straight from the vein. So much was missing, including the warm body it pumped from.

With a devious glint in his ice-blue eyes, Jenner revealed his body, naked and ready. It was difficult not to look at his erection. He was clearly proud of it, allowing everyone a chance to drink in the sight of him. Sure, it was nice, but I'd seen better on each of my men.

"Are you ready for me?" He knelt over Layna on the chaise lounge, caressing her face. She nodded, speechless, kissing his fingers.

I held my breath when he thrust inside her. The sound of my own heart pounded in my ears. Perspiration broke out on my forehead, and I swiped a hand through it. I was certain my companions could hear my heartbeat and smell my lustful hunger.

Arys clasped my free hand in his and squeezed. The quaking hunger raging inside me quelled but not nearly enough. Still, I was grateful for his presence. Thankfully, this time he was keeping my feet on the ground rather than sending me off the deep end.

'You have to keep it together. Don't let Jenner know he's getting to you.' Arys's voice echoed in my head, his mental touch gentle and soothing.

'How is this not getting to you? Don't tell me part of you doesn't want to go up there and join in.' The desperation in my thoughts made me cringe.

Arys stroked his thumb over the back of my hand. 'Are you kidding? Every part of me wants to. I've had centuries to gain control over that urge. He wants to have an effect. Don't let him.'

Jenner claimed Layna's body with total abandon. He pumped into her with furious, fast strokes that forced the cries from her. The lust rolling off the audience was enough to choke me. I half expected them to start humping each other in the aisles, even though they couldn't feel it the way I could.

'If we don't get out of here, I may climb in your lap and ride you right here.' I let him feel the immensity of the need driving me. 'This is seriously disturbing. He's a fool to do this shit in front of humans.'

'Oh, he is many things. A fool is the least of them.'

I couldn't sit still. Watching a vampire I didn't know have sex with a woman I would never know was uncomfortable. However, knowing what was coming made it almost painful.

Shaz shifted in his seat, a small growl rumbled in his throat. This was bad. We should never have brought him here. He wasn't ready for something this intense. I eyed him anxiously, waiting for him to lose it. He held himself together though. Lucky him, he also didn't have to feel it the way I did.

A war was going on inside me. I had been the victim and the vampire. In that moment, I couldn't decide which I wanted to be.

Jenner flipped Layna over, forcing her up on her knees. Gripping her hips, he pounded into her with an urgency I felt in my stomach. The sound of his hand slapping her ass echoed. She screamed and moaned, his name an unintelligible ramble on her lips.

I tapped my feet on the floor, nearly fidgeting myself out of my seat. I tried drinking more of the blood in my glass, but it wasn't what I wanted. Setting it down, I stared anywhere but at the stage. My gaze kept coming back to it. Dammit, I wanted to watch Jenner bleed her.

He shoved a hand into her hair and jerked her head back. Baring her neck, he ensured the audience had a good view. I licked my lips, leaning forward. Arys's grip on my hand tightened. Eroticism oozed from the stage. The pornographic display was more than an act. It was an expression of true passion. To Jenner, this was performance art; to me, it was a gross glamorization of what we were.

Layna closed her eyes in bliss before Jenner leaned in for the bite. He sank fangs into her neck, and blood spilled down her chest. The hum of energy was loud in my ears, deafening. My breath came fast. I was losing the battle of temptation. Again. I didn't make a conscious decision to leap out of my seat. Simply riding the high of Jenner's power wasn't enough. I needed the climactic release that came with the kill.

Arys was ready. He caught me around the waist and dragged me onto his lap, fighting to keep me in his chair with him. Rational thought had stopped. Between the power, the sex and the blood, there was no room left for me. I was all monster.

Jenner raised his head to survey the crowd. His mouth dripped scarlet. His gaze landed upon me, and he winked.

"Alexa, it's all an illusion," Arys hissed in my ear. "You're letting him manipulate you. You are my wolf, and you are stronger than that. Resist him."

Jez leaned away from us but watched with wide eyes. Shaz was tense, ready to help Arys pin me down like a mental patient. Arys's touch was calming despite the power that sparked between us. I was stronger with him. I clung to that. I sat stiffly with Arys's arms around me. The erection beneath me revealed that he hadn't gone entirely unaffected either. We watched in strained silence as Jenner feasted in all ways upon his prey. I needed this to be over.

Layna collapsed on the chaise lounge, a dopey smile on her face. Jenner licked and sucked at the wound, encouraging the flow to continue. Just when I thought my head might explode, a large velvet curtain descended to hide the stage from sight. The spotlight blinked out and darkness fell.

A soft moan echoed from behind the curtain. The twenty-minute show had felt like hours. Finally, it was over. If she wasn't dead yet, she soon would be.

Chapter Five

Several seconds passed before the lights came on. Ushers appeared to herd everyone out a rear exit, opposite the way we'd come in. Except for us.

Roscoe approached from a door behind the stage. Leather clad and bearded, he strode toward us with a swagger that made me certain he owned a motorbike. He headed us off before I could follow the rest of the crowd. Too bad.

We were on our feet, looking at one another with wide eyes. Arys held tight to my arm, keeping me close. He pushed a calming energy into me, and I grabbed on as if it were a life raft during a flood. I vibrated so hard with the effort it took to hold myself together that my teeth nearly rattled.

"Jenner wants to see you backstage," Roscoe said, the dim light glinting off his golden fang. He waited expectantly for us to get moving.

Arys fell into step beside the burly vampire, walking with an angry stride. "When the hell did he start this crazy train? Feeding in front of humans is ballsy. He should know better."

"He does." Roscoe shrugged. "He just doesn't care."

Backstage was a dressing room clearly designed for private parties of the bloodletting kind. Spacious and open, swanky sofas lined the walls. The carpet was dark and lush. But in my current state of mind, the vampiress feeding from a half-naked man captured my attention. This place was going to be the death of me.

Sloane looked up abruptly as we entered. She released her hold on the man's bleeding arm and gave him a shove. "Go now. I'll send for you later."

He slipped by us and out the door without a backward glance. Sloane licked the small drops of blood from her lips with a dainty swipe of her tongue. She smiled and reached to smooth her hair.

"Have a seat." She gestured to the sofas and matching easy chair. "Jenner's just cleaning up from his performance."

"Performance?" Arys refused to sit. He stood stiffly, arms crossed and jaw clenched. "Is that what he calls it?"

Sloane eyed him, amusement shining in her cerulean eyes. "Death is an art, baby. You know that. You do it better than any of us."

"Don't sweet talk me, Sloane. I'm not in the mood. You're an idiot to participate in this exploitation."

I chose not to follow Arys's lead. My legs were shaking, and my entire body hummed with the pent up power I'd called during Jenner's little show. I needed to sit down. Shaz sat beside me, but Jez placed herself opposite Arys where she could watch both Sloane and the door.

Roscoe leaned against the doorframe, staring at his cell phone. There was something about vampires and technology that made me giggle. Some of them were adept at change; others were so behind the times it was laughable.

"If anyone is being exploited, it's the mortal suckers that show up to see something they can only read about in trendy books that pollute the beauty of what we are." Sloane crossed one leg over the other, turning that simple action into a sensual display. "Simmer down, Arys. You saw his tame show. That was nothing. People love it. They tell themselves it's not real, that it's an act, the illusions of Vegas. But they know the truth. Deep down inside. And they enjoy it."

"Why are you still here?" Arys asked, pinning her with a knowing stare. "You used to talk so much about leaving."

"As did you," she agreed. "I suppose you had a reason to go. Everything I have is here."

They fell silent, both of them remembering a time before any of the shifters present had lived. Though she was otherwise cool and composed, a dark shadow passed through Sloane's eyes.

Just when the silence became ridiculously awkward, Jenner swept into the room. His hair was disheveled, but he was dressed, thankfully. Exuding a heavy, sticky sweet energy, he glided through the room as if his feet never touched the ground.

Swiftly, he caught Sloane around the waist and lifted her out of the chair before sitting down himself with her on his lap. An irritated frown creased her brow, but she settled in against him, going so far as to sling an arm around his neck.

"Did you enjoy the show?" Jenner directed his question at Arys. Then his shifty eyes slid over me on the couch. "I know you did." When I didn't respond, he added, "Hot damn, those eyes are fascinating."

With the power raging through me, my eyes had to be Arys's vampire blue. I relaxed into the couch and brazenly reached out metaphysically to taste Jenner. It was rude, but I didn't care. Manners didn't strike me as the kind of thing Jenner cultivated.

His power was vast, impressive. It felt like Harley's, which was a bit different from how Arys felt. I could only assume that Arys's link to me gave him a different flavor. The power was deep and alluring, beckoning to me. He was likely the most powerful vampire in the city, as long as Arys wasn't around.

He sat there watching me as I psychically prodded him, not attempting to shield against me. "Find anything you like?"

"Nothing I haven't seen before." I was flippant, wanting him to know he couldn't play with me. His sire had loved to play. Harley had caused all kinds of hell for me. I wouldn't allow Jenner to do the same.

Trailing a hand up and down Sloane's thigh, Jenner grinned. "My turn."

I raised a hand in invitation, allowing him to feel me out. It wasn't too invasive since I didn't resist. Jenner's metaphysical touch was sensual, bathing me in heat. He lingered longer than necessary, but I remained without reaction.

"I bet you taste as good as you feel." Jenner's gaze strayed to my neck, seeking what lay beneath the choker I wore. "You're dangerous though. I suppose a smart vampire wouldn't want to tangle with you. They all seem to end up dead."

I waved a hand dismissively. "Only the ones that hurt me or try to use me as leverage because they're too weak to earn their power. I'm actually quite a nice person when I'm not being treated like an object." I swung my foot and ran a hand through my hair, beaming at him as if I knew something he didn't know.

"I'll bet you are."

"Is there a reason for this, Jenner?" Arys cut in, impatient with the way we were sniffing one another out. "The phony chatter, it's not necessary. I'd hate to think I sat through staring at your bare ass for nothing. Make with the threats so we can get down to business."

Jenner's low laugh was like the smooth skin of a snake, wrapping around me in places that could not be touched. "I just wanted to welcome you to my city, and to tell you to hurry up and get the hell out of it." His expression never changed, but the atmosphere grew heavy with malice.

Sloane stiffened noticeably, her eyes darting from Jenner to Arys. I didn't move a muscle though I was ready to react. As were Jez and Shaz, I was sure.

"Ah ok," Arys said with a nod and a smirk. "So this is the part where you parade around like a self-appointed god and try to run me out of town. Predictable, yet entertaining. What else have you got?"

Roscoe snickered but said nothing. Jenner shot him a dark glare.

It wasn't hard to figure him out. He thought we were here to make a play for Harley's territory. We weren't. At least, I hadn't thought so. The challenge Arys issued made me second-guess that.

"Does it have to come to that?" Jenner captured Sloane's hand and decorated it with small kisses. She pressed her lips together tightly.

"This isn't your city, Jenner. It was Harley's. He was the master vampire. You have no more right to his authority than any of us." With a slow, calculated gait, Arys came to stand beside my end of the couch.

A dangerous light flashed through Jenner's ice-cold eyes. "You're the reason he's dead. You turned your back on this city and forfeited any right you may have had to it. Get out before I forget that I once called you brother."

This was going from sketchy to downright deadly fast. Arys's growing rage echoed within me. He drew on our connection, and my stomach clenched. It took a lot for him to get to the point of tapping our shared power. I knew Harley was still, and maybe always would be, a touchy subject for him. Perhaps it was worse than I thought.

"Can I just state for the record that we came to Vegas as tourists?" I interjected, sliding a glance at Arys. "At least, I did."

"Like hell you did," Jenner spat. "You came to finish what you started when you murdered my sire."

Oh boy, here we go. I somehow managed to resist the urge to roll my eyes. "Let me remind you that Harley came to my city to force me into a blood bond. I had every right to defend myself. I am not sorry, and I don't give a rat's ass about what he left behind here."

Jenner mulled that over, clearly unhappy with my refusal to be apologetic. He fell silent, almost sullen. He pressed Sloane's hand to his face, thoughtfully staring at me with a devilish spark in his eyes.

At last, he dragged his gaze back to Arys, his expression changing to one of violent accusation. "How could you let her do it? He loved you."

Arys perched on the arm of the couch beside me, shaking his head. Sorrow flickered briefly in his eyes. "We've been over this. I told you last time I came that he brought it on himself. I stopped her once. I told him I wouldn't stop her again."

"He was so hard headed when it came to you, Arys," Sloane said with a sigh. "Nothing we said or did would stop him from going after you once he learned that you'd actually found her."

I frowned, unhappy with being talked about as if I wasn't present. Apparently, every vampire in Harley's little blood-sucking family knew about Arys's dreams and visions of me from before I was born. I didn't get the feeling they understood it though.

"Yes," Jenner added bitterly. "Nothing could come between Harley and his favorite." He pinned me with a chilling stare. "Nothing except you."

Sibling rivalry. Typical enough, yet Jenner's words still sent a chill through me. I'd have thought they would be beyond this kind of thing. I guess hundreds of years only intensified those things rather than erased them.

I leaned forward on the couch, never taking my eyes off Jenner. "What is it that really bothers you? That you weren't Harley's favorite? Or that I killed him? Claire and Maxwell failed to take me down. So will you. Think carefully about what you want to do here."

It was a ballsy thing to say, and I was more than a little concerned it would blow up in my face; however, he had me backed into a corner here. If I didn't come out swinging, Jenner would have the advantage, and he would know it.

Jenner sat stiff in his chair. He dropped Sloane's hand and clenched his into a fist. His power filled the room, a growing heat that quickly became scorching hot.

"I like her," Roscoe said with a nod in Arys's direction. "This bloodline could use a woman like her. Sorry, Sloane."

She huffed and stuck her nose in the air, refusing to acknowledge his comment. As far as I knew, she was the only existing female in Harley's bloodline until I turned.

"This isn't your city." Jenner's voice rose in a near shout. "Harley's dead, and now it's mine. Arys, take your wolf and leave. This is not your home anymore."

"No, it's not. But I won't be ordered around. I wouldn't take that shit from Harley, and I sure as hell won't take it from you." Arys exuded an outward calm; though I knew inside, he was roiling. "You think playing on stage with humans is the way to run this place? You can't just walk away from a blood ring. You're not ready for this city, Jenner."

Jenner exploded from his chair. Shoving Sloane aside, he hurled a slap of power at Arys who caught it, neutralizing the attack. The close proximity to the shot caused my body to tingle.

Arys rose, meeting Jenner in the center of the sitting area. They stared into each other, and something unspoken passed between them.

"Three of our vampires, including our sire, are dead because of her," shouted Jenner. "You are obligated to make it right. So either you came here to do that, or you came to challenge my authority."

Shaz was tense beside me. We exchanged a look, and I gave a slight shake of my head. It wasn't time to jump in yet, though the room was overflowing with tense vampire energy. Sloane backed away slowly to linger near the door with Roscoe. Jez did the same, keeping her distance from all vampires present.

Arys was tapping so much power it made me lightheaded. He considered Jenner's demands with a grave expression. "I loved him too, you know. But it happened, and it's over. How the hell do you expect me to make something like that right?"

"A life for a life. Put one of your shifters in the ring to fight to the death."

Jenner's words rang in my ears, but I had to replay it a few times in my head to be sure I'd heard his insane declaration correctly. The silence was deafening. A tirade lurked on the tip of my tongue as every dirty word I wanted to say came to mind.

"You've lost your fucking mind." The atmosphere pulsed with Arys's vehement declaration.

"You've clearly forgotten how we do things in Sin City. Either play to win or admit defeat and walk away."

"I always win. You should know that by now." A growl laced Arys's words, an echo of my wolf that lurked in him. It was a remnant of my wolf that was, at times, a little too real for Arys to control.

Arys smacked Jenner with a jolt of energy that sparked with gold and blue. It was just enough to knock Jenner back a few feet. That was all it took to incite a violent reaction. The next shot landed along with a punch. Arys staggered back from the blow, his jaw bruised. His eyes were solid blue wolf when he lunged at Jenner.

The two of them grappled with both power and fists. They knocked over the chair Jenner had been sitting on before crashing into a small side table. A flurry of curses and uttered threats filled the air.

"My God, you guys, stop it!" Sloane shrieked, her voice shrill. "You're acting like spoiled children." With a wave of her hand, she lashed out at them in an attempt to pull them apart, but they carried on as if she'd never touched them.

The musky scent of vampire blood tickled my nose. Each of them was bleeding at this point, never ceasing in their assault of one another. Clearly, their issues went deeper than Arys's return to the city.

"You're a motherfucking traitor, Sindarys! You owe us." Jenner's use of Arys's full name shouldn't have been surprising. It reminded me that there were people who knew him from long ago. He had several lifetimes with these vampires, long before me.

"If I owe you anything, it's an ass-kicking that finally puts you in your place." With a tug on the power flowing between us, Arys flung a potentially deadly psi ball.

Either uncanny skill or dumb luck allowed Jenner to deflect the shot. He sent it crashing into the wall where it blew open a basketball-sized hole. Drywall and paint chips rained down in a pile of dust on the carpet.

I was done waiting. They were going to kill each other. I focused hard on both vampires and, with a flick of my wrist, flung them apart. Arys tumbled over the sofa opposite me and hit the floor while Jenner grunted as he slid down the wall next to the gaping hole.

"Now both of you just calm the fuck down. Don't make me hit you again." My words ended on a growl. Power thrummed through me. Looking back and forth between the two cocky vampires, I dared them to call my bluff.

Jenner regained his footing but remained where he was, leaning against the damaged wall. A slow grin lit up his face. Damn vampires. It took a lot more than a slap of power to intimidate or control them. He was going to test my limits severely before this night was through; I could feel it.

"Oh, please do," he invited, going so far as to beckon with a finger. "If that's a taste of how you'd kill me, I can safely say I will die with a smile and a hard on."

"You're a pig." My lip curled in disgust. Though I might not say so aloud, Jenner and Arys were a lot alike in their smarmy conceit. I expected a comment like that from Arys; from him it was laughable, but from Jenner it was just gross.

"And you're a little wolf playing vampire. It's cute, really. But ultimately pointless. You're not one of us." A deadly glare replaced Jenner's grin, and he advanced on me with slow, careful steps.

Arys was at my side, fingers alight with a golden-blue fire. "You're right, Jenner. Alexa is not one of us. She's more than we are. Why else would she have been able to kill Harley? You'll be next if you continue this nonsense."

"I'd like to make it clear that Harley is the one who taught me how to kill him," I said. "You may want to chew on that for a bit."

"Are you implying that my sire wanted you to kill him?" Jenner's voice rose to a thunderous volume. "You think he wanted a hybrid mutation like you to take over his business? Not a chance in hell. You won't make it out of town without paying for what you did to him."

"I'm not implying a damn thing. Harley knew what he was risking by getting close to me. Do you?" I spoke through clenched teeth, finding it hard to hold the wolf back. I wanted to claw Jenner's eyes out.

Sloane placed herself in front of Jenner. She touched his face, bringing his gaze to hers. "Jenner, be reasonable. Arys has never shown an interest in running Vegas. But he's here for whatever reason. Maybe he can help us. Maybe if he knew—"

"Shut your damn fool mouth," Jenner hissed. Grabbing her arm, he gave her a teeth-rattling shake. "I don't need Arys to ride in here on his fucking high horse and save the day. My business is my business."

Arys and I exchanged a look. Sloane was resistant, struggling against Jenner as she looked to Arys for help.

"It's not only your business, Jenner." Sloane jerked free of him and turned to us, a desperate plea in her eyes. "We're in trouble, Arys. Since Harley's death, things have gotten so bad. It's the blood ring. We want out, and they won't let us go—"

The crack of Jenner's hand against her face was startling. She hit the floor fast and hard. A curse fell from her lips. In a blur of speed she was up, seething with fangs bared. But she didn't say another word. Instead, she fled the room.

Everything happened fast then. Arys and Jenner were in each other's face again, their shouts echoing through the room. The power level rose to the point of giving me a smashing headache. Jenner met Arys's demand for an explanation with his own demands for blood and retribution. Shaz moved back a safe distance but was ready to jump in. The vampire pissing contest spiraled out of control.

Roscoe spoke up, his voice gruff but commanding, even amid the noise. "You're brothers. There is no reason for this animosity."

"Our brotherhood ended long ago." Jenner's nostrils flared, and he huffed. "I have no love left for the one who went out of his way to take everything from me."

Yep, pissing contest. I somehow fought back the urge to roll my eyes. I couldn't even begin to pretend to understand men, let alone men who were also monsters. Times like this, I thought maybe Jez had the better deal. No male bullshit.

"Hey, it wasn't me who slept with your fiancée the night you were engaged," Arys replied with a bitter laugh. "That was Maxwell."

"No, you're the one who married her instead, before you killed her, you son of a bitch." Jenner dropped that bomb as if he'd been waiting a very long time to utter the words. It spoke volumes in regards to the hatred he carried like a flaming torch for Arys.

My jaw dropped. A memory slammed into me like a bullet train, a swarm of images that left me shaken and breathless. I had seen the photographic proof of Jenner's claim. A year ago, one of Arys's spurned lovers had sought to have him killed. She showed me the photo of Arys and his young blonde bride. I'd never had the guts to question him further on that. Now I didn't have to.

I stumbled back a few steps, my hand going to my head as I struggled to see the room before me. Being forced to relive Arys's memories as if I were there was a torment like no other. I always saw through his eyes, feeling what he felt. He had fallen for Jenner's bride to be because she reminded him of the woman he had so recently begun to dream about, a woman destiny claimed he would never unite with.

"Alexa? Are you ok?" Shaz shook me, lightly slapping my face.

Laughter rang in my ears. With girlish giggles, she gazed up at Arys, batting her eyes. Within six months of their marriage, he had already decided it was over. Rather than ease his pain, she had made it worse.

Blood sprayed and laughter became screams. Arys's slaughter was vicious, a frantic attempt to rid himself of a woman he was destined to long for but never know. To rid himself of me.

The memory faded, though the scent of blood and fear lingered inside me. Remnants of the vampire's violence brought forth my wolf with a snarl. My four fangs filled my mouth, two on the top and bottom. Fists clenched, my claws sliced the palms of my hands.

"I'm fine," I whispered, waving away Shaz's concern. I was keenly aware of everyone's eyes on me. It took great effort not to let my gaze fall accusingly upon Arys.

Jenner was eyeing me up, nodding in silent appraisal. "I want both wolves. One for Harley, the other for the woman I loved and lost to you."

"Not a chance in hell," Arys fired back.

"Then you've made your choice." Jenner lunged, but Roscoe was just suddenly there, shoving him back. His large stature made his presence heavy, looming.

He gave both vampires a shove, creating more distance between them. I stayed close to Arys, ready to slap him with a psi ball if necessary. I couldn't let him start a war that would have every vampire in the building on our asses. We'd never make it out alive.

"There's gotta be a better way to handle this," Roscoe insisted. A rough edge to his tone made me think he was more than just a yes man. "I'm not going to stand by while the two of you throw down. Be reasonable."

Roscoe shared a look with Jenner, and something passed between the two of them. Jenner appeared reluctant, glancing uncertainly around the room. His vehemence was palpable. Vengeance guided him now. Such a demanding force wouldn't often be denied.

Holding my breath, I waited anxiously to see where this was going. I was dying to shout an, "I told you so," at Arys. Coming here had been idiocy.

"Alright, fine," Jenner finally relented, oozing self-satisfaction. "No violent display of power. Let's make it a little more interesting. Cards. You and me, Arys. Let's play some poker. It is Vegas after all."

The intrigue, which lit up Arys's eyes with a devilish blue spark, set off warning bells in my head. "What are the stakes?" he asked, and I knew then he was going for it.

My stomach clenched. This wasn't exactly a better alternative to beating the hell out of one another. Meeting the eyes of my white wolf, I saw my concern reflected back at me.

"If you win, you and your companions can walk out of here unharmed. You'll be free to go about the city as you please." Jenner beamed as if his offer was too good to refuse. Then he gleefully dropped the bomb that stole my voice. "If I win, I make your wolves part of the entertainment."

Chapter Six

"Is that the best you can do?" Arys raised a dark brow and shook his head. He was going to give it to Jenner now, or so I thought. Imagine my surprise when instead he added, "Let's revise that somewhat. If I win, not only do I walk free and clear of here, but I take control of the club."

I gaped at him, trying to process the total lunacy coming out of his mouth. "Are you serious?"

"Come on, Arys. What the fuck?" Shaz was on his feet, having reached his limit.

Arys shushed us both with a hand, never taking his eyes off Jenner. I had a sinking feeling that Arys's ego was about to make a deal I'd regret. Jenner's stony silence had all of us fixed on him, waiting. Roscoe shrugged as if to say Arys had every right to make his own demands.

"Deal." Jenner extended a hand to Arys. "You must be awfully confident in your abilities to so easily agree to a bet that puts your precious Alexa on the line."

"I never say no to a good poker game. Especially one I know I can win." With a smile that oozed conceit, Arys grasped the other vampire's hand. They shook, so simply sealing a deal that put Shaz and me on the line.

I wanted to be stunned, but I knew my twin flame well. This was very much in his nature. The fact that I didn't agree with his choice meant nothing. It was just another conflict of many that we would have.

"Is this for real?" Jez piped up, regarding the vampires present with the wary distrust of a cat feeling cornered.

"Selfish fucking vampire," Shaz muttered, his fists clenched and knuckles white. "I'm not even surprised anymore by your willingness to sell us out."

"Settle down, pup. Everything is under control. I've got this." Arys dismissed Shaz with a look, but in my mind he pleaded, 'Trust me.'

I didn't. Not this time. Too much was left to chance, this could go all wrong too many ways. And far too much delight danced on Jenner's smug face. I had no response. What could I say to the man who had just gambled with my life?

"Oh God, do I ever need a drink," I muttered. Running a hand through my hair in exasperation, I headed for the door with every intention of appeasing that need.

Jez was quick to join me in my escape. "Right there with ya."

"Wonderful idea," said Jenner. "Why don't we all take a few minutes to do that? I could go for a drink myself. Roscoe, get a private table ready for us. Keep the blood and booze flowing." Crooking his finger in invitation, he added, "You're here now, Arys. You made that choice. So you might as well enjoy the place."

Arys caught up to me, taking my hand in his and holding tight when I attempted to shake him off. It was growing increasingly hard to rein in my temper. Showing Jenner a united front was going to be tough when all I wanted to do was bitch slap Arys upside the head.

"Let's go upstairs," he whispered in my ear. "No matter what happens here tonight, we both need to be at full strength. No arguments."

"We? I didn't hear anything about you being forced into this circus of maniacs." I was bitter, and he knew it. It was evident in the way he gripped my hand tighter, silently pleading with me to give him the benefit of the doubt.

His voice in my head was soft, a gentle touch that conveyed more than words spoken aloud. 'You killed the one vampire who was stronger than every vampire in this city. I trust that you will be able to handle Jenner, whether I win or lose.'

'Losing is an option? What the hell were you thinking?'

'I can't walk away from his challenge, Alexa. I hope you understand. You know I'd never let anything happen to you.'

This was his family, his entire history. I had no choice but to understand, even though I didn't. I had to put my faith in Arys's uncanny ability to kick some serious ass at poker and hope for the best.

Jenner swept past us. "Don't sully yourself with the humans upstairs. The den has all you need. Come, let me show you the changes I've made." He fully expected that we'd follow.

I sighed and glanced at each of my companions in turn. Before I could proclaim my intent to tell Jenner to shove it, Arys dragged me along behind the conceited vamp.

'He has no idea what we are going to do to him.' Arys's voice echoed through my mind. He was seething and doing his best to keep from unleashing his wrath.

'We? Wanna fill me in?' I didn't like the sound of this.

We walked as a group through the theatre and back through the fight room. Roscoe said something about having someone set up a table before he disappeared, leaving us alone with Jenner. The two wolves in the cage were going hard. Their snaps and snarls were audible despite the cheers from the crowd. There was blood on the air.

I looked longingly at the elevator door as we passed, wishing we could leave. Wishing we had never come. I caught Shaz's eye, worried about what was to come. He mustered a small smile and a half-hearted shrug. He was fearless.

'I knew this would happen if we came to this city,' Arys continued. 'It had to eventually. It's ours. Rightfully, it belongs to us.'

'I don't want it.' I didn't. Arys had to know that. He was letting his personal feelings affect his decisions. There was no way he really wanted to run a city like Vegas. 'I'll never live here, Arys. It's not home.'

A muscle twitched in his jaw, but he didn't answer. Sure, I was his other half, but that didn't mean I was going to take over an entire city just to prove a point to Jenner. They were like brothers, sired by the same vampire, battling for supremacy. I didn't want any part in that. Of course, if anything happened to Shaz, I would make Jenner sorry he'd ever met me.

We crossed through the fight room to a solid metal door on the other side. Jenner punched in a security code, and it opened. Immediately, a rush of erotic energy overwhelmed me. It hit me like a punch in the stomach.

"I think you'll find the den to be more inviting than it used to be," Jenner announced with a snake-like smile. "Perhaps your friends will want to play."

He ushered us in and let the heavy door close. I took one look at the den of sin, and panic surged forth. I wasn't surprised by what was going on, but I was horrified because I knew what it was going to do to Shaz and to me.

An orgy of vampires and humans was taking place. Naked bodies covered a large circle shaped bed in the center of the room. They spilled off onto the floor, too lost in their search for pleasure to care. Sloane was happily basking in their midst. Groans and cries from so many created an eerie melody. The scent of sweat and blood mingled with the sex-soaked energy, attacking every one of my weaknesses at once. I turned wide eyes to Shaz, fearful of what I might find.

His expression was pained. After becoming addicted to the rush of a vampire's bite and the pull of power that goes with it, Shaz had faced the hard road of going clean. However, that didn't mean the temptation was gone. The beat of his heart grew rapid. For the first time since we'd arrived at The Wicked Kiss, Shaz was having a strong reaction.

Yet again, so was I. All I saw when I looked at him was a man that I could fuck and bleed. The influence in the room was intense and demanding. I had already fought so hard to deny the bloodlust. Now it swallowed me whole.

"Alexa, don't." Arys grabbed my arm with both hands before I could lunge at Shaz.

My white wolf stood there staring at me with pupils so huge his eyes were black. He shook his head, and his breath came fast. He backed toward the door, unable to tear his gaze away from the obscene scenario.

Jez latched onto Shaz's arm, holding him tight as she dragged him to the door. Jenner's satisfied laughter followed them out.

"I apologize," he chuckled. "I didn't realize he was so easily affected."

"He's a former blood whore, Jenner. Have some class." Even as Arys uttered the command, he too was falling under the hypnotic spell. As his pupils dilated, stimulated by many hungers, his eyes darkened. His arms tightened possessively around me.

Jenner ignored Arys, choosing instead to join Sloane in the mass of bodies. He buried his face in her cleavage and reached beneath her skirt. In moments, they had a naked woman on the bed between them. She was terrible at staying mad, though I had let my anger melt away at the touch of a vampire lover too.

I didn't want to watch, but I couldn't look away. The den itself wasn't all that large. A dozen or more people engaged in bloodletting and orgasms. It was a feast of body and power, one that would give even the strongest vampire a high that would last for hours, maybe even days.

"I can't…" My head spun as I fought the bloodlust. No use. The fight drained from me.

"It's ok. I'm right here." With his lips pressed to my ear, Arys slid a hand up my bare arm to touch the choker hiding my throat. He held me close, murmuring words that were supposed to calm me but only stoked the fire burning between us.

"I'm not participating in this." I had enough sanity left to state my refusal.

Relief crashed through me when Arys whispered his agreement. "Follow my lead."

He gravitated closer to a group of three humping their brains out on the floor at the foot of the bed. There was a small ripple of power as he reached out to them. Almost immediately, one of the two men turned to look at us. His eyes were glazed and somewhat unfocused. He was in deep.

Without speaking, he reached for me, and Arys intercepted him. Gazing deep into the man's vacant eyes, he said, "You're going to bleed for us now. And you're going to love it."

Arys didn't wait for a response. He bit into the man's wrist and shoved it toward me before moving on to plunge fangs into his throat. Our victim groaned, and his knees buckled. We followed him down to the carpet, kneeling beside him.

I pressed my lips to the vampire bite and gasped when the scarlet nectar hit my tongue. Straight from the vein, warm and flavored with his sexual desire, it was exactly what I needed to get through the rest of this night. I pulled his sensual energy into me, devouring it as I sucked at the bloody wound.

The only thing that could have taken me to greater heights was if Arys had been buried inside me. Sensing my need, he stroked a hand through my hair, his fingers entangled in my blonde tresses. Feasting on the wildly erotic storm of energy was exhilarating. I'd never experienced anything quite like it. So many people, both human and vampire, each of them giving off a heady rush of desire, it was a high unlike any other I'd known thus far. I fell through the clouds, plummeting in a free fall, never to land. Freedom.

Our victim twitched between us, crying out. I felt the approach of his climax. Though we never touched him anywhere else, he was reacting to a touch that was deeper and a thousand times more intimate.

I dropped his wrist and sucked in a deep breath. My heart thundered in my ears so I had to strain to hear anything else. Shoving away from the bleeding, writhing man, I fell on my butt in my haste to put distance between us.

Power surged through me, seeking an outlet. I was all fangs and claws, unable to fight back the wolf while the vampire side of me ruled. The good news was that if things got ugly with Jenner later, I'd be primed and ready to blow.

My vision swam as I tried to focus. Jenner and Sloane were a blur along with the many bodies surrounding them. He had his face buried between her thighs while she sucked ferociously at their victim's neck. I'd seen more than enough of Jenner's sexcapades for one night. I watched with a combination of intrigue and apprehension when Arys lifted his head and his crazed blue eyes landed on me. Abandoning the man we'd just fed on, he crossed the short distance to where I sat on the floor, bewildered.

He hovered over me on hands and knees. I gazed up at him, trembling in anticipation. His kiss was electric, a passionate claiming of my mouth. I clung to him, excited when he grabbed my arm and bared the soft inside of my wrist.

Arys bit gently at my flesh, a small bite that left me wanting more. A sound that was both pain and pleasure spilled from me. I ached for him, needing so much more than I was receiving. This was not the place for that.

Unfortunately, this was exactly the place for that, just not for me. As I held tight to my dark vampire, soaring on clouds while he tasted my blood, I lost myself. The euphoria claimed me, and I fell hard. I had to enjoy it while I could. Eventually the rush would fade, and I'd have to come back down to earth where reality would bitch slap me as it so often did.

* * * *

We found Shaz and Jez seated at a back corner poker table in the casino upstairs. Both full and empty glasses and bottles littered the table. In the center sat a deck of cards with The Wicked Kiss logo on the back. They had certainly managed to keep busy in our absence.

Shaz stared straight ahead, his chin propped in one hand and a beer bottle in the other. Rolling wolf eyes my way, he said, "It didn't take the two of you long to make yourselves at home."

I opened my mouth to reply and found I had nothing to say to that. He was right. Instead of muttering a half-assed defense, I eyed up the drink selection.

"When you get the itch, you scratch." Arys shrugged. "That's just the way it is, pup."

Shaz glared darkly in response but said nothing. He shoved a glass toward me, and I sat next to him, accepting the whiskey. The tension was thick.

I braced myself for rejection and reached out to touch Shaz's arm. "I never would have led you into that if I'd known what we were walking into. I'm sorry."

He sighed and shook his head dismissively. "It's fine. Don't apologize." He set the beer down and grabbed my hand. His wolf was strong, raging beneath the surface, spoiling for a fight. It worried me.

"I was starting to think we'd lost you. No more splitting up." Jez shook a finger at me, her words slightly slurred. The empty cocktail glasses piled up in front of her were shocking. Just how long had we been in the den of debauchery?

"Yeah, I'm thinking that's a good plan." I gave her a critical once over. This friggin' place was eating us all alive. "How many have you had, Jez?"

She tipped her head back and laughed uproariously as if I'd just told the world's funniest joke. It stopped as fast as it had started. "This is Vegas, Alexa. Counting drinks is not allowed. You just keep 'em coming until you hit the floor."

"Let's start counting, ok? I don't want to drag your unconscious ass out of here." I reached across the table to slide the last full cocktail away from Jez. She moved fast, intercepting the motion with her cat reflexes. Nice to see she was still alert and reactive.

She shook a finger at me and took a large sip of booze. "I want to get my dance on. This crap is really not my idea of a good time." She gestured erratically to the poker table with a grimace. "Come dance with me."

I wasn't leaving. I needed to see this poker game for myself. This kind of thing could be prone to shenanigans.

Arys gripped the back of the chair next to me. Instead of sitting down, he stood rigid, watching Jenner and Sloane's approach. They sauntered over, beaming with self-satisfaction.

"Finished so soon?" Jenner asked with a sly grin. "I don't recall your appetite being so easily sated, Arys."

"No more games." Arys shook his head, and his eyes blazed. "No more snide fucking comments. I'm done with it."

"Oh, I see." Jenner nodded knowingly. "You love the changes I've made to the place. And you hate that, huh? Figures. You always were the spoiled brother, unable to let me have my moment to shine."

Arys huffed and shoved a hand through his hair. He stared at the floor as if unable to bring himself to look at the taunting vampire. A muscle in his jaw twitched. "Let's just get this over with."

With a snap of his fingers and a few orders barked at the nearest waitress, Jenner quickly had the table cleared and readied for a poker game. He took a seat and gestured for Arys to sit across from him, leaving the rest of us crowded around the side opposite the dealer.

I sat stiffly, studying each vampire in turn. They bickered over the trustworthiness of a dealer employed by Jenner. A snappy reminder from Shaz that shifters could smell a lie brought that argument to an end.

I'll be the first to admit that I don't know a whole hell of a lot about poker. However, I did know enough to understand why Arys was so damn good at it. But was he better than a Las Vegas vampire who had as many years of experience playing the game?

Taking a sip, the whiskey burned, but it was smooth. Focusing on that, I tried not to entertain the fearful thought that whispered in the back of my mind, *What did Jenner have planned for me if Arys lost?*

No matter what happened, my friends had my back. Shaz was hovering on the edge of wolf, ready to lose it the moment the time was right. Jez's feline gaze was narrowed, watchful of the activity around us. Of course, that would have been a tad more reassuring if she hadn't been well on her way to Margaritaville.

I struggled to focus. My head swam as I rode the blood high. A strange giggle escaped me. The power flowed through me, a constant force that drew my gaze hungrily to the mortal occupants of the table.

Then there was Jenner. With two cards in hand, he met my gaze and winked. Didn't he know I could have him if I wanted to? The urge to lure him in was strong. It was a damn good thing that I'd left Kale back home. I would never have been able to stop myself from playing with him.

"This is like watching late night poker on TV, but better because I have a never ending supply of cocktails." Jez cackled, throwing more liquor down her throat.

"You so need to be cut off," I murmured softly, but her wildcat ears easily heard me.

"And you need to join the party. By the end of the night, this place will be yours." She shoved a shooter across the table and raised one to match in cheers.

Jenner tossed his cards down, folding. The dealer gathered the cards while Arys slid the small pot close. So far so good, but this was still just the beginning.

"Are you hens going to cluck the whole time we're playing?" Jenner asked, tossing more chips into the center. "Why don't you go find a way to entertain yourselves?"

Arys bet a frightfully large amount as I tried not to choke on my whiskey. "Show the ladies some respect. They'll be the ones kicking your ass when you lose this joke of a game."

Cards were dealt, and bets were raised. The dealer revealed the first few cards, and I held my breath. Neither vampire folded. I grabbed the shot glass before me and downed it. Tequila. Immediately I thought of Willow. It was his favorite.

When the dealer revealed the fifth card without anyone folding, each vamp was forced to show his cards. Jenner's flush beat Arys's three of a kind, and I felt the color drain from my face as Jenner dragged a pile of chips to his side.

"Keep talking, Arys. Keep talking." Jenner waved over a passing waitress and without a word, bit into her wrist. Not a drop hit the table. He licked the small wound, dragging his tongue over her vein. Then he gifted her with a slap on the ass and sent her on her way.

Arys never missed a beat as the poker game continued. More than once, he made a bet that could seriously compromise his chances of winning without blinking an eye. I, on the other hand, swallowed whiskey by the glass as I tried to drown my growing panic.

For a while, it felt like nothing was happening. Cocky opening bets became small cautious bets and bluffs to feel one another out. The tension was making me ill. Dragging it out like this was growing painful though neither vampire seemed to share my unease. Jez amused herself by silently feigning death by boredom every time someone folded or took a ridiculous amount of time to make a decision. Finally, I couldn't take it anymore either. I walked away from the table with her hot on my heels.

"Holy shit, could those two possibly be more intense?" She briskly rubbed her arms. "They're totally ruining this trip for us. I knew we should have left your vampire at home."

"Hey, don't blame me for this. You're the one who insisted on coming to Vegas." My skin prickled as well, flush with goose bumps. Sitting between two powerful vampires in conflict wasn't easy. "I wish they had just beat the hell out of one another. The waiting is killing me."

Jez crooked a finger, beckoning to a passing waitress. A devilish smile lit up her face. This city was quickly bringing out the inner monster in all of us. "You know Arys wouldn't play a game he couldn't win," she chided. "Have a little faith in him. His arrogance can be backed up with legit skill."

"We can't assume anything. There is always a chance he will lose. Then what? I join them?" I indicated the vampiress showgirls seducing human men with ease on the other side of the building.

With a brow raised in speculative interest, Jez eyed the scantily clad vampires. "I don't think you'd be so lucky. Jenner's idea of entertainment seems to involve an audience and theatrics."

"He can kill me. There's no way in hell I'm doing that." My words came out in a hush. I couldn't bring myself to go down that road right now.

"Think I can buy a lap dance without having to give up any blood?"

I followed Jez's gaze to the redhead gyrating on a table. Annoyance struck me and I frowned. Then I shrugged it off, feeling like an ass. Jez shouldn't have to suffer because of vampire business that didn't involve her. She needed to cut loose and heal after a horrible loss.

"Only one way to find out." I gave her a playful push. "Go ahead. Have fun and be careful. You know where to find me."

Taking a little walk around the casino gave me a chance to ready myself to return to the poker table. It also gave me an excuse to call and check in on things back home.

I hit Kale's number in the contact list and then drifted between slot machines, listening to it ring. An older couple shouted in glee as they won two hundred dollars. A solitary man a few machines down from them swore and punched the air before lighting a cigarette and puffing angrily away. He caught me watching and made a crude penis pulling gesture. Somehow I walked on without stuffing his head up his ass.

"Miss me already?" Kale purred into my ear. "Or just checking to make sure I'm still functioning on a semi-sane level?"

My breath caught, and I had a guilty sense of relief at the sound of his voice. "Maybe a little of both. Is that ok?"

The background noise grew quieter as I awaited his reply. "You're a masochist, Alexa. How is Vegas treating you so far?"

"Vegas is fabulous. The vampires, however, are a serious pain in the ass." I leaned against a slot machine and peered across the distance into the poker area. The thought of returning to that table filled me with dread.

Kale laughed, a light sound that was reminiscent of who he used to be. The sarcasm that followed reminded me how greatly he'd changed. "You mean Arys's vampire family didn't accept you with open arms? Color me shocked. So, how much trouble are you in?"

He could try all he liked to convince me that his love for me had twisted into something ugly during his time locked up by the FPA, but the fact that he bothered to ask told me otherwise. I allowed myself a small smile.

"I'm not sure yet," I said with a bitter laugh. "I'll let you know when the poker game deciding my fate is over."

"Nothing says love quite like using your lady as a poker bet. Classy. And to think, you could be here instead. With me."

"So you can taunt me into driving a stake through your heart?" I scoffed. "That's not a game I want to keep playing. I think my chances of winning are better here."

"Our game is far from over." The promises hidden within Kale's statement echoed across the distance between us.

There was an awkward pause where neither of us spoke. I grasped for words, wondering why I'd thought this call would make me feel better. Somehow, I couldn't accept that things between Kale and me were so irreparably damaged.

"Anyway," I stammered. "I just wanted to make sure things were all good there. So have a good night and, um, try not to kill anybody."

Before I could hang up Kale said, "Alexa…don't get killed, ok? I like you with a heartbeat."

The last bit was cryptic, spoken with a smile judging by the lilt to his tone. It sent a chill through me that left me staring at the phone long after he'd hung up.

I ambled up to the poker table, doing my best to take my sweet time. Only Shaz glanced up at my approach. The two vampires locked in card combat had eyes only for each other. Sloane had vacated, leaving the men without a voice of reason. I guess it would have to be me. Joy.

"So, what did I miss?" I slid into the chair beside Shaz, taking note of the amount of chips in each vampire's possession. Things were not looking good.

"Besides some arrogant bets that didn't pay off? Not much." He stared pointedly at Arys who scowled. "He might be able to bluff a good game back home, but I think he's met his match here."

"It's a game of strategy, pup. I know what I'm doing. Would you care to get in on this?" Arys asked snidely, his temper short.

Shaz ran a finger through the condensation on his beer bottle. He wore a bored expression. "Not at all. I'll leave the stupid decisions in your hands. You're doing a great job so far." He followed up with a sarcastic thumbs up.

I studied him in small glances so he wouldn't notice. He hadn't been back long, but after a month in the wilderness, spending much of his time as wolf, Shaz had come back with some serious attitude. Of course, he'd always been confrontational with Arys.

"Game of strategy, huh?" Jenner's laughter rang with satisfaction. Slapping his cards down on the table, he snickered. "You've lost your touch, my friend."

A straight flush mocked us from the tabletop. I watched with growing horror as Arys's chances of winning grew smaller. He stared in disbelief. Jenner was kicking his ass. If Arys didn't win a few hands, it was over.

Jenner toyed with his chips, picking up a stack and letting it slide through his fingers. The sound they made grated on my senses, an endless clink that quickly got under my skin.

"Maybe it's karma," Jenner offered, sliding the chips faster, louder. "You fucked me over, and now it's your turn, Arys. Let's end this."

"Yeah, why not?" Shaz chimed in. "Some of us don't have precious time to waste."

Arys met my gaze. Other than the muscle twitching in his clenched jaw, he was unreadable. I half expected him to touch my mind, to say something. He didn't.

Instead, Jenner asked me, "What do you think, sweetheart? Feeling lucky?" Confidence oozed from him.

I ignored him and his cocky smile. Intimidating me wasn't necessary. I was already afraid. However, I was also ready to fight. The wolf paced inside me, certain she'd get her shot at Jenner yet.

Everyone stared at me, awaiting my response. My head swam from the booze and blood. The noise and lights assaulting my senses had begun to dull. All things considered, I was feeling pretty good.

To Arys I said, "Do whatever you gotta do, babe," staying committed to our united front.

Arys flung ten grand in chips down, a challenge adorning his handsome face. I didn't know what cards the dealer had dealt him, but he seemed happy with it. Waiting for Jenner to decide if he was bluffing had me on pins and needles. Unable to stay seated, I paced the length of the table. Jenner's eyes flashed in irritation so I shot him a snide smile. Perspiration greased my palms. Calming breaths did nothing to help.

They played a few more hands with neither vampire sustaining much damage. Then, the cards stopped in a long pause as decisions were made.

I didn't have the patience for this shit. The waitress brought me another whiskey, which I eagerly snatched. A cloud of perfume surrounded her, taunting me with a hint of musk and human. Our fingers touched as I accepted the drink, and my gaze fell to her neck.

"Can I offer you anything else?" She asked, tilting her head to reveal two bites hidden beneath her hair. Jenner must pay these people damn good.

"No," I snapped, more forcefully than intended. "Thank you."

It took a moment to regain my composure. The heady atmosphere of the club made it difficult. Talking myself down from the ledge became a lot easier when Jenner's triumphant shout broke through my thoughts.

"Victory has never felt so fucking good!" he crowed.

The cards said it all. Arys stared in stony silence at the pair of kings in his hand. They were shitty cards, especially compared to Jenner's flush. Arys's arrogance had been the driving force behind his decision to settle it this way. He had never really believed he would lose.

It was over. Jenner had his vengeance victory. Hooray for vendettas.

Chapter Seven

I wanted to be surprised. Really, I did. But I wasn't.

"Fina-fucking-lly," Shaz muttered. Tipping his beer to his lips, he settled back into his seat with an uncharacteristically sly smile. "What a boring way to settle a score."

My jaw dropped. Where the hell was this attitude coming from?

"The excitement starts now." Like a kid on Christmas, Jenner was unable to contain his glee. His fang-flashing smile was so wide I thought his head might split in two. Icy blue gaze locked on Shaz, he cackled, "In fact, it can start with you."

"Alright, Jenner, you made your point." Arys tried quickly to intervene. "I owe you. Fair enough. Leave him out of it."

"You married my fiancée! And killed her. Your wolves killed Harley." The dangerous vibe seeping from Jenner had the little hairs on my arms standing on end. Pointing a finger at Shaz, he barked, "You're going in the ring."

I stood back and watched the vampires dissolve into slinging barbs and threats. Chairs abandoned and power raging, they took turns promising one another a slow, painful death.

Searching the crowd for Jez, I spotted her near the stage with Sloane. The two of them were draped all over each other, giggling and talking. I didn't trust Sloane's intentions, but I had no time for that now.

"Boys, boys, boys," I tsked, stepping in between the raging vampires. "There's got to be a better solution."

Despite the knot forming in my stomach, I stayed calm, refusing to let my emotions show. Putting Shaz in the fight cage was cruel in the worst way. It couldn't happen. There was no way I could allow that. As my mind raced, struggling to come up with an amicable alternative, Shaz blew that plan to hell.

"I'd be happy to show you how I tore Harley's throat out," he proclaimed, slamming his beer bottle onto the poker table. He sneered at Jenner. "I wasn't afraid of Harley, and I'm not afraid of you. Put me in the ring."

Everyone fell quiet. Forgetting Arys entirely, Jenner slithered over to Shaz, eyeing him up like a prize-winning piece of meat.

"Well, look at the balls on this one," Jenner mused. "I'm tempted to put money on you myself. Too bad I don't want you to actually walk out of that ring alive."

"I guess you're going to be disappointed then. Might as well place your bet." Arms crossed, the wolf shining in his eyes, Shaz stood relaxed, ready even. Not a shred of fear emanated from him.

Arys looked as stunned as I was. Our eyes met, and I shrugged. This side of Shaz was new to me too.

"Shaz, you don't have to agree to this," Arys said. "I won't let him force you into anything."

Shaz scoffed, looking insulted. "Did I stutter? I said I want to do it. Don't talk down to me, Arys."

"Are you out of your mind?" I asked, incredulous. There weren't words enough for the flurry of questions I wanted to hurl at him.

With a snap of Jenner's fingers, three vampires from his security team surrounded Shaz. Both Arys and I took a defensive stance, but the blond wolf waved us away.

"My guys here will take you down to get ready for the fight," explained Jenner. "Drink, shower, beat the hell out of one of them, I don't care. Do whatever you need to do to be at your best. I want to see a good show."

"Oh, you will." Shaz went with them willingly. The wolf was heavy in him, creeping close to the surface. His green eyes almost glowed.

I stepped in front of him, refusing to let him just walk away like this. "Wait. There has to be another way. You don't have to do this. Why would you want to?"

Shaz touched my cheek; something almost wistful crossed his face. Then it was gone, and I saw only wolf. "Don't do anything to stop this, Lex. I mean it. Consider that a command from your pack Alpha."

He leaned in to press a brief but surprisingly deep and sensual kiss to my lips before following the security guys through the crowd. I gaped after him, speechless and a little pissed off.

"I don't have a pack," I mumbled when I found my voice, but he was already beyond earshot.

I looked to Arys for help. He merely shrugged and sat heavily in the chair Shaz had just vacated. I was torn, wanting to go after him. Did he really expect me to just sit back and let this happen? And more importantly, did he seriously just give me an order?

"Let him go, Alexa," Arys said. Like many times before, it made me wonder if the mental wall between us was more transparent than I thought. "Shaz came back with something to prove. Like any other animal, he's going to run around marking his territory and generally ticking everyone else off. And you have to let him."

I looked longingly after Shaz, knowing I had to let him go. He was an Alpha wolf. He'd be fine. Right?

Remembering my drunken leopard friend, I searched the crowd for Jez who had vanished from sight. In her inebriated state, she'd never be able to fight off a vampire, especially not one like Sloane. No vampire made by Harley could be trusted.

"I should find Jez. How long do I have until Shaz fights?" I couldn't believe I was asking so casually with such acceptance. This was so wrong.

Jenner perched on the edge of the poker table, watching me fidget with my whiskey glass. "Your friend will be safe with Sloane. I promise. In fact, she'll have the time of her life."

"That's what I'm afraid of." Swirling the deep gold liquor in my glass, I grasped my power, making my eyes bleed to wolf and then to glow Arys's vampire blue. I peered into Jenner, hoping he saw the resolve in my eyes. "If anything happens to either Jez or Shaz, I will kill you. And if I go down trying, I'll still find a way to take you with me."

We shared a moment then, Jenner and I. For a brief space in time, I think he truly believed I could and would be the one to end him. Then he shrugged off the dazed wonder and replaced it with a smarmy sneer.

"Your wolf fights next. So we should probably head down there. I like a ringside view."

Without waiting, Jenner headed for the elevator. Angry and cursing up a storm beneath my breath, I followed with one last glance back for Jez who was still missing with Sloane.

Re-entering the fight arena made my knees shake. I walked in a surreal haze. The harsh sting of reality sought to cut through the remains of the euphoric buzz. It had faded along with the effects of the whiskey like a short-lived illusion shattered by impending doom. The usual.

I did my best to tune out Jenner's gloating. He led us to a VIP section near the fight cage where we sat on velvet sofas and watched the current fight while waitresses offered their blood to us.

"Spit it out," Jenner said to Arys. A cheer from the crowd drowned out his words. "There's something you want to say. I can see it all over you."

Arys sat stiffly, his arms crossed, eyeing Jenner like a snake in the grass. "Harley kept the shady activity much quieter than this. How do you do this every night without the FPA shutting it down?"

"Harley's activity was filthy. That blood ring was too dirty, even for me. And I like it dirty. The FPA was happy to let me do whatever I wanted with the place after his death. I have a little arrangement with them. I withdrew from the blood ring, and they leave me and the club alone." Jenner was pleased with himself.

Arys had tried to shut down Harley's blood ring soon after his death. He'd failed. I found it hard to believe Jenner was able to dissolve something so many vampires were determined to hold onto.

"So Harley's death worked out quite nicely for you. How convenient," Arys said with an eye roll. "Must be good for business to have the FPA on your payroll."

"You're having problems with your local sector, I presume. A little bargaining can go a long way. Try it."

"If only it were that easy," I interjected, reconsidering the whiskey.

"Oh, but it is." Jenner was just so sure of himself. Arrogant as all get out, he spoke with condescension. "Everyone needs something they can only get from someone else. It's business."

"What about demons?" I countered, knowing he wouldn't have a smarmy answer for that. "Is there much demon activity here? Seems pointless. Everyone is already sinning."

His gaze dropped pointedly to the black dragon wrapped around my forearm. "I don't associate with them. Nobody with any sense would get caught up with demons."

The slimy son of a bitch didn't know a damn thing about my deal with Shya. My temper flared, and I was contemplating slashing Jenner's throat with my claws when Arys cut in. "How did you dissolve Harley's blood ring?" he asked. "Claire and Maxwell were desperate to keep that going. I can't imagine they were the only ones."

A shadow flickered across Jenner's face. "I took care of it."

He was being purposely vague with good reason, I was sure. The blood ring Harley had been running was vile, a twisted supply and demand of victims for fetish kills. Children, virgins, redheads, whatever a vampire wanted in a victim, they could find. It was truly sickening. Discovering that Jenner had hated it would have made me muster an iota of respect for him if he hadn't just endangered my wolf.

"And what does Hurst say about all of this?" The name dropped from Arys like a bomb, causing Jenner to stiffen. It was familiar to me, though like most of Arys's memories, everything about Hurst remained buried.

"He doesn't say much of anything these days." There was, for the first time, a crack in Jenner's tough exterior. He held Arys's gaze, but it seemed hard, as if he wanted to turn away.

"Who's Hurst?" I looked back and forth between them. I hated feeling out of the loop.

"He sired Harley," said Arys. "He's old, much older than me or Jenner. It's been several decades since I've seen him."

"It's been decades since any of us have seen him," Jenner added. "Hurst is the oldest, wisest vampire I know. He's also a recluse, unwilling to deal with the irritation of humanity any longer."

I waited for further explanation but received none. "So," I prodded. "Where is he?"

"Yes," Arys nodded. "I'd like to know that as well. It would be nice to speak to him."

"Nobody sees Hurst unless he initiates it. He's close enough to stay aware of the goings on of the city without being part of it." Jenner held his hands out and shrugged, dismissing the subject.

I ran a finger around the rim of the whiskey glass, pondering what it must be like to have lived so long as a vampire that one tires of existence. It was as fascinating as it was tragic. Many questions danced on the tip of my tongue, none of which Jenner would answer. I didn't bother to ask.

"Does he know I'm here?" Arys asked. There was visible tension in his shoulders. His restraint was going to break at some point. It wouldn't be pretty.

"He probably knew it before I did. Nothing slips past him." An uncaring shrug from Jenner conveyed that he wasn't close with Harley's maker.

Another loud cheer went up from the crowd. The fight announcer's voice boomed through the arena. He pronounced the winner; the fight was over. A dead wolf was dragged from the ring, the victor barely on his feet. Shaz was next.

Dread filled me, and my stomach flipped. Desperation seized me. "Jenner, please, let's work something out, strike a deal of some kind. Shaz doesn't belong in that ring."

He leaned forward, pressing his fingertips together while giving me a thoughtful once over. "I beg to differ. You don't sound too confident in him. Funny considering you were confident in his ability to help you murder my sire. Tell me, Alexa, would you like to take his place?" Raising a dark brow, he flashed a cocky smile at me, but his gaze strayed to Arys for a reaction.

Arys appeared unruffled, but I could feel the hate-filled rage he held tightly reined. With an eerie sense of calm, he said, "He's going to kill anything you put in there with him. Don't think for a minute that we're even after this. I'm going to make you wish I'd never come back here."

"I wish many things. That is already one of them." Jenner was flippant, but his fingers dug into the tabletop. "Don't forget, Arys, we're only halfway done here. I'll have your lady on stage before the night is over."

Before either Arys or I could snark back, the announcer drew our attention back to the ring. His voice thundered through the place, and my strength crumbled.

"Are you ready for the next fight?" He asked, receiving raucous jeers and applause in response. "You know the drill. Take a good look at each opponent and place your bets."

I turned in my chair to see Shaz enter the fight cage. He wore only the long shorts of a boxer. Both hands were clenched into fists as he fixated on his opponent, a thirty-something lanky werewolf with light brown hair and dark eyes that were pure beast. Both men had eyes only for each other. They were ready. I was terrified.

Shaz had a great physique. He'd always been in shape, but his time in the mountains had given him additional muscle and tone. Unfortunately, sheer force wasn't enough to win a fight like this. He had to want it more than his opponent, and he had to be clever in his attacks.

The crowd grew loud with activity as patrons placed their bets with the designated arena bookies. My panic was growing in leaps and bounds. Why was Arys so unaffected? I wanted to shake him.

"Arys," I spoke through gritted teeth. Turning my growing ire on Jenner, I said, "I won't let him die in there."

Jenner scoffed. "Don't you dare even think about interfering, or I'll toss your ass in there to take on the winner." To Arys he said, "Talk some sense into your woman, brother. She's a loose cannon."

"I'll show you a loose cannon," I roared, on my feet with fangs bared.

"It's Shaz's fight, Alexa," Arys warned. "We must stay out of it. He requested it."

More like demanded it, I thought bitterly. Jenner smirked, and without second-guessing my decision, I tossed the contents of my whiskey glass into his face.

Jenner moved fast, a blur of motion. He grabbed me by the throat and jerked me close. Whiskey dripped from his face. "You have no idea who you're fucking with, little wolf. I could have you on your knees begging me for your pathetic life before Arys could so much as blink."

That was clearly an exaggeration. In a reflexive reaction, I smashed my knee into Jenner's groin with enough force to drop him.

When he stared up at me in open-mouthed surprise, I placed a hand on his forehead and reached for his power. It recognized me, bending easily to my will. I put the squeeze on him, focusing on his lifeless heart.

"This is how I killed Harley," I said slyly. "A power push that caused his heart to explode. And that's what I'll do to you if you ever touch me again."

A handful of Jenner's vampires surged forward from their place in the crowd, ready to protect the master of their city. I stopped them with a hand, sweeping my power out like a wave crashing over each of them in turn. Drawing on my link to Arys, I took them all down.

Taking advantage of my small lapse in focus, Jenner slapped me with a psi ball I never saw coming. It slammed into my chest, knocking me breathless. I lost my balance and stumbled backwards. Arys's quick catch kept me from falling.

"Enough!" Arys threw an energy wall up between me and Jenner, who got to his feet, cursing up a storm.

I took a few deep breaths, ensuring I could still breathe. That attack had carried some serious weight. Jenner was no lightweight, being almost as powerful as Arys. I would have to be more cautious during our next face off.

Tearing through Arys's barrier was tempting. I could do it because of our bond. Instead, I spun on my heel and stormed off across the room. I was fuming, wishing I could sink claws into Jenner until he screamed like a little bitch.

Passing a waitress with a tray laden with cocktails, I swiped one and asked her to bring me something stronger. Too bad I'd wasted a drink on that sniveling vampire.

I planted myself on the opposite side of the room against the back wall where I could see everything. Arys and Jenner were right where I'd left them, heads close together as they spat profanities at each other.

I turned my attention to the two wolves inside the cage. They both moved in place, predatory and anxious to fight. The announcer stepped back into the center of the ring, and the crowd's excitement grew. I groaned.

"I hope you've all placed your bets. Now let's see what kind of beasts we're gambling with here." The announcer gestured to each man to shift. They did without hesitation, leaving their shorts in tattered pieces. The crowd loved this. "At the sound of the bell, the fight begins. It ends when one of you is dead. Good luck. Fight hard."

The announcer left the ring. Apprehension was heavy as the crowd waited for the bell. I closed my eyes, willing myself to wake up from this horrible dream. The waitress returned with my whiskey, forcing me to look. I exchanged the empty cocktail glass for the double shot of rye, dropped her a tip and sighed.

The bell rang. I almost choked on the liquor. *Aw hell, here we go.*

Shaz hung back circling the outside of the ring. His opponent opted for the rush attack. The brown wolf flung himself at Shaz, snarling and snapping. He was too aggressive too soon. His timing was wrong and instead of sinking fangs, he ran face first into the cage. Shaz leaped on his back, getting in a few good bites before bounding backwards to circle again.

The brown wolf wasn't so quick to make a move this time. He hung back, watching Shaz, seeking a way to his throat. I held my glass so tight I thought I felt it crack. Remembering to breathe would be a good idea.

Incessant shouts from the audience rang out, demanding blood. The majority of the crowd was human, slick businessmen in their pricey suits, seeking a bigger thrill than any human club could offer them. Monsters. Every damn one of us. Being human didn't change that. Somehow, it made it worse.

Shaz moved fast, feinting left then right, then going left again. He leaped, crashing against the other wolf with all of his weight. The two of them tumbled across the ring in a brown and white ball of fur.

A yelp cut through the myriad of voices. I recognized it as Shaz. My stomach dropped, and I leaned heavily against the wall at my back. My hands hummed with energy. I could stop this. I could do it right now.

The wolves sprang apart. Blood stained the floor. Shaz's blood. A whimper rose in my throat. My wolf was desperate to fight at his side.

The whiskey burned my throat. I tried to concentrate on the hot sensation as it scorched a path to my stomach. If Shaz came out of this unscathed, I was going to shake him until his teeth rattled. No, *when* he came out of this. When.

There was a burning hot fury emanating from Shaz when he lunged again at the brown wolf. He was forceful, pinning his opponent against the cage. They struggled there, each seeking to gain the advantage over the other.

I tore my gaze away, staring at my feet but seeing only the outcome I feared most playing out in my mind. Good Lord, why did we come here? I had known there would be trouble. If something happened to Shaz, I would never forgive myself.

"There isn't a single part of me that doesn't believe he'll win this." Arys's voice infused me with a sense of calm. Lost in thought, I hadn't noticed his approach. He leaned on the wall next to me and slung an arm around my shoulders. I stood stiffly, unable to relax against him.

"I know I should think that too. Shaz can hold his own. It's just the 'what ifs' that are killing me. I feel like I'm going to throw up. I won't watch him die, Arys."

"You won't have to. That wolf has a lot of rage to get out. There's no better place for it than here."

In silence, we stood there, watching the wolves viciously tear into one another. Every blow that the brown wolf landed had me cringing. It took all of my strength to restrain myself. It would be so easy to toss some power into that cage, to separate them or kill the brown wolf.

"Don't even think it," Arys said, anticipating my intentions. "Not only would it cause more hassle with Jenner, but it would undermine Shaz as a man. He doesn't need you to save him."

I bristled, hating the truth in Arys's words. It was so crappy of him to play the man card, but I understood. Shaz had to do this, to defend his choice to help me take Harley down. It was his way of showing Jenner and every other vampire in their bloodline that he was an Alpha wolf for a damn good reason. I didn't have to like it, but I had to stay out of it. Damn, that sucked.

The brown wolf went down beneath Shaz, his legs kicking as he desperately tried to dislodge his attacker. Blood sprayed. He was definitely hurt. Was it enough?

Shaz backed off to assess his opponent's injuries, a mistake on his part. The brown wolf sprang, sudden and swift. He timed his attack perfectly. Fangs bared, he bit into the side of Shaz's neck. The snow-white fur quickly became bright scarlet as his blood flowed.

He went down hard, unable to shake the brown wolf's hold. The audience was on its feet, arms raised. Boos and cheers rang out, as the gamblers shouted for their wolf to win.

I rushed forward, shoving through people to get closer to the ring. A security guard stepped in my path, pushing me back. I tossed him aside, wrapping my fingers around the cold metal of the cage. Power filled me so hard and fast I gasped.

"You really want to make this night of hell never ending, don't you?" Arys pried my fingers off the cage and pulled me into his arms, easily overpowering me physically.

"We have to help him. Before it's too late." I was frantic, struggling to escape. My gaze locked on Shaz. *Get up*, I willed him. *Get up now!*

His jade-green eyes found me there, near the ring. He had a hardness that I'd never seen. In a move that astonished me along with most of the crowd, he twisted his body, fast and smooth. The action tossed the brown wolf over him, onto his back. On his feet once again, Shaz struck twice, then a third time, finding that sweet, vulnerable spot. He buried his fangs in the brown wolf's throat and tore.

There was so much blood. The sticky sweet scent mingled with the booze, sweat and various colognes to make an aroma cocktail that sickened me as it enticed. Both wolves were bleeding but only one was still standing.

I could have cried with relief. Still, Shaz wasn't out of the woods yet. He was unsteady on his feet and bleeding profusely.

"That's not much blood," Arys whispered in my ear. "It's the white fur. It makes it look worse than it is."

"Stop doing that. Stay out of my head." Again, I tried to be free of his hold, but his grip remained firm. The whiskey glass fell from my hand to shatter as it hit the floor.

I waited several heart-stopping moments for a referee to enter the ring and proclaim the brown wolf dead. About half the crowd cheered in victory, having placed their bets on my white wolf. The wolf within me cheered with them though she had more to lose than cold, empty cash.

Only when Shaz exited the fight cage did Arys finally release me. I made my way to him, tossing people out of the way as I went. He padded over to a bench off to the side laden with towels, water and his clothing. The shift back to human tore a shout from him. I fell to my knees before him, reaching to take his face in my hands.

"Let me see," I said, breathy and scared.

His neck was a raw mess. Several bites marred his body, some mere flesh wounds and others more than a little serious. His face too bore evidence of the fight. Bruises lined his jaw and nose, spreading out beneath his eyes. A cut on his eyebrow dripped steadily.

"I'm ok," he tried to reassure me, wincing when I ran a hand over his ribs. Grasping my hand, he rose, pulling me up with him. "I just need to get dressed and chill for a minute. Can you get me a Scotch?"

"You want a drink? Shaz, you could have a concussion. Or worse." I turned to Arys who stood protectively nearby. "You should try to heal him."

"No," Shaz said. He pulled his pants on, grimacing as he moved. "I'm fine. Really. We heal fast. It's all good."

I saw the truth in his eyes, the unspoken words. He wasn't ready for Arys to touch him like that, with the rush of power. I didn't want to accept that his previous addiction would prevent him from receiving much needed help. Avoiding the rush couldn't possibly be more important than his life.

"It would be best to stop the bleeding." Arys advised, ignoring the warning look Shaz shot him. "Don't forget where you are, pup. In a place like this, you're a delicacy."

"I'll take my chances." Turning his back on us, Shaz cleaned his wounds with the towel.

We couldn't force him to do a damn thing. Rather than push the subject, I ordered him a damn Scotch. He cleaned up reasonably well other than the brutal facial injuries and the blood spatters that stained his platinum hair. Back in his suit, collar open, he exuded an air of disaffected cool. He was too calm for someone who had just killed without reason.

I exchanged a look with Arys who shook his head and shrugged. What had just happened deeply disturbed me.

After a few quiet minutes of sipping his Scotch, Shaz surveyed the room and said, "Well since we're here, we might as well party."

Chapter Eight

I gaped at him, questioning his sanity. "What the fuck, Shaz? Did you get your brain rattled in there?"

"I just fought for my life. Now I want to celebrate the fact that I'm still standing here." Shaz turned to flag down another waitress.

"What you need to be doing right now is healing," I insisted. "And resting. In bed, after a hot shower."

His jade-green gaze swung back to me, and a mischievous smile graced his lips. "Will you play nurse for me?"

Before I could answer, Jenner strolled up. His expression was guarded, unreadable. "You got lucky," he said to Shaz, taking in his injuries with interest. "Congratulations."

"It had nothing to do with luck." Shaz leveled his gaze at the haughty vampire, challenging him with a look. "You think you know werewolves? Well, you don't know me."

Jenner nodded approvingly, and he offered Shaz a hand. "You proved yourself to be the better wolf. I applaud your integrity. Let me know if you're ever in need of a change of scenery. I'll have a job for you." I wouldn't have thought a vampire more arrogant than Arys could exist. Yet, here he was.

"You're assuming you'll still be in charge of this place in the future. How cute," I quipped. It might have been bad form to taunt the vampire who'd promised to cast me in his theatre of bloodlust and melodrama, but I'd tired of his showboating.

"You wanna make a move on my territory, Alexa?" Jenner stepped up close, forcing me to crane my neck to meet his gaze. "After you grace my stage, you'll be begging to be one of my girls."

"I won't be the one begging." It was a promise I intended to keep. Jenner would be sorry he'd won that poker game.

When I didn't call my power or so much as nudge him, Jenner backed off. This was fun for him, his pathetic attempt at playing with Arys's toys as a means of revenge. One thing about vampires, they never got over anything. They had too much time to dwell on past wrongs.

"The midnight show gets the biggest crowd. They'll be getting a treat tonight." Jenner waved over a waitress who set down her tray and slid into his arms. He swept her hair aside and kissed her neck. She quickly fell under his influence, grinding her pelvis against him.

I turned away before he bit her. It wouldn't be long until the clock struck twelve. That didn't leave me a lot of time to ensure Shaz was really alright and decide what to do about Jenner. I wasn't going to play the swooning victim for him.

Jenner offered the wrist of the waitress to Arys who declined. He wanted to taste her though. I could see it all over him.

"You're not doing to Alexa what we saw you do on stage earlier," Arys said, warning in his tone. "I'll call it quits on this game of yours and kill you right here."

A frown creased Jenner's brow. Dragging his tongue over the matching punctures he'd given the waitress, he mumbled against her skin. "Why no, of course not. Every vampire that tastes her blood seems to die or become pathetically addicted to her." His head snapped up quickly then, and he pinned me with a hungry stare. "Too bad. I'll have to watch the two of you together instead."

"Excuse me?" The numbing effects of the alcohol wore off quickly at that sobering remark. It took effort to look Jenner in the eyes rather than ogle the crimson drop sliding down the waitress's neck.

"Arys Knight united with his other half after all this time…yeah that's something I want to see in action. I imagine a witness can come away from that quite affected." Having finished with his nibble, Jenner gave the waitress a light pat on the behind and sent her on her way.

He didn't notice the way Shaz's gaze dropped to the floor. Yeah, one could say bystanders could easily get swept up in the rush of what Arys and I commanded. Shaz knew it very well.

I expected Arys to protest, but instead he shrugged, bored. "Let's just get this over with. Then we're even, and we're done. Is that clear, Jenner?"

"Crystal."

We were far from done with Jenner. Of that, I was certain.

"I'm not an exhibitionist," I protested. "There's no way I'm putting my private life on display so you and your audience can get off on it. You're disgusting, Jenner."

Shaz's scoffing laughter caused my eyebrows to shoot straight up in disbelief. Sucking back the Scotch, he winced as his sore face reminded him that laughing was a privilege. "It won't be so bad, Lex," he offered. "Just take one for the team. The sooner we're done here, the sooner we can enjoy the rest of the city."

"Take one for the team?" I repeated, searching Shaz for any sign of the wolf I thought I knew. "Who are you?"

Before I could lay into Shaz for his rash and absurd behavior, Arys caught my arm and steered me away. When we were a safe distance away, I opened my mouth to let him have it. He clapped a hand over my lips to muffle my bitching.

"It's just another vampire power trip, ok? Remember that. Everything that's happened tonight, it's all about power. Because we've got it, and he's desperate to hang on to it." Arys paused, waiting until I nodded in understanding. "Jenner thinks by coming on strong he can intimidate us. So we play his game. But we play it our way."

Chewing my lower lip in frustration, I turned the possible outcomes of this scenario over in my head. There was no way through without stepping miles out of my comfort zone.

I groaned and might have even pouted a bit. "Why did Shaz automatically get the cage fight? Because he's a man? I'm sensing a bit of a double standard here."

"There isn't a man in this room who has the power you have. Succubus and wolf. Do what you do best. Let's teach Jenner to be careful what he wishes for."

My head swam as the crash from the blood high began. Human blood might sate one hunger, but it was just the beginning. Power was more addictive than blood. An essential life force like blood, power begged to be tasted.

"Do you trust me?" With a gentle hand on my cheek, Arys locked eyes with me, searching for assurance.

Talk about a loaded question. Too many times, he'd made choices that I didn't agree with, choices that significantly increased the danger in our lives. Yet, so had I.

"Yes," I said, leaning into his caress. "I trust you."

* * * *

I watched from backstage as the theatre filled with people. It was a relatively small theatre compared to most, but still a crowd of people waited to watch some authentic vampire activity. My stomach dropped to my knees.

"I change my mind. I can't do this."

"Sure you can. It will be fun." Arys lounged on the sofa, exuding a calm that I did not share. He'd taken off his jacket and opened his shirt to reveal more of his hairless chest. His gaze followed me as I flitted anxiously about the room. "Relax, Alexa. I'll guide you. It'll be fine. You might even like it." With a wink and a sexy snicker, he beckoned me over.

I shook my head, unable to sit down. Pacing a hole in the carpet and wringing my hands wasn't getting me anywhere, but it gave me something to do while I waited for Jenner to turn me into a carnival act. Step right up and watch the werewolf get fucked and bled by the vampire destined to love and kill her. There's a crowd drawing tagline if I ever heard one.

The door opened, and Jenner stood in its frame with his arms crossed. "Remember, I've got your wolf out there. So don't try anything stupid."

"Like what?" I challenged, swallowing my fear despite how it choked me. When he shot me a dark glare, I added, "Hey, my definition of stupid is likely much different from yours."

"Just get your ass in gear. I got the crowd warmed up for you. They're eager to see such a unique pairing. As am I."

My main motivation to walk out of that room and on to the stage to be part of this wackjob show was Shaz. He was in rough shape, pouring liquor on the pain and feeding his new bad attitude.

Jenner's security guys surrounded him and promised that they would add to his injuries if I gave them a reason to.

"What exactly are you expecting to see?" I followed Jenner down the hall while furiously rubbing my moist palms on my skirt. Calm and cool, I had this. That's one of the lies I told myself to combat my nerves.

"I expect to see something that makes me want to touch myself while watching you. Along with everyone else in the room. That's what they're here for."

Finding me so close, he fell back to walk beside me. Smart vampire. It was in his best interest to avoid having me at his back. I wasn't above a cheap, come from behind kind of shot. We stopped at the rear entry to the stage. I was doing a pretty good job of keeping it together. I hadn't run shrieking from the theatre yet, although my confidence would have fared better if my knees weren't quivering.

Arys took my hand, sliding his fingers between mine. A spark of blue and gold flashed like lightning between us. Calm flowed through me, and our contact strengthened me.

"Oh, come on now, Jenner," Arys taunted. "This won't be the first time you've gotten off to me. We both know what this is really about."

The temperature around us rose several degrees in response to Jenner's immediate anger. His fists clenched, and he hissed, "Fuck you," before storming up the steps to the stage.

"What the hell was that about?" I whispered as Jenner announced us to the crowd.

"Cheap shot. Don't worry about it."

I resisted when he tugged me up the stairs. "Did you have a thing with him or something?"

"No. Geez, Alexa, I haven't fucked everyone in my past."

Before I could question him further, Arys dragged me into the spotlight where I stood numb, like a deer in the headlights. The audience was silent, watching us curiously. Their energy hummed like a swarm of insects. I rubbed my arms as if that would wipe the annoying prickle of it away. My mouth was so dry I couldn't swallow. Stage fright gripped me hard as I stared at the onlookers staring back at me. I was sure I'd faint right then and there. Like the fight arena, most of the audience was human. However, I noted an increased vampire presence compared to the earlier show. Shaz was out there. The blinding spotlight kept him hidden in the dark, but I could feel his wolf's energy.

Jenner stood backstage in the shadows just beyond the stage lighting. I couldn't see him, but I could feel the weight of his gaze. He was going to be pissed when I vomited all over the place.

Arys was smooth, acknowledging the crowd with a glance and then dismissing them entirely. He turned me to face him, putting the onlookers to my right. My gaze darted from the spotlight where we stood to the chaise lounge several feet away. Overwhelmed wasn't the right word.

'I can't do this,' I seized hold of the mental door between us and slammed it open.

'Trust me.'

Lifting my hand, Arys kissed my palm before doing the same to my fingertips. I was painfully aware of the many eyes upon me, watching for my reaction. A gasp slipped out, embarrassingly loud in the silent theatre.

Heat started in the center of my hand. A familiar push of dizzying energy accompanied the growing warmth. I began to relax. It had been a while since Arys had manipulated me, and I almost fell under his thrall, unaware that it was happening.

I stared into his eyes, tumbling headlong into those drowning midnight orbs. Turning my arm to expose my wrist, he dragged his lips over the pulse beating there, never breaking eye contact.

'Aw, Arys, no fair.' I tried to say the words aloud, but his actions had stolen my breath. All I mustered was a barely audible, "Why?"

"Because you're mine," he said for the benefit of the crowd. To only me, he whispered through my mind, 'I want you to enjoy this.'

The fear and unease dissolved with every touch of his mouth on my skin. It was a dirty move for Arys to turn his power on me that way. I fell under his influence, becoming the glamoured victim he wanted me to be. The vampire essence within me was no match for Arys. Not until death.

I too had wielded this power over someone else. It felt amazing to be on either side of the vampire and victim power play, at least until the high wore off. Then came the remorse and awkward moments with friends. Or maybe that was just me.

The warm, wet touch of his tongue commanded my full attention. He sucked at my wrist, plumping the veins nicely. Anticipation thrilled through me as I waited to see if he would bite so soon. The audience was tense, wondering the same thing.

Arys knew how to work the rush though, and he ever so gently dragged his fangs over my flesh instead. The growing heat crawled up my arm to engulf my whole body. I had no idea how far Arys was willing to take this. And as the haze of lusty need gripped me, I didn't care.

The seconds felt like hours under his careful touch. Leaving my wrist unmarked, Arys moved to the sensitive inner crook of my elbow. Again, he teased my senses with a flick of his tongue. If having me beg for his bite was what he wanted, he would make it happen.

It no longer occurred to me to be unnerved by the watching crowd. Only one person had seen Arys and me in action. He was currently numbing out in the audience, saddled with security. How would Shaz feel watching now that he wasn't part of it?

Soft music began to play, echoing throughout the theatre. It broke up the stillness but encouraged the mood. Only when Arys pressed his lips to mine did I realize I was holding my breath. It slipped out as a ragged sigh.

His kiss was aggressive, a commanding assault on my mouth. Desire flared its wings wide within me, tickling my insides like butterflies. Deep within my core, I felt it, a yearning for him that could never be matched nor fully sated.

"Do you feel that?" He whispered against my lips. "I'm inside every part of you."

The power built harder, faster and stronger every time we called it together. It had started to feel second nature, which was a nice change from the earlier confusion and mayhem.

Arys's pupils were huge, excitement making his eyes a deep, drowning black. Nobody would be left untouched by the high when he was done here. I tried to pull him in for more, but he avoided my grasp, slipping around to stand behind me. His chest was firm against my back. Pulling my hair aside, he stripped me of the choker, baring my neck. His arms went around me. Holding me tight, Arys breathed deeply of my scent. He groaned, a low sound rife with hunger, a sexy murmur in my ear.

'Show Jenner why he should fear you. Make him yours.'

Those unspoken words floated through my mind. The intent behind them was clear. I gazed into the shadows where Jenner lurked, focusing on his energy among the masses. Intrigue, attraction and wariness flavored his energy. The hunger wore many faces. With just the thought planted in my head, the vampire in me snapped to attention. Jenner…yeah I wanted a taste of that.

I sucked in a deep breath; I shouldn't do what I was about to do, yet caught up in the moment the way I was, I couldn't think of a single reason why not. In a sober state, I never would have considered claiming Jenner. Sure, I'd seduced a five hundred year old vampire who possessed a respectable amount of power, but we already had a personal relationship. Jenner was a stranger I knew only in someone else's memories. He was also of a very strong bloodline. One I shared. Could I do it? Only one way to find out.

The power swelled between Arys and me, causing the lights to flicker. I reached out metaphysically to Jenner while also beckoning him with a finger. Right away, I sensed his resistance. A challenge.

Arys's hand in my hair was possessive. Clutching my long locks, he ran his tongue along the side of my neck. A familiar and welcome tingle began in my loins. I rubbed myself against his evident arousal. A rush of excitement brought a mischievous smile to my face.

I peered into the darkened place where I knew Jenner stood. His energy was tense but ablaze with intrigue. How long could he hold out?

"Jenner." His name was a faint whisper on my lips. Again, I beckoned to him.

Grasping the irresistible force, I held a hand up and blew an invisible kiss across the stage. The power swirled and danced around as it sought and found my target. My power wrapped around Jenner, drawing him into my thrall.

The audience grew restless. Affected by the brewing storm around us, they squirmed in their seats and spoke in hushed whispers to one another. When Jenner stepped into view, they all fell quiet again.

His shoulders were stiff. He moved with a graceless gait as he fought the pull. It was no use. No matter how much Jenner may have meant it when he said he didn't want to taste my blood, he was a vampire, and ultimately, it was always about the blood.

Desire burned in his icy blue eyes. A pained expression crossed his face. His attempts to resist us were weakening. Arys's satisfaction echoed in my mind. Having Jenner fall victim to us pleased him more than giving him a beating ever could. He kept the sex-charged energy flowing while I gave it focus and intent. We worked so well together, finding the perfect natural rhythm.

A cool breeze swept through the theatre. I held a hand out to Jenner and laughed as Arys kissed the ticklish spot on the back of my neck. Arys's hunger for me was palpable, and I knew Jenner felt it too. Jenner took my hand, and the power leaped from me to him. It wound through all three of us, taking us higher.

"Well, I'll be damned," Jenner murmured. He rubbed my hand against his face, inhaling the scent of the blood pumping beneath the surface of my skin. The scruffy bit of facial hair he sported was softer than I expected.

"Do you want to taste me?" The question came unbidden. I slipped into the zone, to the strange place I went when the vampiric power consumed me.

"No, I don't want to," he said, a crack in his voice. "I need to. And I hate you for that."

I hushed him with a finger against his lips. His words were a little too close to something I'd heard from someone else. This wasn't the time to question the morals of my actions. Power was the only thing vampires understood.

A shudder racked me as Arys nipped playfully at my neck. The touch of his fangs and tongue on my jugular vein had me ready for him. The chaise lounge was starting to look inviting.

I pulled Jenner forward, planting one hell of a kiss on him. I breathed the manipulative force through him, dragging him deeper under. A quick nip of his lip spilled enough blood for me to get a taste of him. With my curiosity sated, I offered him my wrist.

He grasped it tight, eyes locked on Arys, waiting for him to spill the first drop. I licked my lips, my breath thin and choppy. With my free hand I reached back to stroke a finger along Arys's face.

Arys's low chuckle echoed around us, though I wasn't sure if it had only been inside my head. His bite forced a cry from me and nearly drove me to my knees except he had wrapped an arm securely around me.

Without hesitation, Jenner followed suit and sunk fangs into my wrist. I watched those sharp points pierce my vein. The blood burst forth, and like a good performer, he ensured the audience got a good view before covering the wound with his mouth. At the first taste of my blood, Jenner's head snapped up, and he stared at me like he was seeing a ghost. He mumbled something that didn't sound like English and dropped to his knees before me. Never loosening his hold on my arm, he licked the crimson flow and groaned.

I grew dizzy, not from blood loss but from the heady rush of having two vampires feast upon me. It was exhilarating, a storm of overwhelming sensations.

Wind whipped through the theatre, howling like the creepy breeze in a horror film. It took me several moments to realize the howl came from Shaz. After a month away from us, he was still ours. Would any amount of time ever change that?

Arys's hard-on pressed against my rear end. I wanted him to take me in all ways.

'Sorry, my wolf,' he spoke inside my mind. 'You want it now, but I'd catch hell for it later.'

A pout curved my lips. His denial displeased me. He bit me a second time, and my displeasure was swept away on a sigh.

Jenner responded to the call of my desire. With one hand, he gripped my wrist while the other slid up the inside of my leg. From calf to thigh, he touched me with the brazenness of one completely under my spell.

I caught a glimpse of the spade tattooed on the back of his hand before it disappeared beneath the hem of my skirt. His skin was hot on mine.

Impatiently, I waited for him to find the throbbing ache between my legs. The arousal of both vampires created an intoxicating buffet of energy for me to devour. Despite what they took from me, they gave as much in return. A beautiful arc of power encompassed the three of us, spilling over to the audience who had grown increasingly restless.

"Touch me," I commanded Jenner. My patience had run out.

I gazed down at him, watching him lick every drop of my blood that dared to attempt escape. Our eyes locked, blue on blue. Staring up at me like a smitten fool, Jenner slid his hand toward the warm place nestled between my thighs.

There was no time to enjoy the shock of pleasure. The bliss moment was shattered suddenly, our spell broken by the explosion that rocked the building.

Chapter Nine

The theatre shook from the blast. I tumbled off the stage and hit the floor hard with Jenner crashing down on top of me. Winded and stunned, my mind scrambled to make sense of what had just happened. People screamed and rushed for the exits. Smoke began to seep into the room, coming from the arena. The wall between the two rooms still stood, indicating a small blast.

"What the fuck was that?" I said through strangled breaths.

Jenner shoved himself off me and hauled me to my feet. I searched frantically for Arys and Shaz, finding neither of them in the crowd's mad dash to escape.

"You need to take the fire exit and get upstairs," Jenner shouted over the commotion. "Find Sloane. Take her and your friend and get out of here. Go to Planet Hollywood and find Roscoe. Send him here." He indicated the emergency exit at the back of the theatre and gave me a push to get moving.

I remained rooted to the spot, refusing to go alone. "I'm not leaving without Arys and Shaz."

"Trust me, you don't want to be here right now," Jenner hissed, giving me another shove. "The blood ring we've all pissed off is behind this. They're probably storming the building. Do you know what they'll do to you if they find out you're here? Get out. Now."

Terror shook me, urging me to heed his warning and head for the door. But where were Shaz and Arys? I couldn't go without them.

'Run, Alexa.' Arys's voice was loud and clear in my mind. 'Listen to Jenner and go. I'm needed here.'

'No,' I resisted, searching the smoky haze for him. 'I'm not leaving you guys. They'll kill you both if you stay.'

'Jenner and I can handle this, especially with your blood in our veins. I promise. I'll keep the pup safe.'

I couldn't stand the thought of leaving without them. Panicked humans tripped me up, and smoke burnt my lungs. There was so much I hadn't told Shaz, so many things I hadn't said since he got back. So much he didn't know.

'You'll get your chance to tell him. Now get the hell out of here.'

The house lights came on, and I spotted Arys on the opposite side of the theatre, headed for the door connecting to the arena. He paused to look over at me. I shook my head, unwilling to be parted.

Then the door burst open, and he was under siege by several vampires packing weaponry. Jenner was a blur as he flew past me to come to Arys's aid. He shouted at me to get moving and instinct told me to listen.

I ran for the fire exit, dodging people as I went. The invading vampires had already taken down some of the remaining audience members. I'd almost reached the door when a hand closed on my arm. Shaz jerked me into his arms and hugged me tight. Then just as fast, he shoved something into my hand and kissed me.

"I'm staying with Arys," he said. "You need to find Jez."

"It's the blood ring, Shaz. They'll find out who you are. You've got to come with me." I tried to drag him along with me, but he resisted.

"No, I should be here. As long as they don't get a hold of you, I can handle it. Ok? Now go. I love you."

He was gone before I could reply. I opened my hand to find the hotel room key card. Mine was in my shoulder bag backstage along with my phone and wallet. I had no choice but to leave without those things.

I ran, easily outrunning those who hadn't yet made it out. More than once, I had to toss people aside when they risked blocking the way. Taking the stairs two at a time, I quickly reached the top floor.

My feet barely touched the floor as I moved with stealth and speed. The best of both monsters were alive in me, wolf and vampire, fueled by the power we'd called. Despite the drawbacks, having the strengths of both sure had its perks.

The fire escape continued up to the roof. It was likely our only way out. I opened the door to the top floor quietly, listening and sensing. There was no sign of the security guys that had been stationed here. Erotic energy hit me like the wave of heat when opening an oven door. It was raw and hot. But that was all. The chaos of the underground floor did not resonate here.

I moved with silent steps down the hall, seeking Sloane's room. Not one door had her name. My heartbeat thundered in my ears. I had to focus, somehow, to sift through the myriad of energies, seeking Jez.

Standing in the middle of the hall with no quick hiding place terrified me. I kept expecting someone to come storming up the stairs from the main floor. Creeping to the top of the stairs, I gazed down, finding the club operating as if nothing was occurring downstairs. What the hell?

Then a smoke bomb went off in the middle of the dance floor, and commotion broke out all across the main level. Good Lord, I hoped Jez wasn't down there.

I moved back into the hall, away from the stairs. *Jez, Jez, Jez.* I chanted her name to myself, seeking her shifter vibe. There! I followed my senses to a door that said Lady Melanie.

There was no time for manners or knocking. The lock gave way easily enough under my adrenaline and power-charged strength, and I burst into the room. It was nice, much nicer than the rooms back home. Soft beige carpet squished beneath my feet. A flat screen TV hung on the wall across from a king-size bed adorned with satin sheets and a mountain of pillows. A mirror above the bed reflected the image of entangled limbs and luscious hair.

"Alexa? What the fuck? Knock much?" Jez was understandably confused and embarrassed. She looked up from between Sloane's legs, and I did my best to avert my eyes.

"We've got trouble. Blood ring trouble. We have to get out of the building."

"What?" Sloane was up off the bed instantly grabbing her clothing from the floor. "Where's Jenner?"

"He's downstairs with Arys. They were under attack by a swarm of angry vampires. They told me to run, to find Roscoe and to take you with me." I motioned frantically for Jez to spring into action. She did, thankfully steadier on her feet than she had been earlier.

Sloane shook her head and smoothed her dress back into place. "I can't leave Jenner. You two go. I'll try to find a way to keep the peace here."

"Keep the peace?" I asked, incredulous. "It's total chaos down there. This is what you wanted Arys to help with, isn't it? The blood ring won't let you out."

"There's only one way out. Nobody just walks away from an operation like that and lives to tell the tale." Sloane sniffed at the air, scenting my bloody wounds. She took a step toward me, and I held her off with a raised hand. "I can smell Jenner on you."

"Yeah well, if we all live through this night, then he can tell you all about that." I knew that look, the flash of hunger in her eyes. She couldn't help it. It was in her nature. "Come on, Jez. We gotta go."

She dressed in record time. Golden hair disheveled and lipstick smeared, Jez looked very much like a woman who just had a fun-filled romp with a lover. In about five seconds, she'd be running for her life.

"Are you sure you won't come with us?" Jez turned back to Sloane, concern heavy in her green eyes.

"I belong here, whether Jenner likes it or not. Just go while you still can." As if it were an afterthought, Sloane pulled Jez close and planted a serious kiss on her. "When this shit is settled, we're going to finish what we started here."

Jez caught a strand of Sloane's blonde hair, twisting it around her finger. "You got it."

I would have objected to that if I hadn't been in such a rush to get moving. Grabbing Jez's hand, I dragged her into the hall. Several doors were now open as vampires and their willing victims surfaced to see what was going on.

We ran down the hall back to the fire exit where we took the stairs to the roof. As we rounded the landing, we ran right into a crossbow-toting blood ring member. He advanced on us with a grim smile, aiming the crossbow at my head.

Jez didn't hesitate. She sprang forward and slammed her fist into his throat, following up with an elbow to his face then a knee to his groin. He grunted and stumbled down the remaining stairs toward us.

The crossbow went off, and I ducked, narrowly avoiding the flying bolt. It lodged in the wall behind me. I jerked it free while Jez continued her assault. The vampire was strong; he recovered quickly. He smashed her in the face with the crossbow. Her insanely high heels failed her, and she fell on the landing, almost tumbling down the stairs. I slammed him with a psi ball, immobilizing him long enough to plunge the bolt into his heart. I didn't wait for the ash and dust of his remains to settle. I got Jez on her feet, and we surged ahead to the rooftop.

"Are you ok?" I asked, afraid to look back in case we were being pursued. So far so good.

"I've had worse."

We found the fire escape mounted on the side of the building and wasted no time getting down to the ground. Jez kicked off her heels, carrying them as we descended. My lungs heaved, and a bitter taste filled my mouth. I breathed a sigh of relief when we made it down without another encounter.

We waited in the dark space between The Wicked Kiss and the neighboring building. Nobody came down after us. Leaning against the concrete wall, I focused on taking a few deep calming breaths. It didn't work.

"What the hell happened to you?" Jez spoke in a hushed tone. She gestured to the vampire bites decorating my neck and wrist. I was glad to see she didn't have any. Sloane was lucky.

"Do you realize how long you've been upstairs with her?" I whispered furiously. "Arys lost the poker game. Shit got stupid. You missed Shaz's cage fight."

Her eyes widened. "Are you kidding me? He won, right? Come on; tell me about it while we walk. You've got to get cleaned up, and we need a plan."

Leaving Arys and Shaz behind felt all kinds of wrong.

I pressed a hand to my neck. The bleeding had stopped. Arranging my hair to hide the wounds would have to do.

Carefully, we made our way down The Strip toward Caesars. We blended easily into the thick, human street traffic. Traffic was heavy on the street as well as the sidewalks and pedways. At times, the bodies were crammed together like the mosh pit at a rock concert. Blasting them all out of my way would have taken just a thought with well-guided intentions. It was hard to swallow the urge and maintain a firm hold on my patience.

It felt like ages before we finally crossed the pedway from the Bellagio hotel to Caesars and broke free of the throng. Caesars Palace loomed large before us. It stood against the Vegas night sky, boasting of beauty, intrigue and adventure.

As we walked, I spoke quickly, giving Jez a basic rundown on what she'd missed.

"You weren't really going to let Jenner get you off, were you?" She asked, her voice loud enough to draw the attention of a few passersby.

I gaped at her. "That's what you focused on out of everything I told you?"

"Well, yeah. You've never had two vampires before. That's gotta be a rush." She held the hotel door open, allowing me to go first. "Wait, you haven't been with two vampires, have you? Because I'd be pissed if you kept something that juicy to yourself."

The icy blast of the air conditioning was a refreshing slap in the face, a sharp contrast to the desert heat outside. We entered the busy lobby where people milled about, checking in and taking photos in front of the fountain with people dressed up as Caesar and Cleopatra.

We veered left, past the twenty-four hour bar and the Starbucks, to the elevator that would take us to our room. I kept my head down, hoping to go unnoticed with my bloodstained attire and fresh wounds.

"No, I have definitely not been with two vampires at the same time. And I was not going to let Jenner get any farther than he did." It felt like a lie, so I changed the subject, embarrassed at how affected I was by my own succubus power. It was a real double-edged sword. "How are you feeling? I need you alert."

"Uh huh," she nodded knowingly, giving me a pointed look. "You smell like lies. You wanted them both, you filthy little energy sucker."

"Jez!"

"I feel fine. In fact, I'm ready for another round."

The elevator door slid open, and we almost collided with a family of four in their haste to pile in. I rushed by a little girl who peered up at me with wide-eyed wonder. I tucked my injured wrist close to my body and averted my gaze.

"I don't think you're taking this seriously, Jez," I said when we were safely inside the hotel room. "Things got bad back there. Really bad."

I sat on the couch and then stood up again. Putting my head in my hands, I closed my eyes and focused on Arys. 'Tell me you're all right.'

It was easy to slip into his head. Though he didn't directly acknowledge my presence, he knew I was there. I saw the destruction and chaos through his eyes.

He was in the arena, backed into a corner with Jenner, Shaz and several Wicked Kiss vampires. Tense, with fists clenched, Arys had a lot more fight left in him. But the intruding vampires had the upper hand, because they had Sloane.

She was on her knees between several of them, with more than enough strong hands to subdue her. Blood dripped from her nose. It took a lot to hurt a vampire. They hadn't wasted their time giving her a beating. I wondered if they'd found her or if she'd gone to them.

"Now Jenner, I know this one here is your favorite. So be a good boy and offer me a deal I can't refuse. Or we'd be happy to finish what we started with your little casino here." This came from a mean looking vampire who stood apart from the rest, establishing himself as the leader. He was tall and slender with a gaunt face. Hard set, dark eyes shone with ruthlessness. A gun glinted in his hand. It appeared to have been modified, most likely to make it deadly to vampires. The average handgun is little danger to the supernatural.

"Let's sit down and talk about this, Linden," Jenner pleaded, trying to sound like he wasn't. "It wasn't necessary for you to come in here and trash my livelihood."

"Funny. That didn't sound like an offer. You can do better than that." Linden's vicious stare swung to Arys. It felt like he could see me there, behind Arys's eyes. "And you...man am I glad to see you. You have one more wolf for me, yes? Where is she?"

Arys smiled, chuckling as if he had a great secret he wasn't about to share. "It's a busy city. She could be anywhere. I'm sure she's planning your death right about now."

Linden gave a slight nod to one of his guys who raised a crossbow and fired. The bolt struck Arys in the arm he raised to block. I felt the pain as if it were my own, though he didn't so much as flinch.

Arys's fingertips burned with ready power. Linden's man reloaded the crossbow and trained it on Shaz.

"Go ahead," Linden said. "We'll wait while you take your shot. Then I'll have your wolf crippled."

Panic thrilled through me, spilling into Arys through my thoughts. He considered doing it, certain he could take them all out. They had muscle but no real power.

He relented, dropping his hold on the power he'd tapped. I knew he'd done it for me. His decision earned him a crack in the head with a crossbow from the closest weapon-wielding vamp.

A bright light flashed behind my eyes. I cried out in pain and dropped to my knees. I was thrust out of Arys's head, whether by his doing or my own, I wasn't sure.

"Alexa?" Jez was beside me, pushing hair back from my face. "What happened? Is it Arys?"

I nodded and dug my fingers into the carpet. Blinking rapidly, I concentrated hard on the hotel room around me, disoriented as Arys and The Wicked Kiss slipped away. "Yeah. I connected with him, but he's gone now. Everyone is ok, but it's pretty bad over there." I repeated to her what I'd seen as she helped me to my feet. "We have to find Roscoe. And get ready for a fight."

"What exactly are the three of us going to do? We can't take on that many vampires. Can we?"

"We might have to try. Roscoe should have a better idea of what we're facing. There's got to be someone else in this city he can call on for help." *I hope.*

I retreated to the washroom where I washed the blood from my skin and freshened up before heading to the bedroom to change. Jeans and a racer back tank top were much more fight friendly than a skirt. I slid a chunky silver bracelet on to hide the bite on my wrist. My hair did a decent job concealing the others.

Returning to the empty living room, I stared out the floor-to-ceiling window at The Strip. The Bellagio fountain was on. The water shimmered with bright lights as it leaped and danced. It was enchanting. I gazed at the fountain and wondered how the hell I was going to help Arys and Shaz without ending up in the blood ring's clutches myself.

When Jez re-entered from her adjoined room, she too wore jeans. Along with a Batman t-shirt, ass-kicking boots, and a high ponytail, she looked ready to lay down a beating.

She strode over to the minibar and appraised the interior. Plucking a bottle from its place, she studied the label.

"Twenty seconds," I warned.

"No worries." She twisted the lid off and took a swig. "I don't need that long to decide."

"Look, Jez, I know that it's Vegas and that you can process booze like a champ, but I'm not sure this is the time for that." I couldn't help but be concerned. Our group had just been split in half. I needed her alert and at my side.

Without warning, Jez tossed a bottle of imported beer my way. "I can't think of a better time for a drink."

I turned the bottle over in my hands a few times before opening it. The girl had a point. "Alright, let's go find Roscoe."

I felt naked without my phone and wallet. They were both inside my shoulder bag back at the club. Slipping Shaz's key card into my back pocket, I closed the hotel door behind us, fearing I might not return.

* * * *

After battling not one but two pedways jam-packed with warm, blood-filled bodies, we were walking through Planet Hollywood.

"So where do we start?" Jez asked, surveying the casino.

It was a nice place, like most casinos, full of lights, noise and tourists. It was also big enough that simply walking around looking for the vampire would be a waste of time.

"I think I can find him." I reached out metaphysically, feeling for any vampire energy in the building. There were a few in the vicinity, but that familiar flavor of vampire energy drew me to Roscoe. "This way."

We weaved between slot machines, taking careful note of our surroundings. The pull led us away from the main casino and into a more adult-only area called The Pleasure Pit. It was a sensory overload. There was an abundance of glowing pink, heart-shaped signs boasting the casino's name. It was certainly an interesting place. All of the dealers were gorgeous women clad in very little. Wearing even less were the ladies dancing and gyrating on poles at various points around the casino.

"Holy shit, why have I not been here before?" Jez gushed. "I think this might be my new favorite place."

"Settle down, wildcat. Let's try to keep it to one woman a night, shall we?" I grinned, shaking my head.

The casino was busy. It came as no surprise that the patrons were mostly male. Following the trace I had on Roscoe's energy, I led the way through to a Blackjack table where we found him flirting with the dealer.

He appeared mildly surprised to see us though surely he'd felt me when I metaphysically reached for him. He looked past me, clearly expecting Arys to be on my heels.

"What are you doing here?" Roscoe got right to the point. I enjoyed a man who doesn't beat around the bush.

"Jenner sent me," I said, studying the two other men seated at the table, both human. They didn't seem to be with Roscoe. "There's some shit going down at the club. You might want to check it out."

I was wary of saying too much in front of the humans present, but none of them paid much attention to us. Roscoe nodded and tapped his cards. The dealer laid another card on the table. Bust.

Roscoe turned in his seat to face us. He raised a hand, signaling to a waitress. "Bring these two a drink. It's on me."

"No, thanks. I'm good," I protested at the same time Jez said, "I'll have a long island iced tea." I shot her a frown, which was wasted on her. Ignoring me, she added, "She'll have the same."

"So what happened?" Roscoe prompted. "Did Jenner and Arys finally kill one another? That's been a long time coming."

The dealer glanced up at that. It didn't sit well with me. I wasn't discussing vampire politics with so many humans within earshot.

"Is there somewhere else we could talk about this?" Maybe I was being paranoid, but we had enough trouble already. Jenner might have had the Vegas FPA in his pocket, yet that didn't mean they'd be happy with me speaking so candidly in public. And one thing I did not need was to catch hell from my local sector when I got home.

Roscoe rolled his eyes. "Whatever's going on over there, it must be good. Go grab a seat at those slot machines over there. I'm on a bit of a roll here. I'll join you in a few."

Was he kidding me? I glared and opened my mouth to tell him to fuck the cards. Jez steered me away before I could blast him.

"We don't have the fucking time for this," I fumed.

"No, we don't. Either he doesn't give a shit, or he doesn't think it's his problem. Losing your temper on him won't help though. Let's give him a few minutes, then we walk. We can handle this without him." Jez dropped into a seat in front of a slot machine and produced a twenty.

Reluctantly, I sat at the machine next to her and watched her play. I considered reaching out to Arys but feared the connection would drop me again. Or worse, distract him when he needed focus. I squirmed, impatient and anxious.

Jez had played her way down to three remaining dollars when Roscoe sidled up with drinks in hand. He set them in front of us and took the free chair beside me.

"This better be worth interrupting my game. Did you see the fox working the table? I want a nip of that." He grinned wide, flashing me a glimpse of gold fang.

I wasn't sharing his mischievous humor. "The blood ring launched some kind of attack on the club. They're over there with Arys and Jenner right now doing God knows what. We made it out, but they stayed. They need us."

Roscoe's head bobbed. "Uh huh. I warned Jenner that this would happen. He was so insistent on getting out of the blood ring. He failed to secure his replacement. It was only a matter of time until they came to collect."

I stared at him as if he'd sprouted a second, even stupider, head. "Ok, so what are we going to do about it?"

"We?" He chuckled. "Jenner should have known better. You don't just tell an organization like that you won't be supplying them anymore. Not without finding a supplier to fill the hole. He'll have to do some fast talking to weasel his way out of this one." Roscoe's throaty laugh picked at my nerves. This was a joke to him.

"I thought you were Jenner's right hand. Doesn't that mean you should be there with him instead of Arys?" Jez piped up. She sipped from the long island iced tea and made a small noise of satisfaction. "Damn, this is good."

With a shrug, he popped some money into the slot machine. "I am Jenner's right hand. He's like a brother to me. He's also a know-it-all who gets too arrogant for his own good."

"Sounds like every other vampire in your bloodline," I muttered, tasting the iced tea. It was pretty darn good. Sweet and smooth.

"Yes, it does. Harley wasn't big on the meek and mild type." The vampire's gaze traveled over me, lingering on my breasts before meeting my eyes. I raised a brow in question. He didn't bother to fake being apologetic. "I bet he really liked you. When he wasn't busy hating you, of course."

"That mother fucker tried to blood bond me against my will. He was a selfish monster who saw us all as toys to collect, but he didn't want us to play with each other. Twisted bastard."

The slot machine made a bunch of noise, and Roscoe swore appreciatively as his money doubled. "Harley got what he deserved. But if anyone asks, I never said that." He laughed and gave me a nudge that almost knocked me off my chair.

"And what about Arys and Jenner? Do they deserve whatever's happening to them right now?" I asked.

Roscoe tapped away at the screen of his machine, silently playing a few hands of video poker. When I was ready to flick him in the forehead, he drawled, "Aw, they'll be fine. They're no use to the blood ring dead. If anything, Arys's presence will keep them interested in working out a deal."

For someone who had come to Caesars to threaten us as soon as we'd arrived, Roscoe wasn't showing much concern now that Jenner was facing serious trouble.

"I can see this was a waste of valuable time." The words felt funny in my mouth, like I was speaking with a cotton ball on my tongue. "Forget we even came."

When I stood up, the room tilted dangerously. I grabbed onto my chair to keep from going down, barely keeping myself off the floor. What the hell?

"What the fuck...did you put in our drinks?" Jez's demand came out slurred. The half-empty glass slipped from her hand. It spilled on the floor, and she went down with it.

I made a clumsy attempt to grab for her. Everything spun. I tried to stay on my feet, but it was difficult to tell which way was up. The disorienting sensations grew quickly, stealing my ability to speak coherently.

"Shifter sedative," he said with a sly grin. "Handy little mix of wolfsbane and a tranquilizer strong enough to take down a bear. Sorry ladies, can't have you getting in the way."

The last thing I saw was Roscoe's mildly amused face. Then the black abyss of drug-induced unconsciousness swallowed me whole.

Chapter Ten

Blood filled my mouth. My head ached, and my heavy eyelids refused to open. Pain shot through my joints when I tried to move. After several attempts, my eyes opened and focused, but my head still refused to lift. My cheek felt raw and scratchy from being mushed into the carpet. *Where the hell am I?*

When I caught sight of my surroundings, I lowered my head back to the floor and counted to ten. This was bad. Really bad. I was in an unfamiliar hotel room, surrounded by bodies. Everything was so red. Blood spattered the floor, the walls, and the bed.

The last thing I remembered was blacking out in Planet Hollywood. Wolfsbane. There were so many stories about it, most of them very old and likely untrue. I had never encountered it until now. I hoped never to have it inside me again.

I struggled to sit up, immediately horrified and shocked by the realization that I was naked. My horror grew as I counted five bodies splayed out in various displays of grotesque violence and death. The room was nice, not a penthouse but not a slum either. A small party had been taking place. Bottles and glasses littered a small coffee table, complete with perfectly cut lines of white powder. It wasn't hard to put together what had happened: I'd torn them to pieces.

A frantic glance around the room revealed what was left of my clothes. Scraps of fabric littered the space not yet occupied by body parts. I surveyed the destruction and knew with absolute certainty that the vampire in me had nothing to do with this. It was all wolf.

Voices in the hallway beyond the hotel door infused me with panic. It got me on my feet, albeit unsteadily, and ready to take on whoever walked through. But nobody did. The voices passed by.

"Oh, fuck me," I muttered, stepping around what was left of my victims. Using a scrap of fabric from the floor, I slowly opened the door just enough to ensure the 'Do Not Disturb' sign was on the other side.

Satisfied that it was, I locked the door and stared at the mess. All of the victims were men. I must have interrupted a boy's night out. I had to get out of there. I needed to find Jez.

Part of me wanted to sink to the bloody carpet and cry. In just one night, Vegas had separated me from everyone I loved. I was alone, and they were God only knew where. In fact, where the hell was I?

The room service menu on the table said Paris Las Vegas.

"What the hell?" I whispered, needing to hear a sound in the silent room, even if it was only the sound of my own voice.

Somehow, I'd managed to go from Planet Hollywood down the block to Paris Las Vegas in a total blackout. It wasn't all that far but felt like miles since I couldn't recall a second of it. Then I'd murdered a group of guys just trying to get their party on. I wracked my brain trying to remember, but it was all a blank.

I reached out to Arys, finding nothing. No response. No contact. He was either shutting me out or unconscious. If he were dead, I would know. I had to do something before it got to that point.

First things first, clean up. A visit to the bathroom resulted in another shock; seeing myself as a monster was never easy. A quick but thorough rinse in the shower washed away the blood, but the stain of shame remained. How could I have done this?

As ill as it made me, I had no choice but to swipe a t-shirt and a pair of sweatpants from a dead guy's suitcase. Standing awkwardly in pants that were way too long for my short frame and a baggy shirt that felt like a dress, I dreaded what I had to do next.

Searching the scene for any shred of my DNA made my stomach churn. More than a few times, I wanted to toss my cookies. Getting up close with each victim allowed me to see the gaping holes in their throats, the random chucks of flesh strewn about. I did manage to find my hotel key card though.

A slow clap broke the silence. I whirled around with a yelp to find Falon appraising my handiwork. As much as I hated the fallen angel, right then I was almost happy to see him.

"Holy shit, Alexa, you have been a bad little wolf," he said, a trace of awe in his tone. "I never imagined you were capable of such destruction. I'm impressed. What do you know? You may be useful after all."

"What are you doing here? Did Shya send you?" I was afraid to blink, fearing he would disappear, that perhaps I was so desperate I was imagining him.

"Of course. Your vampire contacted Shya in a fit because you weren't answering your phone. He was so sure you were in danger." Falon's silver wings tucked in snug against his back. He walked through the room, examining the slaughter. "Shya couldn't risk that so, like usual, he sent me to see what stupid shit you pulled this time."

"My vampire?" It took me a moment to realize he meant Kale. I watched Falon lean in close over one guy whose neck was torn so wide his head barely hung on. "Don't touch anything! Please. Just…help me."

Falon's silver gaze landed on me, ice cold and brimming with judgment. "Why should I? You're alive. In fact, you're the only one here who still is. Looks like you're just fine to me. I'll be sure to let Shya know."

"No, please," I almost shouted. "Don't leave. I need help. I don't know where Jez is. I'm missing the last two hours because some son of a bitch vampire drugged me with wolfsbane. And I can't reach Arys. The local blood ring has him and Shaz."

"When you fuck things up you don't half ass it, do you?" With a shake of his head, Falon snickered. He plucked a piece of ash blonde fur from between a dead man's fingers. "I don't know how you've managed to survive this long. It's uncanny."

"And you're an asshole, but I'm willing to overlook that this time." My relief at seeing a familiar face was fading fast.

His grin vanished. "I can't wait until Shya's done with you. The moment he is, and I do mean the very moment, I'll be there. And you'll be sorry."

"I'm already sorry," I snapped. A shock of pain wracked my brain. I muttered obscenities until it passed.

We glared at one another, each trying to muster greater vehemence in our eyes. Finally, I sighed and shrugged. Falon wasn't worth the precious time that I had to find my friends.

"Just leave, Falon. We both know this is the last place you want to be."

Ignoring his hateful stare, I went back to studying the bodies for any trace of werewolf that would give me away to the local FPA. After several silent minutes, Falon sighed dramatically and shouldered me aside.

"Get out of here, Alexa. Go find your twin so Shya doesn't rain down hell upon either of us. I can't stay long so let me take care of this while I can." The air in the room grew thick as Falon's power rose.

"What are you going to do?" I asked, hesitant, afraid to hear the answer.

Falon turned a wicked smile my way and shook his head. "What do you think I'm going to do? I'm here to clean up your mess. Now beat it."

I couldn't trust him, not for a second. Nor could I trust Shya, a demon who only wanted Arys and me alive because of the rare power we possessed. But I wasn't in a position to argue.

"Fine." I tugged on my boots, the only item not destroyed by my violent wolf shift. I felt ten times more ridiculous than I looked. "Thanks. I guess."

I was almost to the door when he said, "Here. I'm sure you're going to need this." A thud on the floor and the sharp ting of metal spun me around. My dagger, the Dragon Claw, lay on the floor near my feet. I'd never been so happy to see the demon-forged weapon.

"You were going to let me walk out of here without handing it over, weren't you?" I picked the dagger up, satisfied with the way it hummed at my touch. It had been made just for me, with a piece of my hair to bind its magic to mine. With just a nick of the blade, it could kill a vampire.

"I'd love to sabotage you, Hound. You're the enemy, no matter what Shya thinks he can gain from you. But I don't call the shots."

I stared at the dagger. It wasn't small by any means. "How am I going to carry this around the city? I don't have my leather jacket with me." I eyed up the black trench coat Falon wore. It would work. "Let me have your jacket."

"Not a chance. It's your problem." He turned his back on me, dismissing me without another word.

"I don't have time for this shit. Give me your jacket." I grabbed his sleeve and whirled him around. If I had to tear it off his body, I would.

He raised a hand to fend me off. I grabbed on and refused to be budged. "Falon stop being such a dick. Can you hate me later? I don't have time for this."

He gave me a shove that sent me tripping over a body. I fell on my butt in a puddle of blood. "Oh this is just great. Just fucking fabulous."

With a snarl, I came at him with the Dragon Claw held high. Mocking laughter was the response I got. Angered and impatient, I swung the blade, forcing him to sidestep the attack.

"You can't kill me," he gasped out, almost doubled over with laughter. God I hated him. "You stupid wolf."

"I don't know. Can angels function without a head?"

I swung again, and he easily caught the blade. It sliced into his palm. I tried to jerk it away, but he held tight. The force of his anger thrummed through the blade, down the handle into my arm. It seared through me, scorching every nerve as it climbed to my shoulder.

"You underestimate me, Alexa. One day, that's going to stop."

"You keep singing that song, and it's getting old. Let go of my dagger you fence riding piece of shit."

"Oh, is that what you think?" Falon released the dagger with a push of power that forced a shriek from me. "You think fallen angels are simply undecided? I promise you we know exactly where we stand. Your precious Willow included."

"What does Willow have to do with this?" I held my arm with teeth clenched, willing the pain to fade.

Falon studied me. Whatever he saw, it shut him up. In a fast, fluid motion, he stripped off the jacket and tossed it. "Never mind. You have places to be. Clock's ticking."

The smarmy ass knew he had piqued my curiosity, and I couldn't do a damned thing about it. He was right. I had to go. I quickly rigged the dagger's scabbard around my waist, hiding it with Falon's jacket, which was long enough to fall almost to my ankles. Without another word or a backward glance, I darted into the hall and followed the signs to the elevator.

Paris Las Vegas was a nice hotel. There was much to look at. If circumstances had been different, I'd have loved to browse around. As it was, I ran through the lobby to the street beyond.

My body was sore from the violent shift to wolf and back. It didn't usually hurt like this. I ran through the streets, dodging tourists, until I made it back to Caesars where I ditched the huge men's clothing for my own lightweight yoga pants and another bra and tank top. I swapped my boots for runners and chugged back a bottle of water.

At this rate, I was going to be out of clothes in no time. I was in and out of the suite in three minutes flat, running with Falon's coattails flapping behind me. I had no starting point for finding Jez. My only guess was that Roscoe still had her. So I was going to The Wicked Kiss.

The street outside the club was empty. An eerie quiet hovered around the building. Knowing the rooftop access would likely have locked behind us when we left, I crept around to the back.

Two vampires wearing staff t-shirts stood watch at the back door. I stepped out of the shadows, careful to keep the dagger concealed. They stiffened at my approach, exchanging a look with one another. I held my hands up and moved slowly.

"I'm Arys Knight's wolf. I'm here to find him."

"You won't find him here," said the taller of the two. He frowned down at me, sniffing openly in my direction. "Linden and his guys dragged Arys and Jenner out of here over an hour ago. They took the blond wolf too."

Panic seized my heart. Moving them to another location could only mean bad things. Linden and his blood ring were going to kill them.

"What about Sloane?"

"She's here. Recovering."

"Can I see her?" My question was received with skepticism and raised eyebrows. "I'm no threat to her. If you want Jenner back here in one piece, you have to let me speak to Sloane."

They exchanged another look. The silent one shrugged. The tall guy nodded and stepped aside to let me through. I half expected them to follow me, but they remained at their post.

I entered into the back of the club behind the stage, fully anticipating a scene of horror and destruction. Instead, I found the place partying as if the earlier intrusion had never happened. Most of the damage had been cleaned up. Music pounded out of the speakers. People filled the dance floor, and vampire showgirls worked the room. The sheer normalcy was all kinds of fucked up.

The elevator was off limits and besides I had no key card to access it. Slipping into the fire exit stairwell, I made my way down.

The lower level was in much worse shape than upstairs. Evidence of the attack remained in the theatre. Even as I walked through the dust and debris, staff members were hard at work cleaning up. A few of them looked up as I entered. I rushed into the backstage dressing room where I'd left my bag. It was still there, much to my relief. But so was Sloane, and she looked like death. I clutched my bag to me, grateful to find my phone and wallet still inside. I didn't dare take my eyes off Sloane.

"Alexa?" She looked up from the neck of the man she was draining. Her eyes were dull and unfocused.

Someone had done a number on her. She had been stripped of her power, sucked so dry she was little more than a skeletal figure. Her skin clung to her bones, creating sharp angles in her face. Dirty and tattered, her dress barely fit her bony frame. I couldn't recall ever seeing a vampire so drained.

"Sloane, are you alright? What happened? Where are Arys and Jenner?" I stopped dead in my tracks when her parched gaze landed on my throat.

"Linden took them. He's going to kill them." She pushed the unconscious man aside, and he hit the floor with a thump. Peering up at me with sunken eyes, Sloane tried to get up only to collapse back into the chair. "Help me up?" She extended a scrawny arm that wavered uncontrollably. Blood smeared her lips along with what was left of her lipstick. She was truly a ghastly sight.

"I think you need to rest. Finish your…" I gestured to the fallen man and took a step back, unwilling to let her touch me. Hunger blazed in her glassy blue orbs. I probably smelled like a prime meal to her, a sirloin steak to a starving man. She was starved for both blood and the living energy within it. There was no trusting any vampire in such a state. "Can you tell me where Linden would have taken them?"

"No." It seemed to take great effort for her to mutter that one word. She licked her lips, staring at my neck with undisguised bloodlust. "Please, just help me to the bed upstairs."

"Roscoe. Has he been here?" I asked. No way was I touching her. "That bastard drugged me and took Jez. I need to find him. I think he's working with the blood ring."

Her arm dropped to her lap, and she looked positively defeated. She stared right through me, and I was sure she hadn't heard a word I said. I repeated myself, resisting the urge to shake her. She'd likely crumble to dust in my hands.

"You smell so good. So strong. If you could spare just a little, just a few drops, I could be better. I could help you."

Weakness had given her a one-track mind. She was giving me nothing. Frustration shook me. My mind raced, trying to formulate a way to find my loved ones in this city of insanity. I pulled out my phone, careful to keep an eye on Sloane. There were fifteen missed calls from Kale and four voicemails. It wasn't his number I selected from my contacts list though.

I called every one of my missing people. Voicemail for both Shaz and Jez while Arys's phone was off. *Fuck!* I made a hasty decision to call on someone I didn't know I could trust. I was running low on options.

I listened to it ring, holding my breath for a response. On the third ring, a rough, angry voice barked, "O'Brien! This had better be good. Some of us actually sleep at night."

"Briggs, thank God you answered. I need a favor." The urge to cheer was quickly squelched by tentative worry.

"Favors don't come for free, O'Brien. What do you want?" Agent Thomas Briggs of the Edmonton FPA was a hard man, a real ball-buster. Still, he was human, and I knew I had his attention even if it was only from sheer curiosity.

In my peripheral vision, Sloane struggled to stand. If she got up, I'd have to sit her ass back down.

"I need you to track a few cell numbers for me." Explaining my situation as briefly as possible, I felt the weight of it all hit me suddenly, a ton of bricks weighing on my mental faculties.

I could practically hear Briggs shaking his head at me. "You sure you're not supposed to be a cat shifter? If anyone needs nine lives, it's you." He gave a short, sharp bark of a laugh. "Want me to contact someone at the Vegas HQ?"

"No," I said too quickly. "I don't need the Feds involved. This is vampire business. I just need the one favor. Please." I didn't mention that the Vegas FPA had vampire ties that made them even less trustworthy than my home team.

"Fine. I'll let you know if I turn up any locations. Remember, O'Brien, I'm entitled to a favor from you now."

"That sounds like something a demon would say."

"Does it? I guess you would know. I'll be in touch."

He hung up before I could tell him to hurry. I dropped my phone into my bag and turned to Sloane in time to see her launch her pitiful self at me with a snarl. Hands curled into claws, she managed to rake the side of my face before I grabbed her around the throat.

She put up a good struggle. Bloodlust and weakness had stripped away the vibrant sophistication she'd carried so naturally, leaving her a hollow shell hungry for only one thing. With a push of power, I shoved Sloane back into the chair. Her back arched, and she let out a wail. It took more effort to subdue her than her skeletal appearance led me to believe.

"Sloane, snap out of it. Tell me where I can find Roscoe." I gave her a shake and a slap. Her energy was so fragile, it bent so easily to my will. She calmed, blinking at me in wide-eyed confusion. "Where is Roscoe? If you want to help Jenner then you have to tell me how to find Roscoe."

I was almost shouting at her. She blinked a few times then nodded vigorously. "Roscoe has a place at The Golden Nugget. He hunts Fremont Street." Her eyes rolled back in her head, and she moaned. "Just a taste, Alexa, please."

"Trust me, you don't want my blood. You'll thank me later." I left her there mumbling and pleading. Though I owed her nothing, I paused long enough to instruct a staff member to get her upstairs and to keep a steady supply of blood flowing.

I moved as fast as my legs could carry me. Like a bat out of hell, I dashed from the building down the street to Paris Las Vegas where I was able to get a taxi. The cab driver kept flashing me suspicious glances in the rearview mirror, and I realized my wounded neck was exposed. Arranging my hair to hide it, I hoped he would be smart enough to keep his mouth shut. It couldn't have been the weirdest thing a Las Vegas taxi driver saw in a night.

His foot grew heavier on the gas pedal, and in five minutes, I was at my destination. "Have a nice night," I said, tossing some cash and all but leaping out of the vehicle.

I reached out to feel the vicinity for Roscoe, for anything vampy at all. Making my way down Fremont Street, I checked and rechecked my phone, hoping for something from Briggs. Nothing yet.

Though the wolfsbane had done a real number on me, the effects had mostly worn off. I felt pretty damn good, and I attributed that to my vampire side. Perhaps the two co-existed better than I thought.

Fremont Street was a brilliant, loud and chaotic party place. A street party had never looked so good. For several blocks beneath a large, well-lit canopy laid more shops, casinos and street performers than one could possibly enjoy in just one night. A live band drew a healthy crowd, while incredibly talented dancers earned dollar bills for their efforts.

It had a different vibe than The Strip. A bit more casual and laid back, Fremont Street boasted a family friendly atmosphere. I passed more than one baby stroller as I hastily made my way from one end to the other.

Worry nagged me. Jez was out there somewhere. I could only wonder what effect the wolfsbane had on her, a naturally born shifter. I prayed her resistance had been better than mine.

As I passed the stage where a live band performed a Maroon 5 cover, an older lady danced directly into my path. Petite with short blonde hair, large earrings dangled from her lobes. Her eyes were wide, pupils huge. The scent of narcotics in her system had me trying to dodge her. She moved with me, a crooked smile on her thin lips.

"You can't save everybody," she cackled, her body jerking and twisting in a bizarre stoner's dance. "You can't even save yourself."

"What the hell are you talking about?" I snapped.

Her eerie grin grew wider, revealing yellow teeth. "A vampire queen with no throne is no queen at all."

She danced away into the throng of people gathered around the stage, leaving me staring after her in bewilderment. I continued on, turning over her words in my head. It could have been the intoxicated ramble of a woman on drugs, but I didn't think so. Narcotics had a way of opening the mind up to things nobody should ever have access to. Sinister things that speak horrible truths.

The urge to keep peering over my shoulder was strong. She had made me uneasy. I couldn't shake the feeling of being watched. The more distance I covered, the more certain I was that someone was following me. I opened myself up metaphysically to feel my stalker out. Familiar blood. Roscoe had found me first.

I kept my pace steady, hurried but not erratic. Leading him off the street into one of the casinos would give me a chance to confront him with fewer witnesses. Weaving my way through slot machines, my pulse pounded in anticipation of when he would jump me.

When his meaty hand came down on my shoulder, I was ready. I grabbed his wrist and jerked him forward, bending so he went over my back and hit the floor in front of me. I was on him fast, a knee on his chest and a clawed hand around his throat.

"I'm happy to see you don't really know as much about me as you think you do," I growled. "Where the fuck is Jez?"

"The leopard?" He grunted as my claws pierced his flesh. "Hell if I know. You both went down from the wolfsbane, and I didn't stick around to find out what happened next."

"Don't fucking lie to me. I will kill you right here. I don't give a damn how many cameras see me do it."

"I'm not lying. I tried to stop you from interfering in business that doesn't concern you. That's all." He clutched my arm in a desperate attempt to dislodge it from around his neck.

"And Jenner and Arys? Where were they taken?"

Roscoe's lips formed a thin white line, and he shook his head as much as he was able. He offered me nothing.

Fine. I could do this the hard way. I thrust a surge of fury-driven energy deep inside him, focusing on his cold, dead heart. And then I squeezed until blood filled his eyes and pooled in his mouth.

"Are you willing to die to keep that secret?" I asked, a cold smile tugging at my lips. "This just gets easier every time I do it. You're about two seconds from being a pile of dust."

A strangled cry escaped him. "The desert." He coughed and spat blood. "They'll be staked down in the desert for sunrise."

The blood drained from my face, and my breath came faster. "Get up, nice and slow. You're going to take me to them."

I let Roscoe up, releasing my hold on him. He wiped the blood from his eyes and mouth with the back of his sleeve, glaring angrily. "I don't know where they are. You're on your own."

"Why would you sell Jenner out like that? What happened to being his right hand?"

With a shrug of his wide shoulders, Roscoe pinned me with a fierce stare. "Survival of the fittest, I suppose. He wanted to pull out of the blood ring, but Harley started that ring decades ago. It wasn't about to die off because Jenner didn't want to play dirty anymore. I had to make the choice that best suited my needs."

I wanted so badly to plunge the Dragon Claw into his guts and watch the horror and shock flash across his face when he realized he was dead. However, it was a big weapon, too big to flash inside the casino.

My phone rang, the vibration in my bag alerting me to it. I made the mistake of going for it, giving Roscoe his chance to bolt. He slammed his elbow into my face, and I dropped to my knees. He was gone before I could regain my focus.

Chapter Eleven

It was Briggs.

"Hey, O'Brien I have a trace for you. We only picked up data on one phone. The other two are offline, possibly destroyed. The one we found is registered to a Jezebel St. Claire out of Edmonton."

"Yeah," I gasped, holding my battered nose. A few scarlet drops stained my palm. "What's the address?"

"Fremont Street. At The Golden Nugget. I'll keep trying on those other two. Can't promise anything though."

So Jez was here. Roscoe had lied. Next time I saw him, he was getting acquainted with the Dragon Claw. "Thanks, Briggs. I appreciate this. I know you didn't have to do it."

"Are you ok?" He asked upon hearing the pain in my voice.

"Just took an elbow to the nose, actually. But I'm fine, thanks. Call me if you find anything else."

There was hesitation on the line. Instead of hanging up, Briggs tentatively said, "You know, O'Brien, we may be able to offer assistance. Just say the word."

I chuckled in spite of everything. "I'm not quite desperate enough to take you up on that. But I'll keep it in mind."

"You do that."

Vampire politics were difficult enough. The last thing I wanted or needed was the Feds getting further into my business than they already were. Briggs had a hard-on for supernatural info. He'd take anything he could get. But he wouldn't be getting it from me.

Evidently, Briggs believed I could be recruited to the predominantly human government organization, most likely because he had so easily recruited my younger sister, Juliet. I had seen enough of the FPA to know I was safer with the demons.

By the time I made it to The Golden Nugget, my lungs were heaving. I sprinted down floor after floor looking for Jez. Sensing vampires came easier. I could feel every vampire in the city if I concentrated hard enough. However, I was still able to pick out that earthy Were vibe when close enough.

Human. That's all I could feel and smell. With a flurry of choice curse words, I continued up to the next floor. That's when the heady scent of wildcat tickled my nose. I knocked on the door and waited. No one answered. I studied the lock, feeling less than confident. Jez wasn't alone in there. I could feel the vampire with her.

I'd used my telekinetic abilities to manipulate locks before, but never had I tried it on a hotel room key card lock. Kicking the door down would have been easier. Taking a deep breath, I steeled my nerves and focused my energy on the lock. It wouldn't give. I banged a fist on the door in frustration. Then I tried again. No deal.

"For fuck's sakes," I swore.

"Do you need help?" I turned to find a lady wearing housekeeping garb, pushing a cart filled with cleaning supplies. Here was my chance to get into that room.

"Yes, I do." I approached her slowly, a huge smile pasted on my face. It was time to draw on the vampire glamour that I rarely used. It wasn't my strongest skill. I gazed into her eyes and encouraged the thrall. "I must have lost my keycard somewhere. Can you let me in?"

She blinked a few times, seemingly puzzled. Then her pupils dilated, and her shoulders relaxed. "Of course, dear. That won't be a problem."

I waited with growing impatience for her to open the door. The lock released, and I grasped the door handle, waiting for her to move along down the hall in a mesmerized stupor. It wouldn't last long.

"Thank you, Arys," I muttered beneath my breath. As much as I feared the vampire essence that possessed me, it was growing harder to loathe it.

Shoving the door open, I flicked on the light and prepared to draw my dagger. Of all the scenarios that had flashed through my mind, this was not one of them. Jez was most certainly inside the hotel room. She was furry on four legs, a gorgeous leopard, not entirely out of place in a city like this. She was also mauling the shit out of a vampire.

It was a nice room, painted in dark colors with a carpet to match. The king size bed was accompanied by a couch and coffee table placed before the window. The minibar was housed in an elaborate entertainment unit boasting a big, flat screen TV.

What my gaze was drawn to most of all was the writhing vampire flailing about on the floor. She had already torn his throat out which explained the lack of screams. From the twisted agony on his bloody face, he was in absolute hell.

"Holy shit." I closed the door firmly behind me.

Jez had done a real number on him. One of his hands lay several feet from his body, and she was currently working on a leg. What the fuck did he do to her?

She rounded on me with a snarl. Those green eyes sparkled with ruthless fury until she saw that it was me. Then she cleared the distance in a single leap, knocking me down in her haste to greet me. The golden black pattern on her svelte frame rippled. She was so rare, so gorgeous. I was a little jealous.

"I think it's time to put this guy out of his misery." I stood and drew the Dragon Claw from its sheath. "We have to get out of here before Roscoe comes back with reinforcements."

The shift was fast and fluid. In just seconds, her body reformed, leaving her naked and quaking on the floor. I wasted no time in slicing the vampire's head off. Immediately, he went up in a small puff of dust and ash.

"Lex? What happened to you?" Jez's voice was rough, as if she'd just chain-smoked a carton of cigarettes. "I woke up here, and that fucking scumbag vampire was standing guard."

I went through the bathroom and the small linen closet until I found a bathrobe. I wrapped it around her and pulled her up. She was a little shaky but appeared unharmed. "Did he hurt you? Do you remember anything from the past few hours?"

"No, it's a total blank. I woke up with that crazy shithead leering at me. He said he was to watch me while Roscoe hunted you down."

"That's strange. I just had a run in with Roscoe. Once I put the squeeze on him, he wanted nothing to do with me." I gathered the few things of Jez's that I could find while she washed the blood from her face and hands. "We have to go. Arys is going to burn at sunrise unless I can find him first."

"Have I mentioned yet how sorry I am for dragging you to this godforsaken fucking city?" Bitterness laced her tone. "I can't go out like this."

"We'll grab something from a shop downstairs. You're not going to like it though."

She emerged from the bathroom wearing a frown. Her face, free of makeup, radiated an innocence that red lipstick and mascara hid well. I couldn't understand why she wanted to hide such pure beauty beneath a crimson veil.

"Great, so I get to wear tacky Vegas tourist attire while we save your boyfriend. Give me what you're wearing. You obviously had time to go back to the hotel."

"Jez! We have to move it before anyone else shows up here."

"Alright, alright." She swiped her purse from my hands and tied the robe tighter. "So what happened to you anyway?"

By the time we purchased a Las Vegas t-shirt and Capri sweatpants, I'd filled her in on my brief time alone. Admitting to the death of almost half a dozen humans left me feeling hollow inside. I knew it wasn't entirely my fault, yet I couldn't shake the certainty that it had left a stain on my soul that would never wash clean.

Right there on Fremont Street, Jez slid the clothing on beneath the robe before ditching it in a trashcan. "Good Lord, I feel like the 'fashion don't' page in a magazine. When I get home I'm burning these ugly rags."

"The fun of being a shifter, huh?"

We hurried to the front of the hotel where the taxi line was thirty people long. I glanced around frantically with no real plan and mounting panic. I didn't know what to do.

"Over there." Jez pointed to a small line of limos. "The windows are blacked out. That's what we need. Go do that handy vampire glamour thing on the driver."

It was a start. I jerked open the driver door, almost giving the guy behind the wheel a heart attack.

"Can I help you, ladies?" He straightened his tie and smiled. "I'm afraid I'm waiting for a client at the moment, but if you'd like to book me for another time—"

I took a deep breath, finding it impossible to stay calm. *Focus*, I told myself.

"You're going to get out of the car and go inside the hotel. Have a drink, play some slots. Forget you ever saw us." A gentle push of power and a suggestive gaze earned me the same dopey expression the housekeeping lady had had, but I still held my breath in hopes that the glamour had worked. It was growing harder to achieve the same effect, taking more effort. The energy feed in the theatre earlier had done me wonders, but it was fading fast now. I could only handle so much in a night.

"Right, sure, ok." The driver slid out of the car and walked away with a robotic gait. I let my breath out in a giant sigh of relief.

"You drive," I said to Jez. "I need to concentrate on finding Arys."

Driving a stolen limo through Las Vegas had most definitely not been on my agenda for this vacation. Of course, nothing that had happened so far had been on my agenda.

"You're getting good at this vampire shit," Jez remarked, adjusting the mirrors. "Scary good."

"Fabulous. I'm thrilled." I squeezed my eyes shut against the ache that surfaced at the back of my skull. My mortal body simply couldn't handle so much undead power.

"Where to?"

"No idea. Just drive."

With my face in my hands, I concentrated on deep, even breaths. Arys. I let his name whisper through my mind. That should have been enough to open the mental door between us, but it remained firmly closed.

"He's shutting me out," I groaned. "He thinks he's going to die with the sunrise, and he doesn't want me to feel it."

"Is that how it works?" Jez was aghast. "Shit. Everything comes with a price, huh?"

If he wouldn't let me connect with him, there was only one way to find him. I would have to sift through every vampire aura in the city until I found those that reflected Harley's blood. This process of elimination might just make my head explode.

Sunrise was less than an hour away. The pressure was building, threatening my fragile grip on sanity. I'd already lost myself to the primal rage that lurked inside me all the time. It was a miracle I'd come back to myself at all after what I'd done to those men at Paris Las Vegas. I had to hold it together. Shaz and Arys needed me.

Letting my breath out slowly, I reached out to touch the City of Sin. Much like at home, The Wicked Kiss housed more vampires than any other dwelling. It shone like a beacon in my mind's eye.

I turned my attention from it, seeking common blood elsewhere. A tug on my thoughts from Fremont Street showed me where Roscoe was. He was likely laying low, ready to vacate the street when dawn broke. I was so far from done with him.

The ache in my head grew until a wave of agony crashed over me. My breaths came faster and shorter until I grew dizzy. Arys was out there. I knew it. *Where?* I pleaded to the powers that be. *Show me where.* Power filled the car, thick and pulsating, making it hard to suck air into my lungs. Something warm and wet slid between my hands to splatter my lap; my nose was bleeding profusely. Just when my pained groan became a wail, when I thought for sure it was over and that I'd killed us all by coming here, I felt him.

It wasn't like pointing out a location on a map. Instead, I felt the pull deep within me. My entire being called to him and received an answer. Our bond was forever. Nothing could break it or hide it, not even Arys himself.

"This way." I waved a hand erratically, and Jez took a sharp and sudden turn. Several other drivers honked and gestured angrily as we careened around a corner in the big stretch limo.

Jez pulled a small packet of tissues from her purse and shoved it into my hands. "You're scaring me now. That's more blood than usual."

I opened my eyes to find my hands held a scarlet puddle. Despite the tissue I pressed to my face, the blood kept coming. "I can't let go of the hold I have on him, and it hurts like a bitch." The pounding of my heart echoed in my ears, drowning out the sound of honks and jeers in traffic. Jez maneuvered the big car with as much finesse as she drove her old Jeep back home, which wasn't saying a lot. *Please, don't crash,* I tried to say, but the words wouldn't come out. It took every bit of strength to stay tuned to Arys's energy. I couldn't afford to lose him now. "Left up ahead," I gasped. "Follow it out of the city."

Jez's concern was palpable. She continued to shoot me worried glances. "Next time you can choose where we go. I promise. Just don't spontaneously combust or anything. Ok?"

"I'll see what I can do," I said with a wry smile that made my face ache.

With the squeal of tires, we jerked to a halt. Jez laid on the horn and stuck her hand out the window to flip someone the bird. "The cab drivers are fucking nuts here."

"What if we don't make it in time?" I looked to the east, searching the sky for signs of the coming morning. "What if I lose him?"

"That won't happen, Alexa. Stay positive. We proved already tonight that we're a force to be reckoned with. You can't give up now. You have to blow this blood ring apart. And you need Arys to do it." Jez's hand was warm on my arm as she gave it a squeeze. "By the time we leave, you will own this city."

"I'm glad one of us is so sure." I clenched my teeth and choked back a pained cry. The brain-shattering sensation was near blinding.

It felt like forever before we exited the city limits. The desert stretched wide around us. Mountains stood tall in the distance. It would have been beautiful at any other time. As we drew closer, the pressure in my head began to ease. I could almost breathe again. I continued to direct Jez, who did a great job of navigating with little more than random arm waves to go on. We turned off the main route and followed a secondary road for several miles. We were close now.

"Over there. That house." A cool wind blew through me, chilling my insides. It was a confirmation that nearly brought me to tears. He was here.

The house was a small, two level with an attached garage. If the ramshackle exterior and the old rusted car outside were any indication, the place was abandoned. But not empty.

"There are vampires here," I said. "They must be watching from inside."

"To make sure their enemies burn." Jez nodded. "Makes sense. I doubt the head honchos would do a job like that. Whoever is here will be small time. Let's take them out."

I balled up the tissue and dropped it on the floor, satisfied that my nose had finally stopped bleeding. "Are you sure you're up for that after the wolfsbane?"

"Please," she scoffed. "That may have slowed down a regular shifter, but neither you or I are quite normal, are we? That idiot said he gave us enough to drop a bear. Should have used the elephant dose."

I stared at the house as we came to a stop. The sun was just emerging over the horizon. It was dark enough still for the vampires inside to come out and stop us. That was a chance I'd have to take.

"Watch your back. They have weapons."

There was no way to creep up to the house, no possible way to hide our arrival. We stepped out of the car with a score to settle. I held the Dragon Claw in one hand and a blazing blue and gold psi ball in the other.

Keeping our distance from the house, we went around to the back. The rising metaphysical wind tossed my hair. Every step I took toward Arys increased my strength.

I didn't see him right away. It took scouring the desert land behind the house to spot the two figures on the ground in the distance. My heart sank at the realization that Shaz wasn't there.

I broke into a run, fully expecting the crossbow bolt that whizzed over my head. The shot was way off. Three vampires burst out of the house. Preternatural speed made them a blur of motion.

"Keep going," I shouted to Jez before jerking to a halt. With fangs bared, I turned to face my opponents.

The psi ball exploded on the ground before them. A cloud of dust rose up to engulf the two it knocked down. The third quickly became acquainted with the dagger blade as I slid it into his belly.

Without waiting for his ashen remains to settle, I advanced on the other two. "Which one of you wants to die first?" I pinned them with a steady push of power. Fueled by adrenaline and sheer will, it held, though I was going to feel it later. Both vampires were frozen in place. One sneered at me while the other quaked in terror. I preferred the latter. "Alright, together then." With a swipe of my blade, I decapitated them both. More dust for the desert floor.

I hurried after Jez, thankful for the easy kill; those were very rare these days. She shouted at me to hurry. The sun's golden glow lit up the horizon. It was close now, just a matter of minutes until the open desert land was awash in its light.

When I came upon the two vampires, bile rose in my throat. Jenner and Arys were staked to the ground. Their captors had driven a pair of lengthy chunks of wood through their middles and into the ground beneath them. Hands outstretched at either side, iron nails pierced each palm, ensuring they stayed put.

There was blood, a lot of it, as well as cuts and bruises from what looked like someone's torture fun. I froze, staring at Arys's battered face. Then I snapped into action, moving to help Jez tug the first big stake free. It took both of us, since the stake was embedded deeply within the earth. The shout that it tore from Arys almost doubled me over. I had never seen him in such pain. It hurt me both emotionally and physically, a phantom pain that almost drove me to my knees. It didn't take long to free him. Getting him on his feet was another thing. I tried to get him to lean on me, but he shook his head and rolled onto his side.

"Jenner." Arys's word was barely audible.

I looked at Jenner with his one eye swollen shut and stake protruding from his middle. Part of me was perfectly willing to walk away and let the fucker burn. He was the one who had made himself a foe from the moment we'd landed in town. He'd pissed off the blood ring and withheld that information from us. I had no reason to save him. Except Arys. Jez awaited my decision. She shrugged, fine with it either way. Jenner rolled his one good eye toward me, knowing damn well his life was in my hands.

"Fuck." I shot a glance toward the horizon, and my panic grew. "Fine. Let's hurry."

Together Jez and I tore the stake free, almost falling on our asses when it burst out of the ground. We each grabbed a nail and yanked it from a hand. Even with our superhuman strength, carrying the weight of an injured vampire was not easy. Every step we took caused them further agony. The limo looked so damn far away. Could we make it in time?

"Come on," I urged Arys on. "We're almost there."

Every anguished sound that came from him was like a knife in my gut. Sure, I'd seen Arys take a few hits but nothing like this. Perhaps part of me hadn't believed it was possible for him to be anything other than the dominant force. Seeing him so close to death had awakened a new kind of terror in me.

I could feel the rising sun chasing us to the car. I urged Arys along, caring more about his overall safety than his current level of injury. He could survive being impaled through the stomach. No vampire could survive the sun.

A horrible memory flashed through my mind. I'd watched one of the blood ring vamps die by sunlight, and I'd never witnessed a nastier vampire death. The thought spurred me on, giving me the extra strength I needed.

We reached the limo as the warm glow broke fully over the horizon. The UV rays hurt my eyes, so I wasn't surprised when both vampires cried out. I flung the back door open and shoved Arys inside, stepping back to allow Jenner through. Jez slammed the door shut, and I sank to the ground, leaning against the back tire.

"Thank you, God," I whispered. Panting and repeating my prayer of gratitude, I realized that tears rolled down my face.

"Should we go inside? Might be something worth swiping in there." Jez extended a hand, which I gratefully accepted.

"If we make it home, I'm going to stay in bed for a week," I declared.

"If? No, you mean when. When we get home. Which we will."

The house was just as derelict inside as out. Nobody had lived there for a very long time. There was little evidence of the vampires who had claimed it, so they weren't total idiots. We picked up a crossbow, half a dozen bolts and a gun with wooden bullets.

I had no use for guns. Jez inspected it, shrugged and said, "Why not? It's not like customs let us bring our own weapons through."

I got into the back of the limousine with the guys while Jez took us back to Caesars. They splayed out in the roomy backseat across from one another. I knelt on the floor in front of Arys, afraid to touch him for fear of hurting him.

"Why did you shut me out?" I hadn't meant for those to be my first words to him after such an ordeal, but his isolation had hurt me.

He tried to touch me, and even though the wounds in his hands had already begun to heal, he was simply too weak. I leaned in closer and carefully held his hand to my face.

"I had to," he said, wincing with each word. "Didn't want you to feel it. I was afraid I'd take you with me." What it felt like to feel him die, that's what he meant. Like he had felt Harley die when I killed him.

Guilt slithered in among my many emotions. Our bond was deep enough that, as a mortal, his death could take me down too. Then I'd be here as a vampire without him. The thought was horrifying.

"Don't ever do that again." My voice broke, and I rested my forehead against his. I didn't want to ask, but I needed to know. "Where's Shaz?"

Arys shook his head, defeated and ashamed. "They have him. He'll go to the highest bidder. Eventually."

"What?" I sat back on the floor in shock. The blood ring had Shaz. If they knew he was one of Harley's killers, then there's no telling what kind of hell he would go through before they killed him. "Do they know who he is?"

"Oh yeah," Jenner chimed in with a groan. "They know. And they're looking for you."

Chapter Twelve

"Do they know we're here?" Jez asked through a mouthful of chicken. "Is it safe to sleep?"

"They don't know you're at this hotel. And I doubt they'd waste time and resources tracking you by day. As far as I know, they don't have a lot of daywalkers in their employ." Jenner watched Jez eat with blatant disgust. He lay sprawled on the couch, shirtless and ghostly white.

Returning to Caesars had been simple enough. Pulling the limo up to the entry just beneath the Augustus Tower elevator had given us enough shade to get the wounded vampires safely inside. Now we tackled the task of healing them by nightfall and somehow resting up. Fatigue teased me, making my eyelids heavy. My mind refused to give in. How could I sleep when Shaz was out there?

I nibbled on a chicken wing. I should have been ravenous after the night I'd just had, but the constant turning of my stomach made it hard to swallow.

Jenner watched us eat; his face twisted into a grimace. "That's just about the ugliest thing I've seen in ages. When do I get to eat?"

Jez had wasted no time ordering room service and digging in to the meat dishes on the cart. She shot Jenner a dirty look and flung a chicken bone at him. "Stop fucking watching us then."

"Should be any time now," Arys said. His blue gaze strayed to the door. He too lay haphazardly along the opposite end of the couch. Dark circles lined his eyes though most of the bruises and gashes had faded. The gaping hole in his sternum had closed. It was covered with a thick, pink scar.

The healing time of a vampire far exceeded that of a wolf. An injury that would take a human weeks to heal would take me a few days, though for Arys, it could be just minutes or hours. However, without blood, healing would take longer, especially as far as his metaphysical abilities went. To help replace the energy that the vamps had expended, we were expecting four escorts to arrive at any moment.

I shifted in my chair, uncomfortable and sore. Feeling stiff and tired, I shoved my plate back onto the room service cart, opting for water instead.

"Do we have a plan?" I inquired when I noticed Arys watching me. He was going to get after me about eating if I didn't change the subject. "Do we even know where to find them?"

"We don't find them. We let them find us." His knowing gaze strayed from me to the room service cart. "Between now and nightfall, we regain our strength and rest up."

"Do we absolutely have to keep him?" Jez gestured to Jenner with her fork, and he scowled. "I don't like the way he's looking at me."

"Yes, we do," I said, shooting a warning look Jenner's way. "He owes us for this entire night of hell."

Jenner sat up straighter, brow raised. "Excuse me? I told you to leave town. You chose to stay. Not my problem."

"You withheld information that endangered us all," I snapped, my fists clenched. "Not to mention that bullshit you pulled with the poker game."

Jenner's mirthless laugh warmed the atmosphere. "I won that game fair and fucking square."

"Yes, but it shouldn't have happened in the first place." I was far too exhausted to waste energy on anger, but Jenner was the one I blamed for whatever Shaz was going through right that moment.

Arys sighed and held up a hand. "There's no point arguing. What's done is done. We must focus on the next step."

"I say me and Jez find them. Today. Take them out during daylight." Even as I said it, I knew I wouldn't have the strength. I just hated feeling so helpless.

"Like hell you will," Arys objected. "You're not going anywhere without me, not as long as we're in this city."

I expected to find that blue spark burning in his eyes, the one that preceded every fight we ever had. Instead, I found concern. He had thought it was over. I couldn't blame him for feeling so protective. Running off without him to confront the blood ring vamps would be stupid.

"I just can't stand the thought of Shaz being out there." I hung my head so my hair fell to hide my face as I blinked back tears.

Arys reached out to touch my thigh. His hand was cold, a sure indicator he needed to feed. There was a knock on the door at the same moment my cell phone rang. Both Arys and Jenner rose. I didn't want to watch them steal the life force from unsuspecting women so I slipped away to the bathroom to talk in private.

"You really know how to make a guy crazy, don't you?" Kale's low, smooth tone greeted me. "I must have called you a dozen times."

"More than that actually." I found myself smiling. He almost sounded like himself again rather than the manic fiend I'd left behind. It was an illusion though. Kale would never come back from the kind of crazy that claimed him.

"Obviously, you're still alive. Is everything ok? I knew you wouldn't want me to send Falon, but the only way to find you was through Shya's demon mark."

I repeated the events of the evening while stripping down for a shower. It was odd speaking to Kale as if nothing had changed between us when in fact everything had. It was tough.

Since the night he had violated me and tried to kill me, I'd struggled to accept that the friend he had been was dead to me now. The promise he had made echoed in my mind as we talked. Kale had declared his intent to force me to release him by driving a stake through his heart. He intended for me to put him out of his misery.

"You're strong. You'll play the heroine and save Shaz. No worries."

I laughed bitterly, examining the bruises marring my naked flesh in the mirror. "Right, no worries."

"It's what you do though, isn't it? You put yourself in danger to save those you love." Something in his voice, a crack of emotion, told me he wasn't just talking about Shaz.

The sound of girlish giggles echoed from beyond the door, followed by Jez's sarcastic tone. Blood was about to be spilled in the living room, and I was hiding out in the washroom. Pitiful.

"Kale, I'm sorry about what happened with the FPA. I went in there for you, twice, and I failed. It's because of me that they drove you so crazy." Slowly I dragged a brush through my tangled hair. I waited nervously for his response.

"They didn't drive me crazy, Alexa. Somebody else did that long ago. Your blood opened a door I'd thought was closed forever. The FPA just made me feel ok with it again." He was flippant, speaking like it was no big deal. Shit happens.

I set the phone down and put it on speaker. Needing to feel normal, I washed the remnants of smeared makeup from my face. "You sound fine right now. Like the Kale I first met."

"That's because there's fourteen hundred miles between us."

Very unnerving. I stared at the phone, glad I couldn't peer into his mismatched eyes. "Is that what it takes for you to talk to me without wanting to kill me?" I blurted the question, knowing I shouldn't be asking it.

His silence frightened me. I was tempted to hang up, however, that would only postpone this conversation for a face-to-face encounter. "You don't want to know what it takes." The devious chuckle that followed sent a shiver down my spine. His voice dropped even lower when he said, "If only it was as simple as merely wanting to kill you."

He would lose his grip on the precarious scrap of sanity that somehow kept him from being a ravenous, unstoppable killing machine. That day would come. I knew it in every part of me, and selfishly, I prayed I wouldn't be around to see it.

"And here I thought you called because you cared," I said, using snide derision to cover up my hurt.

"Oh, but I do care. In fact, I care so much for you, Alexa, that I dusted a vampire to defend your baby sister's honor when she passed through looking for you."

That raised a red flag. A lump formed in my throat, and I swallowed hard. "Don't touch my sister, Kale. I know you want to get to me and make me take you out, but that is not the way to do it." As much as I tried to stay calm, I was sure he could hear the panic in my voice. I wasn't sure how much more I could take. Vampires were going to be my undoing. Sometimes all I wanted was to go back to the days of just being wolf. The days when I hunted vampires, before I knew I would be one of them.

"I'm hurt that you would immediately jump to such a conclusion," he said with feigned emotion. Like flipping a switch, his tone changed, becoming serious and sobered. "I said I'd make you crazy. I never said I would break your heart." His words were like a dagger, sharp and slicing deep. I never knew what to expect from him anymore. Such a declaration wasn't it.

I opened my mouth to say something, anything, to maybe apologize or plead my case. I didn't know. He never gave me the chance.

"I'm glad you made it through the night in one piece," he continued. "You sound tired. Go get some rest."

He hung up, saving me from having to form words. It was starting to grow harder to recall when we last had a normal conversation. One of these days, I would let myself mourn the loss of what had never been and never could be. Maybe.

A shriek rang out, quickly silenced by a hungry vampire. A tremor rocked me. The tantric pull of incubus energy caused me to break out in goose bumps. I turned on the shower, ignoring the urge to go out there and throw myself into the sex-charged bloodletting.

The hot spray felt heavenly. Shoving all thought aside, I washed my hair and scrubbed my skin clean. More than once, emotion threatened to overwhelm me. I crammed it back down to the depths it had risen from. I stood in the steamy water long after I'd finished washing up. I wasn't ready to get out and face reality yet.

The bathroom door opened, and Arys slipped inside. He wasted no time shedding his clothing. The large black dragon on his back drew my gaze. I scowled. I detested the constant reminders we both bore of Shya's influence in our lives.

Nonetheless, I drank in the sight of his hard body. The large stake scar was no longer visible. His skin was flawless, without any sign of the abuse he'd endured. He hummed with renewed energy.

Arys's skin was warm when he joined me in the shower. Pulling me into his arms, he murmured, "I need to feel you."

Throwing my arms around his neck, I kissed him with a sudden yearning intensity. He tasted like blood. "You scared the hell out of me. Don't ever do that again. You can't shut me out. I still found you."

He buried his face in my neck and inhaled my scent. His arms tightened around my waist. "I didn't want to hurt you. We still don't know every aspect of our link. I was terrified if I'd died, then it would take you with me."

That hadn't crossed my mind when Jez and I had been rushing out of the city in search of him. It was a chilling possibility. As rare as twin flames were, we had no way of knowing for sure how the death of one twin would affect the other. Especially considering Arys had died a human death long before I'd ever been born. Based on the yin yang theory that bound our power, we could only exist together by maintaining a balance. However, we were two separate beings born at very different times.

"Promise me you won't do that again," I insisted, sliding a hand up into his wet hair. A shudder racked me as Arys gently pushed healing energy through me. I wasn't in bad shape physically though it did wonders to help my metaphysical weakness.

"I promise." The hot caress of his lips on my skin freed me from the chains of fear and worry. His erection pressed against me, thick and ready. "Oh God, how I need you."

His hands found my breasts. I made a small noise of contentment when he rubbed my nipples into taut points. Comfort was temporary but necessary. I needed him too.

It felt so good to put my hands on Arys. When I left his side back at The Wicked Kiss, I hadn't ever really believed I wouldn't see him again. Now that I was standing there with him, it started to sink in. We had come so close to being parted.

I kissed him again. Slow and sensual, our tongues entangled in an erotic dance. Things were bad, damn bad, but I was starting to get used to that feeling. Only moments like this would keep me sane, so I threw myself into loving my dark vampire.

Arys slid a hand between my legs. He stroked me with a finger, knowing exactly how I liked to be touched. A shock of pleasure slammed through me.

Every place our slippery, wet skin made contact created another spark. We were soon alight with the fire that united us.

Arys lifted my leg, hooking it over his forearm. He positioned himself so that he held my weight as he thrust inside me. The shower tile was cool against my back. The hot water cascaded over us, plastering my hair to my face. He pushed it aside with a gentle hand. Our eyes locked, and the heat between us grew as if we'd thrown gasoline on the flames of our passion. Every stroke of his rigid length coaxed a small sound of delight from me.

It didn't take long for the steady push and pull of rising power to restore my strength. Feeding off our lovemaking wasn't new for either of us. It was a fantastic way to build and devour much needed energy. And it was a hell of a lot of fun too.

I clung to Arys, my senses on overload. All I could see, feel, smell and taste was him. The sound of his satisfied groans drove my own desire higher.

"Growl for me, Alexa," he murmured. The force behind his thrust grew aggressive as he guided me to the edge of bliss. "I need to hear you."

My moans became cries. With clawed fingertips, I scratched bloody grooves into Arys's well-muscled back. Climax shook me. Spasms within me held Arys deep, bringing him over the edge in a harmonious sharing of ecstasy. My cries turned to growls, and I nipped at his neck and shoulders. Oh how I ached for this man.

Once wasn't enough for Arys. After leaving the shower and toweling off, he lifted me onto the bathroom counter and resumed his claiming of my body. The counter was the perfect height, allowing him to step between my legs. I was still ready for him, hungry for the joy and completion only he could give me.

The rush of soaring power grew dizzying with Arys buried inside me. A potent, writhing force, it caused the lights to flicker, and elsewhere in the suite, I felt Jenner react to what we called.

I dragged my hands down Arys's chest, reveling in the heady masculine feel of him. His fingers entangled in my hair, his lips on my neck. Being with him took me to places I'd never dreamed of. Our connection went far beyond the physical. It had taken some time to adjust to having him be part of me. Perhaps I never fully would. I could definitely never say it was boring.

When at last we were spent, I rested my head against his chest for several long, blessedly silent minutes. I took that precious time to memorize again how he felt. I was afraid that one day a memory would be all I had.

* * * *

"So they were going to kill you just because you wanted out?" Jez's eyes were wide despite the yawn she stifled. "Damn. And I thought vampires were bad on their own. They sound pretty fucking scary in an organized group."

Jenner paused in his impatient pacing around the living room. "They were going to kill me because I didn't secure their supply first. I'm welcome to leave but not without finding someone to take my place. I meant to. I got caught up in giving the club a makeover. Besides, it wouldn't have been my problem if Harley were still alive."

His pale-blue gaze swung to me. It was hard to read. Accusation lurked in those depths, but so did something else. Something I'd only seen in the eyes of one other person; Kale's gorgeous eyes exuded that same dark infatuation when he looked at me. I had claimed Jenner as mine with my blood and power. In the moment, it had felt right, necessary even. Too late now for regrets. I hated what I'd done to Kale, but Jenner, he'd had it coming.

"Well Harley's dead, and I'm not sorry about it," I snapped, tired and irritable. "So I suggest you get over it and focus on the here and now, so you don't end up the same way."

It was early morning, still well before noon. Sleep was calling me. Arys and Jenner had retold the tale of their evening. We were discussing our plans for the following night.

I curled up on Arys's lap, wrapped in a hotel bathrobe. Jez wore the same, her hair tied atop her head. She too wore the signs of fatigue. Jenner was a restless mess, unable to sit still. He appeared uncomfortable in the borrowed clothes he wore, clearly out of his element here with us.

"Don't make the mistake of thinking I'm the only one whose head is on the chopping block," Jenner warned. "At least if I go out, it'll be fast. Can't say the same for you."

Amusement played about his face, his lips twisting as he hid a smirk. I pinned Arys with a look. "What the hell is he talking about?"

Arys glowered at Jenner. "Linden has plans for you. Plans he enjoyed telling me about in great detail while his guys were staking me down in the desert." Arys glanced away, as if he couldn't stand to think about it. "There's no way I can convince you to stay here while I go for Shaz, is there?"

"I'm not staying here," I insisted with a shake of my head. "Tell me what Linden said."

The vampires exchanged a look. Jenner wore a haughty expression.

Arys shrugged. "He said that he has special plans for Harley's killers. If he gets his chance, he'll bleed you, torture you, pass you around. But he won't kill you. Even if you beg him to." Arys rubbed his forehead and swore. "I don't want to think about it. It's not going to happen."

"Holy shit, that's screwed up," Jez muttered. "I can't believe those fuckers almost had me. I'm damn glad I never killed Harley."

I bit my lower lip, an anxious habit I'd had since childhood. "Is that what he's doing to Shaz right now?"

I looked from one vampire to the other. Jenner resumed his slow pace around the living room, avoiding my eyes. Arys let me see the truth. There was no hiding what he really felt from me.

"Alexa," he said, taking my hand. "I'm so sorry. I wish I was able to get him out of there. We were outnumbered in every way. I called on all the power I safely could without drawing on you. There were just too many of them."

Jez visibly paled. "Who the hell are these guys?"

"I think we can take them, together," Arys declared, his eyes flashing with determination. "We're stronger together. Still, we may need to up the ante, bring in more firepower."

I didn't like the sound of that. "Why does that sound like something I'm gonna hate?"

"I think you should take blood from one of the angels." Arys dropped his little bomb and waited for my protests.

A frown creased my brow as I considered it. Jez snickered and taunted me about getting wrinkles, which only made me frown harder.

Taking blood from an angel was dangerous. However, it did have its advantages, like the ability to set things on fire with only a thought. What made it so deadly was that only angels could fully master their power. In the hands of anyone else, especially a mortal, it was a disaster waiting to happen.

"I don't know, Arys." I shook my head, pondering. I snuggled in a little closer, seeking reassurance in his embrace. "That's risky. And I don't want to go there with Willow. It's so…personal."

Taking blood and power was deeply, painfully intimate. My succubus nature only heightened that effect. Recalling Falon's erection pressed between my thighs made me shudder. The worst part was that I had wanted him too. *Ew, gross.* Power was like any other intoxicant. The high could lead one to do things later regretted.

"Then take Falon's blood. Forcefully if need be." Arys was too flippant. He hadn't been the one to taste angel's blood. He didn't understand how different it was.

"Easy for you to say; you didn't feel what I felt."

"Why not just use a blade on Willow to take his blood? No contact." Jez's point was valid. Unfortunately, it didn't work that way.

Jenner fielded that question, jumping in before I could find a way to explain. "Not possible. Physical contact is essential. Blood is just one part of the feed for vampires like us. It'll sustain us but it doesn't empower us. We need the energy of the life force. It's got to be a hands-on process."

I felt awkward. Remembering what had happened between Jenner and me brought a rush of heat to my cheeks. It was far too easy to get caught up in the rush when the power was running high.

Jez yawned, and I immediately did the same.

"Go get some rest." Arys brushed a soft kiss across my forehead. "You and Jez take our bedroom. Jenner and I will take her room. I'm not leaving him unattended with either of you."

I knew what that meant. "You're calling more escorts here, aren't you?"

"We're not killing. I need to be at full strength. So do you."

"Forget it." I got to my feet but shot Arys a warning look. I was having flashbacks to the time I had walked in on he and Harley sharing a victim. "I'm not being part of that. Better be careful."

"Always," came his cautious reply.

An unspoken understanding passed between us. Though Arys had stopped bedding his victims when he and I'd bonded, he still drove them into a sexual and sometimes terrorized frenzy in order to sate his hunger. I preferred not to know the details of those encounters.

Jenner's laugh sent a prickle of annoyance through me. He was clearly entertained. "I never thought I'd see the day when Arys Knight put himself on a leash for a woman. Keep in mind that when you turn, Alexa, he will no longer find total fulfillment in you. You will both be forced to find that in humankind."

My temper flared. "Better get your fill of escorts, Jenner. If I need to steal strength from anyone later, it's going to be you." If Arys hadn't been in the room I'd have been quite tempted to throw open the curtains and roast Jenner's snarky ass. I turned away before I could see the glare he shot at my back. I felt the weight of it though.

Jez followed me with another series of yawns. Closing the door, she gave a self-deprecating laugh and said, "Um, so have I mentioned how sorry I am for insisting we come here for a getaway? I fucked up."

"No, you didn't fuck up." I tossed the pillows off the bed and rumpled the blankets so they weren't so annoyingly perfect. "I had to meet Jenner at some point." I threw my hands up in surrender and stared at the bed.

Jez saw my face fall, and her smile disappeared. "Hey, Lex, it's going to be ok. I'm sure of it." She pulled me in for a hug, stroking a hand through my damp hair.

She smelled good, like earth and animal. It made my wolf whine and paw at my insides. We didn't have to be pack to share that connection. It made me miss Shaz. I'd never get used to being without him.

"I think I need to be wolf." Too much time in the vampire world was weighing on my beast. I longed for the forest, missing the tickle of pine and animal musk in my nose.

Jez nodded emphatically. "I totally understand. Let's do it."

It was so nice to have people who understood the many parts of me. I was grateful. Though, it would have been nice to have just one person who understood them all.

It didn't take long for sleep to drag me under. I welcomed it, needing the brief reprieve from the real world. Jez's gold and black head rested on my back. We curled up on the bed together, a wolf and a leopard.

I was sure it still wasn't the weirdest thing that had happened in that hotel bed.

Chapter Thirteen

"Shut it down, Jenner." Arys's tone held no room for argument.

"Not a chance. Nothing stops this club from operating."

The two of them glared daggers at one another. The Wicked Kiss was running like a well-oiled machine. The nightclub owner in me was more than a little envious of just how smooth Jenner's club ran compared to mine.

"Nothing? How about death?" Arys inquired.

"Try it." There was no budging Jenner. "This place operates twenty-four hours. No exceptions."

We sat at a table on the main floor. No evidence remained of last night's chaos. I refused to go downstairs again. Not only did it cater to a crowd that I wanted no part of, but it made escape harder.

"How do you know Linden will even come?" I asked nervously, nursing my second coffee. No liquor for me, I needed to stay alert. "What if he just takes Shaz and calls it even? We could be wasting time sitting here waiting."

Jenner looked like himself again. Being back here did something for him. It wasn't just his appearance. He thrived off this place. Dressed in his own attire of dark pants and a black t-shirt that showed off his many tattoos, he gave off an air of confidence he hadn't had early that morning back at Caesars. His dark hair was slicked into place. Not a scratch remained from his injuries.

"Call it even?" He chuckled. "Oh, that won't happen. Besides, you're the one with the rare blood. Maybe it wouldn't be so bad for them all to get a taste. I don't think he has a clue what it will do to him."

"Did you?" I pinned him with a predatory gaze. He was lucky I didn't smack him for a stupid remark like that.

Refusing to acknowledge me, he walked away to consult with the security guys working the door. Despite my increasing unease, I was still able to snicker to myself. It wasn't often I got the upper hand over a powerful vampire. I was going to enjoy it while I could.

"I have a bad feeling about this, Arys." I tapped my fingernails on the tabletop, the rhythm increasing with my apprehension. "It's not going to play out the way you think it is."

"I know." Arys had yet to sit. He was up and down, unable to let his guard down for even a second. On high alert, he scanned the vicinity constantly, ready for anything. He was in a foul mood. Not that I could blame him. I wasn't too thrilled myself.

Jez and Sloane lingered a few tables over, speaking in low tones. It wasn't my business what Jez did and who she did it with. I just hoped she didn't get hurt.

Sloane had recovered as well. She didn't say a word about trying to attack me in her weakened state. Whatever. I could pretend it didn't happen. It wasn't important right now. But if she ever came at me again, she'd be sorry. Likewise if she hurt Jez in any way.

The air rippled, and I groaned. I didn't want to do this.

Falon appeared wearing his usual scowl. He wasn't any happier about this than I was. Good.

"All right wolf, let's get this over with. I may vomit just thinking about letting your lips touch me again."

I turned a pout on Arys, pleading with my eyes. "Aw, don't make me do this."

"I'm not making you do anything." He gave Falon a stiff nod before sliding into the seat next to mine. "We're powerful enough to blow Linden's world apart. But he's going to come prepared and so should we. As a succubus with both light and dark power, I think you're the only one who can do it."

Arys wouldn't be so insistent if he didn't truly think it was necessary. My resistance was personal. I had to suck it up and get over it. This was for Shaz. My personal comfort meant nothing compared to his safety.

The things I'd heard about the blood ring were beyond horrifying. These vampires preyed on specific kinds of victims, fetish kills that would turn the strongest stomach. I could not afford to take them lightly.

"Fine," I relented. I could do it for Shaz. To Falon, I said, "What are you getting out of this?"

I hadn't had any part in this arrangement. Naturally, I was suspicious. Demons didn't do a damn thing without getting something in return. Falon may not be full demon yet, but he might as well have been. He was his own brand of evil.

"That's between me and Shya. Lucky you. Off the hook this time. I've been given the not so important job of being your back up." Falon looked positively miserable when he added, "Lucky me."

"If Shya gives such a damn about keeping me alive, why does he always send you? Why not make an appearance himself?" I never knew what to think when it came to Shya. The demon was unpredictable and downright wicked.

Falon shook his head of fair hair. "I can't answer for him. He's a bit of a need to know kind of guy, if you haven't noticed. Besides, do you really want him here?"

"Good point."

It had been a couple weeks since I'd seen Shya. He saved me from certain death and made Arys promise to pay the price. The demon was easily the last person I wanted to see. Going home meant having to deal with Shya. I had left to get a break from him and the promise of my death playing a role in some master plan of his. I couldn't escape that damn demon anywhere. Even now, he was interfering by sending Falon to shadow me. Good for me now, bad for me later. The time was coming when Shya and I would really throw down, come hell or high water. Quite possibly literally.

"How much time do you think we have?" I asked Arys, trying to play it cool in front of Falon. He didn't need to know my insides were in knots.

"It's hard to say. Better to be ready than to allow them the element of surprise. It worked too well for them last night." Slipping a hand into my hair, Arys pulled me close, pressing his lips to mine. "No matter what, don't make it easy for Linden to find your weaknesses."

I shook my head, knowing full well that was impossible. Linden already had one of my weaknesses in his possession.

Rising, I gestured to Falon. "Are you sure you want to do this?"

"I'm sure that I don't want to do this, but seeing as it's not quite my choice, let's just make it fast." He rolled up a sleeve and offered his wrist to me.

Swallowing hard, I took his forearm and stroked a finger over the veins beneath the surface of his skin. Blood that had never been human called to me with the promise of power born of a different realm. Being able to manipulate such forces was both a gift and a curse.

The weight of Arys's gaze caused me to hesitate. "Are you sure you want to watch this?" I asked, hoping he wouldn't.

"I do." He shrugged unapologetically. Intrigue drew him closer.

I was careful to avoid eye contact with Falon. If it was anything like last time, things were about to get strange. I slid my fingers between his and pushed a breath of power into him. He responded as I'd hoped he would, pushing back with a suffocating breeze of potent energy. Closing my eyes, I reached down deep inside myself to the place where the succubus energy dwelled. It bubbled up in response like a pot boiling over on the stove, spilling over to draw Falon into my thrall.

I bit into his wrist, groaning as the power-charged blood hit my tongue. Falon healed rapidly, forcing me to bite again and again. The bloodlust surged forth and, with it, a hunger for the inhuman strength in every crimson drop.

It didn't take long for the hypnotic pull to catch us both in its grip. Falon's free hand tangled in my hair. My fangs pierced his flesh again, and he gave a ragged sigh. The euphoric charge filled me, empowering me with parts of him that I should never have been able to harness. The limited contact wasn't enough, and I sought to take Falon down beneath me. I had to take him into me in all ways. I needed to explore his illicit desire.

He used the hand in my hair to jerk my head close. His lips were on mine, begging me for more. As powerful as he was, Falon was incapable of resisting my metaphysical call. I forgot about his wrist. His kiss was deep, passionate and demanding. I bit his lip, sucking it into my mouth before going for his throat.

Arys stepped in at the right time. He jerked me out of Falon's arms, preventing me from taking a deadly amount. I stumbled, momentarily dizzy. Then my focus re-centered, and I licked the blood from my lips with a mischievous smile.

"I'm starting to think I should have been present last time this happened." Arys's expression was one of mixed emotion. I knew that glint in his eyes. He had liked what he just saw, but he didn't want to, much like my reaction to Jenner in the theatre.

"Fucking hell," Falon swore. "Why did you kiss me?"

I felt lightheaded and giggly. Falon's power coursed through me, seeking an outlet. Containing it until I needed it most might prove difficult.

"You kissed me, pal. Nice try though. I wouldn't want to admit to that either if I were you."

"If I wasn't here you'd be fucking on the table by now. This can never happen without a neutral third party." Arys pulled me farther away from Falon as if he thought I might just drop my pants and bend over for the asshole angel.

Falon's pale eyes sparked with self-loathing. His reaction to me really made him unhappy. I found it satisfying.

"I'll be around if I'm needed," Falon muttered, barely able to bring himself to look at me. "Breathe a word of this to anyone, and I'll gut you like the animal you are."

He was gone before I could laugh in his scowling face. Too bad.

Someone was watching me intently. A glance about revealed it to be Jenner. He lingered near the door wearing a glower that made his ruggedly handsome features borderline ugly. Of course, he would be affected by what just happened. Our bloodline was the damndest thing.

"How do you feel?" Arys turned my attention back to him. His eyes were wide, pupils dilated with excitement. "Your eyes are silver, and your aura feels…off."

All speaking at once, a crowd of voices accompanied the racing of my heart. I was ready for it this time. The thoughts of so many being freely exuded all around me was still overwhelming though.

"I feel like I could fly if I really wanted to. There's this bizarre sensation, like I'm floating along above the surface rather than actually touching the floor. And I can already hear people's thoughts." Calming breaths. It might have been borrowed power, but it was now mine to do with as I pleased. I would not be bent to its will; I would do the bending this time.

"Stay calm and focused. Of all of us, you have the best chance of putting the fear in these guys. You were born to do this kind of thing." The hug Arys pulled me into was warm and over much too quickly. He put me at arm's length, as if he didn't trust himself to be closer.

A shout from the doorman had us all braced and alert. I slid the Dragon Claw from its sheath before Linden strode through the front entry with four henchmen in tow. I'd expected more.

Pausing in the doorway, he surveyed the quick reparations that had been made since his stunt here last night before looking at each of us in turn. Jenner stood ready with power lighting up his clenched fists. With an air of casual disinterest, Jez held the stolen crossbow in one hand, bolt in the other. It was rare that I saw her truly afraid of anyone. Sloane hung back, behind the rest of us, but I felt her tap her power. The room buzzed with the force of Harley's bloodline. How any one vampire could spawn so many impressive creatures was beyond me. Where did it all come from?

Linden strode through the crowd with a relaxed gait. He held no visible weapons nor did he possess any great metaphysical power. The confidence oozing from him was unsettling. His dark stare fixed on me. Whatever he was thinking, he did a good job of hiding it. I couldn't hear his thoughts.

He stopped several feet away, keeping a safe distance as he looked me over. "I've been looking forward to meeting you, Alexa. You're nothing like how I imagined. I'm pleasantly surprised."

"I'm afraid I can't say the same." My response was ice cold. The only thing stopping me from setting the bastard on fire was Shaz. I needed to know he was alive.

"I'm sure you'd like to know how the white wolf is doing. He's surviving. And he'll walk away alive if you make the right decision." There was grim amusement on Linden's face when he appraised the dagger in my hand. "Pretty blade you've got there."

"Thank you." I tightened my grip on the black jade handle. "Would you like a closer look?"

Linden chuckled, a self-satisfied sound that tested my nerves. "We both know you're not going to use that. Not if you want to see your wolf again, which I assume you do. So let's talk business." He spared a glance for Arys and Jenner. "Nice to see you boys again."

"No armed attack tonight, Linden?" Jenner spoke up. "Did you lose too many crew members fucking up my club?"

Linden clapped his hands together once before spreading them wide in a gesture of not giving a fuck. "I'm not here for you tonight, Jenner. Though seeing as you escaped the sun, we apparently do have unfinished business to settle. You," he continued, pointing at me. "I'm here for you."

I steeled myself, ready for ludicrous demands. "Because I killed Harley."

"Because you put a hole in my business. You owe me." It was so cut and dry according to Linden. "I assume you're willing to do what it takes to keep your wolf alive. Are you willing to take his place?"

I laughed. Excitement gripped me as my borrowed power guided my actions. I took a few steps toward Linden, just enough to make his lackeys bristle. "I'm willing to consider letting you walk out of here and carry on your business. After you bring Shaz to me." I caressed the flat part of the dagger blade with a palm. It hummed with a melody only I could hear. It couldn't wait to taste Linden.

Arys was a silent shadow at my side. If he disagreed with my choice of response, he didn't let on. Smart man.

"I see." Linden nodded knowingly. "You think you have leverage here merely because you're the most powerful one in the room. Power comes in many forms. I have it too. Just like I have your wolf. So you can make a choice. Surrender or fight."

I pretended to consider my options. Linden gave the impression that he always got what he wanted. I would have believed it if one of his guys hadn't been thinking very ugly thoughts about him. Someone in Linden's camp didn't enjoy his role in Linden's successes.

Casting a glance around at Arys and Jez, I found them both awaiting my lead. They trusted me to make the right call. It was a lot of pressure. I had to follow my instinct.

Shaz would never have wanted me to give in to demands. I twirled the Dragon Claw in my right hand and held a flaming psi ball in the other. The flames were a nice touch. I hadn't meant to do that.

"Well, Linden, I think we're going to have to fight."

He nodded his dark head as if he'd expected as much. "Kill me, and you'll never find the wolf. At least, you won't find him alive."

I was done talking. I let the psi ball fly, aiming not for Linden but for the big vampire to his left. It exploded against his chest, and he went down beating at the flames.

We all sprang into motion. Linden rushed to meet me. Drawing a gun, he aimed it at my head but never had a chance to shoot before I kicked it out of his grasp. He swung a heavy fist, and I was quick to avoid it.

Arys and Jenner took on Linden's men while Jez watched our backs. I didn't want to kill them all. Not until I dragged Shaz's location out of somebody. I'd never be able to find him the way I had Arys.

Linden was light on his feet and, like most vampires, graceful in his movements. He made a hell of a dance partner. Having no psychic power didn't stop him from being a good opponent. He kept me moving, always defending myself. It gave me little opportunity to focus the overflow of power slamming around inside me.

An attempt at slamming him with a blast missed the mark and hit a nearby table, causing the tablecloth to erupt into fire. *Oops.* I took a punch to the jaw before catching his arm and twisting. I slammed my foot into the back of Linden's leg, and he went down on his knees.

I held the Dragon Claw to his throat. "Careful, Linden. If you get so much as a scratch from this thing, it's all over for you. Now you're going to tell me where Shaz is."

To his credit, Linden refused to utter a word. Jenner and Arys were throwing Linden's guys around with ease. I took advantage of those vital seconds and shoved power into Linden. I'd force my way into his thoughts if I had to.

His resistance was strong. Too strong. Clearly, this was not the first time he'd taken a metaphysical beating.

"You can't kill me," he chortled, finding humor in near death. "I'm a god in this city. An organization like mine doesn't die if I do. But your wolf does."

Shaz was all he had to use against me. He had banked on it being enough. And it was. It was enough to make me fight harder rather than surrender.

The blood ring was a vile creation that turned the hunt into a fetish. It made children and innocents a target of torture and twisted scenarios. Every vampire involved in that deserved to die.

It took very little effort to take hold of Linden's heart with my mind and squeeze. Falon's power enabled me to do with ease what would have otherwise drained much of my strength.

Linden gasped and made a choking sound. I didn't need him to find Shaz. I could still hunt down Roscoe. Linden's heart was seconds from bursting. It gave me a rush of gleeful anticipation. Unfortunately, my amusement died before he did.

"Let him go, Alexa," Sloane's voice rang out above the rest. The bitch had Linden's fallen gun pressed to Jez's temple.

"You traitorous cunt." Venom dripped from Jenner's words.

"Sorry, baby. I didn't want you to find out this way," Sloane purred. "I took a beating last night to keep it from you. Since you survived, I suppose it would have come out eventually."

I released Linden, having no other choice. Nobody moved except one of his guys who came forward to help him. He waved him off, getting up on his own.

Sloane's betrayal didn't come as much of a shock to me as it apparently did to Jenner. He was aghast, jaw dropped in disbelief. Despite their rocky relationship, he must really love her. She had gone to a lot of trouble to hide her alliance with Linden. I knew she was trouble the first moment I laid eyes on her.

"You know Jenner just because you want out of the game doesn't mean everyone does," Linden said, looking quite pleased with himself. "You should know by now how this works."

"You are one evil bitch, Sloane," Jez said. She was unafraid but smart enough not to try anything rash.

Sloane pressed the gun tighter to Jez's head and shrugged. "I like you, Jez, really I do. I'm sorry we didn't get to finish what we started last night. But a woman has got to look out for herself. I hope you understand."

I exchanged a look with Arys. We could do nothing as long as Sloane could blow Jez's brains out in the blink of an eye. All the power drumming through me was useless with my friend's life on the line. I could blast Sloane in a thought but not without risking a shot going off.

"Now," Linden turned to me with a broad, satisfied smile. "What were you saying about a fight?"

Sloane didn't give me a chance to answer. She slammed the gun into the side of Jez's head so hard the crack was audible over the loud music. Jez went down hard, out cold. Blood stained her golden hair.

"You can walk out of here on your own free will, Alexa. Or I can put a bullet in her brain." Sloane kept the gun trained on the fallen leopard. "Don't even think of using that juice you sucked out of the angel either. My finger just might twitch on the trigger."

I nodded, holding my hands still at my sides. "If you kill Jez, it'll be the last thing you ever do."

"I don't doubt it," Sloane agreed. "But she'll still be dead."

"Fine. Let's go. I'm all yours."

Arys's wrath was tangible. Blue and gold electricity twisted and danced about his fingers. I shook my head, imploring him not to endanger Jez further.

"Let me take Harley's place," he announced, drawing every eye his way. "I'll stay in Vegas and resume his supply to your organization. Just leave my wolves out of it."

Shock and horror slapped me. Arys was either desperate or crazy. It didn't matter though because Linden wasn't buying it. With the confident swagger of one who knew he had won this round, he sidled over to Arys. "You tried to shut my blood ring down once. You let your protégé murder your sire. I would never make the mistake of trusting you. In fact, the sooner you get on a flight out of the country, the better for both of your wolves. I'll consider selling them to some of my less sadistic buyers."

"I'm not going anywhere without Alexa. I'm taking over The Wicked Kiss. Jenner has proven he's not fit to run it. I can be a worthy partner." Calm and cool, Arys almost had me convinced he spoke the truth. He'd damn well better be glad I could tell he was lying.

Linden nodded to his guys, and they surrounded me. Not one of them dared to put their hands on me. Smart.

"I'll be taking what I'm owed and leaving now. Arys, you have twenty-four hours to leave my city. I'm being generous." Linden ushered us toward the exit. I moved woodenly. My legs felt heavy.

Arys moved to stop us. Sloane cocked her weapon.

"Don't!" I shouted. Panic echoed in my voice. "Arys, please. You have to let me go." Silently, just from my mind to his, I added, 'Take care of Jez. I'll find Shaz, and we'll get out. You know Shya won't let me die. I'll be ok.'

Arys backed off, but he was miserable. A storm brewed in his midnight gaze. The echo of my wolf showed in his eyes. 'You better find a way out tonight. I'm not going home without you.'

'I love you.'

He didn't say it back, and in that small slight, his weakness was revealed. It was too easy to take Arys down simply by targeting me. I didn't need his affirmation to know he loved me. His love ran deeper than mine; it had burned much longer.

They took me to a super swanky SUV limo parked outside. I was shoved into a dark leather interior and crammed between Linden's guys. The long black seat ran in an L shape down one side of the vehicle, curving behind the driver. A brightly lit bar filled the space across. TV screens mounted in several places played a muted movie.

The scent of cologne and whiskey permeated the car. I wrinkled my nose and tried not to sneeze. I wasn't afraid, which was a pleasant realization. It might have been the angel blood or possibly the fact that I knew I would die by Arys's hand.

Of course, I was certainly wary. A "mob boss" guy like Linden thrived off the fear of others. Even if he didn't kill me, there was little chance of me emerging from this entirely unscathed.

Sloane slipped into the limo behind Linden, and I groaned inwardly. I couldn't stand to look at her Hollywood-chic face. With her makeup expertly in place and a gown that could have graced a red carpet, I couldn't help but wonder why she fought so hard to hide behind illusion. Besides, her soul was ugly; no amount of cosmetics would hide that.

Linden banged on the partition separating us from the driver, and the SUV lurched forward. Then he nudged a lackey who produced a set of government issued FPA handcuffs designed to inhibit the power of someone like me.

"You're a fucking FPA agent, aren't you? Son of a bitch." I surrounded myself with a shield of energy that cast a warm glow throughout the vehicle.

"I am." Linden nodded and pulled a cell phone from his pocket. "I see you're familiar with these." He gestured to the cuffs. "So you know why I have to insist you wear them. We can all play nice, or I can make a call and have a body part removed from the wolf. Your call."

He held the phone ready, finger poised to hit send. I burned with boiling hot hatred. And I dropped my shield. I held my hands out before me, allowing those wretched cuffs to imprison my power for the third time. Perhaps I should have taken Briggs up on his offer to help. Somehow, I didn't think he knew the Las Vegas unit had a vampire like Linden in their employ, or that he was running a very shady underground side business.

"I'm happy to see you can be reasonable," Linden continued, smiling like I wasn't giving him a death glare. "This doesn't have to be all bad, you know. I have many clients that treat their blood slaves quite well."

"Does the FPA know about your business venture?" I asked, refusing to be intimidated by him in any way. "I didn't think they were into that kind of thing, though from what I've seen, one can never be sure with them."

Linden began to select bottles from the bar, holding them up as an offering. I recognized a pricey whiskey that I used to drink back at Raoul's house, long before he had died. I nodded to that one.

"No, the FPA tries to uphold their squeaky clean mission statement. My business is only mine." He poured a generous amount of whiskey into a crystal glass and pressed it into my hands. "Although, being FPA does have its perks. As you can see."

It certainly did. I wouldn't mind having a set of FPA handcuffs myself, just in case. When I got home, I'd have to see if Briggs would be willing to slip me a pair. He would have his price of course.

I tried to hear the thoughts of those surrounding me. Since Sloane's mention of angel blood, they had all shut up their minds tightly.

Speaking of angels, where the hell was Falon? The asshole had ditched me. Letting Linden sell me off as a blood slave would get me out of his hair. He was probably concocting a story for Shya right now.

Shya was a strange one. He could go from threatening my life to claiming he needed me alive in the same sentence. I didn't doubt that he would come for me at some point. However, I was not his damsel to save, and I would rather die than be further indebted to the demon.

A shrill, piercing screech bounced around inside my head as Falon's blood became too much for my mortal body. It needed release. I sipped the fine whiskey and squinted through the pain.

I swung my accusing stare to Sloane who sat stiffly near the door. As much as I loathed that bitch right then, I knew she was my only shot at manipulating someone on the inside. Whether we liked it or not, we shared a bloodline. Appealing to that side of her might be my only chance at finding an ally among so many monsters.

"What is wrong with you? You betrayed your own blood. For what? Money? Blood? Power? And why the hell would you take a beating to hide your disloyalty if you're so ok with it?"

With an exasperated and forced sigh, she met my eyes. "You wouldn't understand. You haven't lived with them for hundreds of years. You're still new to them, a novelty. That wears off." Her glossy lips pressed tight into a thin red line, and she stared out the window at the bright city lights. She hadn't given me much, but it was enough. She was hurt and lashing out. Maybe I could work with that.

"My girl does what it takes to keep a secret." Linden beamed a fangy grin at Sloane who ignored it. "She knows loyalty comes at a price."

Linden loved to hear the sound of his own voice. He had no trouble carrying on a conversation consisting mostly of his stream of consciousness as we drove through the city. The first prickle of nervousness trickled through me when I noticed the area we had entered. It was littered with large commercial buildings and warehouses with very little human activity, where nobody would hear you scream.

I tossed back the last of the superb whiskey, knowing it might be my last. I wanted to tap Arys's thoughts but decided to wait. I didn't want to interrupt if he was healing Jez.

Jostled along by two big but quiet vampires, I followed Linden into one of the warehouses that looked much like the rest. A building number was its only identification, and I made a point to commit it to memory. There was nothing special about the warehouse. It was big without being massive, drab grey from the concrete walls to the floor and smelled like absolute fear.

Consisting of half a dozen vampires, further security greeted us. Linden spoke in low tones with one of them, and I heard the mention of a white wolf. My guts twisted painfully. I was afraid, not for me, but for Shaz. It had been my call to kill Harley. He didn't deserve to be punished for having my back.

The warehouse was made up primarily of one giant room, which was furnished with many sofas and electronic devices, TVs and such. A long conference style table sat along one wall. Lining the back of the building, a brick room caught my attention. That's where the thick aroma of fear emanated from.

I drifted toward the heavily barred door, needing to see what lie on the other side. A vampire with a fat head on his oddly skinny neck stopped me with a rough hand on my shoulder.

"No, it's fine." Linden glided over, taking my elbow as if we were old friends out for a stroll. "You want to see the wolf. I understand." He barked instructions for the door to be opened.

I held my breath, afraid to inhale too much of the intoxicating scent. Fear was a trigger for both the wolf and the vampire. It stirred my hunger for the hunt.

The door opened, and I was pulled into a dank, dimly lit room. It was filled with people, all human. Old, young, of various ethnic backgrounds, there was much variation. My gaze landed on a woman in the corner, crying and holding her pregnant belly. The vampire side of me had no emotion, no sympathy, but the wolf raged and roared, seeking to break free of its human cage.

"You're the worst kind of evil," I said.

Linden continued as if I hadn't said a word. "That's the bathroom there, if you should need it. Otherwise, I'll take you to the wolf. Naturally, I couldn't leave him in here with the others. Better safe than sorry." The bathroom he pointed out was little more than a filthy toilet and sink with a curtain for a door. I recoiled at the sight of it.

In the back of the grubby room was a row of prison-like cells, each with a flimsy cot and a scrap of cloth that could hardly be called a blanket. They were all empty save one. In the last cell paced a dirty, bloody, but very much alive white wolf.

Chapter Fourteen

I threw myself on the floor beside Shaz the moment the door opened. The heavy bars banged shut as they relocked behind me.

His name was repetition on my lips, and I grabbed a handful of his fur, pressing my face to his. He nuzzled me back, making a low sound between a whine and a growl. Pine, wolf musk and blood. He smelled injured yet alive, but most importantly he smelled like home.

"I'll give you two some time. You should make the most of it. I doubt you will go to the same buyer." Linden turned to go, then paused and glanced back. "There are a great many people interested in you both. I can't wait to hear the offers. Of course, they'll have to wait their turn. I always get the first taste of the high demand ones."

The urge to spit a nasty retort after him was strong. Somehow I held my tongue and watched him go. The human cattle he had piled into this brick prison all turned away from him as he passed. One older man openly prayed out loud as if casting out the devil himself. Linden was unfazed.

"Can you shift?" I asked Shaz when the vampires were gone.

He did so with an agonized howl that became a shout as he resumed human form. Several gasps and shrieks rang out from our fellow captives. One young girl promptly burst into tears. It was easy to forget that the world of vampires and werewolves was brand new to these people.

I grabbed the scrap of blanket from the cot and covered his nakedness with it. Having my hands bound in front of me was a small blessing. I looked him over for any sign of a serious injury. Other than a few vampire bites in miscellaneous places and much bruising, he was in one piece.

Before I could speak again, Shaz kissed me. It was a soft, tender show of emotion. His lips trembled slightly on mine. His weakness was a disadvantage if we were going to fight our way out of here.

"Is there something you need to tell me?" He asked, peering in wonder at my eyes. "I've never seen that before."

"I took blood from Falon," I whispered so I would not be overheard. "It's risky, but it gives me strength and abilities I don't have on my own. Unfortunately, I can't use any power as long as I have these handcuffs on. Tell me what's happened to you."

Shaz leaned heavily against me. Pushing his hands through my hair, he nuzzled me with wolfish affection, sighing as he inhaled my scent. "After they trashed the nightclub, they took Arys and Jenner. Those two put up a good fight, but they were swarmed. Honestly, I think Arys held back because they threatened to kill me. I know he had the power to wipe them all out. He never tried."

I was too stunned to reply. Arys had also said he and Jenner were outnumbered, though he hadn't added much more. I too had believed Arys would be much harder to take down. His power had centuries of growth on mine. Could it be possible that he was willing to face potential death to keep Shaz alive? Or was he merely seeking a way out of what the future held for us?

"I was brought here and have been here since. What happened to Arys?" The concern on Shaz's face was genuine. When did the two of them start to give a damn about each other?

Speaking quickly but quietly, I told him the rushed version of the previous evening leading up to this moment. "If Falon was here, he could get these things off me; he's done it before. But I think that fucker sold me out." What Falon didn't realize was that this meant war. I'd pay him back for leaving me hanging. Somehow.

"We can't let them separate us," Shaz said, desperation in his touch as he wrapped himself around me. "And we can't leave them behind either."

He nodded to the captives huddled outside our cell. Some of them stared at us in raw horror while others were more focused on the door, knowing the true danger lay beyond. I counted half a dozen youth among the mix of adults, about twenty in total. How were we going to get them all out of here? My brain turned over the possibilities. There had to be a way.

An onslaught of thoughts battered me. They came fast, a cacophony of fear and prayers. It was impossible to sort them out or follow one string of thought. It was overwhelming and took great effort to block it out. How could I have forgotten how bad the mind reading aspect was?

Healing Shaz was a priority. I had yet to perfect the skill, but I'd made some progress. Still, as long as I had the damn cuffs on we were screwed.

Another shrill head-splitting wave of pain cut through me as my body rebelled against Falon's caged power. Shaz's jade eyes were wolf and heavy with concern. I thought about how much I'd missed him while he was gone and how I'd known it was best for him, and I felt guilty that he was here now with me. If he had stayed gone, he would be free as a wolf should be. He should never have been a victim of such vampire blood games.

Protector of mankind. The words rose up in my thoughts, an echo of a memory. Willow had said that's what my name meant. I'd scoffed at the time, finding it hard to believe I could ever be anything other than a menace to mankind. Looking at all of those innocent victims, I knew I had to find a way to justify the name I'd been given. The vampire world had swallowed me whole, but I was not one of them. Not yet. I was a Hound of God, a wolf chosen to serve good by battling evil. Linden was evil. I would destroy him.

"Shaz, there's so much I haven't told you since you've been back. I learned a lot while you were gone. You should know. I should tell you." I was rambling uncontrollably. All the things I wanted to say for several weeks now came bubbling up. I was afraid I wouldn't get another chance.

"Hey, slow down." With a finger on my lips, Shaz stopped me. "You can tell me everything after we get out of here." He held me tight, and I tried to focus on his calming scent. The pungent smell of crippling fear was testing my control.

For a long time, we simply held one another. It felt so good to be in his arms. It would have felt better if it had been anywhere else.

A cool wind whispered through me followed by Arys's voice in my head. 'Tell me you're ok.'

'I am for now. I'm with Shaz in a warehouse in some commercial district. But Arys, things are bad. Linden is FPA. He's got me cuffed, and Falon is a no show. How's Jez?'

Arys's displeasure rang in my thoughts. 'She'll be fine. Still a bit out of it. She wants to go after you but can barely stay on her feet. I'm wrestling cocktails out of her hand so I think she'll bounce back. Let me see where you are.'

I opened myself up to him, allowing him to see through my eyes. Together we regarded the miserable humans awaiting their fate. Lingering on the pregnant lady and the youth present, I felt Arys recoil in disgust. He was a brutal, ruthless serial killer, no denying that. But he didn't hunt kids. Ever.

'It gets uglier. I've seen it. I want to come in after you.'

'No, Arys, you can't. You heard Linden. It will just put us at greater risk. And we have innocents here. You and Jenner should hunt down Roscoe. See if there's anything he knows that can give you some kind of leverage over Linden.' I waited for his response. He was quiet in my head though his agitation came across just fine.

'All right. Try to lure Falon, or Shya if you have to. Use that mark. And keep in touch. If anything changes, if Linden does anything to you, I want to know.' There was a pause. 'I can feel the pressure building from Falon's power. It's hurting you.'

It sure was. My head ached, and it was just a matter of time until the nosebleeds started. 'Don't worry about me. I don't die this way. Remember?' I wanted to ask him about sacrificing himself for Shaz, but this wasn't the right time.

'Don't remind me. Be safe. Trust your instinct.' I sensed he wanted to add something else. After a moment he said, 'I love you.' He was gone, slipping away as swift and smooth as he'd slipped in.

Shaz and I moved from the cold stone floor to the bare mattress atop the cot. We huddled there together, watching and waiting for something, anything to happen. The waiting was killing me. I held tight to Shaz's hand and tried to ignore the metal cuffs digging into my wrists.

"When I was in Jasper, there were times when I thought I might not come back," Shaz began. "I spent so much time as wolf that I started to forget human life. But I never forgot you, Lex."

"I counted the days while you were gone." I laughed, a short clipped laugh lacking mirth. "Hell, I counted the hours. I was afraid I would never see you again. When Arys let it slip that the two of you had been in touch, I was pissed. But I understand now."

"I needed to know you were ok. I missed you."

"I missed you too."

"I'll never leave you like that again," he promised, kissing my face. "I know I can be what I need to be. For you. For myself. I think I know who I am now."

I thought about his readiness to fight at Jenner's, his desire for that kill. It made me uneasy. Had Arys and I done that to him, or was he growing into his own as a predator?

"Shaz, you've got to do what's best for you, always. Ok?"

"You are what's best for me. It was always you, Lex. Before there were vampires and demons in our daily lives, there was you and me." His fist clenched in my hair, his mouth warm on my neck.

The genuine affection in his touch washed away the remnants of our past mistakes. For the first time since he'd come back, I saw promise in what we shared. I bit back the onslaught of emotion that threatened. I could cry later. Now, it was time for kicking some ass.

Voices rose beyond the door. Panic seized me. The humans grew louder in their worried protests. Their distressed thoughts were loud inside my head. If only I could silence it.

Linden strode in with two well-dressed vampires in tow. They were clad in black tie attire. Both of them looked our way but were ultimately unimpressed.

Pointing to three different women, Linden said, "You, you and you. Up against the wall. You know the drill." Two of the women were on their feet immediately. The third, a thirty-something with auburn hair, glared at Linden with open hostility. She refused to comply. I watched with trepidation as he grabbed her by the hair and hauled her up. He threw her against the wall, and she stifled a scream. "This one is a fighter," Linden said with a laugh. "Guess we'll have to break that wild spirit."

"You can kill me, but you will never break me," she spat. She stared at the vampires with utter hatred. Her fierceness was admirable.

One of the potential buyers nodded enthusiastically. "I like her already. It's been a while since I've had one that put up a good fight."

I was frozen, helpless, able only to watch. Though I admired her warrior spirit, what she didn't know was that these guys would take their sweet time killing her. They would break her a thousand times over before death freed her.

Linden reached to take her arm, and she spat in his face, following up with a resounding smack that echoed. The sudden rage that burst from him was explosive. The backhand he threw knocked her to the ground with a shriek. I held my breath, fighting back the protests on my tongue.

Everyone else in the room seemed to shrink as far away from the scene as possible. A couple of the kids began to cry. Their thoughts were a mass of confusion, questions that were words and feelings rather than full phrases. The sense of helplessness grew. What could I do to protect them when I couldn't protect myself?

Linden whistled, and a few of his security guys entered. "Teach this one that she's no longer a person. She has no rights. She's just meat."

It was hard to get a good feel of a vampire's age and power without being able to metaphysically touch them. Yet, it appeared that Linden's personnel was primarily muscle, not brand new vampires but not yet a hundred either. If he had any serious power players in his arsenal, they were elsewhere for a reason. These guys seemed like expendable help.

Picking Linden's crew apart wasn't giving me any great insights into him, but it did tell me a little about his people. At his command, right away one of them began to undo his pants, which elicited a series of protests and cries from the captives. Much to my surprise, one vampire agreed with them.

"Not in front of the kids," he said, meeting Linden's stony gaze with one to match.

"Fine. Get them out of here. Find them something to eat. Nobody likes them malnourished." The command was issued as if it had been his idea. Linden wasn't fooling me anymore. He was the boss here, but he didn't call all the shots.

I stared after the vampire now leading the youth from the room that was their prison. Dark haired with a chiseled jaw and confident set to his shoulders, he guided them along with a gentle hand. How curious. I hadn't for a moment expected to find a shred of humanity here among the inhuman. It was a small spark of light in a dark place, and it renewed my hope.

At least it did until the door closed and the sick scenario resumed. It took three vampires to hold her down. She fought so hard. It was amazing. Unfortunately, it earned her a beating. More than one captive was brave enough to intervene. Needless to say, it didn't go well for them. They were tossed aside like ragdolls.

I was on my feet, throwing myself against the bars. "What kind of monster needs to rape a woman like some common thug to make a point? You make a mockery of what it means to be a vampire, Linden. You fucking coward."

"Is that right?" Holding up a hand, he stopped his men from tearing the woman's clothes off. "That's an interesting accusation coming from a creature who is a master of manipulation. Is making a victim want it any less of a violation?"

Guilty as charged. He was right, and I knew it. But I wasn't here to argue right and wrong with this wackjob. "How bad do you want to find out?" I taunted, slamming my cuffs against the bars. The sound reverberated through the room. "Get these off and see for yourself."

He chuckled, an eerie sound that was almost gleeful. "I don't think so. I will however make this personal for you, seeing as you could use a little spirit breaking yourself." Linden nodded to two of his guys. "Bring the male wolf out here."

Linden's clients stood back and watched with interest as Shaz was dragged from the cage. I fought to get out but was forced back by a gun in my face. Any vampire that needed a human weapon to subdue another was a cowardly piece of shit. I would kill them all.

They made Shaz stand there naked in front of everyone with several weapons aimed at him. His expression was hard, unreadable. But his eyes were all wolf.

"Now then, finish what they started," Linden commanded with a gesture to the woman pinned on the floor.

"Are you fucking crazy?" Shaz stood firm, staring down the vampire with ease. "That's not going to happen."

One of Linden's clients spoke up, a strange lilt in his voice. "Make him do it as wolf."

I wanted to vomit. If there had been anything in my stomach, I likely would have. The expression on Shaz's face indicated he felt the same.

"I'm not hurting anyone," Shaz said, stubborn refusal creasing his brow. "I'll die first."

"If you won't do it, I'll have it done to her." Linden pointed a finger at me. I had one for him as well.

"Go ahead and try. You really have no idea what she will do to you." Shaz laughed, something that seemed to surprise some of the vamps. He spoke through bared fangs. "Fuck. You."

Linden's gaze flicked back and forth between Shaz and me. In a blur of motion, Linden threw a punch that knocked Shaz back several feet. He nodded, an unspoken command, and his guys moved in to finish what he started.

They took turns hitting and kicking Shaz. Once he was on the floor, my wolf was throwing herself against my insides, desperate to break free and come to his aid. But she couldn't. Together we were caged, watching and praying.

A whimper sounded low in my throat. I tried to squelch it, knowing my distress was what Linden wanted. Blood red tears brimmed in my eyes, and I blinked them away. They would not fall now.

Unwilling to lay there and die, Shaz shifted to wolf. It gave him a burst of strength, and he rounded on the vampires snarling and snapping. It wasn't enough though. They had already done too much damage. They came at him from every side. The crunch of bone was audible as a booted foot slammed into his ribs again and again. A shrill yelp rang above the cacophony of panicked voices. It was a knife in my heart. My wolf was hurting, and I couldn't get to him.

"That's enough," Linden said, bringing the beating to an end.

"As much fun as this has been, we've got to be going." One of the waiting clients announced. "We'll take that one."

The auburn-haired woman was jerked off the floor and forced from the room after them. I watched her go, feeling like I'd failed her.

"I knew you wouldn't be worth the trouble," Linden said with a scowl my way. "If the interest in you wasn't so high, I would kill you and save myself this hassle."

"You know you can't take me," I spat. "That's why you have me bound and caged, isn't it? I killed Harley, and you know I can kill you. Too bad for you, Linden, your greed has already put the price on your head. I will kill anyone you sell me to, and then I'll come back for you. I promise."

Without a word, he turned his back on me and left. Needing no instruction, his lackeys filed out behind him. When the door closed, I slumped against the bars and sighed.

Shaz's sides heaved. He was on the floor, in and out of consciousness. He needed healing. If I lost him here, if he died this way because of me, I would never forgive myself.

One of the women standing against the wall dropped to her knees beside him. She slid out of her jacket and placed it beneath Shaz's head. He growled and whimpered, yet she was unafraid.

"Are you the same?" She asked, her gentle eyes meeting mine. "A wolf, like he is."

"Yes," I heard myself say. It may have been the very first time I told a human that I was not one of them. "I am."

I was curious about her. Why was she here? It took great effort to search for her thoughts in the mess of voices in my head. They jumbled together until they were just white noise. Then I heard it, her voice. Her kind heart was born of a desire to serve others, to care for them. She was a woman of God, a nun who took care of those in need.

I didn't think I could be any more disgusted with Linden, but I was. That likely meant the woman he had just sold off was one too. Evil wore many faces. At times, it even wore mine. This was my opportunity to be what so many proclaimed me to be, an ambassador of the light.

"We're going to get out of here," I told her. "All of us."

She searched my eyes and bit her lower lip. Then she nodded. We had no choice but to trust each other.

Sloane entered with two of the children in tow. She snapped at them to sit down and behave before gliding over to me. She was careful to stand a few feet away from the bars.

"I know it doesn't mean anything, but I just wanted to apologize. This was never supposed to be personal. I'm sure there's a valid reason why Arys is so in love with you. I'm sure you can be quite lovely." When I didn't respond, she ignored my silent glare and continued. "If you hadn't killed Harley, Jenner and I would never have been at odds. I wouldn't have had to lie to him. You belong here. But Arys is family, so I'm sorry it has to be this way."

"You know Arys. He won't be getting on any plane out of here without me." I curled my fingers around the bars and stared at Sloane like she was prey. Because she was now.

She began to fidget with her blonde waves before brushing a non-existent thread from her skirt. Anything to avoid my eyes. "Yes, well, there are ways of dealing with him. Without you around, there's nothing to stop the sun from having him next time, is there?"

I couldn't bring myself to feign surprise. Vampires were not known for their lasting loyalty. They were very much a dog-eat-dog kind of species.

"Well, seeing as you plan to stand by and benefit from my being sold into slavery, think you can fake some humanity and heal my wolf? He doesn't deserve to suffer." It was a long shot, but I had to try.

Sloane looked confused. She shook her head making her waves bounce. "There are very few healers among our line. I am not one of them."

I bit back an accusation. I had to think back. Had I ever seen another vampire in our bloodline heal other than Arys and Harley? Healing wasn't a trademark of the undead by any means. I had just assumed it was possible with great enough power.

I sat back on the cot, which creaked and groaned under my weight. A spring stuck up through the flimsy mattress into my thigh.

"You know I'm going to kill you, right?" I wanted her to go away. These Vegas vampires were growing tiresome.

She turned to go, pausing by the door. All eyes were on her, the enemy. "If things had been different, I'm sure we would have been great friends, Alexa. This city has been my home for over a century. It took me a long time to rise up in the ranks here. Staying on top meant maintaining ties with Linden. I don't expect you to understand."

"Oh, but I do," I called after her, a menacing grin curved my lips. "I too have a position to protect. It started with your sire. It will continue with you."

Sloane didn't waste time with petty comebacks or elaborate threats. It was nice, almost respectful. She simply left the room without a second glance.

Another wave of pain racked my skull, and a few drops of blood fell from my nose to stain the concrete. I was desperate. Twisting my hands at an awkward angle, I managed to get a clawed fingertip to touch the dragon on my forearm. Blood welled up from the wound. It was immediately followed by a searing pain and the stench of sulfur.

"This has to work," I said through clenched teeth.

It did. The air moved, and for the first time, I was relieved by it. Falon appeared with a curse. He slapped my hand away from the demon mark with a hiss.

"Do you want to reign down hellfire on your ass? Shya will torture you in so many ways for tampering with that mark. As much as I'd love that, I'd probably join you."

"Where the fuck did you go? Were you just going to leave me here to be sold off to some twisted vampire who will use me as a blood slave?" I was furious and also a little scared. I thrust my bound wrists at Falon. "Get these off of me."

Falon's sudden arrival had set off a series of shrieks and wails. He silenced them all with a look. Pinning me with angry silver eyes, he crossed his arms and glared. "Let's get one thing straight. I don't work for you, bitch. I am damn good at what I do. I get shit done, and I don't take orders from hybrid scum."

There was no time to argue. I continued to thrust my cuffed hands at him, clamping my mouth shut so I wouldn't call him the many foul names that came to mind. The kids were traumatized enough as it was.

With a muttered, "Fuck," Falon grasped the cuffs and snapped them off as if they were made of plastic. Power flowed freely through me again, and it took great restraint to keep from setting the cot on fire.

"Thank you." I rubbed my sore wrists and pointed to the locked prison door.

Falon snickered. He produced the Dragon Claw as if from a place unseen and tossed it on the cot. "Shya's instructions were to give you what you need to stay alive. I've done that. Now you're on your own. If you die, it's not my problem." He lowered his voice as if telling a grand secret. "I kind of hope you do."

Gone, just like that. The same vicious side of me that promised Sloane death added payback for Falon to my hit list. I couldn't kill him, but I would find a way to make him sorry for treating me like such shit.

"Was that...? Was he...?" The nun was ghostly pale, gaping in wonder. The name Sue rose up from the myriad of voices. Her name was Sue.

"A demon? Yes. Well, no. But he might as well be." I did a double-take when I saw her hands go together in prayer. "Hey, lady, please do not ever mistake him or anyone like him for a true angel. He is the enemy."

"I never thought they would look so human," she mumbled, blinking rapidly.

"Yeah well, it's a lie."

I concentrated on the lock that stood between me and a shot at freedom. The power went out from me, leaping erratically. It took great strength to focus it on only the lock. This was no time for accidental casualties. There was a spark of gold light and a loud metallic clang. The lock gave way. I bit back a cry of victory.

Carefully, I eased the door open. I kept expecting Linden's lackeys to burst in and catch me. The Dragon Claw felt good in my hand, ready. Unfortunately, it caused some unease in my fellow captives.

"We're getting out of here," I said, looking at them all in turn. "We have to work together."

"How the hell did you do that?" One man with a scruffy beard and a black eye asked as he watched me walk free of the tiny prison cell. "What are you?"

I sighed. It seemed that I could never escape that question. It passed the lips of many when I was around. "I'm a werewolf." A simple answer was the best answer. "I just have a few extra bonus add ons. Upgrades, you could say."

"Like in a video game?" This from the cutest little boy with a Batman t-shirt and the bluest eyes I'd ever seen on a human. "Are you the good guy?"

I stared, frozen, into his innocence. If he knew the many horrific things I'd done, he would definitely categorize me as a villain. In a world of black and white, there was no place for one like me. I walked in both worlds. Everything in me felt inclined to protect him. To protect all of them. Willow was right. I knew it then.

"You got it, kid. I'm one of the good guys."

I knelt beside Shaz, setting the dagger aside. His breath came too fast and shallow. His eyes rolled back in his head. I couldn't get him to look at me.

Healing had proved difficult for me. It came from a place of life and nature, taking precise concentration and intent. I had done it before, with Arys's guidance. Sloane's revelation encouraged me. It meant that the ability to heal had been meant for Arys and me, somehow. It was a gift.

I can do this.

I placed my hands on Shaz, clenching his bloodstained fur between my fingers. Taking several deep breaths, I counted backwards from ten and prayed nobody would come through that door.

It was easy to feel and touch his broken energy. Aligning it to mine, I pushed a gentle, warm flow of light into his battered body. The constant chatter of voices in my head beat at my focus. I fought to shut it out. The wolf within demanded my attention. She heard nothing, saw nothing, only Shaz. The connection between us grew stronger. Power flowed out from me, seeking and finding its target, breathing health and vitality into this wolf that I loved with every part of me left that was wolf and human. The sound of other people's thoughts faded. Shaz was all I knew. My being was devoted to keeping him alive. Nothing else proved stronger than that devotion. I steadied the flow between us, giving all I had until his energy hummed happily once again.

I collapsed beside him, my head in my hands, and blood running steadily from my nose. My ragged breaths became gasps, and I coughed.

Thanks to the angel blood crashing through my veins, the exhaustion was short lived. I recovered quickly. The burn out that followed the inevitable crash from so much power was going to be brutal. So I'd better make it worth it.

Chapter Fifteen

"Trust Shaz," I said. "He'll get you out of here. And take care of each other. Nobody gets left behind."

I stood near the door, speaking to the group of frightened captives. The Dragon Claw was ready in my hand for when the door opened again. At my side was Shaz, as wolf, strong and alert.

I didn't have much of a plan. I would take on Linden and his guys, keep them busy while Shaz led the humans out of the warehouse. It was growing harder to restrain the force within me. If I never took blood from an angel again, it would be too soon.

For the better part of an hour, I'd listened to stories. The men and women told tales of being kidnapped and abused at the hands of Linden and his crew. They'd been lined up against the wall while vampires ogled them. Harsh punishments were handed out to those that dared to fight back.

Linden was a crime lord in his own right. He took human trafficking to another level. Taking him out wouldn't be enough to abolish an organization like this. Still, I couldn't go home and pretend it didn't exist while they treated innocents like cattle.

Innocent blood was on my hands too. I would not make the error of having a holier than thou attitude toward Linden. My mistakes were just that though. Mistakes. When I hunted with the intent to lure and kill, I chose ones with blood on their own hands.

Touching base with Arys, I assured him I was fine. He and Jenner had found Roscoe who had yet to give them anything on Linden. Arys was still of the mind that he needed to come for me. Having to stay away and wait it out was driving him mad. I refused to put the kids at greater risk. There was no way to predict what Linden may do if Arys arrived on the scene.

My palm grew sweaty on the dagger handle. I was nervous but eager. I didn't have to wait much longer for a vampire to return with the rest of the children. Standing behind the door, I waited for it to close and expose me.

I was on the guy before he could react to seeing me out of the cell. Shoving the dagger into its sheath, I grabbed his head and snapped his neck, letting him fall. Then I swiped his phone, keys and gun so they wouldn't be lost in the destruction of his body when I dusted him.

"Who knows how to use this?" I offered the gun to the first guy who held up a hand with a semblance of confidence. "You take the rear. Cover everyone else on the way out. Especially the kids and that lady there." I motioned to the pregnant lady who wore a hard, stern expression. She was braver than I ever would have been in her place. "A gun isn't the best weapon against vampires, but a good face shot or two can buy you some time."

A broken neck also wouldn't keep a vampire down long. A quick swipe of the Dragon Claw's blade ensured he wouldn't be a future problem. His dusty remains had both the kids and adults fascinated. They would never look at the world the same again after this night.

"Stay here until Shaz comes back for you," I reminded them one last time. "We'll clear a path out of the warehouse."

I met Shaz's calm green eyes. He inclined his head in a wolfish nod, and I slowly eased the door open. I could see half of the lengthy table from the tiny crack in the door. Just one vampire sat there. He was engrossed in whatever was on his smartphone screen. A few others lingered near the door. It creaked as I opened it, and they turned to catch me sneaking up on them.

So much for a sneak attack. I flung the door wide, hands crackling with power. Shaz raced past me, lunging at the closest vampire. Hitting him full in the chest, Shaz took him down with a snarl, tearing the guy's throat out with a vicious snap of jaws.

I hit the others with a fiery blast that engulfed them all. An exhilarating rush of power flowed from me, seeking and finding its target. It was a relief to rid myself of the angelic force. It didn't belong to me, and I needed it out of my head.

A shout rang out from the one at the table. I threw a flaming psi ball at his head, and it hit with an uncanny precision and strength. His head burst into flames, the rest of him was quick to follow. The smartphone clattered to the floor.

My last experience with angel blood hadn't gone quite this smooth. Either this was dumb luck or my control was improving. Considering how bad it had once been, this was nice. I could get used to the power.

With the Dragon Claw, I finished off the one with his throat splayed open. Shaz and I turned to find half a dozen or so blocking the main exit. We could handle those odds.

With every shot of Falon's power that I used, the pressure in my head subsided. I hit the entire group of them with a blast that almost winded me. They all went down in a flaming pile. I didn't doubt for a moment that Falon could throw fire. However, I'd never witnessed it myself. I was a little bummed that it wasn't one of my abilities. It was damn handy.

"Go, get them out of here," I told Shaz, turning to find a few more vamps heading in from the back of the building. "I've got these guys."

The newcomers got hit with a face full of fire. One of them fell against the couch, and the flames began to spread. I expected more and found the brief reprieve to be unsettling. Was that all Linden had for manpower here?

I wiped my bleeding nose with the back of my hand. When I became a vampire, I would never miss that side effect of a mortal using immortal power.

Shaz led the captives in a steady line to the front exit. They ran for their lives, following the white wolf that promised them freedom.

Smoke was beginning to fill the warehouse. I coughed and tried to limit my breaths. My eyes burned and began to water. The fire consumed the couch and jumped to the next flammable thing in its path.

I ran back to the prison room to confirm that everyone was out. It was empty. I ran back to the dirty little bathroom to double check. Empty. Relief crushed me.

I turned and fled the room, intent on the exit. Linden stepped out in front of me, and I had to jerk to a halt to avoid colliding with him. On his face was a giant, shit-eating grin, and in his arms was a struggling child.

"Well done, Alexa." The flames cast Linden in a macabre light. "I don't know how you did it, but you certainly are adept at playing the heroine. But you've forgotten one thing. You can't save them all."

The young boy wailed, tears streaming down his chubby cheeks. It was the same kid who had asked me if I was one of the good guys. I didn't give Linden a chance to follow through with his intent or his bad-guy dialogue. I threw myself at him, taking him and the child down to the ground. Landing between us, the kid was fine, just terribly frightened.

Wrapping my hands around Linden's throat, I slammed his skull against the hard floor repeatedly until he released his hold on the boy. Shaz appeared and dragged the kid away by the back of his shirt.

The smoke thickened, making it difficult to see. Every breath made my chest ache. My wolf recoiled, instinctively demanding that we flee the burning building. Letting Linden go to save myself would be a favor to nobody. He would only be free to start anew, in a new building with a new batch of victims. Perhaps he was just one of many involved in this sick business. All it took to send a message to the rest was the right hit. I had to hope Linden was it.

"You should never have let me know you exist," I snarled, slamming his head one more time. Blood stained the floor beneath him.

I set my sights on his heart and reached with my power to destroy it. The flow of energy was smooth and on target, yet it fell flat. Like hitting a psychic wall, my power hit an impenetrable block.

Linden stared up into my confused face and nodded. His voice was strained from my grip on his throat when he croaked, "You're not the only rare breed walking around out there, you know."

Before I could draw the dagger, he slammed a heavy fist into the side of my head. It dazed me, allowing him to roll me to his side. He hit me with a smattering of blows that caused a bright light to flash behind my eyes. I kicked out in his general direction, connecting with his knee. A crack followed by a shriek was always good news.

The sound of the Dragon Claw sliding from its sheath sent a surge of panic through me. I rolled away from Linden and pushed to my feet, but not before my own dagger tasted my blood. It pierced my side, a flesh wound, thanks to quick reflexes. Warm, wet blood seeped through my shirt. Ignoring it, I danced back out of reach as Linden swung the dagger again.

The fire had crawled along the walls to the ceiling, which didn't appear to be made of the sturdiest material. As pieces began to fall and smash against the floor, my need to flee the building grew. Linden had the advantage here; he didn't need to breathe. I coughed harder as my body rejected the smoky air.

"You had help getting this in here. Based on the mark on your arm, I'm thinking demon." Linden cut the air in a figure eight with the Dragon Claw. "So where is this demon now? It doesn't seem that he's coming to save you."

"I don't need a fucking demon to save me." My lungs burned, and I could barely get the words out.

I glanced at the roof above us. It was still holding for now. Maybe I could do something about that. Focusing the last of Falon's power on the roof, I willed it to come down in a burning heap on top of Linden. I planned to go for the door as soon as I felt it give. It might not work—I could be digging my own grave—but keeping him inside was the best way to give the others a chance to flee to safety.

"I change my mind," Linden announced. "I'm going to keep you for myself. It's become very apparent why Harley wanted you so badly. I am going to love breaking you." For a species that was good at secret keeping, they were also very adept gossipers. I should just start assuming anyone that knew Arys or Harley knew way too much about me.

Linden rushed me, breaking my concentration. I threw an arm up to block the Dragon Claw. The blade bit into my forearm, and I yelped. Mother fucker that hurt.

In a desperate move, I swept his legs out from under him with a kick. He lost his balance but recovered quickly. With preternatural speed, he was at my back with the dagger blade pressed to my throat.

"Don't make me kill you," he said, the picture of health compared to my choking, injured self. "We could have fun together. I'll even forget about how many of my men you killed tonight."

I couldn't see his face, but that didn't make him any less threatening. Another series of coughs racked me, and the blade cut into my skin. In response to his offer, I held up a middle finger. The heat was unbearable. Lack of oxygen was making me dizzy. I felt the blade slide across my throat and thought it was all over.

A loud crack from above was accompanied by falling debris. It hit us with more force than I'd anticipated. It knocked the Dragon Claw from Linden's hand, and I scrambled to pick it up. As my fingers closed around the hilt, a large piece of metal crashed into my skull.

Wiping tears from my burning eyes, I whirled to find Linden holding a piece of debris ready for another smack. Unable to breathe, I lurched toward the exit, or at least where I thought it should be. Linden followed, determined to keep me from escaping him. I swung the dagger and just barely missed him. *Shit!*

I fell to my knees, fighting to see my way out and avoid the next blow headed my way. The outline of a wolf loomed in the distance. The exit must have been farther than I thought. Shaz dodged fallen debris and flames as he came to my aid. With fangs bared and a growl rumbling in his throat, he leaped at Linden, knocking him away from me. The two of them struggled. There was a crack of bone.

The roar of flames was loud in my ears. Every snap and crackle promised a horrible fate. I heaved myself toward the door, the dagger dragging on the floor behind me. A hand wrapped around my ankle, jerking me back. Linden fought hard. With Shaz on his back, attacking furiously, he pulled me close. I swung wildly with the dagger, connecting with rubble.

The warehouse groaned. The screech of twisting metal pierced my ears. I looked up in time to see the roof bow dangerously.

If I was going down, I was taking Linden with me. I thrust the dagger forward in a last ditch attempt. Whether it struck home or not, I didn't know. The ceiling came down, and I had only seconds to cover my head with my arms and hope for the best.

* * * *

"I bet you have a bitch of a headache."

The disembodied voice floated above me. I opened my eyes to find Jez's face, upside down as she leaned over to scrutinize me. My vision tilted to one side, and my stomach rolled in a nauseous wave. Contrary to her assumption, my head didn't feel all that bad. In fact, my entire body felt numb. My throat was dry, my mouth like cotton. It took great effort to do more than lay there and groan.

"You were a mess when Shaz dragged you out of that warehouse," Jez continued, brushing the hair back from my face before helping me sip some water. "Bad concussion. Blood, bruises, the works. Arys healed the worst of it. You looked so much worse. Wow, he has a hell of a healing touch, huh? Packs a bit of an erotic punch. I was so not prepared for that."

I rolled over and sat up, unable to focus on the rambling leopard. My head swam. "Can we go home now?"

"You're singing my song," Jez muttered. "I have never wanted my own bed as bad as I do right now."

I was on a bed at The Wicked Kiss. The soft silky feel of the blankets against my skin shouldn't have so easily caught my attention. My club back home was getting a makeover if I had to pay for it myself.

"Where's Shaz? Did he get everyone out of there before the building came down? What happened to Linden?" I swung my legs over the side of the bed and, still feeling good, stood up.

"Downstairs. Yes, he did. And nobody knows. You know vampires, Lex. It takes more than a collapsed building to kill them."

"And Sloane?" I hadn't encountered her during my escape. She and I had a score to settle.

"On the run. Jenner figures she's already out of the state."

It felt so damn good to be free of Falon's manic energy. It would be a cold day in hell before I'd do that again.

I took a few minutes to use the en suite bathroom. It was small yet still somehow maintained a semblance of class. Instead of just a shower, it boasted of a tub big enough for two. A perusal in the mirror showed a pale blonde with disheveled hair and tired brown eyes. Ah brown, that was what I wanted to see. A faint bruise darkened the skin around one eye. A pink scar was all that remained of both dagger wounds.

All things considered, I felt better than I should. I also felt hungry. Demanding nourishment, the bloodlust echoed my mortal hunger.

We went downstairs to where Arys and Shaz sat around a table with Jenner and Roscoe. "They don't have him locked up or something?" I asked Jez as we crossed the noisy dance floor in making our way to them.

She shrugged, her lips twisting into a disapproving grimace. "That's what I said, but apparently being family or whatever gets you some kind of free fuck up pass."

"Not in my family it doesn't."

I stalked through the nightclub with one thing in mind. My pace quickened. I wasn't at full strength, but one should never underestimate how strong rage can make you.

Arys looked up at my approach. His relief immediately turned to shock when I grabbed Roscoe by the throat and dragged him out of his chair. I forced him down on his knees before me.

"Give me one reason to let you live," I growled into his face.

Jenner flew to his feet, and I flung up a hand to ward him off. Without saying a word, Arys shook his head, and Jenner sat back down.

I put the squeeze on Roscoe, just enough to let him know I meant business. He demonstrated his ballsiness by daring to push back. There was no way he could out strength me, and we both knew it. I was the bigger bad here. It had taken me almost a year to see and accept it, but Harley was right when he claimed my power to be bigger than his. That made it bigger than that of every vampire sired by him. Except for Arys.

"Let me try this one more time. Start with the sweet talk or end up as dust in the vacuum."

It was becoming easier all the time to take hold of a vampire's life force and bend it to my will. I turned up the pressure until Roscoe groaned and abandoned his efforts to withstand my assault. Blood filled his eyes, dripped from his nose and trickled from the corner of his mouth. For a moment, it appeared that he chose death.

Then he coughed out a stream of words that ran together. "My loyalty is to this family first. Linden promised to leave Jenner alone if I kept working for the blood ring, rounding up and delivering victims. I never meant you or your friend any harm. You were supposed to be out for a few hours, safe and out of the line of fire." Spitting blood,

Roscoe stared up at me with the intensity I'd come to expect from this damn bloodline.

I loosened my hold, considering his words. "Then why was Jez locked in a hotel room with a vampire standing guard over her while you supposedly looked for me?"

"I was going to stash you both there while you slept it off, but you lost your fucking mind and took off like a rabid maniac." Roscoe's long hair fell forward to hide his face. He peered up at me from under that wild mane. "I fucked up. I get that. Kill me if you're going to but at least believe me."

The light glinted off his gold fang, and at this proximity I was certain it was a replacement rather than merely gold plated. Who did a vampire piss off to have a fang yanked out of his face? Ouch.

"How did you lose the fang?" I asked. Manners went out the window long ago in this place.

"I pissed Harley off one time too many." His grunted response was only mildly surprising. It confirmed what I'd already known about Harley. He was a ruthless bastard.

Playing queen to Arys's king didn't mean acting like a super bitch running a dictatorship. If Arys trusted Roscoe enough to keep him in the fold, then perhaps so should I.

"I don't hand out a lot of second chances," I said. "For instance, Sloane will not be getting one. You, however, don't strike me as a liar. So I'm going to give you the benefit of the doubt. This time. And only this time. You owe me one."

I released him so fast he almost fell backwards. Jenner was glaring daggers my way so I made sure to slide into the chair closest to him at the table.

"Is there something you'd like to talk about, Jenner?" I taunted. "Looks like there's something you want to say."

"So I guess I don't need to ask how you're feeling." Arys's low chuckle was music to my ears. "Jenner and Roscoe are a little unhappy about my choice to re-establish my place in this city. Of course, I'll be doing it from Edmonton, so they should be grateful for that." He gave each vampire in question a pointed look before continuing. "Jenner will stay in charge, but he'll answer to both you and me. And somehow we'll find a way to take down the blood ring."

There was a question in his expression as he awaited my yay or nay. "That sounds fair. Certainly can't hurt to set up a stronghold here too. Two strongholds in two major cities. Couldn't hurt."

From day one in Vegas, I'd been pretty sure Arys was leading up to a takeover of his former home. He'd spent many years here. Naturally, he wanted to stake his own claim now that his sire was gone. Claiming Vegas as ours was not on my list of happy things. However, someone had to do it. If it wasn't us, Linden's crew would continue to run rampant like an infectious disease. Las Vegas had enough crazy shit going on without the growth of that organization.

The glimpse of the blood ring I had seen was small, just a scratch on the surface of their evil. And it was more than enough for me. I couldn't go home and let it keep happening, knowing there was more I could have done.

"I'm not changing The Wicked Kiss." Jenner leaned back with arms crossed, daring me to disagree. "It took months to build that theatre down there and regardless of what you both might think, the people fucking love it."

I couldn't help but laugh. He was incredibly determined. Fierceness flashed in his ice-cold eyes. He would not be denied. "Whatever you want, Jenner," I snickered. "Although there needs to be a few ground rules. Like no killing the people you take on stage."

"I don't kill them all." His protest sounded too much like one I'd heard before.

I cast a glance between Jenner and Arys, rolling my eyes. "What about the wolf fights? To the death seems too harsh. They volunteer, and they leave alive."

The stony mask that encompassed Jenner's face was almost frightening. Void of emotion, he issued a silent challenge. "No deal," he said. "I'm not compromising there."

"What if I'm not giving you a choice?" I countered.

Arys broke in before I could decide to throw Jenner around. "This can be discussed later. What matters now is that we're all on the same page as far as the blood ring is concerned."

The venomous glare Jenner turned on Arys would have intimidated any other vampire. "I don't suppose my opinion really holds any weight now, does it? Especially not now that he wants to see her. I might as well go back to Paris and start over." Emanating waves of contempt, Jenner slumped in his seat.

I hadn't thought vampires to be prone to pouting, but that twisted frown marring his face was definitely a pout. However, his words were far more interesting. "Who wants to see me?" Trepidation made my empty stomach lurch. I just wanted to go home. The sooner, the better.

"Hurst," Arys answered, his jaw clenched as he tried to hide his concern. "He's requested that you be brought to him. To talk."

Harley's maker wanted to see me? Oh, balls. That sucked.

"Nobody can go with you," Arys went on. "He won't allow it. But nobody's forcing you either. It's your call."

I looked around the table at my family, those I'd come with and those that had been forced upon me. Jenner was the only one wearing an openly malicious grin. From the very little I had heard of this vampire, I didn't get the feeling he intended to kill me. It seemed rather unlikely that he wanted to see me at all considering he chose to remove himself from the mortal world. When I gave the question over to instinct, I felt without a doubt that Hurst was someone worthy of my time. There had to be a reason he wanted to see me. I needed to know what that was.

"I'll go. Then I want to get on a plane and go home before this city decides not to let me leave at all."

Chapter Sixteen

The four of us sat around the table, having been abandoned by Jenner and Roscoe who understandably wanted very little to do with us at the moment. For the most part Jez ignored us, tapping out messages on her phone at record speed.

We had taken some time to talk about our plans for The Wicked Kiss Las Vegas, Sloane, and Linden, should he prove to be alive. We all understood that wiping out the blood ring would take time. Shaz had assured me every person from the warehouse had made it to safety. It was a small start but a significant one.

"You have to feed." Arys squinted and braced himself for the blow back.

Instead of snarling at him like usual, I merely sighed and nodded. A healing could only do so much. The hunger burning in my gut demanded sustenance. "I know. Thanks for the reminder, Mom." The snarky comment earned me a middle finger, and I smirked.

"I should come with, keep things under control." Arys started to rise, but Shaz stopped him with a hand.

"No. It should be me. Lex can feed on me."

My protests couldn't come fast enough. I tripped over my tongue in my hurried attempt to deny his offer. "There are too many reasons why that's not going to work. Don't feel like you have to be part of that, Shaz."

"But I do though. You need mortal blood. I'm the only mortal here you can bite without turning them wolf. And honestly, I kind of like that I have something you need that you can't get from him." He jerked a thumb toward Arys who raised a dark brow and shook his head.

"Can't argue with that logic," Jez said without looking up from her phone. I was touched by Shaz's offer. There had once been a time when I could take blood from him without any trouble. Taking energy, however, might be tricky, and the two tended to go hand in hand.

"Are you sure?" I wasn't about to insult him with an outright refusal. Shaz was capable of making his own decisions.

"Of course."

I slapped a hand down on the table, making Jez jump. "Ok, then. Let's do this before I chicken out."

"You guys are so gonna do it," Jez said in a singsong tone. "It's about time too."

Ignoring her, I stood and held a hand out to Shaz. The warmth of his hand in mine drew me to his wolfish scent of pine and forest with a hint of wolf musk. I suddenly could not wait to sink my teeth into that. The bloodlust was bearable still, though it was definitely making itself known. Leaving instructions for Arys to order me a medium rare steak and a salad, I ascended the stairs with Shaz, back up to the room I'd woken up in.

"Are you sure?" I asked again when the door closed. My breath came faster as anticipation thrilled through me.

Shaz laughed and threw a pillow at my head. "Yes, dammit. I know you want to shelter me from this side of you, but you can't." He grew serious, giving me a look filled with wisdom well beyond his years. "I devoted myself to you long ago, Lex. At the time, I was living in a fantasy, thinking we would have this Hollywood happily ever after. I know now that it can't be that way. It can't change how I feel about you though. Nothing can. Not even Arys."

"You should sit down," I said, a lump in my throat. "There are a few things you need to know." I proceeded to tell him everything I had learned in his absence. From the potential loss of my wolf to the foretold future of my death at Arys's hand, I told Shaz everything. Some of it was hard to say and even harder to hear. When I finished, he sat there on the end of the bed in silence. We stared at one another until I was ready to shout at him to say something.

Finally, he did. "If you think any of that is going to scare me off, then you don't know me very well. I'm not going anywhere. Not now, not even if you lose your wolf."

"And if I'm only vampire? What then?" I challenged. "You can't give up your future for me, Shaz. You deserve to be loved by someone who isn't bound to another. You deserve better than me."

His mouth opened in thoughtful wonder, and he nodded knowingly. "Ah, I get it. This is about you chasing me off, setting me free or whatever term you're using to rationalize it. You think I can't love you because of Arys. Actually, I love you in spite of him." Shaz leaned back on the bed and tilted his head to expose his neck, offering it up to me. "I trust that we love each other because we're meant to. I don't need any more than that."

My gaze fixated on the steady pulse pumping beneath his smooth skin. I didn't know why I felt this deep-rooted need to drive him away, to set him free, as he'd said. Especially considering how terribly I'd missed him when he was gone. We had already hurt one another too much. I couldn't be the bringer of anymore of his pain.

"You should need more than that." My voice barely squeaked out. "I can't give you a monogamous, picket fence life."

A flicker of sadness crossed his jade eyes. Then it was gone, blinked away by the wolf looking out at me. "I know."

I crossed the distance between us without hesitation. Climbing onto his lap, I captured his face between my hands and kissed him. The unspoken bond between us grew stronger. We didn't live a life that allowed us to plan for the future. We had to be grateful for this moment right now. It was a tough lesson, but one I was learning.

It had been too long. Too long since I'd touched him. Too long since I'd felt him between my legs. I was taking what he was offering and throwing caution to the wind while doing so. Tasting him kicked my bloodlust into overdrive. I tugged his shirt up over his head and tossed it, wondering where he'd gotten fresh clothes. For that matter, I wasn't even sure it was the same day as our escape. Dragging my hands over his warm skin, I reveled in the way his smell teased my senses. Our kiss was wild, passionate and hungry. It had been a few months since we'd been intimate. It felt like forever.

I nipped at his lips and tongue, drawing out the moment when I would shed his blood. For once, my wolf was perfectly content with the vampire hunger commanding me. In this moment, both sides of me found satisfaction.

Shaz ran his hands up my side, sliding my top up and off. He buried his face in my neck, and I took the opportunity to run my hands through his soft platinum hair. A sigh was the only sound.

With a hand in his hair, I jerked his head back and forced him to meet my eyes. I needed to see the desire burning in him for me. When Shaz had been away, I had let myself imagine this moment, our first time together after so much shit had gone down between us. In my fantasy, it was slow and tender. But this hurried, desperate need for one another, it was so much better.

The sound of his heartbeat quickening had me licking my lips in excitement. We moved in synch, shedding the last of our clothing. When I straddled him, naked, feeling his arousal pressed against me, I could have wept from the solace my wolf knew at last.

There was no hesitation, not so much as a moment of pause. He slipped inside me as I simultaneously went for his neck. Heady wolf blood spurted into my mouth. I moaned in bliss as I took him into me in so many ways.

Carnal and wild, we moved together. Hands on my hips, Shaz guided me. I licked and sucked at the bleeding bite wound. Drinking in the satisfying rush of erotic energy, I feasted on his body and blood.

With a low growl, Shaz flipped us over so I lay beneath him. This was where we paused. He gazed down at me with gorgeous wolf eyes. I smiled.

He thrust into me with the fierceness of the wolf claiming its mate. I raised my hips, matching his rhythm, taking him deep within me. Blood trickled down his neck, and I captured it with my tongue.

The sound of Shaz's low moans in my ear brought me closer to the edge. Knowing he still wanted me after everything was a comfort that I didn't know I needed quite so bad. The past few months had been more difficult than I wanted to admit. Part of me had been afraid we wouldn't be able to do this again; however, no ugly past memories surfaced to ruin it. My senses were on fire for Shaz. The way he smelled, the way he felt, he consumed me.

I fell headlong into the bliss moment far sooner than I'd have liked. Of course, if I had it my way, I would have stayed locked in that room loving Shaz all night. Long after the climactic explosion, we lay together, as if unable to disentangle from one another. It was peaceful and so vital for us both then. Our ragged breaths were loud in the stillness. The room smelled of sweat, blood and sex.

"I missed this." Shaz lay curled around me, his face in my hair. "But damn that was worth waiting for."

"The only thing missing is the forest. Desert life is not for me."

"Better get over it. I have a feeling you'll be back."

I groaned and snuggled in closer. "Don't remind me. Maybe I can just video chat with Jenner. Bitch him out via the internet."

I was determined to suck every iota of gratification possible out of the afterglow. That would have been easier if Arys hadn't banged on the door. Not only did he not wait for a response, he strode right in without an invitation.

"There's a car here to take you to Hurst. Come on. Get dressed." Arys picked my clothes off the floor and flung them at me. He made no attempt to hide his amusement.

"Afterglow much?" I sat up in time to catch my panties with my face. "Arys! That's so rude."

He snickered, and I hid a smile. I was in too good of a mood to pretend to be mad.

Arys couldn't hide his urgency as he ushered me down the stairs. I'd gotten dressed at warp speed. The way he and Jenner spoke of Hurst, one might think him a god. I knew better. However, any vampire that intimidated Arys in any way was one worth being wary of.

"Where's my steak?" I demanded as he dragged me to the exit. "Can you slow down? I hate that you're rushing me like this."

"You can eat later. An offer like this from Hurst is almost never extended. If he wants to see you, it has to be important." He actually began to finger comb my hair as if worried about my appearance.

I slapped his hands away and scowled. "Stop that. What's gotten into you? Should I be worried about this?"

"No, I don't think so." Arys didn't look entirely convinced.

"Great. Let me guess. No weapons."

"Right. The Dragon Claw stays here. Don't tap any power. You won't need to. He would never harm you."

The Dragon Claw had survived the warehouse fire. A weapon forged in the fires of Hell, it would likely survive anything short of the apocalypse. It had become somewhat of a security blanket for me, and I felt naked without it.

"You know, I'm starting to get real sick of the vampires calling all the shots. Shaz and I were having a moment, Arys. We needed that."

"I know. I'm sorry." Confusion marred his features. He seemed to want to tell me something. At last he spit out, "Hurst knows things. Things nobody should know. If he has something to share, it could be vital to us."

I sighed and gave him a gentle cheek caress. "I'm going, ok? Now you get my steak here, so I don't have to stick a foot up your ass when I get back. Oh, and see if you can rebook our flight home. I am fucking done with this city."

"Will do."

Arys walked me to the waiting black town car. The driver gave us a nod, holding the door for me. I couldn't help but note that he was human.

I sat back against the seat as we pulled away from The Wicked Kiss. This damn nightclub chain was starting to take over my existence. I knew there was power in running a place like this. Unfortunately, it always came at a price.

The trek was short. Or at least it felt that way. In no time, we stopped. I recalled no specific details about the location. What the building looked like, where it was located, I remembered none of that.

My memory of meeting Hurst began with a dimly lit library. Candles burned, illuminating the small table where I sat. Oil lamps burned in sconces on the wall. The place seemed void of electricity, something that had to be almost impossible in Vegas.

A polite human man asked if I would like a beverage. I asked for a vanilla latte, surprised when he nodded as if that were no problem.

I didn't have to wait for long before an unseen door hidden in the shadows across the room opened and a robed figure emerged. He made his way slowly toward me, as if he enjoyed taking his time, simply because he could.

Power surrounded him like a fog. Resonating with the skill of several centuries, it hovered the way an aroma lingers in the air. As he drew closer to the light, I saw that his robes were indeed a long cloak that touched the floor as he walked.

The man returned with my latte, placed it before me and slipped away in silence. I barely noticed.

Hurst stepped into the warm candle light. He looked nothing like I'd pictured. Long black hair streaked with silver fell over his shoulders. Lines in his face indicated that he'd been a relatively old man at the time of his turning. A sharp, hawk-like nose gave him a beaked appearance that was somehow both cryptic and endearing. He sank into the chair across from me, gently settling himself like a sheet cascading down upon the bed on laundry day.

I bit my tongue, unsure if I should speak first. I chose to wait. Instantly, he mesmerized me. The air of prestige he commanded was intimidating. I was nothing but a dumb kid next to this guy.

"Alexa, hello." With a twinkle in his hazel eyes, Hurst captured my hand in his and placed a respectful kiss across my knuckles. "I am happy to meet you."

I stared at him in stunned silence. Where was the scorned sire I'd been expecting? The one who would tear a strip out of me for killing a vampire he had made.

"Please," he continued. His voice was low and rough, as if he'd swallowed gravel. "Do not be afraid. I mean you no harm. I am quite delighted to meet Arys's wolf. The underworld speaks of you often. You are known in many parts of the world." That was news to me. Bad news potentially. Already I saw what Arys meant about Hurst's tendency to know things others did not.

"I'm honored to be here, really. Just a little nervous. I'm sure you understand." I sipped the latte, needing a way to keep my hands busy. It was hot, obviously. Burnt taste buds were nobody's friend, but I sucked it up and drank it anyway.

"I'm afraid I don't. You have no need to fear me, or anyone else, for that matter. You are a rare breed. The only one of your kind."

"What does that mean?" I was afraid to ask questions, afraid of the answers.

Hurst studied me, and I tried desperately to keep from squirming under the massive weight of his stare. "No Hounds have walked in the world of the undead. None until you. I understand it must be incredibly difficult for you. Do you have any questions?"

I had many. Where to begin? I started with perhaps the most obvious, the one that nagged me. "Do you hate me for killing Harley?"

He laughed, a gruff sound I'd equate to that of a cement mixer. His gravelly voice was gentle, though, when he replied, "Not at all. It is very easy for the undead to forget that they are not truly immortal. They too can die. Harlan made his own choices. As did you. I feel only sadness that he learned so little in his time."

Huh? Well that was interesting. What made it so puzzling was the way vampires like Jenner carried on about it as if I'd committed some great cardinal sin. Sure Harley was his maker but if Harley's own sire saw it for what it was, why couldn't the others?

"The vampires Harley sired don't seem to feel that way."

"They are immature, self-centered in their view of the world. Pay no mind to them." Hurst's eyes twinkled with age-old wisdom and knowledge of things I would never know. His aged appearance made it easy to forget he was vampire. "They all belong to you though they do not yet know that. In time you will all see."

Whoa. What? His words brought to mind an incident from a year or so ago. A vampire had attacked me, swearing he'd rather die than bow down to me. A shudder racked me at the memory.

I felt calm in Hurst's company. The vampire essence within me knew him. It gave me a strange but welcome reassurance.

"Arys thinks there is a particular reason you wanted to see me," I hedged, hoping he'd take it from there.

Hurst gazed into the darkness lurking at the edge of the candlelight. Shelves of books lined every wall in the room, ceiling to floor. It was the most impressive library I'd ever seen.

"I have read every book in here. And a great many more as well. There is no greater power in this world than that of knowledge. Never forget that, Alexa."

A cool breeze picked up, blowing my hair around my face. The shadows danced beyond the light, writhing and twisting into odd shapes. A book floated through the room, coming to settle between us in the center of the table. The front cover was nothing more than a mysterious symbol. It might have been a letter from an ancient language or a mark of some form of magic. Whatever it was, it began to glow.

"It knows you," Hurst said, causing my stomach to drop. "It's very old. A book of long buried secrets, it has been passed through only the hands of those who can read it."

Gently, as if the pages might crumble at his touch, Hurst opened the book. It was written in an old language, one I did not recognize. I gripped my latte tight, afraid to let it go for fear it would spill.

"What does it say about me?" Oddly enough, the apprehension I'd been feeling was gone in the presence of the book. No longer did I fear the answer. How strange.

"It says many things about many beings. A Hound of God bound to the darkness is indeed one of them. It comes with a warning for you. Beware the angel with black wings."

I pursed my lips, frowning at the book. It didn't take a magic book to make me aware of the dangers of demons. I mean, hello, demons.

"I assume that means Shya." I watched the book closely, wishing I could read it for myself.

"There is danger in assumption." Hurst's wrinkled hands caressed the pages affectionately. "What is it that you fear most?"

I had no response to that. I feared many things. Death at Arys's hand. Failing to carry out the purpose we were created for. The loss of myself, my wolf.

"You have all that you need," he continued. The candle flame flickered in his eyes, creating an eerie but intriguing reflection. "To save your wolf."

I did a double take, blinking rapidly as if that would help me to hear his words again. "What do you mean?"

"It is already within your possession. It calls to you, a piece of the earth. A gift from a friend."

Hope soared, taking flight as I pieced it together. "Lena's amulet. Yes, I have it. What does it do?"

After Lena's death, her daughter Brogan had given me the amulet. It had called to my wolf, vibrating with a joyful, earthy energy. Not knowing what to do with it, I had kept it safe, stored away in my house.

"Your friend foresaw much of what you would face, as many witches have. She gifted you with a piece of earth, enchanted for you and you alone. Wear it. All the time. Die with it on, and it will keep the wolf within you."

Hurst spoke like a grandfather telling children fantastic stories of monsters and magic, things they would never believe. Or perhaps that was just how I felt, like one of those wide-eyed kids, peering at him in dazed wonder.

How had Lena possibly known what I would face? Sure, Arys and I had both encountered witches who knew of our bond and even our fate. Yet this was so outrageous, so hard to believe. Lena had been like a mother to me. Better than my own mother, in fact. To think that she had known, that she had done something so thoughtful for me, it made me want to weep.

"I must inform you, however, that the amulet will only save your wolf. It will not save your light. You sacrificed that part of you when Arys gave you his blood." Hurst watched me closely. Too closely. "There is only one way to save your light. It requires a sacrifice from another. One willing to take your darkness for you."

A heavy weight settled upon me. I stared at the book, and I detested it with every part of my being. What kind of a revelation was that? It was torment, that's what it was. More torment to carry around inside me while I awaited my fate.

"Wow." I let my gaze travel around the grand library. There were no words for what I was feeling. "I appreciate the information, but you should've let me keep thinking there was no way. That's the kind of shit I'd rather not know."

Hurst allowed me a moment to absorb that bombshell. With a gentle smile, he offered, "Ignorance may feel like a protective shell, but it is a cage. You must set yourself free."

Did I have to? I let out a breath in a huff and nodded. "It's hard."

"It is. I know. That's why I wanted to share this with you. Before you return home. You have much to face yet. You must trust that you can."

I drank the rest of my coffee, focusing on the sweet vanilla flavor. It was important for me to find pleasure in simple joys. Those little things were so easily overlooked in the face of greater chaos.

"What if I can't? There's all this talk of me leading vampires and werewolves. What does that even mean? Leading them where? To do what?" My words ended on a shrill note. All the latte bliss moments in the world couldn't keep me grounded in the face of such uncertainty.

Hurst regarded me with a pensive expression. I found his wise, owlish quality to be both puzzling and comforting. Spending so much time cut off from the human world had to do something to the psyche. I could totally see myself ending up that way.

"There are those who see the future, and those who plan the future. Neither are guaranteed. Do not worry yourself with such things. In time, all things will be revealed. Your efforts are better spent on what is soon to come." He patted my hand warmly. "Would you like more coffee?"

"No, thanks. I'm good." What a weird conversation. I was going to be replaying this one in my head for weeks. "And just what is soon to come? You talk like you know."

Hurst clasped his hands together and settled back in his chair. He wore the scent of old books like a second skin. It tickled my nose, and I stifled a sneeze.

"There is much speculation regarding the demon whose mark you bear. The underworld feels he will soon make a move toward greater power. He is feared by many and subject to very few." He paused, and this time he exhibited an air of reservation. "You and Arys must be on guard. He will do all he can to corrupt you both."

I might have been new to this world compared to an old vampire like Hurst, but I wasn't born yesterday. Warning me about Shya was like telling me the sky was blue. Of course, I appreciated the sentiment.

"He already is," I sighed. "But thank you. I appreciate the warning."

"I won't keep you much longer. I'm sure you're eager to get back to your twin flame. It pleases me greatly to hear how well you two have managed your union. It's an honor to my bloodline."

Despite my polite refusal, Hurst's human assistant brought me another coffee and a plate of cookies. Not quite what I would have expected as the guest of a vampire, but I'd happily take it.

As I nibbled an oatmeal cookie, my stomach growled. Arys better have ordered that steak. I eyed Hurst with open curiosity. Making the most of our remaining time was essential.

"What is it about our bloodline that makes us so strong? Did it start with you?" I asked. Arys had never been able to answer that question.

"No, it did not." Hurst stared off into the shadows. Something wistful passed across his face. "As you know, many vampires possess metaphysical attributes of varying degrees. Others possess none at all. Tales from the old world claim the origins of the vampire are linked to a deal made with the devil. Of course, there is no way of knowing for sure."

I stared at him in wonder, my cookie forgotten in my hand. I gestured for him to continue.

"One folk story states that the first vampires were born of demon blood. A king with three daughters made a deal with the devil to preserve his children always by making them immortal. Or as immortal as a human can be. Another story agrees that the first vampires were created from demon blood but created to be an affront to God. More than human but less than demon, and all dark. A mockery of humankind created to prey on humankind. In both, the first generation of vampires each possessed different demon traits. Traits that have been passed on throughout the years as new vampires are made. Some theorize that the strengths of those traits vary based on the strengths of the individual, and I'm inclined to agree with that for the most part."

I felt like a kid on Halloween listening to ghost stories. A strange chill crept through me as I processed his accounts. It wasn't the first time I'd heard tales of vampires being linked to demons. That's where the darkness came from. My body shook as the chill spread, freezing my very bones. I faced every night with a piece of that darkness living inside me. How would I ever be the same when it completely consumed me?

"Our bloodline is currently one of the most powerful in the western world," Hurst continued when I failed to speak. "I'm sure you've seen evidence of that yourself."

"I have," I said softly.

"Which is why you must take care when turning a human. Like your wolf, some people cannot adjust to the power we command." Hurst pushed the plate of cookies closer to me. He met my eyes evenly when he added, "Please give Arys a message for me. Tell him that he must not turn the young male witch."

The blood drained from my face. My gaze fell to the dragon on my forearm. It was a perfect match to the one on Arys's back. The one he had received after making a deal with Shya, a promise to turn Gabriel, a human skilled in the dark arts. At this rate, we were never going to get these damn demon marks removed. We would never be able or willing to give Shya what he expected of us. That problem would have to wait until I was back home after a weeklong snooze in my own bed.

"I'll tell him," I promised. "Thank you, again, for sharing with me. I'm not entirely sure what to do with it all, but I'll figure it out."

"That you will." Hurst rose and called forward his human assistant. "Take Alexa back to her kin, please."

I stood up, my legs wobbly like jelly. The symbol on the old book pulsed, and again I resisted the urge to touch it. It scared me even as it enticed.

Hurst drew me into a surprising hug. His embrace was gentle, comforting. He stroked a hand through my hair and patted my back. "Stay strong, young Hound." He pulled back and gazed down at me. I fell into his hazel eyes, drawn into the abyss of power. He spoke slowly, carefully. "You will not remember this location. You will recall only this room and our discussion. Go now and take care."

The next thing I knew, I was standing outside The Wicked Kiss alone and disoriented.

Chapter Seventeen

Back at Caesars Palace after a long and fabulous day in bed, I groaned and whined in protest to Arys's insistence that we go out.

"Out? Are you kidding me? All we've been is out. I want to go home."

The minibar muffled Jez's snicker and hid her head from sight while she perused the selection. The twenty-second rule had been abandoned. Screw it.

"But now we get to act like tourists, Lex," she said, pulling out two bottles of imported beer. "Like we should have been from the start."

"Might as well kill time before our flight." Arys tried to appeal to my rational side. He didn't know that I had no inclination left to be rational. This trip had drained me of all sense and reasonability. "Besides, I want you to see Vegas. I mean really see The Strip the way you're meant to, without all the vampire politics."

I caught the bottle that Jez slid to me across the table. "I don't know, Arys. Wouldn't you rather stay here and just enjoy the view?" I pointed to the Bellagio fountain across the street. The water was alight, dancing to some song we could not hear within our room.

"I'd rather get down there for a street view. Let's make the most of our last few hours here."

At my request, and with no argument from the others, Arys had rebooked our flight for tonight. Midnight. I was perfectly content to stay at Caesars and be pampered, enjoying the luxury the hotel offered. The city was a daunting place, a haven for vampires. It was also now ours. Or so Arys claimed.

I groaned again, being as stubborn as I could without driving myself crazy. Since my visit with Hurst, I was especially eager to get home. I needed some time alone with my thoughts. There was no place on earth better for that than running through the forest as wolf.

"Do we have to?" I whined.

"Yes," said both Jez and Arys simultaneously.

I gave a scoff of irritation and pushed to my feet. Disappearing from the living room, I went to the bedroom and packed my things. The minute we were set to depart for the airport, I'd be ready. I'd even already called Willow and had him pop in to grab my dagger. Airport security wouldn't have nice things to say about me if they found that in my luggage.

It was a casual dress kind of night, jeans and a black tank top with my ass-kicking boots. I wasn't betting on getting out of Sin City without further trouble. The odds just weren't in my favor.

The door opened, and Arys entered. He had that look in his eyes, the one that said he knew exactly what I was thinking. "You're worrying about what Hurst said, aren't you?" He sat on the bed beside me and gave my hair a playful tug.

"Yes," I said truthfully. "Every damn word."

"Don't. It's not worth it."

"How can you say that?" I asked, aghast at his flippancy. "As far as our deals with Shya go, we are fucked. Totally, completely, horrifically fucked."

Arys's low velvet smooth laugh stroked me in places unseen. Damn him and his impossible sensuality. "We are no such thing. Everything will work itself out. It always does. Haven't you caught on to that by now?"

"Not in the slightest. You're delusional."

"And you're a neurotic head case who wastes too much time and energy on fear. You are the one to be feared. Start believing it." He pulled me in against him and gave me a comforting squeeze. His scent of cologne and hair products teased me. It was one of my favorite smells.

"You can't turn Gabriel, Arys," I whispered, afraid of disturbing the brief moment of peace. "Promise me that you won't."

He took too long in answering. I expected it when he said, "Don't make me promise anything, Alexa. Not with someone like Shya in the picture."

I gave a small growl of frustration. "Fine. But you have to promise me not to tell anyone what Hurst said about losing my light. Nobody can know there's a way to save it. I'm not compromising on this one."

He met my intense gaze, seeing how gravely serious I was. With a nod, he kissed the side of my nose, and I smiled. "Fair enough. That's your secret to share."

I wasn't entirely sure what Hurst had meant by a sacrifice. It didn't matter. I would never allow anyone to sacrifice themselves for me. Never. I carried enough guilt without that weighing on my conscience. If the darkness was bound to claim me, then so be it.

"So where are you taking us tonight?" I forced a smile. This city meant something to Arys; I didn't want to crap all over his attempt to show me what he loved about it.

A brilliant smile broke over his handsome face. It warmed my heart. Taking my hand, he pulled me off the bed and from the room. "To see a little magic. The Vegas kind."

By the time we made it down The Strip to another hotel for the show, I was starting to feel good about playing tourist with the humans. It was what I'd ideally wanted since we arrived.

We were all dressed casual, each of us wearing fight-friendly attire. Hopefully it wouldn't be a requirement for the evening. If I could get out of Vegas without another incident, it would be a miracle.

As we filed into the theatre with hundreds of people excited to see a magic show, the bloodlust didn't taunt me, a pleasant surprise. Surrounded by humans, their hearts pumping crimson joy steadily through their veins, I felt nothing.

My gaze landed on Shaz. Taking blood from him had satisfied the hunger, though at the time, I hadn't known how much. The blood of a shifter was stronger, more potent than human blood. My bloodlust seemed to like it. As it was also an intoxicant to vampires, I'd have to be very careful.

The theatre was loud with many people, all chattering away at once. The air conditioning was especially high, creating an actual chilly breeze. Compared to the heat outside the building, it contrasted greatly. This climate certainly took some getting used to, but it was doing wonders for my hair.

"How much do you want to bet that this guy's not even human?" Jez leaned in to whisper close to my ear.

I'd seen this stuff on TV. Vegas was known for its magicians and illusionists. Many had come before, and many would follow. Parlor tricks that involved a diversion of attention were clever, but they were very human.

"I'll take that bet," I replied.

The theatre dimmed, and everyone fell into a hushed silence. The hum of excitement was lively, tickling my senses in a pleasing manner. The show began, and in no time, the crowd was applauding wildly.

I analyzed everything the magician did and watched every move he made, every hair on his head. A few of his tricks I saw right through. But then the real magic started to happen. We watched attentively as illusion after illusion made me question everything I thought I knew about magic for entertainment purposes. Disappearing from center stage to reappear seconds later in the crowd, that was not a human feat. Levitation could be faked, but in this case, it was very real.

I couldn't resist the urge to take a poke at the guy, just to feel him out a little from where I sat. He would know, but by the time he identified it as me, we would be gone. His energy felt strong and solid, not demon, shifter or vampire. Whatever he was, I had yet to encounter another.

"I don't know what he is," I whispered to Jez, "but it's definitely not human."

"Ha. I knew it."

Las Vegas was built on illusions. It always had been. Everyone wore a human face. How deceiving. There were more supernatural types walking the city streets than I would have guessed, far more than there were back home. How in the hell were Arys and I going to establish a position of power in a place that had more monsters than I knew what to do with?

The show ended, and we exited the theatre. I excused myself to the restroom while the others browsed the merchandise store outside.

After using the facilities, I washed my hands and tried to smooth down a few flyaway strands of hair.

My hackles rose, and immediately I felt eyes upon me. The restroom was empty of anyone but me. Or so I thought. In the mirror, I watched as a stall door behind me opened and Linden strode out. I spun to face him, and he caught me by the throat. Pinning me against the bathroom counter, he gave me a rough shake.

"My, my, fancy meeting you here," he said, his face void of any emotion. His eyes glittered with malevolence.

I'd met more than one vampire in my time who had the ability to withstand my power. They were few and far between, and they were still dead. However, a vampire seldom managed to sneak up on me. Linden was awfully sure of himself merely because I couldn't blast him with my mind. He was forgetting that I was a different kind of monster.

His grip on my throat cut off my air supply. I struggled to stay calm. It was just him and me in here with nothing to stop me from plunging a handful of claws into his guts, which is what I did. Warm and wet, his insides felt slippery as I wriggled my claws. He grunted and bent at the waist, loosening his hold on me. I slammed a knee into his jaw, and he stumbled back.

"Did you come to kill me, Linden? In the ladies room of all places? Geez, that's shady."

He recovered fast, as vampires are wont to do. He managed to grasp enough of my long hair to slam my face into the bathroom counter. Twice.

"I'm a reasonable man, Alexa. I'm also smart enough to know when I've met my match. So consider this a warning. Stop your takeover of The Wicked Kiss, or I will burn it to the ground with Jenner and his crew inside. I will wage a fucking war. Understood?"

Blood poured from my nose and top lip. Holy shit that hurt. My wolf was ready for a fight. Physical brutality was what the wolf did best.

Linden was left holding a handful of my hair as I tore from his grasp. I leaped on him with fangs bared and slashed his face. I followed up with a head butt that made him stumble.

A snarly mess of fangs and claws, I said, "The Wicked Kiss is mine. I killed Harley Kayson. Everything that fucker had belongs to me. If you want it, you'll have to do better than that."

I slashed at him again, going for his throat. He moved suddenly to counterattack, and I got his eye instead. A scream tore from him as my claw sank into the soft tissue, tearing it to shreds. We grappled, a blur in the mirror. I kept expecting the door to open. I had to finish this before that happened.

Linden was strong; his age showed in his attacks. I might not be able to use my power on him, but I could use it to strengthen myself. Tapping the energy lying in wait within my core, I focused it all into my fist.

I punched through his chest with ease, my hand closing on his dead heart. "Surprise," I said cheerfully, despite my bloodied face and missing chunk of hair. "This isn't your city anymore, Linden."

Linden's remaining eye was wide with shock. I yanked his heart free and crushed it in my hand. The bloody, pulpy remains quickly faded to a dusty residue. His body followed suit, hitting the floor in a burst of dust and ash.

"Asshole," I muttered, turning back to the sink to clean up. My body thrummed with the rush of the fight. It was exhilarating.

I'd just finished scrubbing blood from my face and hands when the door opened and three women entered. They all filed into stalls without so much as looking at me. I had a feeling the locals were oblivious to this stuff, used to it after living with it for so long.

My lip bled from where my teeth had gouged it, and my nose swelled, but otherwise, I was no worse for wear. A sore spot on my scalp reminded me to pick the blonde hairs from Linden's ashes and flush them before leaving the restroom.

"What in the fuck?" Jez's loud exclamation drew the eye of bystanders when I emerged. "What happened to you?"

"Linden happened to me."

As I proceeded to tell the brief tale of the bathroom fiasco, Arys led us from the hotel. He was on high alert, continuously checking to see if we were being followed.

"We need to see Jenner before we leave," he said. "Now is the best time for him to make a move against the rest of the blood ring."

"Jenner? Again?" I questioned with a huff. "Fine. But he can come to us. I'm not going back to that place."

"Caesars. Poker room. One hour." Arys passed my phone back after making the call. He and Shaz would have to replace the phones Linden swiped from them. "Let's walk. I want to stop in front of the Bellagio fountain. You have to see it up close."

Walking The Strip at a relaxed pace was nice. It was the first time I'd had a chance to enjoy it. The hectic pace of the last few days hadn't allowed me a chance to appreciate this crazy ass city that never sleeps.

People packed the streets. Families, couples, groups of friends all made their way through the throng, voices raised in jubilance. We couldn't walk for more than a minute without someone shoving escort cards at the guys.

Jez plucked a card from Arys's hand and studied the busty blonde in the photo. "I bet this isn't the girl that shows up when you call."

Arys shrugged "As long as they send a screamer, it's all good."

The two of them shared a laugh while I exchanged an eye roll with Shaz. Nobody could ever say predatory types didn't have a sense of humor.

We passed showgirls posing with tourists for tips and even a few Elvis impersonators traveling as a small pack. The bright lights and constant noise was kind of comforting and much more intense in real life than any movie could portray. I was fascinated by the glitz of The Strip. There was so much to see. Maybe Vegas wasn't so bad after all. Maybe it was just all the damn vampires.

The Eiffel Tower was especially beautiful against the night sky. I gazed up at it, lost in thought, wondering about the men I'd killed in that hotel. It was a lost memory that didn't feel real. Roscoe owed me for that, and I would collect on that debt.

We reached the Bellagio to find the foot traffic very heavy in front of it. All of the tourists and their dogs lined up, waiting for the fountain to go off again.

Two giggling twenty-somethings passed with drink containers bigger than my arm. Jez's gaze followed them with delight. "I must have one of those."

"A girl or a drink?" I asked. It was Jez after all.

Her response was lost in the noise as the fountain lights came on. People chattered excitedly and held up smartphones to take video footage. *God Bless the USA* played over loud speakers, creating a sense of unity among all gathered, regardless of home country. It was nice.

I crammed in against the railing with everyone else. The fountain waters went so high. The Bellagio was gorgeous lit up in the background with the fabulous Caesars Palace just across the street to the right.

For the first time ever, I felt like a tourist, and I loved it. The fountain spray was cool against my skin, a brief reprieve of the desert heat. I watched with as much childlike glee as the next person as the water leaped as high as the Bellagio itself.

"Beautiful," I whispered to myself. That moment in time was something special and maybe even a little magical, which made me wish I could capture the feeling and keep it forever.

"There's nothing quite like it." With a knowing grin, Arys slipped his arms around me from behind. "It's one of my favorite places in all the world. That sounds childish, doesn't it?"

"It does." I laughed and leaned back into his embrace. "But I get it. I really do."

The song ended. The fountain waters fell quiet, and the small lake lay peaceful once again. The crowd began to disperse, and the chatter kicked up a notch. As Arys tugged me away, onward to Caesars, I cast a wistful glance back at the dark water.

Jez stopped to take a photo with some showgirls. Her smile stretched from ear to ear as she snuggled up to the sparkly ladies. It was so simple, to pretend to be one of them. Human. Sometimes it was necessary too, for the good of our own mental health.

The crush of the crowd crossing the pedway to the hotel was as chaotic as it had been the last time I'd crossed. Above the din, I could hear the voice of the guy selling water on the end.

Stepping back into Caesars meant a shot of cold air conditioning in the face. I welcomed it. What I did not welcome was the unfortunate reminder that human life would never be for me. A bride with a handful of flowers cheerfully pranced through the lobby on the arm of her groom. Their friends followed, all dressed to the nines in wedding attire. My gaze went to Shaz who was also watching the happy couple. What was he thinking?

He caught me looking and forced a tight smile. It was still hard to accept, even after so many years. That would never be us.

The Poker Room was loud and busy, much like every other part of the casino. Men and women surrounded the tables and wore very stern expressions.

Jenner sat at one table, alone. In a suit that hid his tattoos, he looked suave, almost sexy. Shaz and Jez excused themselves, leaving the vampire talk to the vampires.

"We're going to watch some dancing girls," Jez said with a wink. "Come find us when you're done with the politics."

I sat across from Jenner, letting Arys take a seat in the middle. I decided to buy into the game. Why should they have all the gambling fun? I'd seen enough of poker to know it was a game of chance but also of strategy. No reason I couldn't hold my own.

"Now, what could be so important that you dragged me over here?" Jenner inquired, peeking at his cards before looking at each of us in turn.

I shot a questioning look to Arys. These casinos were under heavy watch. Could we talk freely about such things here?

"Alexa killed Linden about an hour ago," Arys said brazenly, answering my question. "Is that important enough? We fly out at midnight. I thought it was worth sharing with you first. It changes things."

Jenner was silent. Not only did I have no idea how good his hand was, I had no idea what he was thinking. His poker face was exceptional.

A peek at my own cards revealed an ace and the two of clubs. Folding never crossed my mind. It would be like giving in before I knew what kind of chance I stood. So, when Jenner raised the pot to five grand, I sucked in a deep breath but matched the bet.

"Linden's dead? Good job." His icy gaze swept over me in appraisal. Clearly, someone was still harboring a grudge. Couldn't say I blamed him. "So what now?"

The dealer laid the first three cards on the table, and Arys immediately folded. Big baby.

"Now we take apart the rest of the blood ring before it can recover from the loss. That will be your job. Think you can handle it?" Arys and Jenner shared a look. Something unspoken passed between them.

I was feeling good about my cards so I continued to stay in the game. Big mistake. The dealer laid the last two down, and my certainty changed as Jenner's straight beat my three of a kind. Crap.

"Don't you think it would be easier to take over the blood ring rather than disband it?" Jenner suggested, pulling my chips into his pile, shooting me a smarmy smile as he did so. "At least if we control it, we can make changes. Such as, no more kids."

I chewed my bottom lip, an anxious habit I'd never been able to break. He did have a point, it just sounded so sketchy.

"The only way I'm going to agree to that is if we take it even further," I said, peeking at the new cards I'd been dealt. "No innocents at all."

The lady dealing had the best poker face of us all. She went through the motions of her job without reacting to our conversation. Either she didn't care, or she knew better than to get involved.

Jenner scoffed. "You clearly don't understand how supply and demand works. That's asking too much."

"And you clearly don't understand that I'm not asking." Again, I chose to hold my cards, a pair of fours. Not the best hand by any means but still worth a shot.

Arys watched our exchange with thinly veiled amusement. I think he had been waiting a long time for this moment, when I would become a thorn in the side of his vampire kin.

"You know, Alexa," Arys said with a chuckle after I lost the next hand. "Sometimes you have to fold. It's not always worth the risk."

"Even the shittiest hand has the possibility of being a win," I retorted. "I just have to be a better liar than a vampire."

"Which you aren't," Jenner quipped. "You're still too human."

That shouldn't have been an insult, but for some reason, I took it as one. Jenner wore his disdain of me like a fragrance. He stunk of it. He had every damn right. And yet, he'd put me in a position of having to prove myself to be vampire enough to rule at Arys's side.

I held Jenner's gaze, a coy smile curving my lips. "Did you taste anything human in my blood?" I taunted. Without twitching a finger, I reached out to him with a gentle push of power, just enough to envelope him in a seductive haze. I didn't even have to touch him to make him want me. It was so wrong for so many reasons, yet I felt empowered. This time I raised the bet, feeling a little cocky. Having an advantage felt liberating. It didn't happen often enough.

Jenner stiffened and broke eye contact. "What the hell do you want me to do? Since you're laying claim to this city, that makes the blood ring your damn problem. Not mine."

I let Arys field that one. It was his choice to take control of his former home city. I had my hands full enough with Edmonton. Piling Vegas on top of that was bound to give me a nervous breakdown.

"While I'm away, you will run the city. You will also, however, answer to me. Be my right hand, Jenner. We can reign here, together." Arys tossed some chips in as a bet, but his eyes were on the other vampire.

Jenner mulled over the offer. We played another hand, and I actually won. The thrill was instant and a little addictive. Fun rush, though I'd had better.

"I won't be your whipping boy, Arys. If I act as your right hand, then I get a say in what goes on here too."

"Of course."

"The blood ring relied heavily on us for their supply. We lured people in for them. Now would be a good time to try a takeover. But it's not going to be easy." He looked from Arys to me and back again. "I want one thing. Sloane. When she turns up, I deal with her. Not you guys."

"Fuck that," I protested at the same time Arys said, "Deal."

I shot my twin flame a dark glare. Jenner didn't try to hide his enjoyment of our conflicting responses. I jumped in, just barely restraining myself from an angry tirade.

"You damn well better gain control of that blood ring. No children. No expecting women and no rape or abuse. Or I'll be coming back here for you." My threat lacked the satisfaction I usually felt when issuing one. Leaving the blood business running in any way didn't sit well with me. Still I knew Jenner was right. Something like that couldn't be dissolved overnight.

"Start replacing the innocents with evil doers," Arys added. "There are more than enough here. Rapists, murderers, pimps, whatever. Find them. Sell them. Tell the buyers that's what they get now. If they don't like it, they hunt their own prey, and then you kill them."

Jenner sat back in his chair, fuming. The anger rolled off him like steam. "All I want to do is run The Wicked Kiss, my way. I walked away from the blood ring for a reason."

"Then have Roscoe or someone else do the dirty work. Just get it done." Arys's tone had dropped to a deadly low.

I was with Jenner on this one. I wanted nothing to do with the blood ring. I just wanted it gone.

"So you get to come here, issue commands and leave me with the mess. Sounds about right. You've always been the flighty one." Jenner's insult rolled off Arys who shrugged.

"The mess was here when we arrived," I interjected. "In fact, I'm pretty sure you would be ashes in the desert right now if we hadn't been here." Leaving Jenner brimming with hate and rage was not going to be in anyone's best interest. Swallowing my pride, I angled at a ceasefire. "According to Hurst, our bloodline is crazy powerful. We need to be united, not divided. Especially now."

Jenner's chips clicked together loudly as he threw them down to place a bet. "I have a bad feeling about this."

I laughed bitterly. "I've had that feeling since I got here."

The hunger that burned in his gaze was startling. He watched the pulse in my throat and licked his lips. The backlash from what I'd done to him might be cause for concern. If he went down the same road as Kale…but no, that couldn't happen. Kale's madness was due to much more than a taste of my blood.

"I'd rather die than be yours." Jenner's admission was low, a murmur, yet I heard it clearly.

"You're not the first to tell me that," I quipped. "Should I just kill you now and get it over with then?"

Much to my surprise, Jenner folded. He tossed his cards down and gave up the win, which had he held out, would have been his. His loss felt symbolic.

"God, I hate you," he muttered.

I happily added his chips to my dwindling stack. "Consider me extremely relieved. I've come to learn that a vampire's love is far deadlier than his hatred."

Arys's expression was unreadable. If he was perturbed by my claim, he didn't show it.

"Anything else?" Jenner rose. His poker face no longer in place, he regarded us each with utter contempt.

"We'll be in touch," Arys replied coolly. "Oh, and Jenner, it's not so bad really. Being hers. One day, you might even like it."

There wasn't much Jenner could say. His own game turned on him. If he hadn't forced us to play, he wouldn't have lost. With a glower so hot it almost burned, he stalked out with a hateful, "Go to hell."

"That went well," Arys observed, watching his brother go. "Better than I expected really."

"You shouldn't have said that," I scolded, thinking of Kale. "You don't know what it's like to be mine the way he is. The way Kale is."

"Nobody is yours the way Sinclair is." Arys's expression turned from grim satisfaction to open hostility at the mention of Kale's name. "Don't forget, Alexa. I longed for you before you were even born. There is no one deeper under your spell than me." That knocked me down a peg. I often reminded myself that Arys had waited for me for over a century. His staying power was admirable. I'd have lost my mind years ago.

"You're right. Love is a two way street, and I tend to forget that you've walked it much longer than I have." I went to him, leaning down to slide my arms around him. "I'm sorry, Arys."

He patted my arm and graced me with a tender smile. "Don't be. It's been a hectic few days. Let's go home."

Chapter Eighteen

Damn it felt good to be home. I stretched languorously in my bed, all but hugging the mattress. Well, there may have been a little hugging of the mattress. Leaving home felt nice, but nothing compared to returning.

We had landed in Edmonton before sunrise. Needing some time to myself, I'd sent both of my boys on their way and headed home alone. My mind was cluttered, and I needed some quality time with my pillow in my own house.

It took many attempts to haul my ass out of bed at sundown. The temptation to stay immersed in the soft blankets until hunger forced me out was strong, though not stronger than my insatiable need for knowledge.

I planned a coffee date with Brogan. The talented witch had agreed to meet with me regarding the amulet her mother had left me. Hurst had shed much light upon it, but I needed to know more. I needed verification.

After a hot shower, I applied some smoky eye makeup and blow-dried my hair. All the while, I turned over the events of our trip in my head. I'd known it would be crazy, but it had exceeded my expectations.

Jenner lingered in my thoughts. Part of me wished I could go back in time and undo what I'd done to him. That had to be the scrap of humanity I had left. The side of me that was ruled by the vampire thought his arrogant ass had deserved it. Still, he was under my thrall now, a victim of my manipulation. That had to be all kinds of wrong.

It was bittersweet to have to leave my house so soon after returning. I had recently purchased it, and it still had that new feeling to it. It wasn't lived in enough. I cast a longing look out my living room window at the forest beyond my backyard. The forest was the main reason I had chosen the house, other than the lack of neighbors; the place was just too perfect for someone like me.

Slinging my bag onto my shoulder, I locked up and made the quick trek from my small town to the big city just down the highway. Being on the open road with the local rock station blasting was invigorating. It made it almost possible to ignore the steady hum of the amulet in my bag.

A quick stop at Starbucks for two Frappuccinos, and I was on my way to Toil and Trouble, the small magic shop Brogan had inherited from Lena. It was a cozy little place on the south side of the city. Hopefully it wouldn't be too busy this close to closing time.

The door chime sounded as I entered. The scent of incense greeted me. A table filled with gemstones sat in the center with a sale sign hanging overhead. Shelves lined with spell books hugged the walls. Everything from love charms to voodoo dolls graced Brogan's shop.

"Hey, welcome home!" Brogan called out from the back where she was arranging a jewelry display. "How was the trip? Looks like you made it back in one piece."

"Just barely. The trip was a nightmare." I crossed the store to where she was and handed her a coffee. "You like caramel, right?"

"Love it. Thanks." She took a sip and made a face of pure joy. "So good. Now, tell me about your trip."

I gave her the recap of my Vegas vacation while browsing the aisles. A display case filled with vampire hunting tools caught my eye. "This is new. Isn't it?"

Brogan shrugged. "It's a novelty item. I've had requests for it. Nobody is going to hunt vampires with that stuff. I mean, there's a bottle of holy water in there. That doesn't even work on vampires."

No, it would work on demons or fallen angels though. It piqued my interest that someone had specifically asked for vampire hunting gear though. "Who asked you to order in this stuff?"

"I have no idea. I get calls and emails about stuff like that all the time. Nobody has bought any of it yet though." She paused, scrutinizing the so-called vampire hunter kit. "You don't think it was a serious request, do you?"

"Can't be too careful in this city." A laugh bubbled up. "Next time you get a call like that, refer them to Vegas. The vampire population there is outrageous."

"So the amulet my mom gave you, that's what you want my help with? I can take a look at it, tell you if she spelled it and how—"

She broke off as the door opened with a chime. The telltale pulse of raw power accompanied the new arrival, and I turned to find Gabriel in the entryway. He nodded a grim hello in our direction but said nothing as he made his way to a shelf filled with spelling accessories.

Gabriel was young, just nineteen. He possessed more natural power than any human I'd ever known. Unfortunately, that had made him a target for Shya. The same demon that meddled in my life had lured Gabriel in, tainting him with black magic. I could feel it. The murky pull of darkness cloaked him. Apparently, he was still very much involved with the demon.

"Can I help you find anything?" Brogan approached him cautiously. "I just got some new stones in. And a few new books too."

I hung back, unwilling to get too close. Gabriel was precognitive. With just a touch, he could see glimpses of one's future. Since he had told me he saw me as a vampire, I didn't want to get too close. He'd said it wasn't pretty, whatever that meant. Despite my attempts to keep him away from Shya, Gabriel had willingly become part of the demon's inner circle.

"No, thanks. Just grabbing a few things I'm low on." Gabriel was standoffish, unwilling to engage more than he had to. He gathered several items including black candles, some herbs and a scrying mirror.

Brogan and I exchanged a look. The kid was in over his head, and he didn't realize how deep. I thought about what Hurst had said, his warning that Arys could not turn Gabriel as Shya had made him promise. Gabriel was already too dangerous. Vampirism would take that to a new and alarming level.

After collecting his things, he went to the counter where Brogan joined him. She attempted to engage him in small talk, but he would have none of it. With his long, dyed-black hair falling in his face and black liner smudged around his eyes, he looked like any other Goth kid. I knew better though.

Much to my surprise, he paused on his way out. Turning back to face me, he opened his mouth as if to speak but then thought better of it. For a moment, our gazes locked, and I saw something evil lurking inside him. Before I could say anything, he shoved through the door and disappeared.

"I can't say for sure, but I think he just bought the things needed to do a resurrection spell." Brogan's hazel eyes reflected her concern. "I wish there was something I could do. It's not like I can refuse to sell to him."

"No, definitely don't do that. He'll just get it online or something. At least if he buys it here, we can track what he's using." A resurrection spell? I shook my head and repressed a shudder. That was all kinds of bad news. "I'm sorry, Brogan. I know you're worried about him. I wish there was more we could do."

"There has to be something." She gazed down at her copy of the receipt and frowned. "Well anyway, let's go sit in the back and take a look at that amulet."

I flipped through a book on zombies while she locked up. It was impossible to tell if it was fiction or if the writer had believed every word to be truth. I would certainly take such things with a grain of salt. Although, considering Gabriel was working resurrection spells, perhaps I should consider reading up on zombies more thoroughly. As much as I didn't want to, I would find out why Shya had Gabriel doing such spells. And hopefully, I would find a way to stop it.

We sat at the table in the cluttered back storage room. I pulled the amulet from my bag, more drawn to it now than ever before. The teardrop-shaped, smooth, black stone warmed at my touch.

"Oh yes, I remember this one." Brogan took the amulet and turned it over in careful examination. "It's definitely been spelled. I can do a revelation spell. It should reveal what exactly my mother did to it without touching her spell."

I gestured for her to go ahead. This was not my area of expertise. I watched in silent wonder as Brogan fetched a few supplies. After lighting blue candles and sprinkling some fine powder into the flames, she spoke a phrase in Latin, and the amulet began to glow. My heart jumped when she slowly passed the amulet through the candle flame. To my utter shock, an image began to form on the surface. The faint outline of a yin yang glimmered in the candlelight. I sucked in a breath and held it.

"It's made of black onyx," Brogan began. "A stone meant for grounding, for connection to the earth and its energy. It has the ability to ward off negative energy given off by others. Only natural energy though. It won't do much against someone like Shya."

"Hurst said it will keep my wolf inside me when I die a mortal death. Can you verify that?"

"Yes. It feels like my mom tied the spell to you. I can feel its purpose. It won't be activated until your death. Then it should bind your wolf to the amulet, keeping it safe until your transition is complete." She handed the amulet back with a gentle smile. "My mom always was so good at planning ahead."

"How did she know?" I asked, going back to my final conversations with Lena. She had known about Arys and me. She'd been the first to tell me our bond was meant to be. Could she have known the risk it posed to my wolf?

Brogan shook her blonde head, and her smile grew. "Even now, Mom never stops surprising me. She was so intuitive."

"She gave me the greatest gift. I wish I could thank her." Sorrow gripped me in its rough clutches. Lena's death had come at the hands of two members of the blood ring. I'd killed both Claire and Maxwell, but it would never be enough. I couldn't bring her back.

I gave Brogan's arm a friendly pat. "You know I owe you, right? For life. Seriously. Anything you need, anything I can ever do. Don't hesitate."

She started to protest then thought better of it. "Thank you, Alexa. That means a lot to me. My mom really loved you." A solemn silence fell as we each remembered Lena in our own way. Then Brogan snapped out of it, her cheery tone tight and forced. "Let me turn that amulet into a pendant for you. It's best if you wear it. All the time. Even in the shower."

Just ten minutes later, the shiny onyx stone was ready to wear. Using a special drill made for such things, Brogan drilled a small hole in the top of the teardrop. She slipped it onto a strong piece of leather, which I tied securely around my neck.

The moment the stone lay against my chest, a slight dizzy spell hit me. It aligned itself to the earthy energy of my wolf, and a sense of serene calm spread through me. It felt right. I could have cried with relief. I might lose my light, but I would not lose my wolf.

I gave Brogan a hug and said goodnight. Halfway to the door she stopped me with a frantic plea. "Please let me know if there's anything I can do to help Gabriel. If he's ever in trouble or anything…"

"I'll keep you posted, but I won't get you involved. As long as you're not on anybody's radar, I won't do anything to change that."

As I exited Toil and Trouble, I made a silent vow to keep that promise. Too many people I loved were already under Shya's thumb in one way or another. The precious few that were not part of that needed to stay that way.

I'd told myself that I'd take a few days at home to just chill and recover from Vegas. Still, I found myself driving across the river toward downtown and The Wicked Kiss. Since I was already in the city, I might as well make sure the building was still standing. Leaving Kale in charge in his current mental state was chancy. Seeing him wasn't something I'd been planning to do so soon. As long as we weren't alone together, nothing should come of it. Besides, during the flight home, I'd done some thinking and made some decisions regarding the nightclub Kale and I shared. We had work to do.

By the time I reached the club, I was convinced I should have gone back home to bed. Still, it didn't stop me from getting out of the car. Kale's classic Camaro was in the parking lot. Crap. So much for the hope that he wasn't here. It made me sad, the realization that, every time I came to the Kiss now, I held out hope that it would be at a time when Kale was elsewhere. We had been such close friends once.

It was still early. The place wouldn't be crowded for a few hours yet; the parking lot was especially empty. Suspicious. The guys working the door greeted me as I passed through the lobby. Was it just me or were they stiffer than usual? When I stepped into the heart of the club, I saw why.

The place was a total disaster. Worse than I'd ever seen it, and I'd seen it in pretty rough shape. Tables were not just overturned but smashed. Chairs littered the floor as if they'd been tossed around by a tornado. Broken glass crunched under my feet. The aroma of liquor and blood dominated the air while violence colored the atmosphere.

In the middle of it all stood Kale and Willow. They each looked up at my appearance in jaw-dropped surprise. I'd interrupted their clean up attempt. I stood frozen, staring at them, unable to form words just yet. They exchanged a look with one another.

"Do I even want to know?" I swept through the room, stepping over fragments of table and other miscellaneous debris. Was that a burn mark on the ceiling?

"No," they said in unison before dissolving into nervous laughter. They had definitely not been expecting me.

"You're home sooner than I expected," Kale remarked with a secretive smile. "Glad to see you're relatively unscathed. How was Vegas?"

I stared at the trashed stage, biting back the stream of curses that threatened to spill forth. "It was a fucking gong show. Apparently, I missed something while I was gone. Want to fill me in?"

Willow turned away, hiding what I think was another laugh. He disappeared behind the bar, leaving Kale to answer my questions.

"Not particularly," Kale said with a shrug. "Had a little trouble is all. I took care of it. Nothing for you to concern yourself with."

"Is that so?" I eyed him skeptically. "Looks to me like I was right about leaving you in charge here. Another day or two, and there probably wouldn't even be a building left to trash."

Kale didn't say anything for a moment. He continued to throw pieces of wood and glass into a large pile in the center of the room. The muscles in his arms and back rippled as he did so. He seldom dressed so casually in jeans and a t-shirt, so I allowed myself a moment to enjoy the view.

"Gee, thanks; glad to see you too," he said. His tone dripped sarcasm. "Actually, I'm the reason this place is still standing, among other things. Though I don't expect you to believe that."

Willow emerged from the bar with a tequila in one hand and the Dragon Claw in the other. He passed me the dagger, which I happily accepted. It was so good to have it back in my hands.

"I'm sorry I wasn't able to help when you ran into trouble," he said. "Kale knew you were in trouble, but without a location I couldn't jump to you."

My gaze lingered on Kale who had turned his back on me as he continued to clean up. "No worries. Shya sent Falon, who was a total asshole like usual, but he helped. I'm here now, so it's all good."

"Is it?" Willow questioned, his gold-flecked green eyes intense upon me. "Then why are you back early?"

He walked along beside me as I perused the perimeter, surveying the extent of the damage. I gave him the quick version, aware that Kale's keen ears heard my every word. I wasn't ready to share with anyone what had happened with Jenner.

"You're taking over Las Vegas?" Concern glimmered in Willow's eyes. "Might I suggest you wait until Shya's been dealt with?"

"That's the plan. Vegas is a fucking mess of vampire chaos. I'm not prepared to handle that right now. Someone else will be taking care of it until Arys and I can get back there."

As Willow and I talked, Kale kept working in silence. I wondered what he was thinking. My curiosity was dying to know why Willow was here with him, but I didn't dare ask just yet. Kale was trying to keep something from me, and after the trip I'd just had, I was ok with that.

As I walked through the mess that had been a fully functioning nightclub just days before, I put together a mental list. Jenner's club had intimidated me. It had also made mine look like a sleazy joint compared to his high-class style. I wanted to renovate.

I pulled out my phone and began to take notes. The old booths lining the exterior walls had to go. They were hard and uncomfortable. More furniture was needed and new light fixtures. The current ones were ugly and ancient.

Willow returned to help Kale as I made my way to the back. He was committed to keeping the vampire's secret. Whatever had gone on here, they felt the need to keep it from me. Had it been anyone else, I would have been pissed, but I trusted Willow implicitly.

The back hall was lined with rooms where vampires and willing victims came to play. It was adequate but shady, not much better than a low budget hotel. That was going to change.

I went to the last door at the end of the hall, the one room that was forbidden to all but me. It had been the suite Harley stayed in when he'd come to town. The same room I killed him in. Now it was mine. And as much as I wanted to deny it, I might actually need to make use of it one day. So it might as well be nice. I stood in the doorway, scrutinizing everything from the cheap bedding to the less than impressive en suite bathroom. It was about as good as the one at Linden's warehouse. Unacceptable.

I felt Kale's honey sweet energy draw closer, so it came as no surprise when from right behind me he said, "I'm sorry about the mess. Everything goes to shit when the queen is away."

A chill stole over me. I turned to face him, knowing better than to allow him at my back. "Seriously? What's with everyone and the fucking royalty references lately?"

Kale shrugged and leaned against the doorframe, crossing his arms. "I guess you're the only one still in denial about it."

"Apparently so." With a raised brow I gave him a critical once over. He was unpredictable, and sadly, I couldn't trust him anymore, not since his promise to force my hand, to make me stake him.

My phone rang, startling me as it blasted a Weird Al Yankovic song. *Damn you, Arys.* That vampire thought he was so funny. One of these days, I was going to bust him messing with my ringtone, and then he'd be sorry.

"Alexa, you're home!" My best friend Kylarai gushed excitedly in my ear. "I've been dying to share my news with you. Is this a bad time?"

I glanced at Kale who likely could hear every word she said. He wore a bored expression.

"Not at all. What's up? You sound like you're going to explode. Must be good news." I tensed, waiting for her to tell me something amazing, because I sure could use some good news.

"You're not going to believe this. I could just pee my pants with glee." Her giggle brought a smile to my face. She took a deep, audible breath and said in a rush, "I'm engaged!" It was better than good news. It was fantastic.

"Aw, congratulations. Nobody deserves it more than you. He's such a great guy." My words were sincere. I couldn't be happier for her.

After many failed relationships, including a previous marriage, Kylarai had connected immediately with Coby. Having survived my attack on him several months ago, he'd come into our pack as a wary but gentle soul. They hadn't been together long, but they were a perfect match.

"You don't think we're rushing it, do you?" Ky asked uncertainly. "I know it's only been a couple of months, but it feels right, you know? And I really want to have an autumn wedding."

"Autumn? It's practically the end of summer. That doesn't give you much time to plan."

"I know. That's why I need your help. The engagement party is next weekend. I figured you'd be back by then."

My heart jumped for her. It gave me hope, seeing how my attack on Coby had led to their engagement. Maybe good could come from bad after all.

"I don't think it's too fast if you believe in your heart that he's the one," I said, my voice catching. The weight of Kale's stare was suddenly too much to take. "Anything you need, just let me know. I'm here to help."

"You'll be my maid of honor, right?"

Her hopeful request made it hard to swallow. Emotion choked me. "Yeah, of course I will."

Tears pricked the back of my eyes, and I blinked them away. This was so good for her. I squashed the tiny thread of envy that wove its way through me. I was genuinely happy for her.

After I hung up, I dragged my gaze back to Kale's.

He nodded and forced a tight smile. "Kylarai's getting married. How wonderful for her. She's the kindest soul I've ever met. I hope they find much happiness together." There was no lie in him. Despite their very brief fling, Kale had always hoped Ky would find the man she belonged with.

"Yeah, me too."

"I guess some people get their happy ending after all."

His comment struck too close to home. This was not a conversation I wanted to be having. "I want to renovate," I said, hoping to change the subject. "This place needed work before you trashed it. So we might as well take advantage of the mess and turn it into something better."

Kale smirked openly. "You saw the Vegas club and felt inferior, huh? That's ok. I get it. I've seen it. So, what did you have in mind?"

"I don't feel inferior to the Vegas vampires," I said hotly, my cheeks flushed. "I just think the place needs a makeover. Will you help?"

The weight of his brown and blue gaze was heavy as he considered my request. He stared at me until I grew twitchy. "Sure. Why not?"

I shielded hard against the onslaught of energy seeping from him. It was too tempting. He gave off a hungry vibe, one that made me wonder if he'd been feeding. Someone as mentally fragile as him was dangerous enough when well fed. If he denied himself too long, he could be absolutely deadly.

"Good. We can start with the club and work our way back here. That should keep you busy." I walked around the room to put some distance between us. I didn't like the way he was watching me.

"Right. Because keeping me busy will change things." Something in his tone set my skin to crawling. I looked at him sharply. He was still leaning in the doorframe, casual and calm, but there was something malevolent lurking beneath the surface.

"I've had the worst week ever. The last thing I need is to come home to your crazy ass spewing ugly promises. Can't you let it go?" I was tired of vampires and their personal vendettas. Was it really so impossible for them to let go of a grudge?

"Let it go?" He repeated. His shoulders stiffened despite his relaxed pose. "You've made a slave of me, and you want me to just get over it? That's not how this works, Alexa."

"Evidently." I sighed. "Kale, please, you have to understand that I would never have intentionally done anything to hurt you. Things are happening, big things that I can't control. I need you with me, not against me."

"Well, if the queen needs something, then who am I to deny her?" Bitterness laced his words. Emotion stormed him, a conflict of feelings that battered my shields.

I shook my head, his name a whisper on my lips. "What can I do to change this vengeful need you have? We were friends once. Partners."

"We were lovers too. Once. For a brief moment." His gaze dropped, and he stared at the floor. "I'm sorry it is the way it is. You claimed me. You drew me in, and you made me yours. It was purely intentional, and we both know it. There is no changing something like that. It is what it is."

I couldn't dispute his claim. I had done exactly what he said. The worst part? I didn't regret it. Not really. This selfish little part of me wanted Kale to be mine in whatever way I could have him. Of the two of us, I was the worst monster. "You're right." I relented, leaning against the wall opposite him. "I'm a selfish bitch as far as you're concerned, Kale. And I don't know why."

His head came up suddenly, and he fixed me with a stare so intense it made me uneasy. "You know why. You will probably never admit it to either of us, but you know why." A bark of hostile laughter racked him. "Arys must just fucking love that you want me as bad as I want you."

Ignoring that last jab, I tried to push the conversation to a conclusion. "So that's it then? You carry on this game of crazy vampire until I get sick of it and stake you?"

"Something like that."

"I don't understand why."

"Don't you? Think about it. Think about belonging to someone with every part of your being. Think about needing someone so bad, and never being able to have them." There was pain in his eyes, quickly replaced by rage. He was so very unstable. "There is no moving on for our kind. Humans are gifted with short-term memories and fickle hearts. But us, when we love, it is always forever."

His declaration stole my breath as an ill sensation developed in my gut. His reference to our kind, as if I were already vampire, chilled me to the bone. I imagined having to watch Arys bond with someone else while I remained his always, and I knew that whatever Kale was going through, I would never understand.

An apology wasn't going to cut it, not for something like this. Sorry would be a greater insult than silence. So I said nothing. After the silence grew unbearable, I gathered myself and left the room. Kale moved aside to let me pass.

It hurt me to know how much I was hurting him. What hurt most of all was knowing I could do nothing to change it, nothing to save him. Only death would bring him relief. And that, I could not give him.

"Hey, Alexa," he called after me. "Welcome home."

Chapter Nineteen

I sipped a cold beer and eyed the TV in the corner of the bar, the cause of so much shouting among the patrons. Sports lounges really weren't my kind of place. I waited for Agent Thomas Briggs to arrive for this little meeting he'd insisted upon.

Arys sat beside me, watching the big screen with veiled interest. He might be a big bad vampire, but I'd seen him rant and rave at the TV during an intense game. There had been no convincing him to let me handle Briggs alone. He was determined to show this city our united front, to spread and enforce the word that we were in power here. I imagined that wouldn't go over too well with others.

"We've barely been back a week, and the FPA is already demanding secret meetings in neutral locations. That's bullshit. They want you bad, and I don't trust how far they're willing to go to get you." A muscle in Arys's jaw twitched, a sure indicator that his temper was on a short leash.

"Briggs is as bad as Shya when it comes to collecting people," I said with a shrug. "He's an idiot if he thinks I can be persuaded to work for the government. I think the demon is less corrupt."

Arys's blue gaze traveled over the other lounge occupants. He scrutinized them each in turn, as if deciding if they met his criteria for a potential victim, whatever those criteria were. Every time I thought I knew, the vampire surprised me. His boundaries were few and far between.

"Jenner did one thing right," Arys mused. "Getting the FPA on his pay roll was a smart move. Harley never bothered with such things. He preferred his FPA encounters to be bloody."

The lounge door opened, and Briggs strode in, looking every bit as much like a movie Fed as I'd ever seen him. With his dark hair cropped short, tailored suit hugging his body like a glove and sunglasses hiding his brown eyes, he had a real *Men in Black* thing going.

At his side was my younger sister and fellow werewolf, Juliet O'Brien. Brunette curls gave her a soft edge that was otherwise missing in her stiff appearance. In jeans and a leather jacket, she exuded a sense of badass that didn't match her federal agent status. She was wolf and family. She shouldn't be with them. But she was. And I would have been too if the FPA had it their way.

"Something tells me that Briggs isn't the kind of guy that can be bought," I said beneath my breath.

Arys gave my thigh a squeeze and murmured, "We'll see about that."

Juliet and Briggs slid into the booth across from us. A waitress promptly appeared to take their order. Juliet requested an iced tea, while Briggs barked a short order for coffee.

"Thank you for being so accommodating," Briggs said when the waitress had departed. "I appreciate it."

His gaze flicked from me to Arys, and I saw the derision in his eyes. If he'd had it his way, Arys wouldn't be here. Briggs wouldn't be the first to find dealing with the vampire to be difficult, maybe even unbearable. Arys didn't like to play nice with very many people.

I exchanged small talk with my sister, feeling somewhat awkward but finding genuine warmth in her smile. Things had been strained between us since I'd discovered she survived the wolf attack that turned us both. The Feds had raised her into someone I couldn't trust. That was so hard. Slowly, we were getting to know one another again.

Arys waited until the waitress had come and gone again. Then he leaned forward and said, "Start talking, Briggs. Why did you call this little gathering? I'm sure it wasn't because you missed us so damn much while we were away."

"Not at all." Briggs removed his shades and set them on the table beside his coffee cup. "I don't want to be here anymore than you do. When we get reports, I have no choice but to follow up."

"What now?" I had a sinking feeling that I knew where this was going.

Briggs gave me a level stare. As pretentious as the Fed could be, he was a pretty straight shooter, a no nonsense kind of guy, and I could respect that, even when he accused me of murder.

"Did you kill a federal agent in Las Vegas?" His question was for me. The way he said it came off as more of a statement than a question.

I took a long, slow sip of beer, choosing my words carefully before responding. Good news sure traveled fast. "I killed a vampire in Las Vegas. One who was running a very sick and fucking twisted blood ring. If he happened to be a Fed, then that's on you guys. Not me."

"Son of a bitch." Briggs took a swig of coffee, putting his mug down so hard it splashed over the edge. "It's a crime to kill a federal agent, even one that isn't human."

Arys's energy buzzed with displeasure. "Is it not also illegal to traffic human beings? Are you saying that you turn a blind eye to agents involved in such activity?"

"No. Of course not. That kind of shit is inexcusable." Briggs scowled into his mug. "Can you provide some kind of proof of this allegation?"

I didn't know whether to laugh in his face or claw his eyes out. "Are you kidding me? I shouldn't have to prove that one of your guys was up to no good. That's the FPA's problem. Which we are solving by taking over the blood ring with the intent to disband it entirely. If anything, you should have come here to thank me, not question me."

Juliet shifted in her seat, glancing uneasily from Briggs to me. There was something in the way she looked at him, something not entirely professional. Were they sleeping together? Sure Briggs was a hottie with that creamy dark skin, deep voice and intense government persona, but Juliet was playing with fire. It wasn't my business though. My opinion would stay right where it was, in my head.

"Lexi, we take it very seriously when our agents are suspected of being involved in something illegal. There is no law against killing a vampire, but you must understand why we need to follow up on this." Juliet appealed to my sensible side, hoping I'd respond favorably.

She wouldn't look at Arys for long. Despite her tough exterior, he intimidated her. They hadn't really met under the best circumstances.

"Sure. I just don't understand why you need me to do that. The way I see it, I did you guys a favor." I fixed Briggs with an ice-cold stare, daring him to make this my problem. "The entire Las Vegas FPA is corrupt. They've been in bed with the vampires there for a while now. So forgive me if I don't feel bad about dispatching one of their sorry asses from the planet."

Briggs seemed to be exerting great effort in keeping his jaw from dropping. The grip on his mug tightened, and his slow, steady breathing was incredibly forced. He looked to Juliet who shook her head. Nope. I wasn't lying.

"What the hell are you talking about?"

Arys nudged me under the table. Maybe I shouldn't have shared Jenner's business transactions with Briggs, but I wanted him to know that the FPA as a whole had much bigger problems than me killing one measly vampire.

"Come now, Agent Briggs," Arys said in his best placating tone. "Don't pretend such corruption is unheard of in your organization. I'm sure the place is built on it."

Briggs's temper flared. He pounded a fist on the table, almost upsetting my beer bottle. "I can assure you, Mr. Knight, that no agent works with the enemy without just cause."

"The enemy?" I repeated, incredulous at his broad description for an entire species. "That's how you classify us? Well, now that I know where we stand, I'm pretty sure it's safe to say we can never and will never be able to work together. On anything. Not even Shya."

"It's a general fucking term, O'Brien," Briggs snarled, directing his angry gaze my way. "You are a goddamn monster, in case you've forgotten."

Rage roared beneath the surface of my skin, threatening to burst forth like lava. Briggs was going to get burned if he didn't watch it. "The worst monster I see here is the one throwing the word around while trying desperately to paint Feds as puritans. Get off your fucking high horse, Briggs." I was seething. Letting him enrage me was playing right into his hands. A few calming breaths did little to help.

"Ok, let's just keep things calm here." Juliet held up a hand, demanding attention. "There is no reason we can't discuss this rationally. Alexa, we'll look into your claims. But please, can you agree to allow us to handle it next time you come across something as serious as a blood ring headed by an agent?"

I stared at her like she was speaking another language. "Um, what? No, I can't agree to anything so absolutely ludicrous. That fucker had children. Do you understand what that means? Vampires trafficking kids. Entertain that thought for a minute, will you?" I leaned back in my seat, arms crossed, angry gaze leveled on Briggs. If he was going to make me get graphic, I would. But I think he knew better than to push me on this.

After a few minutes of strained silence, Briggs relented. "You're right, O'Brien. That's some sick shit. Putting a stop to it should be a priority. I'll take a look at the Las Vegas department myself, see what's going on there."

"And?" I was suspicious. He had changed his tune too easily.

"And I suppose I'll do what I can to get the higher ups off your case. You made a call you thought was best that ultimately served the safety of the public. It wouldn't be fair to hassle you further on this."

I gawked at him, unsure of where this change of attitude had come from. Maybe sleeping with my sister was changing Briggs's opinion of me. One could only hope. Although if that was the case, things could get sour very quickly if it didn't work out with them.

"Thank you." I raised my beer bottle to him before finishing the last of the brew. "You're all wrong about me, Briggs. I am not the enemy. I don't know why I have to keep saying so."

"That's the way the world works." He shrugged. "We're all the villain in somebody's story. Get over it."

Arys snickered. He knew that Briggs was pushing all the wrong buttons. "You're talking the wrong crap to the wrong woman, my friend. Stop while you're ahead."

"Nobody here is a villain," Juliet insisted, her gaze lingering on Arys. "Not even you. Otherwise, you wouldn't be so dedicated to taking care of my sister. There's no reason that we can't work together for the good of this city."

I was starting to get the feeling that this meeting had never been about Linden's murder. It was just a ploy for Briggs to get me face to face so he could grill me further about Shya. "Don't start with the Shya talk again," I warned. "I have nothing to share with you."

Briggs swore and set his mug down hard, rattling the unused silverware. He was very comfortable in his bad cop role. "You know he's up to something. We need your help to stop him."

"Stop him from what?" Arys inquired with a raised brow and half smile.

"We don't know, and we don't want to find out the hard way." Briggs turned his angry stare on the vampire where it was completely wasted. "You both have the opportunity to do some good here. Choose carefully what side you want to be on."

I'd about had it with Briggs. He was so sure of himself, so sure he knew where Arys and I stood. Because we had power and were inhuman, he put us in a box with Shya, assuming us to be the same. I was done with that shit. "You don't know what the fuck you're talking about," I spat. "Do you think I walk around with a demon mark on my arm because I like it? Just because I won't work for you doesn't mean I'm working for Shya. There are many things you don't know about me, which is exactly how I'd like to keep it. Stay out of my way, Briggs, and I'll stay out of yours."

"It's too late for that now," he said lazily, unfazed by my wrath. "Besides, you owe me a favor."

So I did. Having him track Jez's phone in Vegas had come at a price. "And what might that be?"

Briggs gave Juliet a nudge, and she slid out of the booth, her iced tea mostly untouched. With a nod to Arys, he turned his intense stare on me. "I'll let you know."

Tossing a few bucks down to cover their drinks, Briggs ushered Juliet from the lounge without a look back. She paused in the doorway to motion that she would call me.

I slumped in my seat and sighed, trying to remember why I'd been in such a rush to get home. The Vegas vampires weren't looking so bad now.

* * * *

Home alone with a pizza and the TV remote. It was as close to normal as things got, and it didn't happen often.

I reclined on the couch, watching a rerun of *The Walking Dead*. I couldn't remember the last time I permitted myself to have a lazy night. After the meeting with Briggs, I'd said fuck it and came home while Arys went to the local bar to play poker with his human card buddies.

Tomorrow night was Kylarai's engagement party. It was going to open the door on a new phase of life for her. It was also going to mean many hours of wedding planning. She meant the world to me. I'd do all I could to help, though I imagined she was already on top of everything.

The sound of the zombie apocalypse was accompanied by the yips and howls of coyotes outside. They would lurk around my yard and make noise as long as there was no sign of me. When I ran as wolf, they were long gone.

Staring brainlessly at the television felt really damn nice. The absence of thought was rare and welcome. It didn't take long for the images on the screen to blur as my eyelids drooped.

I was still exhausted from the trip. It was going to take some time to recover. Las Vegas was like a never-ending hangover. I could still feel it in me days later. Slumber beckoned, and I happily succumbed.

My dreams were mostly made up of random images, things I would never remember upon waking. Then the haze in my subconscious cleared, and I found myself gazing down at the inviting form of a scantily clad woman. She lay sprawled across a bed, staring up at me with terror in her wide eyes. Her dark hair was in disarray, and her body bore the marks of abuse. Her lips moved, but I ignored her pleas for mercy. If I allowed myself to enjoy her desperation, it would drive me over the edge much too quickly.

I'd had this dream before. If in fact, it was a dream at all. It wasn't the first time I'd slipped into Arys's thoughts without trying.

An overturned lamp cast a dim glow from where it lay on the floor. A small television played with the sound on mute. I didn't spare a glance at the screen; it was irrelevant. I advanced on her with lips peeled back to expose my fangs. I itched for the moment when they would pierce her flesh. The pulsing vein in her throat beckoned me, demanding I taste her.

There was no second thoughts, no consideration that I would not do this. She was already mine.

Inside Arys's mind, I was a silent passenger, feeling only what he felt. The promise of ecstasy fed my excited anticipation. It was growing increasingly difficult to drag this out. Rushing the moment her blood would flow was not to my tastes. However, one could only withhold the hunger for so long before snapping.

I tired of her shrieks and pleas, seeking to change her tune. A caress in the right place, a few whispered words in her ear, and she was a writhing mess of lust, begging me to fulfill her unholy need.

She reached up to entangle her hand in my long locks. Seeing the ash blonde strands wrapped around her fingers gave me pause. It struck me that something wasn't right here, but the bloodlust's demand washed away my confusion.

Her smooth skin was hot beneath my tongue. I licked and sucked at her jugular, groaning in need. I couldn't wait anymore. Sinking my fangs, I laughed wickedly as her moans mingled with cries. Blood burst from the vein to coat my tongue. I drank deeply, finding satisfaction at last. The dizzying storm of energy swept me up in its thrall. Fear, desire, excitement. All delectable flavors of the feed, each encouraging my hunger for all she had to give.

Never did it occur to me to stop. Not until I heard her heart stutter in its final throes. Her grip on me grew slack, and she lay motionless beneath me. I jerked back with a sigh, riding the high of the kill. Satisfied, I lay beside her lifeless body, watching the stars explode behind my eyes.

There was no guilt, no remorse of any kind. There never was in Arys's memories, not since the very beginning, three centuries ago. It merely was what it was, a moment of bliss that I was surely entitled to after so much hunger.

At last, I slipped off the bed and gathered myself. I turned to go and caught sight of myself in her bedroom mirror. It was not Arys's reflection I saw but my own. Staring back at me was my own face, lips bloodstained, and eyes that seemed to glow a deep vampire blue. My cheeks were flushed with stolen blood. Beneath my upper lip were two small and perfect fangs.

How could it be that this was not Arys's memory at all? The vampiress staring back at me was indeed me, though gazing at her, I felt detached, like she was someone else entirely.

As I backed away from the mirror in fright, my reflection did not do the same. She merely watched me with a devilish smile. I turned to run, but to where, I didn't know. All I knew was that I had to escape this place.

I awoke with a start. A noise had disturbed me. Lunging off the couch, I almost face planted on the floor when the raised bottom of the recliner tripped me up. Dazed from the sudden interruption of sleep, I pushed to my feet and whirled around to find Falon standing in the attached kitchen.

"For fuck's sakes, Falon." My shout bordered on hysterical. As far as rude awakenings go, this had to be one of the worst. "What the hell are you doing in my house?"

"Watching you sleep," he said, lifting one shoulder in a half-assed shrug. "You snore. I think you drool too. It's an ugly sight."

"Get out of my house," I seethed. "You're not welcome here. Ever. Got it?" There was something incredibly unsettling about Falon watching me sleep. It gave me the creeps in a big way.

"Hey, I knocked on the door. Nobody answered. So I let myself in."

"Liar."

"Ok, I'm lying. I came in because I have a message from Shya, and you won't answer his calls. Deal with it."

"I don't want to talk to Shya, and I sure as shit don't want to talk to you. Get out."

He walked around my living room, scrutinizing photos and touching objects on the shelf beside the TV. The bastard seemed to feed off my anger, so I kept my tirade to myself and watched him, waiting for him to get to the point.

"You don't have to talk. Just listen." Falon turned to me with a photo in his hand. It was of Shaz and me, taken long before I had known of Shya's role in my life. "You almost look innocent here. So misleading."

"You know what? I'm going to call Shya right now. I'd rather listen to his crap than yours." I rummaged through my shoulder bag for my phone, hoping it would get Falon to leave.

"Don't waste your time. He's unavailable at the moment. Which is why I'm playing messenger. Lucky us, huh?"

"Indeed." A growl laced my word. Arms crossed, I tapped a foot impatiently.

Falon returned the photo to its place before slipping back into the kitchen to peer into the fridge. He was trying to antagonize me, clearly. It was working. I wanted to kick him in the ass when he bent over to ogle my leftovers.

"Spinach?" His voice was muffled by the refrigerator. "Funny. I didn't imagine wolves to be veggie eaters. Definitely not surprised by all the booze. I suppose it helps, to drink your problems away. Might as well do as much of that as you can. You may not have much time left for such human vices."

He was hitting too close to home after the dream I'd just had. Since I still hadn't had a chance to process it, I was reluctant to talk about such things. As hard as it was to bite back the flood of curse words dancing on the tip of my tongue, I kept quiet and waited. Eventually he would have to tire of this game. Right?

After criticizing my groceries, furniture and even my attire, Falon grew bored of hearing himself talk. "Shya wants you to stay in town. After all the crap in Vegas, he insists that you stay local for a while. He wants you close."

"And he couldn't leave that in a message on my voicemail?" It was getting harder and harder to resist the urge to throw a dirty dish from the sink at him.

Falon gave me one of his famous glares, the kind that implied I was a total idiot and a waste of his precious time. "Your voicemail is always full. I'm sure you do that on purpose. And no, unfortunately, there's more."

He stepped toward me with an intimidating gait. Instinctively, I backed away, into the living room. I held up a hand to ward him off, a blue and gold psi ball blazed in my palm.

It did nothing to deter him. "Don't even try it," he warned. "I'll strip your power and leave you here crying and weak."

"What are you doing?" I gasped when he seized my arm. Turning it over so the dragon on my inner forearm was exposed, Falon dragged a finger over the winged beast, drawing some kind of symbol over top of it. I shuddered at his touch.

Nothing visible appeared, but I could feel the dark magic take hold. It burned, searing my flesh until I yelped. Although it hurt, it was nothing compared to having the dragon first etched into my forearm.

"Just a little binding so you stay put," Falon said, releasing me. "Try to leave, and it will cause you crippling pain. So please do be your stubborn self and find out the hard way. I'd love to see that."

I held my arm close, focusing on slow, steady breaths until the burning subsided. Falon left without another word. Only the sound of feathers ruffling accompanied his departure.

A binding to keep me in town? What kind of fuckery was that? I sank slowly down on the arm of the couch. Shya wanted me close bad enough to bind me. The heavy meaning of that action set bats loose inside me. My insides turned. It could only mean one thing. The time was near when he would use my death as planned to open the seal that held the scroll he so desperately sought. Had he found it already then?

A knot of panic choked me. The dream now held meaning. For a year, I'd known that I would one day rise as a vampire. Now it felt real. Things were changing and fast. Had the dream merely been a frightened projection of my subconscious, or was it a vision of what was to come?

Chapter Twenty

A house full of werewolves can make for an interesting party. The engagement party for Kylarai and Coby was off to a great start. Being there with them was easily the highlight of my whole week.

The heavenly aroma of barbecued meat tantalized my senses. It mingled with the scent of coffee, liquor and wolf. Gifts were stacked in the living room despite Ky's insistence that nobody bring any. Mine was among them, a gift certificate to a local home decor store where I knew Kylarai loved to shop.

The entire town pack was there. It had been awkward to walk into Kylarai's house, knowing what they all thought of me. Thankfully, our differences were set aside for the night. We were there to celebrate a friend. That's all that mattered.

"Are you going to run with us tonight?" Shaz leaned in close, gracing me with his musky wolf scent.

"As long as nobody has a problem with that."

Shaz pulled me in close for a nuzzle. "Well, I'm Alpha, and I say that anyone with a problem can take it up with me."

I eyed the wolves of my former pack, expecting animosity but finding none. Being kicked out of my own pack had been damn hard, though I knew it was best for everyone. For the most part my former pack was polite, greeting me as I passed, asking how I was. We all knew it was just for show. Facing them all like this made it feel very fresh.

If I'd been any one of them, I would have felt the same way. I was a liability. No longer able to promise them safety, it just made sense that I had to go. Still, I had never been a lone wolf. Until now.

A cool blast of air entered through the open patio door. People went back and forth from the house to the yard, voices raised in joyful chatter. Everyone had hugs and words of encouragement for the happy couple. I awaited my own moment with them.

I sipped from a glass of whiskey on the rocks. Falon's words flashed back to me as I savored the burn. He was right. My time for human vices was running out. I might as well make the most of it. Abandoning the notion of sipping, I slammed back the drink and rose to get another.

"Thank you for coming." Coby's gentle tone grabbed my attention.

He was standing in the kitchen, leaning on the partition that separated the small cooking area from the dining room. Short brown hair and a scruffy five o'clock shadow made him ruggedly handsome. His hazel eyes showed his gentle nature. Still a new wolf, turned by me during a fit of vampiric hunger, Coby had been adjusting well in recent weeks.

Setting my drink on the counter, I threw my arms around him in a warm hug. "I wouldn't have missed it for anything. I'm so happy for you both."

He tensed at first, then relaxed and slipped his arms around me. The embrace was brief but warm and meaningful. He and I would always be linked in some way. His forgiveness of my attack meant a lot to me.

"Alexa, I want to thank you, for everything. But especially for Kylarai. Your encouragement really helped me get the balls to ask her out in the first place." He smiled, a sheepish grin that exuded joy. "I've never been much of a love at first sight kind of guy. Not until now."

"I couldn't hand pick a better man for Kylarai than you." It was true. Ky had been hungry for love, seeking it in humans and even Kale. Her last relationship had ended badly. The fact that she even had the guts to try again spoke volumes.

Coby glanced around, ensuring nobody was paying us any attention. "Look, I know things are gonna get bad for you. Kylarai has shared a lot with me; I hope you don't mind. I just want you to know that I'm here for you. If you need me to back you up, on anything, don't hesitate to say the word."

I could have cried. We were not incredibly close by any means. For a while, I'd fully expected Coby to harbor a grudge toward me. So this proclamation gave me the warm and fuzzies in a big way. There were no words for what I was feeling. In a house filled with wolves who had cast me out, here was the only one with a good reason to do so, offering me friendship.

I hugged him again, so tight he made a pained sound. "Thank you," I whispered, turning away before I could tear up. He slipped outside to tend the barbecue, leaving me alone.

Shouts and laughter filled the house. It was a heartwarming sound. I stood in the kitchen drinking whiskey and reveling in the sound and smell of so many wolves. It brought forth the beast within, keeping the bloodlust buried.

"Why are you hiding in here by yourself?" Kylarai appeared with an empty appetizer plate in hand. She gave me a once over and set the plate down. "What's wrong?"

"Nothing. Really. Congratulations, again. I'm so happy for you." I pulled her in for a hug, savoring her familiar scent of wolf and flowers.

"Thank you. Now tell me what's wrong." She turned to the fridge and began to pile more appetizers onto the plate, but her grey eyes were on me. "Don't bullshit me either. You guys don't call me a mother hen for nothing."

I smiled. She was so intuitive when it came to Shaz and me. She knew us so well. "I'm fine, I promise. Just recovering from a vacation that was anything but relaxing."

"And?" She prodded.

It was tempting to tell her about my dream and the growing suspicion that my mortal days were dwindling. She knew everything else already. Kylarai was family, like a sister to me. She was also a worrier.

"And nothing. I swear. Just hiding in the kitchen because I feel like everyone else is looking at me, waiting for me to snap and bleed someone."

She frowned, and her lips quirked. She knew I was hiding something. But it was only because I didn't want to ruin her big night or the excitement of planning her wedding.

"You owe me a girls' night," she said, picking up the plate full of appetizers. "We haven't done that in a while. Then you're going to tell me everything."

"Deal."

We stood there chatting and munching appetizers until Coby appeared in the doorway, beckoning Ky with a finger and a naughty smile. With a girlish giggle, she ditched the appetizers on the table and disappeared outside with him.

After another glass of whiskey, I gravitated toward the patio door. The heavy energy of so many wolves drew me to the backyard where a few people were abandoning clothes and human form in favor of being furry on four legs.

Ky and Coby stood by the fire pit. He had his arms around her from behind, and her head rested on his chest. The orange glow of the flames lit up her smile. They looked great together.

Watching the wolves shift was breathtaking. One by one, they ceased eating, laughing and chatting to embrace the change. Graceful and smooth, every one of them, as they descended to the grass on all fours. It was a fast, fluid shift that encompassed every reformation of the body but much too fast for the eye to follow. The human to wolf visual was enchanting.

"Do you want to join them?" Shaz approached with a wild glint in his eyes. He followed my gaze, looking out at the pack that was now his. "It's been a while since we've all been together like this."

That was true. There'd been a time when we had run together on a regular basis, especially on full moons. Now I ran alone more often than not. "Yes, I do. Can you believe I'm almost afraid to be here with them?" I laughed bitterly. "They were right to kick me out. I'm not one of them anymore."

Shaz turned me to face him. With a finger beneath my chin, he forced me to meet his eyes. "They were never right to kick you out. You led them, protected them. You helped them to live the comfortable life they have here. When they should have supported you, they abandoned you. They don't deserve to have you lead them."

The intensity in his gaze rocked me. There was such vehemence in his words. A spark of anger lit up his brilliant eyes, and I watched as they bled to wolf.

"I don't deserve you," I said softly.

"You know there's no way in hell they would have pulled that shit if I'd been around to put a stop to it. Things have changed so much since Raoul died." Shaz stared longingly out the window to the field and forest beyond Kylarai's backyard.

It had been very different when Raoul led the pack. He was a strong leader who was always willing to do what was best for the wolves in his pack. Except for me, I guess. Our relationship had been warped by the history he'd shared with my mother. Too bad I hadn't known that until after he died.

In the year or more since his passing, I had changed and so had the town wolves. They knew I was bonded to a vampire, one they all saw as a threat. Being spurned by them had stung, but ultimately, it had meant very little. They didn't really know a damn thing about me.

"Let's go. I've been waiting impatiently for this all day." Shaz led me outside, down the patio steps to the grass that was beginning to yellow with the promise of summer's end.

A smile tugged at my lips as a memory surfaced. Shaz and Arys had really gone at it out here. While beating the hell out of one another, they'd torn the wooden railing off in a tumble down the stairs.

Noticing my reminiscent expression, Shaz chuckled. "I'd like to think I would have won that fight. If Kylarai hadn't broken it up."

"You guys have come a long way," I replied. "I'm impressed."

"Yeah, well...there's a lot you don't see."

"What is that supposed to mean?"

He used disrobing as a means of distraction. "Nothing at all."

Slowly, Shaz peeled off his t-shirt and hung it on the railing. He'd bulked up during his extended time as wolf in the mountains. His firm physique rippled with hard muscles that demanded my attention. It was impossible to resist running my hands over his chest, down his stomach.

"Hey, guys, save it for the forest," Kylarai called from across the yard. "No hanky-panky in the yard."

"You heard the lady," Shaz said, playfully pushing me away. "Hands off."

When he dropped his pants next, I was in a hurry to join him. I disrobed fast, feeling the exhilarating rush of my wolf rising to the surface.

"Are you coming?" I asked Ky and Coby, noting that everyone else had made their way across the field toward the tree line.

"Sure," Coby said with a mischievous grin. "We'll be right behind you."

My hungry gaze wandered over Shaz. My wolf couldn't have been happier to be there with her mate. Something had changed in him while he was away. It was more than merely his physique. There was a new understanding in him and a newfound aggression that was courageous but not careless.

I knew damn well that he and Arys discussed me when I was not around. I couldn't fault them for it either. Still, I wondered what it was that initiated the change in Shaz.

Before I could reach for him again, Shaz darted away and dropped to his knees, becoming wolf before touching the ground. He playfully nipped at my ankles and smacked me with his tail.

"I'll give you a head start," I said, nodding toward the tree line.

He didn't have to be told twice. Turning tail, he fled from the yard and into the night. It was an old game for us, racing to a particular tree on the edge of the forest. I was the reigning champion. It had been a long time since we'd raced and just been wolf with the others.

Embracing the change was like opening a floodgate. The wolf rose up, bursting forth, freed from its human prison. My body reknit and reformed, a sensation that hurt for just a second before it was replaced by the satisfying release, like that of having a good stretch.

Leaving Coby and Ky behind, I raced after the shock of white fur in the distance. No, I could most definitely never live in Las Vegas. The desert may have been the home of my vampiric origins, but it was foreign land to my wolf. First and foremost, I would always be wolf. The black onyx amulet hung around my neck, bouncing gently against my chest as I ran. Brogan had said to wear it, and I feared taking it off for even a minute.

Shaz was bigger and faster, but he didn't have my desire to win. The dirt kicked up beneath my feet as I flew across the field with the forest in my sights. Running on two legs never felt as good or as natural since I'd become wolf. This was what I was meant to be. I would not lose it. I caught up to Shaz easily and was ready to overtake him. Instead, I hung back and let him have the win.

He turned to me with accusation in his eyes. Then he jumped on me, knocking me to the ground beneath of flurry of playful bites and nips. He knew I had let him win.

Running in the forest always gave me this deep-seated longing, this need to be there always. And like other times when the vampire world had become too much, I considered staying there among the trees, with those who called the forest home.

If only it could be so simple.

The forest was alive with the sound of wolves, raising their melodious voices to the sky. There was no sound like it. It banished my insecurity. I didn't have to belong to this pack to know that I was every bit as much a wolf as they were.

I followed Shaz as he bounded through the brush and thick patches of trees, tracking various scents that caught his attention. The hoot of an owl drew my eye to a large tree branch overhead. The majestic bird stared down at me. It was a special moment in time, not my first encounter with a bird of prey and hopefully not my last. We shared an acknowledgment of one another, an unspoken respect.

I trotted off, thinking about how nature was superior to both humans and vampires. Here in the wild, we recognized each other, and we all knew our roles. It was peaceful. And if I could use anything in my life just then, it was peace.

When I found Shaz, he was having a stare down with a frightened rabbit. The little thing was quivering in fright, frozen solid, eyes wide with fear. Shaz moved slowly, lying down in the faded grass. After several moments, the rabbit broke from its position and fled down a nearby hole in the ground.

My heart skipped a beat. I went to Shaz and nuzzled him with wolf kisses. He was still the sweetest man I knew, and yet, he was also a killer, ready to take on anyone, man, wolf or vampire, if it was the right thing to do.

Eventually we made our way to the clearing. It was a place among the trees that the pack used as a meeting point. Shaz raised his muzzle and howled. The sound shook me. There was nothing more heart wrenching. His cry was echoed by the pack. One by one, they began to arrive in the clearing, forming a circle around us. He was calling them to us, and upon realizing that, my nerves began to take hold. What was he doing?

When everyone was gathered, Shaz shifted back to human form. Standing in the center of the circle of beasts, he made eye contact with them each in turn.

I remained as wolf, slinking out of the center, doing my best to blend in with the others. He was the Alpha here with Kylarai, should she choose to keep the position of Alpha female. I had no authority here now.

"I've gathered you all here together for a reason," Shaz began when all the wolves were settled. "To begin, I'd like to congratulate Coby and Kylarai on their engagement. We all wish you both the best. Know that this is your family, and we love you. Always."

The wolves made a bunch of noise, yips and howls, proclaiming their agreement. Kylarai and Coby stood together, two brown wolves that couldn't stop gazing longingly at each other.

When the noise died down, Shaz continued, "As you all know, I've recently returned from spending some time away. During that time, I've come to realize many things. One of those things is that I can no longer be the Alpha of this pack."

This announcement was met with much shock and confusion. Holding up a hand for silence, Shaz held a hand out to Ky and Coby. "Kylarai is your current Alpha female. I would like to hand the Alpha male title over to Coby. If anyone has a problem with that, come forward now or forever keep your silence."

I tensed, hopeful that nobody would dare to defy Shaz's wish. As it was, the small town pack was composed of everyday types, teachers, lawyers, soccer moms. Nobody moved.

We all stared at Shaz. I couldn't believe he was walking out on them. Something had changed in him. I saw it in Vegas when he killed in Jenner's death fight. I was still trying to decide if I should be worried about his easy acceptance of that situation.

Satisfied that nobody dared to challenge Coby as the new Alpha, he beckoned both wolves forward. "My place is no longer here with you all. I belong with Alexa. Most of you don't really understand who she is, you only see what she is." He paused, allowing that to sink in. "Welcome your new Alpha couple. And obey them always. They'll take care of you."

He backed out of the center of the circle, gesturing for Coby and Kylarai to take his place there. They did so with some hesitation.

They were evidently as surprised by this announcement as the rest of us.

The pack raised their voices in tribute to their new leaders. I joined them, happy to see Kylarai take on the leadership role I knew she'd been born for. This was for the best. Neither I nor Shaz could bring trouble to them if we were no longer part of them. Still, I felt bad for Shaz. He deserved to have a pack to call his own.

Resuming his wolf form, Shaz nudged my flank and bounded into the trees. I followed, dying to ask him a dozen questions. We went a good mile or more from the others, stopping only after their voices had faded in the distance.

Certain that we were alone, I shifted, needing a human voice. At my request, he followed suit.

"Why didn't you tell me you were going to do that?" I demanded. The ground was cold under my feet. A twig poked into my heel, but I barely noticed.

"So you could try to talk me out of it?" He asked with a chuckle. "No way. I know you, Lex."

"But, why? You fought for that pack. They're yours."

"Not anymore. I needed to do it. My place is with you." He placed a finger on my lips, muffling my protests. "We need to make contact with the city wolves. You need to reach out to them, and I'll be by your side when you do it."

"It's not going to be that simple." I pushed his hand away but held it tight.

"Nothing ever is."

"Being with me means being in the world of vampires."

"It always has. You've never been just a wolf, Alexa. I've always accepted that."

What more could I say? Shaz had made his choice. He knew what he risked. There was no point in arguing or begging him to change his mind. So I did the only thing I could. I kissed him.

His tongue slipped between my lips, delving hungrily into my mouth. This time when I ran my hands over him, he didn't push me away.

Passion and instinct drove us to the forest floor. I couldn't get enough of the way he felt. My hand closed around his shaft, and I was pleased to find him already hard for me. His soft moan encouraged me as I stroked him. We lay together, surrounded by nature while love and desire consumed us. His mouth was hot on my neck and chest as he licked and nipped my sensitive flesh.

I needed to have him, here in the forest, where we belonged. Unlike our last encounter, I was not the aggressor. There was no bloodlust present within me nor did I see him as prey. Instead, I wanted him to claim me.

Shaz didn't need my submission. Already he was taking a dominant stance, reaching between my thighs to slide his fingers inside me. His mouth claimed my nipple while his fingers worked magic. Deciding I was ready for him, Shaz nudged my legs apart. He entered me with a slick thrust. That first stroke was my favorite. Having him inside me brought a happy sigh to my lips.

It had been so long since we'd made love like this, under the stars. We moved together, our pace frenzied but tender. Claws and fangs gave an aggressive edge to the carnal act, but there was genuine emotion behind every touch, every kiss and bite.

The masculine scent of him was mouthwatering. All I could taste, breathe and feel was Shaz. I was a willing slave to the passion that consumed us.

Face to face, we gazed into one another. My breath came faster, and my heart pounded in my ears. The cool night air was a soothing caress on my sweaty skin. My white wolf possessed my body, making it his in every way. We had both needed this moment.

Learning to live in the moment was starting to come easier. My future might have been predestined in many ways, such as my link to Arys or being a Hound of God. However, I knew that nothing was written in stone. Things could always change. We all had choices to make that would alter what came next.

Choosing to embrace it all, good and bad, risks and benefits, I was determined to move forward bravely. I was tired of being afraid, tired of expecting the worst. I had a job to do, and I was going to see it through. Even if it killed me.

Shaz's devotion would never cease to surprise me. In recent days, he seemed more sure of our role together than I ever had. He had always been the balance I needed, the one who kept me from being consumed by Arys's darkness. Maybe it wouldn't always be so, but I would never forget the lengths he was willing to go to for me.

Being there in his arms, gazing up into his fabulous green eyes, I was able to submit myself to whatever lay ahead. I found strength in those who loved me, my friends and family. Their willingness to back me, regardless of what that meant, was more than I would ever deserve. And I cherished it. I would do anything for any one of them. We were stronger together.

Still, I knew deep in my heart that when push came to shove, I would have to walk this dark path alone.

Epilogue

A loud clatter followed by a bang had me cringing. The last of the old furniture and tables were being hauled out of The Wicked Kiss. I was happier than I thought I'd be to see them go.

I had wasted no time in following through with my plans to renovate. Whatever had gone on here in my absence was still a mystery to me. Kale and Willow seemed to be the only ones to know the exact story, and neither of them was talking.

I snuck a sidelong glance at Willow who sat perched on a barstool beside me, watching the vampires on my staff tear apart my nightclub. In his hand was a tequila, like usual. I would never understand how he could drink that awful swill.

"Still not talking, huh?" I teased, knowing he wouldn't spill Kale's secret.

"There's nothing to talk about. I promise." He ducked his dirty-blond head to hide a grin. "So, tell me what you plan to do about Jenner and the Vegas club."

While we watched the loud and sometimes destructive activity in the club, I had filled him in on the details of my trip. I had also told him about the dream I had a few nights ago. Even Arys and Shaz didn't know about that. Not yet.

"Vegas is Arys's problem right now," I said, frowning into my whiskey glass. "I have enough to deal with here. How the hell can I run two cities when I have yet to run one? And who knows? I might be dead soon. Then neither city will be my problem."

Willow's silver wings were absent from sight though I could almost hear them rustle as he shifted on his stool. He gave me a look I was starting to know well. It meant he was about to get serious on me.

"You think the dream means you're going to die soon?" He asked, his tone gentle and warm. "Dreams are open to interpretation. They can mean almost anything. Try not to read too much into it."

Falon's words haunted me every time I gazed into the dark gold liquor in my glass. He represented everything I feared and loathed. Being one of Shya's minions didn't appeal to me. I would rather truly be dead than enslaved to a demon.

The dragon on my forearm itched and burned, as if aware of my thoughts. More than once, I had toyed with the thought of digging it out of my flesh with a claw. The only thing stopping me was knowing that Shya would make me pay for it. He had still not shown up unexpectedly nor had he continued to call. It was starting to make me nervous. I wished he would just get it over with already.

Since returning from Las Vegas, I felt like I was stuck in some kind of limbo. Waiting for something to happen was not my strong suit. I'd rather make things happen. In this case, my hands were tied. I could do nothing until Shya made the first move. Then I could only react and hope that it was enough.

Of course, there were other things to keep me busy. I had no intention of remaining idle. Shya was seeking something, a scroll. It went without saying that I would be wise to seek it as well. Seeing as the bastard planned to use my death to open the seal barring it, I had as much reason to desire its location as he did.

"I don't think I'm jumping to the wrong conclusion, Willow. I can feel it. It's going to happen soon." I took a deep breath and blurted, "I'm scared."

It was a confession I don't think I would have made to anyone else. Arys had a way of knowing my feelings due to our bond, but even he did not know my every thought. An admission of fear felt like an admission of weakness. I detested it.

Willow scooted his stool closer so he could put a friendly arm around my shoulders and pull me in against him. His touch was comforting like a warm blanket on a rainy day.

"I know," he said, resting his head against mine. "It's ok to be scared, Alexa. It means you still feel something. You still care. It's a good thing."

"Doesn't feel too damn good."

There was another crash as a broken table came apart on its way out the door. It would be a relief when this was done. I planned to keep the club operating during renovations, which would prove difficult but had to be done. It would have been nice if Kale had been here to help oversee things. Wherever he was, I probably didn't want to know.

He too had been keeping his distance. That was likely for the best. There were only so many ways and so many times I could apologize for taking Shya's mark to save him. I would never be sorry for saving him, no matter how hard Kale tried to make me regret that choice.

Baggage. We all had it. Mine was starting to get pretty heavy. I shuddered to imagine what it would be like after centuries as a vampire. I couldn't picture it.

The Wicked Kiss was almost bare. The floors were being redone as soon as the painting was finished. No carpet. It was too easily dirtied up in a place like this. Kale had little input to give despite the building's ownership being in his name, so I'd chosen a nice, non-slip luxury vinyl tile to do the main party area in, including the dance floor. The old, hard booth seats were being replaced with softer seats that were more couch-like rather than bench-like. I was still picking out furniture for the lounge area behind the bar. I sighed when I remembered that the paint color for the walls had yet to be selected. There was a lot of work ahead, and yet I was kind of excited about it.

The regular patrons that couldn't stay away were crowded around the bar, squeezing in wherever they could. If they could see the Vegas club, they'd all be on the next flight out. Jenner had much to be proud of.

Thinking about Vegas brought something to mind, something I'd forgotten about until now. I met Willow's gold and green gaze. I had to ask.

"Willow, there was something Falon said in Vegas. It struck me as kind of odd. He told me that all fallen angels know exactly where they stand. You included. What does that mean?" There. I asked, despite the nagging little voice that insisted I didn't want an answer to Falon's cryptic shit.

Much to my surprise, Willow got very quiet. He looked away, staring at the crew tearing out the old dance floor, and I didn't like that he was purposely avoiding eye contact. "Don't listen to a word that comes out of Falon's mouth," he said. "We all had a purpose before the fall, and some of us still have a purpose now. You can't let him get inside your head. That's what he wants."

"At this point, there are so many people inside my head I don't think there's room left for me," I joked, finding it close enough to the truth to make it hard to laugh.

Willow chose an interesting way of avoiding my question. He hadn't really given me an answer. Which perhaps was answer enough. For whatever reason, Willow didn't want to talk about it. Fair enough. I understood that some subjects were sensitive for him. Clearly, this was one of them.

Busying myself with the makeover of the club had worked wonders to keep my mind occupied. Too much time to think was a very bad thing. Eventually, the club would be finished. Then I'd have to find something else to do. Drinking myself stupid with Willow was always an option. Might as well do it while I still could.

Pretending the Las Vegas club was someone else's problem was a delusion that would soon grow tired. It was mine now, and so was Jenner. I would walk among the glamour of The Strip once again, and next time, I might be one of the many vampires hunting the streets of Sin City. I had done my best to avoid thinking about it since coming home because I knew that taking control of Vegas was for the best. Harley had made a mess of it. Now he was gone, and we were left to clean up after him. And we would.

Arys loved that damn city. I could see why. Standing in front of the Bellagio fountain, I'd known a sense of wonder I hadn't felt in a very long time. It was an illusion, much like everything else in Las Vegas.

Vampires in Vegas and a demon at home made my to-do list daunting, to say the least. I chewed my bottom lip, lost in thought. Was it possible to intertwine the two? To harness the power of the Sin City vampires from a distance? The wheels in my brain turned. An idea began to take form, one that surely was far too outrageous to work. It was one that would simmer on the backburner of my mind.

I was startled from my thoughts by an attractive young man. He paid no attention to the drink in my hand, unaware that I was not what he was seeking. Brazen and more than a little drunk, he asked me if I was seeking a playmate for the night.

For a split second, I was tempted to say yes. My gaze went to the pulse throbbing in his neck, and I hungrily licked my lips. "Sorry, handsome. I'm not what you're looking for tonight. Not if you want to leave here alive."

After he had moved on to another, I groaned and gave Willow's arm a squeeze. "Oh, God, I wanted to devour that guy. I'm going to be the worst kind of vampire."

"You turned him away. That counts for something."

"Yeah, this time."

With a sigh and a bitter laugh, I wasted no time in acquiring a refill. The whiskey was going down fast and smooth tonight. My mortal life was slipping away. I could feel it. Every night the void grew.

Now that I had tuned in to the blood rushing through the human bodies around us, I couldn't focus on anything else. The dream from a few nights ago came back to haunt me. Sinking fangs, spilling blood, it's what I craved.

"I think I need some air." I slid off the stool and headed for the exit. Willow fell into step beside me, a comforting shadow at my side.

There was a bite to the night air. Fall was approaching fast. I embraced the chill. Feeling it meant I was still mortal, human in some small way. I clung to that.

The scent of cigarettes tainted the air. I wrinkled my nose and flashed a mock glare at Willow. "Why do you do that?"

Puffing away on a smoke, he leaned against the building and shrugged. "Because I can. It's not like it's going to kill me. And it goes well with the tequila."

Laughter released some of the tension I'd been holding. I was able to relax. Standing in the parking lot after drinking with a fallen angel, all I could do was laugh.

The Feds would be calling in their favor in the near future. Shya openly admitted his plan to sacrifice me for access to greater power. Not to mention the forbidden vampire lover intent on making me crazy. One might say I had a lot on my plate.

None of it mattered. It didn't. Because once it did, I would be made powerless. The fact that I was still standing, still ready to fight, that meant something. I was a Hound of God, the light half of a twin flame. I didn't come this far to die without fulfilling my purpose. Whether that was to clean up Vegas or to find a way to stop Shya, I didn't know. But I was ready to find out.

I could do this. No, I would do this.

One day at a time.

Check out TrinaMLee.com for information and excerpts from Sunset to Sunrise, Alexa O'Brien Huntress Book 7.5, a Kale Sinclair novella.

About the Author

Trina M. Lee was born in Edmonton, Alberta Canada. Writing fiction since childhood, a fascination with the supernatural developed in her early teen years and an immersion in paranormal fiction began. Trina enjoys hearing from readers and has an active social media presence.

Website: TrinaMLee.com
Facebook: Facebook.com/AuthorTrinaMLee
Twitter: Twitter.com/TrinaMLee

5201176R00139

Printed in Great Britain
by Amazon.co.uk, Ltd.,
Marston Gate.